Cover design by Nina Patel

Edited by Kate Keysell Copy Editing

Books by the same author

Lost in a Hurricane
Deathbed Confessions
The Unfolding Path
Farewell Bright Star

It's the world's oldest secret.....

...and the world is about to find out

Covenant
of
Silence

To

Jim Larkin

Just ahead of us on the road,
as he was in life.

It's the world's oldest secret.....

...and the world is about to find out

Covenant
of
Silence

Peter Larner

1

Hallet is guilty, that much is certain.

In a rare, tranquil moment of uninterrupted silence, Bertoni endeavoured to hold onto that thought. It provided a calming influence on an otherwise stressful day. He needed to avoid unnecessary conjecture and dispel any alternative theories, as these would serve only to lower his self esteem and raise his blood pressure in equal measure. But optimism was an infrequent visitor to his misanthropic world and it sat as uneasily as he did in the opulently furnished waiting room.

The confined ambience of a windowless room enclosed within a large office building managed to mute the relentless sound of the traffic in the unseen streets and made him feel uncomfortable. Absolute quiet wasn't crucial, just the soft sounds of the natural world, rather than the manufactured chattering of the modern one.

It was an important meeting and he wondered whether he should have put a clean shirt on this morning. He wanted to get up and look out of a window, but was denied this simple pleasure. The wood-panelled Georgian room lingered in a bygone age, oblivious to a twenty-first century discernible only by the faint humming of the traffic outside. A childhood memory of hushed ages past hovered in the mind of one who could remember an era when owning a car was less commonplace and owning two was unheard of.

Bertoni struggled to enjoy his moment of calm, even if it had been augmented by meandering through the streets of his youth. Offices didn't sound like offices anymore in his view. A modern office environment had been dehumanised by the introduction of computers and sterilised through the perfectibility of automation. Gone were the rhythmic clicking of typewriter keys and the strident, shrill bell of a telephone, superseded by a restrained and gentle purring. He closed his eyes for a moment and, with an artificial stream of cold air brushing his face, any lingering background noise was muffled by the freshly fallen snow of his adolescence. But snow, on the hottest day of the year, soon melts and his calmness dissolved just as quickly as more familiar feelings of apprehension returned. He slipped from that temporary arbour of solace and almost spoke the words out loud in a futile effort to overpower his lack of conviction. Hallet is guilty. He had means, motive and opportunity. It was textbook stuff and there was no room for error. The three foundation blocks of a successful prosecution are means, motive and opportunity. That's what they taught Bertoni at Hendon.

Did Hallet have the means to commit the crime? Yes, he did. Did he have the motive? Certainly. And the opportunity? Well he didn't have an alibi, so the opportunity was clearly there. But, if Bertoni was so sure of Hallet's guilt, why did he spend so much time deliberating the point in his mind? After all, DNA evidence can't lie.

Bertoni thought about moving his seat. He was trapped in the line of fire from the air-conditioning unit opposite him and, in spite of the surrogate supply of fresh air, he still felt claustrophobic. He felt the need to see, as well as feel, the open air as he looked around his oppressive surroundings. But, ever the martyr, he remained in his seat and checked his watch. Redpath looked quizzically at the large clock on the wall that seemed to have been missed by his boss, but Bertoni was hoping that it was wrong.

The detective inspector glanced over at his sergeant and wondered why he looked so relaxed. Either Chief Superintendent Bent had developed a sense of humour, or he truly believed that contrasting temperaments would somehow produce results. Opposites might attract in a scientific sense, Bertoni thought, but they are likely only to create tension and discord where personalities are involved. In the classroom, such corrupting influences would be kept apart. Bertoni's experience, patience and tolerance were tainted only by the cynicism that experience brings, whereas Redpath was young, petulant and impulsive.

Hallet is guilty, Bertoni repeated to himself, perhaps hoping to assert the statement's voracity. This was a well-earned result, but the DI's experience told him that it wasn't over until the judge said 'Take him down'.

Two more years of work and mortgage repayments and he could retire to his holiday home in Tenerife. Bertoni had served his time, just as Hallet was going to serve his.

Of course, the police had never found the murder weapon, so there was no evidence to support the means to commit murder, but then Hallet had no alibi, so he had the opportunity. And he certainly had the motive; after all, Kosoto had murdered his daughter. Bertoni had no children of his own but could imagine the overwhelming desire for revenge in such a situation. Producing the murder weapon would help, but it's not a prerequisite for a conviction. Anyway, he assured himself, leaving all that aside, there was the DNA evidence. The forensic officer had found Hallet's DNA on Kosoto's body, yet the ex-serviceman denied ever meeting the victim or visiting the scene of the murder. Like most things in life, that little fact bothered Bertoni. It nagged away, feeding on his doubts. Why did Hallet deny going to Wharf Street? And why did he deny ever meeting Kosoto? If he had only conceded these two important points, he would have made Bertoni's task much more difficult. But an absolute denial was incompatible with the scientific evidence. Of course, it still wouldn't explain how Hallet's DNA was found in one of the wounds inflicted on Kosoto, but he only managed to attract attention to himself by denying he had ever been to the house where his DNA was found. Still, thought Bertoni, he was a first-timer. He wasn't a professional killer. This was a crime of passion, carried out in the heat of the moment, so he was bound to make mistakes.

Bertoni thought he heard some activity in the reception area outside but the voices suggested it was just the mail being delivered. He sighed and the tediousness of the situation collided with a disturbing notion. For one fleeting moment an explanation occurred to the seasoned detective that might make sense of the conflicting evidence. Cally planted Hallet's DNA. This alternative explanation wasn't any more plausible. There was no reason for Cally to plant evidence. But then, how much did Bertoni know about his young forensic officer? This is the only scenario that would explain Hallet's continual denial of visiting Wharf Street.

Anyway, thought Bertoni, where is Cally? His dark imagination began to invent all types of reasons for Cally's absence from such an important meeting. She had planted the DNA evidence and now she had lost her nerve. Hallet is two weeks away from trial and Cally has lost her nerve. He retrieved his mobile phone from a jacket pocket and thought about calling her. A sign on the wall said that all mobile phones should be switched off. Bertoni followed the instruction and looked around the room, trying to forget his foolish suspicions and doubts about what was, after all, a most straightforward case of murder.

There were doors on three of the four walls in the waiting room where the two men sat. One door led out of the building, through the reception where they had arrived twenty minutes earlier. Halfway up another there was a nameplate indicating it was the office of T.C.A. Cruickshank, QC and the third, which stood ajar, housed his secretary, a rather austere, middle-aged woman whose querulous nature was subdued only by her superciliousness. A water cooler stood in one corner of the room and broke the silence by gurgling occasionally. Bertoni thought about retrieving a cup of water but couldn't see anywhere to dispose of the empty cup, so he stayed seated, crossed his legs and sighed.

It was a slow day. At least that was Steve Redpath's assessment. Sitting in a leather armchair in a building that was fully air-conditioned might not be as exciting as chasing villains, but he couldn't understand why his boss was in such a hurry to get the meeting over with. There were worse things they could be doing. Ashley Bertoni, however, was familiar with Theo Cruikshank QC and had often felt the lash of his harsh words in the past. So he, at least, could appreciate how unwise it was to keep their host waiting.

The door from the reception opened but it wasn't their colleague, Cally Boyce. This woman was much older, aloof and matronly. She was carrying the post.

"Mr Cruickshank will see you when you are all here," she said, with a rather disappointing expression on her face and an emphasis on the word 'all'. And with that said, she delivered the post to her boss and retired back through the door that had previously been ajar. It was closed behind her.

A few minutes elapsed and Cally arrived, puffing and panting and gathering her papers together as she tried to shut the door without dropping her handbag.

"You're late," said Ashley as he shuffled on his seat. Cally knew she was late, so the statement served only to relieve his tension.

"Tyler had to get up early this morning to go to a seminar," she said in mitigation, "and he didn't reset the alarm."

"It's never your fault, is it, Cally?" said Bertoni, sounding like a reproachful father.

"Well, PC Saunders isn't here yet anyway," she said looking around the room and placing her paperwork on an empty chair.

"Saunders is on holiday," replied Bertoni severely, "Cruickshank saw him last week. It's just us today." The room fell silent only momentarily and Steve smiled, content in the firm belief that women were like fish out of water in the police force.

While Cally continued to argue her case with Bertoni about how hot it was outside and how she had run all the way from the underground station, Steve got up and, rather unwisely in Ashley's view, knocked on Cruickshank's office door, before opening it slightly and telling the occupant that Cally had arrived. Redpath spoke in the rough tones of London's east end, which stood in stark contrast to the rounded vowels of the Oxford-educated lawyer.

"Oh, right then," called back Cruickshank, rather sarcastically, "I'll stop what I'm doing, shall I?" adding brutally, "now that you have finally condescended to arrive."

6

The matronly secretary had heard the exchange of words and entered the room.

"I'm sorry, Mr Cruickshank," she said before closing his door and ushering Steve back to his seat in the waiting room. Bertoni sent a loaded and disapproving look at his junior, who returned to his seat, unmoved by the experience.

Five minutes passed before the QC opened his door and beckoned his three visitors to enter, glaring at Redpath as he did so. Bertoni stood back and watched Cally follow Cruickshank into the room. Steve swaggered as if into a bar in some Quentin Tarantino movie and took a seat. Bertoni looked at Redpath's face and was struck by his youthful self-confidence, wondering when and where he had lost such assurance. Envious of his young colleague's blissful indifference to the challenge that faced him and determined not to postpone the execution any longer, the DI gathered his thoughts and experience about him like a comfort blanket and took his seat. Bertoni's glass was never half full. He never expected a good day. He expected the worst and didn't waste time hoping for anything else.

Cruickshank was elegantly dressed and deeply tanned, having just returned from his annual summer holiday in the West Indies. Everyone sat and waited in silence for the secretary to arrive with tea and coffee. There were some biscuits on a plate, but they all seemed a little hesitant to be the first to take one. All except Steve of course who, indifferent to Mr Cruickshank's scowls, reached forward and took the only bourbon. His host's left eye began to twitch.

"Perhaps we can get started now," said the pinstriped barrister, adding, "The Crown versus David Hallet."

He lifted the cup and saucer to chest height, sipped his coffee and continued in a manner that seemed determined to conclude the meeting as quickly as possible.

"The trial is set for the Old Bailey beginning on..." he hesitated as he flicked through the papers on his desk. "Tuesday 2 September. You all need to be available on days one and two."

Cally fumbled in her handbag for her diary, much to the annoyance of Ashley, who mimicked his host's polite handling of a cup and saucer.

Cruickshank explained that PC Saunders would be the first witness for the prosecution.

"It was only Saunders being proactive that caused the body to be found in the first place." As he spoke, he continuously looked through his papers to remind himself of the names of the various people involved.

"Apparently, the local police station received regular calls from a Mrs Myers, who lives at 68 Wharf Street. She is the chairman of the local Neighbourhood Watch, although it seems she may have been the only member." He paused. "Anyway, she regularly called the police to complain about number 1 being used as a drug den."

Cruickshank went on to explain that the house had been empty for many years and was a base for drug dealers to sell their wares. But, when Mrs Myers failed to call for over a week, Constable Saunders decided to call on her. It seems he was worried about her. He knew she never went on holiday so feared he might find her dead in her home. Instead he learned from her that there had been no activity at number 1 for more than a week. Suspicious of this, Saunders visited the derelict house and found the body of Nelson Kosoto.

"Saunders's evidence will give us a sound start," said Cruickshank assuredly. "His proactive approach to policing shows the force in a good light. That gives us a platform."

Redpath lifted the coffee cup, leaving the saucer on the table and drank from it loudly before placing it back on the saucer.

Cruickshank ignored his noisy guest and rose from his seat to begin relaying the merits of his case, in greater detail, to his tiny audience. With theatrical enunciation he saw himself as Schofield playing Hamlet for the Royal Shakespeare Company. Unfulfilled, youthful and unrealised ambitions lost to the theatre and now wasted on those who would be extras in his next performance.

It was some time before the QC paused to allow any of his visitors to speak. Detective Inspector Bertoni would follow Saunders into the box and provide more of the background to the investigation. It was important, stressed the barrister, that Bertoni began at the very beginning, with the dark history of 1 Wharf Street. The house was a detached, listed property that was built in the mid-nineteenth century. It had been the scene of a murder back then, when its first resident was killed. Then, one hundred and fifty years later, two more murders were committed there. First, on December 8 last year, Charlene Hallet was hacked to death in a frenzied attack. Then, on February 12, Charlene's father used the same weapon to murder Nelson Kosoto, who had initially been arrested for Charlene's murder, but later released without charge. It was for Bertoni to set out this bleak history to the jury, under the gentle prompting of Theo Cruickshank.

It was important, Cruickshank reminded Bertoni, that this part of the prosecution evidence fully explored the connection between the two murders to establish a clear motive. As he spoke, he crossed the room to switch on the TV that stood there. He picked up the remote control and turned on the DVD player.

"I intend to submit your TV interview on the BBC as evidence, Detective Inspector."

He pressed play and the four of them sat in silence to listen to Bertoni's interview after Kosoto had been released without charge following questioning by the police for the murder of Charlene Hallet.

"Your last words set the motive up very well, I think," he added and turned the volume up to ensure nobody missed the section he was referring to.

"Now that Mr Kosoto has been released without charge, are your enquiries continuing, Detective Inspector?" asked the young interviewer. The fifty-six-year-old police officer replied quietly but firmly.

"We are not looking for anyone else in connection with this crime."

Cruickshank switched off the TV and returned to his desk as the others turned their chairs back to face him.

"I think we'll end your evidence there," said the QC, before turning to look at the younger of the two police officers. He reminded both officers that he would begin the questioning by asking them for their name, rank and experience.

"Now, Sergeant Redpath," he said, "you were shot once, I believe." Steve nodded. "Good," said Cruickshank, which brought a smile to Cally's face.

"Well, not good you were shot, of course, but good in that it engages the jury. We won't dwell on it, but we will certainly mention it."

He explained to Redpath that he wanted him to focus on the evidence of the mobile phone and also the murder weapon.

"The murder weapon wasn't found," stated Cally.

"Yes, that's why I want to link the two. We can confuse the jury when it comes to physical evidence."

"Well," explained Steve, "we never found the murder weapon, but we knew what it was, a machete."

"Yes," replied Cruickshank, "the defence will focus on that. The machete isn't the weapon of choice for your average adult, white male."

Redpath laughed quietly to himself before making a rather rash comment.

"And I thought it was the police who were supposed to be institutionally racist," he said.

Cruickshank jumped up from his seat.

"Never, never say anything like that in *my* courtroom," he demanded, with the emphasis on the 'my'.

Redpath sat still, silent and suitably chastened.

"We will move on very swiftly," advised Cruickshank, "from the absent murder weapon, to the mobile phone."

"Yes," said Redpath, "we found a mobile telephone on Kosoto's body. On it was a text message that said, "'You,' which was like a letter 'u' in the text message, 'You fucked with the wrong people.' Is it alright to say 'fucked'?" he asked.

"Yes," replied Cruickshank, "but it's always useful simply to look at the judge as you do so; a sort of acknowledgement that you are giving evidence verbatim. He'll nod back to indicate that he realises you don't use that kind of language in your normal speech." A few eyebrows were raised in the room.

Cruickshank told them that he would then ask Redpath whether he had established who sent that message. He suggested that Redpath was then to refer to his notebook and tell the jury that the message had been sent from a pay-as-you-go mobile telephone that was purchased by the accused, David Hallet.

"In my view, a visible reference to any contemporaneous notes always adds emphasis and gives the jury time to take the evidence in," explained the lawyer, before finishing his coffee and checking his notes again.

"Okay," said Cruickshank, "and I will then refer to various exhibits that establish Hallet purchasing that telephone. Again, the mobile phone that Hallet used was never recovered, but I don't want us to dwell on that. Keep referring to the mobile phone found on the body of Kosoto."

It is important, he warned the three witnesses, that they refer to the murdered man as Nelson Kosoto or, even better, the young Mr Kosoto.

"The prosecution will want to ensure the jury is aware of Kosoto's history of drug dealing but, in my experience, it does not serve them well to destroy the memory of a murder victim."

"Can I just ask something?" asked Cally.

"If you must, Miss Boyce," answered a rather impatient Cruickshank.

"Do you not think it was a funny thing for Hallet to text Kosoto? I mean," she added, turning to Steve Redpath, "in all the time you spent interviewing Hallet, did he ever swear?"

But before Steve could answer, Cruickshank had intervened, his eye twitching nervously.

"Miss Boyce, can I suggest that you confine your comments to matters of forensic evidence?" He wasn't asking, or even suggesting. The tone of his voice said she should keep her opinion to herself.

"In my experience," he added, "very few accused men use foul language in the witness box. The jury would not know whether he used that language in common parlance or not. But they will assume he did, which adds to our case."

"Yes, but…" she said, but Cruickshank was adamant.

"Miss Boyce. I will ask you about your qualifications and your role in working for the police in your capacity as a forensic scientist. Please refer us to the university you attended, the degree qualification, your experiences in previous murder cases and *the evidence* in this particular case."

He reminded her that he would ask the questions and she should simply answer them. There was, after all, he assured her, overwhelming forensic evidence. Hallet had denied ever visiting 1 Wharf Street. He denied ever meeting Mr Kosoto and he denied ever sending the victim a threatening text message.

"Yet, we have irrefutable evidence to the contrary. This not only condemns the accused but identifies him as a habitual liar."

Bertoni's thoughts wandered back to the waiting room. If Cally had planted the DNA evidence, now was the time to confess. But, in the two seconds that Cruickshank allowed her before continuing his performance, there was no such response. The experienced detective looked deep into her eyes for any sign of fear. But there was none.

"Your evidence is crucial to this case, Miss Boyce, so please don't let me down. Hallet's DNA was on the wall against which Mr Kosoto was murdered and, indeed, it was found in the very cuts the machete made to the wallpaper and in the very wounds on the body of the victim. The case for the prosecution rests on your evidence."

"Yes, I understand," she replied.

"Okay," the QC replied, "if there are no other questions, I shall see you all on 2 September."

13

Other questions, thought Cally, any questions might have been useful.

"Oh, just one point before you leave," said Cruickshank, "there is no need to dwell too long on Hallet's lack of an alibi. His wife will be called as a witness for the defence and we have sworn evidence from her that her husband was out 'driving around' on the night of Kosoto's murder."

"Yes," replied Bertoni, "she said in her statement that her husband never got over the death of their daughter and used to spend his evenings simply driving around."

"That's good," said Cruickshank, before bidding them farewell. "See you in court."

David Hallet had been remanded in custody for the past three months at Maidstone Prison. It wasn't the softest option for a remand prisoner, but then he had committed murder. The team hadn't visited him for several weeks. He had never shown any signs of pleading guilty, nor had he tried to bargain for manslaughter. Bertoni believed he may try for diminished responsibility but, judging by his appearance on the last visit, this didn't seem likely.

Maidstone had a reputation for toughness but Hallet seemed unaffected by his long stay there. He wasn't the archetypal hard man but he seemed to be coping with the experience very well.

There were no plans to see him again, so the team could relax and spend the next two weeks building their case and practise giving their evidence. A conviction would look good on all of their CVs and there was a good chance they could close the Charlene Hallet case on the basis that Kosoto must have committed her murder and paid the ultimate penalty: death at the hands of the victim's father. An eye for an eye and a hacking to death was punished in the same fashion and with the same machete if Cally's investigation was correct.

Hallet's defence counsel had maintained throughout that the evidence against his client was circumstantial. The absence of an alibi simply established that nobody could prove where he was. This was not proof that he was at Wharf Street murdering Nelson Kosoto. He dismissed the text message with the same casual disregard. Hallet had purchased the mobile phone for his daughter, as many parents do. There was no evidence that he sent a threatening text message on that same mobile phone to Kosoto. The mobile phone, like the murder weapon, had never been produced by the police. Kosoto was a drugs baron, who lived life close to the edge with tragic consequences. Kosoto lived by the sword and, sadly, died by it too. The police had produced no weapon and no evidence that Hallet had committed this crime. The suggestion of a motive and the absence of an alibi did not, in his view, represent sufficient justification for a guilty verdict.

~~~ الـ صمت من الـ عهد ~~~

With the rest of the day free, Steve and Ashley headed off to the nearest pub, but Cally needed to get back to the house to tidy up. Galen was coming round for dinner that evening and she had rushed out this morning, leaving the bed unmade and dirty laundry littering the place. Not the ambience for a quiet dinner at home with an old school friend.

Cally was looking for the corkscrew and had spent ten minutes emptying the contents of various drawers, finding a collection of space-wasting objects including an egg-shaped brooch. She couldn't recall seeing it before so assumed it must belong to Tyler. It seemed a little effeminate for her boyfriend

15

and wondered, for a moment, about buying a chain for it, as a surprise present. But she couldn't remember ever seeing him wearing it. She rolled it in her hand. It was old and discoloured. She rubbed it on her sleeve. It was purple with a small link at the top that, presumably, was for a chain. She held it up and thought again about buying a chain. It was a little too bohemian for Tyler, she thought. So she consigned it back to the drawer and continued her search for the corkscrew.

Galen arrived in a t-shirt and jeans, as instructed, shortly after seven o'clock. He kissed Cally on both cheeks, with his standard apology.

"Sorry, you always get two from me. All those years spent at the English College in Rome."

He slumped into the armchair, rather heavily for such a small frame. His long sojourn in Italy had turned his skin to a dark olive colour. He was tall, with a slender physique and handsome enough to cause people to sigh, as if to say 'what a waste' when they learned he was a Catholic priest. But Galen would simply laugh at such comments that categorised celibacy as a disease rather than a lifestyle choice. He knew that neither Cally nor Tyler ever thought this way. They appreciated his conviction and admired his dedication.

"Dinner will be another half an hour," explained Cally, "what would you like to drink?"

"Cold beer if you have one. It was hot and sticky on the underground. The heat is so different in London compared with Rome. It can be the same temperature but it feels quite different," he called to her in the kitchen.

"That'll be the humidity."

"Probably."

Cally opened the fridge and returned with two bottles of cold beer. She sat opposite Galen, looked at him and smiled.

"So, how's your new parish, then?"

"Interesting. There's a primary school next door, so I'm a school governor. There's a mixed age profile at mass, with a couple of funerals a month and a wedding next week. Commuter belt so the parishioners are not short of a few bob. Decent collection. I was blown away by the amount raised for the African drought collection last week. Nearly £2,000." He paused, realising he was talking too much. "Anyway, never mind me, how are you?"

Cally knew that Galen had not called her by chance. Tyler had probably phoned him to say that she didn't like being in the house on her own while he was away. She lifted the bottle to her mouth and took a mouthful of beer.

"I'm fine too," she said, adding, "it's kind of you to call round. You must come back some time when Tyler is at home." She then wondered how her friend might interpret that slightly ill-chosen comment.

She explained that Tyler was attending a seminar on gene research in Stratford-upon-Avon. He would be away for two nights, but it was essential for his work. He needed to keep up-to-date with new technologies and ideas.

"I thought he was the one with all the ideas," he replied, adding, "why Stratford? Are they examining Hamlet's skull?"

"No. Stratford is just central for everyone, geographically. Although most of them live and work in London and others fly in from abroad. Anyway, it was Yorrick's skull, not Hamlet's."

"What's Superboy working on at the moment, then?" asked Galen, ignoring the literary correction.

"He never tells me. He's normally always working on something that is commercially sensitive."

"What, he never discusses his work with you?"

"No."

17

Cally got up to check something in the kitchen.

"Doesn't that worry you?" he called to her.

"Why?" she asked, wondering where this was leading.

"Well, do you talk to him about your work?"

"Of course I do," she said returning to the room.

"There you are then, your work has a high level of sensitivity too, doesn't it?" he said. "Of course everyone discusses their work with their partner."

"How would you know, Galen?" she answered, turning on him.

There was a pause in the conversation.

"I'm sorry. You're right," he answered eventually.

"No, I'm not right. You're probably much better at relationships than Tyler or I am. I'm sorry."

She explained that her relationship with Tyler was unique.

"Every marriage is its own mystery," she said.

"Marriage?"

"Don't get excited, Galen, it's a euphemism. Marriage in its broadest sense." She paused. "We're not getting married," she proclaimed to emphasise the point.

They smiled at each other and remembered how they had always argued when they were younger. They were both strong characters and they often clashed when together.

"What made you become a priest, Galen?" She was suddenly conscious that she had never asked such a simple question of her friend. Of course, they had discussed it, but she had never understood what caused him to take such a dramatic step in his life.

He paused and wondered whether she would understand his answer. It sounded a bit over-sentimental, a little too heavy for a midweek chat.

"I came out of the confessional one day and saw the image of Our Lady glide across the altar."

"Why did it happen that time, do you think?" she asked without hesitation.

"I don't know. I've thought about that many times. Perhaps I was in a state of perfect grace for the first time in my existence."

"That's a strange term to use. Why do you say existence and not life?"

"I feel that this life is just part of the journey. I think I might be coming towards the end of that journey."

"And you think this journey begins with a calling by Mary, walking across the altar in front of you?"

"I don't know, Cally."

"Perhaps it's another Mary that is calling you. Someone else, from deeper in the past. Deep in the early part of your journey."

Galen wanted to change the subject. It was getting too heavy. Never discuss religion or politics, he thought. But it was difficult when you were a priest. People expect you to talk endlessly about religion.

"Is Tyler's job safe?" Galen asked after a few minutes.

"Well, not as safe as yours, I suppose but, yes, he's doing very well."

"He always was a swot at school. Do you remember all the prizes he used to win for science and maths?"

Cally nodded and sipped her beer. She, too, realised that the conversation was getting a little too deep, so she decided to seek Galen's advice on the David Hallet case. She explained her concerns about the weapon used, the text message, the wording of that message and the lack of any evidence other than the DNA she found at the scene and, of course, the motive.

The weapon could easily be explained, thought Galen. David Hallet visited 1 Wharf Street to see Nelson Kosoto and, perhaps, kill him in revenge for killing his daughter. After all, the police had told everyone that they were not looking for anyone else in connection with the murder of Charlene. What sort of message did that send to David Hallet? The machete could easily have belonged to Nelson but David Hallet got it off him and killed him with it.

"But what about the text message?" asked Cally. She repeated what had been said and felt a little embarrassed for swearing in front of a priest, even one she had known since school days.

"He was angry."

"No, Galen, in all the months this enquiry has been going on I have never heard David Hallet swear once. He was interviewed relentlessly for two days. He was deliberately kept under pressure. He never swore in all that time. He would have said 'You messed with the wrong person', not 'You fucked with the wrong people.'".

"But then there's the DNA, Cally. You say it was on the body and on the wall of the room. How positive is that sort of evidence? Can there be any doubt about it?"

"No," she answered in a resigned tone and went into the kitchen to get Galen another beer before serving dinner. They were just about to sit down to eat when a text message arrived on Cally's phone.

"Anything important?" asked Galen as she went to retrieve the message.

"Not sure, it's from Chief Superintendent Bent asking me to meet him in his office in the morning."

"That's an unfortunate name for a copper isn't it? He must take a lot of stick."

But Cally admitted that she didn't see much of the head of the murder squad. Galen noticed that she looked a little concerned but she clearly did not know what the meeting was about.

After they finished their meal, Cally received a call from Steve Redpath to check whether she had received the text message from Bent and to say that Bertoni wanted to meet up before they spoke to the chief superintendent.

"I'll pick you up about eight and then we can drive round to collect Ashley and chat on the way."

"Where does Ashley live?" she asked.

"In the past most of the time," came the sarcastic reply. "See you at eight."

Hearing that Cally had an important interview in the morning was just the excuse Galen needed to leave earlier than planned. They shared a risotto and a bottle of white wine, reminiscing about their school days and spoke a little more about the Hallet case. But, after Galen had shown her all the latest apps on his Blackberry and bored her with his nerdish interest in all things IT, he looked at the clock and talked about leaving. Cally still enjoyed his company and their friendship went back a long way. They agreed to meet up again soon, when Tyler was around.

~~~ الـ صمت من الـ عهد ~~~

Tyler wasn't shy but he didn't really like meeting people for the first time. It was one of his many irrational fears, like heights and dying in a fire. He thought that perhaps he was once abused as a child but he couldn't have been because he was sure he wouldn't forget something like that. He would have remembered that. But then he convinced himself that

21

maybe he had subconsciously removed it. It felt so real, like some holiday incident in the dark, distant past. The mind works in funny ways, he thought, before finally convincing himself that perhaps it was the product of one of his dreams.

Tyler had become a little blasé about seminars. His job required him to keep up-to-date with the latest techniques and ideas on genetic research, so he was a frequent attendee at such events. They were normally a mix of regulars, slightly outnumbered by the newcomers and trade magazine reporters looking for a page filler. As soon as he had checked in to the hotel and unpacked, he sent a text to Galen to make sure he was joining Cally for dinner. He almost always received an immediate reply from Galen, who may not be the only Catholic priest with a Blackberry but was probably the most nerdish of computer freaks who had responded to the calling.

"Def," came the immediate and abridged text response.

It seemed a bit early for a drink, but there is little else to do when you are away from home on business in a strange hotel. It was a very hot day and he was on expenses. So Tyler checked his iphone, answered a couple of email messages and walked down to the bar. He hesitated when the barman asked what he wanted to drink. He looked at his watch, surveyed the room and, in spite of the fact that the other customers were partaking in afternoon tea, he ordered a pint of cold lager.

"Hi," said a voice sitting at a table behind him.

A man of about the same age as him stood up and walked over with his hand held out. Tyler didn't recognise him but took his hand and shook it anyway.

"Paul Gilligan," he said. "Are you attending the conference?"

Tyler nodded, introduced himself and asked if Paul wanted a drink.

"It's a bit early but, okay, yeah I'll have a beer too."

He spoke with a slight accent that Tyler didn't recognise. His olive complexion suggested that he wasn't English.

"Who are you with?" asked Tyler.

"Nobody."

"No," said Tyler, "I mean, what company are you with?"

Paul laughed. "Still nobody, then," he replied. "I'm a freelance journalist."

"In England?"

"No, I've been in the States for a while. I tend to travel quite a lot."

"So what are you doing at this seminar?"

"A piece for *Research Today*. And you?"

"I'm a molecular biologist with Double Helix Limited in London."

The bar was quiet. Two women sat by the window drinking coffee and a TV played silently in the otherwise empty lounge.

Tyler and Paul shared another two drinks before they thought about getting changed for dinner. Just as they were preparing to leave another young and clearly foreign man joined them at the bar. He ordered a coffee from the barman and asked if they were attending the conference. Not wishing to appear rude, Tyler offered to pay for the coffee and ordered two more drinks for Paul and himself.

The man introduced himself as Piruz Yilmaz but preferred to be called Perry. He was originally from Turgutreis in Turkey but was working for Codon Genetics Limited, which was a competitor of Tyler's employer and was also based in London.

The three men enjoyed a few jokes and exchanged memories of previous seminars. But Tyler had never seen either of them before. Other people attending the seminar began to join them at the bar at various intervals and, in the end, they skipped dinner and instead grabbed some bar snacks and continued drinking. Tyler met a young woman specialising in genetically modified food, an older man who was developing medical applications for genetic disorders and an enthusiastic young man in glasses with a bright green pullover and even brighter ginger hair. Alex was working in species conservation and Tyler hoped that the conference would not spend too much time on animal genealogy as it had little bearing on his work. Only a few of the delegates accepted Tyler's over-simplified description of himself as a molecular biologist without wanting to know more. There were a great many attendees who were in research, but none working in such an advanced field as Tyler. It took him a while to shrug off the determined, but rather boring, Alex and the drinking session went on until quite late, with Perry and Paul joining Tyler as the last guests to leave the bar.

~~~ الـ صمت من الـ عهد ~~~

After collecting Bertoni, Steve and Cally drove directly to a café in Hackney, which the men appeared to be familiar with. Cally asked for a coffee and the two men ordered full English breakfasts before settling down to discuss the purpose of the meeting with Bent.

The cafe was crowded but they managed to find a vacant table in the corner. Delivery drivers and construction workers made up the greater part of the clientele, many of whom knew they had been joined by 'Old Bill'. The cacophony of chattering voices seemed to quieten once the three began their rather furtive-looking discussion.

"My sister's boy," began Bertoni quietly and in deference to the listening multitude, "is a uniform down at H division in Bow. He phoned me last night, just after I received the text from Bent." He paused to scoop up a forkful of beans.

"And?" asked Cally impatiently.

"And?" questioned Bertoni firmly. "And we are in deep shit," he said, barely raising his head six inches above the plate. He checked the room to see if anyone he knew was present and, satisfied that most had stopped listening, continued.

"Our friends at Bow have picked up a dealer called Leroy Livingstone, otherwise known as Bunny, for the murder of Charlene Hallet and," he added after he had secured their full attention, "the murder of Nelson Kosoto."

"They're having a laugh," replied Redpath loudly enough to startle the other customers. And, if raised voices failed to attract their attention, his slamming his knife and fork down on the laminated table top certainly did. "We're only two weeks from taking David Hallet to court for the murder of Kosoto. What the bloody hell are they thinking?"

"My sister's boy tells me that they found a machete on him and they are convinced it is the murder weapon used on both Charlene and Kosoto."

Redpath protested that H division should have brought the machete directly to them.

"I've had a bad feeling about this one for some time," confessed Bertoni ruefully.

~ ~ ~ سـكون حالة مـ يـ ثاق~ ~ ~

Tyler awoke in the early hours of the morning in a strange and eerily quiet hotel bedroom that was in absolute darkness except for a series of red numbers some feet away. 3, 4, 5. He sat up in the bed wondering what had happened to 1 and 2. He squinted his sleepy eyes and 5 disappeared, replaced by 6 and, next to the shadowy outline of a TV on the other side of the room, the red lights on an alarm clock told him it was 3:46. He flopped back on the bed but any tiredness had been drained from him. Fragments of his discussion in the bar a few hours earlier filtered through the silence. He had said too much, been too frank. Or, at least, that was his recollection. He thought about the people he had met and tried to recall their names. There was someone called Alex who had ginger hair and wore a bright green jumper. He was a very serious young man with no sense of humour. Then there was a guy called Paul from a magazine and another called Perry, whose real name was foreign. Tyler's mind was stirring into life now. Piruz, that was it and Perry's boss was there too. A tall, elegant-looking man named Oliver. Tyler searched his memory. Oliver Carmichael. Didn't he ask a lot of questions? Discretion was indeed the better part of valour, but Tyler had swopped discretion for several pints of lager during a very long session in the bar. He was trying to recall what they were talking about when he suddenly thought of Cally. He couldn't remember calling her. He hadn't phoned her to say goodnight. In fact, he hadn't made contact at all. She would be worried. He was worried. She was seeing Galen, so that was alright. He didn't want to disturb their dinner together. He lay there, excusing his error, but confusion was replaced by regret. He tried to go back to sleep but it was too late. He had to recall the events of the previous evening. Had he been indiscreet? Had he told his employer's biggest competitor anything about his latest project? More importantly, had he mentioned anything about his recent discovery? After all, he hadn't even told his boss about it yet. Eventually he fell back into a disturbed sleep and woke as the bright sunlight crashed through the window into his room.

Tyler waited until after breakfast before ringing Cally, just in case anyone mentioned anything about their conversations the night before. He thought he might need someone to confide in if he had, indeed, embarrassed himself. But, although several people he failed to recognise nodded to him and said good morning, nobody joined him at his table for breakfast, so it seemed his fears may have been misplaced. He found a quiet area in reception from which to call Cally on his mobile before the seminar began. It rang a couple of times and went to voicemail.

At the coffee break Tyler checked his mobile phone and there was a brief message from Cally telling him about her appointment with Bent. He didn't get to speak to her until that evening. Cally told him about her day but he didn't want to worry her about any possible indiscretion on his part in the hotel bar. Tyler believed that some things, like work and dreams, were best not shared until he had resolved them in his own mind. He needed to think this situation through and he began by ensuring he stayed sober that night.

~~~ صمتال من ال عهد ~~~

The team found themselves in a different waiting room, expecting another difficult time from someone in authority. They were a little early, so Bertoni went off to find a toilet. He had no idea how long the meeting with Bent might last and his bladder wasn't as resilient as it was in his youth. Steve was still smouldering after receiving a reprimand from Ashley in the car for spending too much time sending personal text messages on his phone.

"Is he okay?" asked Cally quietly, noticing how uncharacteristically tetchy Bertoni was.

"I can't remember the last time he was okay," answered Redpath caustically. "I don't suppose he's been okay since they introduced decimalisation."

"He was probably more comfortable in the twentieth century. The modern world, the internet, iphones and the like are just a mystery to him, but he manages without them; everyone did years ago. There's fear in not understanding things, Steve; show some patience."

"He's a dinosaur, Cally. But it's not just that. It's his whole approach to life." He paused for a moment trying to recall an incident earlier that week. "The other day, he used the word 'forefend'. Nobody uses the word 'forefend'."

"There's nothing terrible in that, Steve. Just because he still speaks in Elizabethan English."

"What? Heavens, 'forefend'! Who uses that language anymore?"

Cally reminded her colleague that Ashley was late coming into the police force. He was a secondary school teacher until he was nearly thirty, which is why he now needs to work until he is almost sixty before he can retire.

Bertoni came ambling back down the corridor and his two associates both manufactured a smile as he sat down. His experience and intuition told him they had been talking about him or collaborating about something. It didn't bother him. He was just pleased they weren't arguing. They all sat in silence for a few moments before they heard the scraping sound of furniture from inside the office. Frighteningly, thought Bertoni, the worse thing was not that they might imprison an innocent man, but that the guilty man would be free to kill again.

Cally and her colleagues were ushered into Chief Superintendent Bent's office and introduced to Alastair Pennington-Brown, who was head of the chambers where Cruickshank worked. Bright sunshine burst through the large window directly into the faces of Bertoni and his team as they sat facing the two men. They shuffled on their chairs in an attempt to avoid the blinding light. Pennington-Brown was made invisible by the brightness.

As they moved their seats, Bent immediately went on the offensive, explaining to them that, with a name like Bent, he had spent his entire career staying absolutely in line with procedure. It was clear that he had begun many such talks in this way. It sounded a little stale to Cally, as if he was reciting his favourite poem.

"I'm so straight," he pointed out, "that you could use me as a plumb line. And I expect my officers to behave in precisely the same way. The very minimum I expect from my team is full compliance with the Police and Criminal Evidence Act." His tone suggested that they had failed to do this in the Hallet case. He wanted to impress Pennington-Brown and reinforce his image as a tough, uncompromising cop.

Redpath manufactured an expression of confusion on his face, suggesting he didn't understand what Bent was talking about. But this served only to upset Bent and the senior officer began pointing directly at him.

"Don't even think about going there, Sergeant," he began. "If you believe for one minute that your hangdog look can fool me, think again. I've been doing this job for long enough to know that you guys all knew exactly what this meeting was about before coming here. You're detectives for Christ's sake. Not very good ones, but detectives all the same."

"Sorry, Sir," mumbled Redpath.

"In any case," added Bent, "Bertoni's nephew works over at H division. Bertoni probably knew about this debacle before I did. Now let's get one thing straight. What we need, from this point on, is total honesty."

This sounded like a policy statement rather than a heartfelt declaration. Honesty was a rare quality in a policeman, especially one who had made chief superintendent.

Bent sat down next to his guest, straightened his jacket and spoke quietly.

"I am going to ask you this question only once. And that doesn't mean once today. It means once only. This is your only chance."

Bertoni uncrossed his legs and Redpath raised his head as if he was about to be shot by a firing squad. But this was a different kind of firing squad.

"Did any of you plant Hallet's DNA on Kosoto's body?"

"Absolutely not, Sir," answered Cally immediately.

"No way!" screamed Redpath.

"Sir, I can absolutely assure you," began Bertoni, before they were all interrupted by Bent, who seemed intent on bringing the meeting to a premature end.

"Detective Inspector Bertoni and Sergeant Redpath, you are both suspended on full pay while this matter is investigated."

"What about her?" asked Redpath, standing up and pointing at Cally, "she's the bloody forensic officer." Cally looked shocked and disappointed at her colleague's attack.

"I'm not finished with Miss Boyce," answered Bent and Redpath thought he had scored a point. He was wrong.

"Nor am I finished with you, Sergeant," he continued. "I will call you to give a full account in a few days' time."

After the two officers had been unceremoniously despatched from the office, Bent and Pennington-Brown questioned Cally for another hour. The second voice continued to be made invisible by the sunlight. They wanted to know every detail of her forensic investigation, particularly how David Hallet's DNA was found both in the shoulder wound of Nelson Kosoto and on the torn wallpaper in the house at Wharf Street.

In view of what had happened to her colleagues, Cally tried to anticipate the end of the interview. She wanted to prevent Bent from suspending her. She had avoided interrupting him during the interview but this was too important not to risk upsetting him. He turned to look at Pennington-Brown and his expression was asking his guest if he had any more questions. He didn't and Cally seized her opportunity.

"I'd like to take some holiday," she blurted out, before realising that this may have sounded like an admission of guilt or, at least, complicity on her part. He looked at her suspiciously.

"Please don't suspend me, Sir. I can't have that on my CV. I've got my whole career ahead of me," she pleaded.

"I'm glad you think you might still have a career, Miss Boyce," replied Bent.

"You're optimistic if nothing else," added Pennington-Brown as he stood up and picked up his briefcase.

Cally turned to say goodbye.

"Look," said Bent, "I don't care if you are on holiday or suspended from your feet until you tell me the truth, but you will make yourself readily available for my questioning whenever and wherever I demand it."

"Of course, Sir," she answered hesitantly, before turning to look directly at Pennington-Brown. "I just don't want this to end up as a witch hunt." She regretted her words immediately.

"My purpose," explained the quietly spoken lawyer, "is to sustain the good reputation of my chambers, Miss Boyce. Chief Superintendent Bent's motive is to do the same for the name of the force. Personally, I have no interest whatsoever in your career, but it must be apparent to you that the future of this enterprise is important to us all. We have no interest in burning you at the stake, if only to protect our own good names." He shook hands with Bent, ignored Cally and left the room.

Tyler placed the slim desk diary back into his briefcase, pensively fingering its dappled, leather surface as he did so. It was a Christmas present from one of the suppliers. It was a deep red colour and had his name and qualifications embossed in gold leaf on the cover. It seemed a shame not to use it, even though he had no need to record appointments. His engagements were kept on the computer. But he had decided to keep the diary anyway and write an entry each day about the dreams that haunted him at night. He determined not to look back, not to reread the entries until the year had ended. Then, in a quiet moment, when the New Year began, he would read it and try to learn what the dreams meant; try to understand who the young woman was and perhaps, through this, learn something about himself. He wondered where Cally was and what she was doing and then he remembered their conversation of the previous evening and hoped that she had not been suspended.

~~~ ال صمت من ال عهد ~~~

To weep seems ludicrous and immature but I am consumed by an inexplicable feeling of loss. I want to cry but, in the light of day, it seems absurd to do so over a dream.

Someone, a young woman who lives in a contrived, illusory world created by my dreams, vanishes on my awakening and leaves me with a sense of unknowing, a sensation of wondering when I might see her again or whether I will ever see her again. Dreams are so fragile and uncontrollable.

Idyllic rural scenes of a harvest are replaced in an instant by a house on fire. I shrink from it, for the heat seems real. I am standing at a distance looking on, watching the flames engulf the house and the people inside it. Strangely there is no screaming, no attempt to escape the burning building. Then the face of a young woman appears at an open window. I know her. She stands, patiently, stoically, looking at me, wishing me well without speaking. But I know what she is thinking. She feels only kindness towards me and yet I do nothing to save her because she does not want to be saved from the flames.

The woman is similar to Cally, but she is not Cally. Like an analogous double, a lookalike, although the likeness is less about actual appearance or mannerisms than a perception of similarity. A perceived likeness rather than one of identity. Perhaps I have been thinking too much about clones lately and they are now occupying my dreams. No, it is not her looks or features, but her actions that are congruent with Cally's behaviour.

The scene changes and I am now facing a steep mountain path. Looking upwards, people are falling over the cliff towards me. I'm not sure where I am or even if it is a real place or somewhere created by my imagination. All I do know is that she is no longer here. There were storms, fires and earthquakes but these had passed. It is calm and silent and the sun is setting behind me. Covered by clouds it moves too quickly to be real. It is raining and getting dark. I am scrambling up the rocky mountain path and goats are running and scattering as I approach them. I finally arrive at the top of the hill.

33

There is a house and an old well. Previous dreams had similar pastoral scenes but these were generally happy times. Times of blissful autumn harvests and joy. And, even though she was not there, I could feel her presence and still felt happy. But not this time, this time, on that windswept mountain top, there is only pain.

2

There were once twin girls born in the settlement city of Metapontum. They were alike in every respect but character. And it was this singular difference that attracted them to the master. Through the grace of contentedness Aspasia saw beauty and love in all things, whereas Kalisto questioned the reason for all things. Through that same grace of contentedness, which had long since been lost to the greater part of humanity, Aspasia acceded in all matters to her sister, who was older by just one hour. This, she did not out of deference or respect for her sister, but because she had resigned herself, from an early age, to be the handmaid of providence.

A column of students, all similarly dressed in a white robe tied loosely at the waist with a cord, strode two-abreast behind an elegant elderly gentleman. Some chatted quietly and others, of a more studious inclination, observed the people as they approached the gates of the city. All wore sandals and a few had coloured braiding to their tunics to denote seniority.

The sisters, along with the other followers of the master, needed to walk quickly to keep up as, even in his old age, he was spritely of foot. They walked in the shade of the tall plane trees that lined the pathway and, as they approached the large and ornately sculptured arched entrance to the city, the incoherent sound of voices grew louder, sounding like a rock fall from one of the neighbouring mountains that overlooked the city. Kalisto left the orderly column of walkers and wandered out of the shade into the sunlight. After many days of torrential rainstorms, she longed to feel the warmth of the sun on her face.

Through the throng of people who filled the market square ran a young man who was eager to join the group. His dark complexion and slender physique was immediately recognisable to the sisters. Gallus wore a broad smile and waved to the twins as he approached.

"It's a hot day for running, Gallus," said Aspasia, as he joined them.

"I awoke late," he confessed quietly, in case the master should hear him.

"At least he *can* run," commented Kalisto in a derisory tone, "unlike his lame friend Tiro."

Her barbed words did not go unnoticed by the master, who fired a glare at his uncharitable student. Kalisto was unmoved by the reproachful look, but Aspasia simply and obediently chose silence. As the group reached the entrance to the Temple of the Muses, the master stopped. It occurred to him that one of his students should not enter this sacred place with bitterness in her heart. So he signalled to the others to go ahead and took a few moments to counsel Kalisto.

Gallus and the others obeyed instinctively, but Aspasia stood still, torn between compliance with the master and allegiance to her sister. After brief consideration, she chose to wait just inside the temple entrance but signalled to Gallus to go ahead. Her languid, dark brown eyes belied a lively mind and loving heart. As with all discernible features, Kalisto shared her sister's eyes. But, to the perceptive onlooker, Aspasia's eyes gifted an assurance of unmeasured love and, although this was absent in the eyes of her sister, for those who knew her well there lay a promise of that same enduring love. That look of indifference from Kalisto was a temporary resident of her soul, as was the callousness of her heart.

"Why do you despise those weaker than yourself so much?" the master asked.

Kalisto shrugged petulantly and remained indifferent to his words. But he waited patiently for her answer. The congregation could wait. The salvation of a single soul took precedence.

"Do we continue to feed the runt of a litter?" she asked, "even though we know its weakness will cause it to die anyway?"

The master gently took her hands in his. He was fleet of foot, but, in his old age, his grip was poor. Her large dark brown eyes tried to look away but he waited until she was looking directly at him.

"Tiro was not born with his affliction," he said, explaining something that she was already aware of. "Another traveller along life's way caused his lameness. Has he not, therefore, suffered enough?"

"Life itself seems unfair to me," she answered. "If it permits the weak to survive and even succeed."

Aspasia had ventured closer to the pair. She loved her sister but would never contradict the master.

"He does not seek sympathy for his condition," she offered, hoping not to attract the disapproval of the master for her boldness. "Tiro works hard and is as industrious as any young man in the region," she added.

As the three stood there, with the master pondering whether to prevent the dark heart of Kalisto from entering the temple, Ceranus, the chief magistrate and his assistant, Kassandros, passed by. Aspasia bowed her head as they did so, but her sister simply raised her eyebrows at her sister's acquiescence and stared Ceranus in the eyes. They frowned and glared at the master's inability to regulate his students.

"Why does that man devote so much of his valuable time to such unworthy souls?" asked Ceranus in a rhetorical tone.

Kassandros mumbled an obsequious response and the two entered the temple and took their places on the front pews. Only the master knew why he paid so much attention to the twins. They represented an important dimension to his own continuing studies. For, in spite of his wide renown for wisdom, he still thirsted for greater knowledge and longed to fully understand the infinite secrets of the transmigration of the human soul. In Aspasia, he saw a soul on its final step towards eternal peace and, in Kalisto, he saw a soul at the beginning of that same journey; a spirit that stood at the threshold of metanoia. The fact that they were twins served only to increase his curiosity.

"Kalisto," he eventually said, "when you express opinions about others, such comments say more about you than they do about the other person. You have a great distance to travel and your journey will take you from selfishness to selflessness for I have no doubt that God's grace will reach your heart. You will meet a great many people on the way. It is what they think of you, rather than what you think of them, that will matter."

Kalisto sighed. Her sister took her hand and led her into the temple, taking a seat at the rear as was the custom for women, particularly those so young.

The master observed Aspasia's actions and determined that forgiveness was a prerequisite of a soul on its final journey through a world of time and space.

The Temple of the Muses lacked the grandeur of the temples in Samos, where many of the residents of Metapontum had emigrated from. But then the coastline was not as pleasing either and the city inferior to that of their homeland. The roof was sufficiently high to give it a sense of majesty but it lacked the opulence of the temples in Greece. The open casements were placed strategically to ensure that the fading light of the sun was directed along the main aisle during the late afternoon at this time of year. The main interior remained cool throughout the hottest of days. Pilgrims, it was often said, visited the temple to escape the heat of day, rather than to seek the grace and mercy of the gods.

Ceranus and Kassandros did not stay for the whole of the master's homily. They both feared his wisdom and believed he had the power to see into their hearts like a spy of the gods. Other than those who had shared in the execution of those deeds, the true darkness of their souls had been revealed only to their victims, for they had left no witnesses to their foul acts. In any case, the chief magistrate had many spies of his own who would report every movement and every word spoken by the master. Whatever the content of his homily, it would soon be reported to Ceranus. To attend the lecture would only give legitimacy to his words. So, they deliberately rose to their feet as he approached the podium and left the temple. A few others, who sought to endear themselves to the city's magistrates, left with them.

The congregation, which now consisted mainly of students, sat in subdued anticipation as the master rose to speak.

"We, each of us, abide in enforced exile from our true homeland," he began. "We shape our present and temporary home with immorality and malevolence. But God himself shares in the responsibility for this."

There was a restrained groan at the reference to 'God', rather than 'the gods', but they failed to understand that he referred to their true home with God, not Greece. He acknowledged their groans with a riposte.

"Yes, a single God created this world. A world of space and time. A world that relies on the interaction of opposites. Light and dark; hot and cold; dry and wet; heavy and light; quickness and slowness; and, of course, male and female. These opposites were created for a reason."

"Before the world began, before the universe existed, there was only good and evil, opposites pitched in an eternal conflict. Good devised a way to entrap evil and created time and space for this purpose alone. Millions of years later, when creation was ready, man was given wisdom from the Tree of Knowledge and the gift of metanoia by the Tree of Life. Evil could not resist the urge to corrupt and good, as recompense for inflicting this on the world, granted man eternal life through metanoia."

But the congregation did not understand the meaning of the word 'metanoia' and many shook their heads in disbelief at what the master was saying.

The master thought about completing his lecture but could see the frustration and discord about him and decided not to continue by telling them that the soul transmigrated seven times before returning to be part of good itself. Some members of the crowd got up and left the temple. Others jeered at him and were unsettled by his talk of a single, omnipotent God.

He paused as if he felt impelled to say something but was constrained by some great force not to do so. Knowledge of the significance of seven would only endanger the few who were prepared to listen, such as Aspasia.

"When we meet next week," he said, "I shall reveal something of great magnitude to you. This news will cause you to understand more fully why we will all, eventually, leave this place of evil and return to our true home. The truth is at the gates of the citadel," he added before leaving the platform.

As the master was speaking, darkness enveloped the temple and the sky outside rumbled prophetically. As he finished, the casements and alcoves were lit up for a second by a lightning flash and a loud crash exploded a few seconds later. Through the open doors the congregation could see a tempestuous storm raging outside. As the sisters sheltered from the heavy rain the master walked over to Kalisto and gave her a sheet of parchment.

"On the way home," he told her, "I want you to tear small pieces from this parchment and cast them to the wind."

"For what purpose?" she asked him.

"When you return to the temple tomorrow, I want you to collect all the pieces and return them to me."

"But that's impossible," she began to say before realising the important lesson she was being taught.

"Yes," said the master, "and so it is with words. Once spoken, they are cast onto the winds and cannot be retrieved. The harm they do cannot be undone."

Leaving the girl to think on his words, the master waited for the storm to subside and took the time to ask Gallus about Tiro, a friend of his, who had been absent. Gallus explained that if his friend failed to work, he was not fed. For him to attend a lecture would require him to fast.

"The mind needs to be fed too, Gallus, and fasting harms nobody."

"It is difficult for him," explained the young man. "Moliones is a hard taskmaster. In any case, Master, the heavy rainstorms of the past few days have destroyed part of the path that leads from the mountain to the city."

"Then take some of the students and repair it, Gallus. If we wait for Ceranus to attend to it, those who live on the mountain will be there until next spring."

~~~ الـ صـمت من الـ عهد ~~~

Now, at that time, a wealthy merchant was visiting Metapontum to trade his wares. The fame and reputation of the master had spread far and wide and Nathaniel of Capernaum was eager to meet with and learn from him. And the master, in full knowledge of the criticism it would bring, was pleased to invite the traveller to stay at his home. From the knowledge he had gained, Nathaniel believed that his host shared his interest in geometry and astronomy and was similarly beguiled by the significance of numbers. The decision to invite a Jew into his house did not go unnoticed by the narrow-minded inhabitants of Metapontum and it was soon brought to the attention of the chief magistrate himself.

For his part, too, Nathaniel recognised the danger that his host courted by welcoming a Jew into his home.

"You place yourself at great risk by opening your door to an infidel," the visitor said when they first met.

"I am often accused of being an infidel myself," he answered generously.

"You could be sentenced to death and yet you have nothing to gain from inviting me to your home. It is not modesty that prompts my words, but truth, for there is nothing I can teach the great master, whose fame knows no borders."

42

Nathaniel was just pleased to have been invited to meet the renowned man at a private audience. He looked forward to relating the details of his meeting with his host on returning to his homeland.

"I have little left to address before I die," said the master. "And death itself holds no fear for me. Besides, my friend, we are talking only of numbers, are we not?"

"Ah, yes, your number theorem. But take care, your wisdom far outweighs my limited knowledge of the subject."

But he soon understood and appreciated the simplicity that his host could bring to the issue.

The master went on to clarify his considered view that numbers had personalities and represented different aspects of life. He explained that the number one represented unity, two diversity and three harmony because it was the sum of unity and diversity. Four represented justice and retribution, five marriage and six creation.

"Numbers are male and female," he confirmed. "Two is the first female number and three the first male, so five represents marriage and six creation because it is the sum of the first male and female numbers, plus one." His voice was calm and authoritative. There was no doubt in his tone. He was absolutely convinced of the conclusions he had reached.

"Understanding the true meaning of numbers can help us come to terms with life and, more importantly, death."

Nathaniel had never considered the way numbers might be related to and have influence on the world and matters ethereal.

"We are all to perish, Sir," answered the Jew. "When Adam sinned, man was separated from God; condemned to die once the Tree of Life was taken from him."

"It was not just the Tree of Life that was taken from us, Nathaniel."

The expression on Nathaniel's face asked for more information.

"There were two trees in the Garden of Eden. The Tree of Life *and* the Tree of Knowledge. The latter is now lost to mankind, Nathaniel." The master spoke quietly, but with authority and assurance. He stared trance-like as he continued speaking. "The knowledge of metanoia; the knowledge of the transmigration of the soul, the message that eternal life is the inheritance of everyone, or every soul to be more accurate. The reward for every soul that transverses this world seven times. Our prize for enduring the challenges of a world of time and space, created by the eternal and all-knowing God, to enthral and entrap the eternal enemy, evil." The master blinked and shook his head, realising he had probably said too much.

His guest implored him to expand on his words but he would add little more to his statement at that time. "Do your own scriptures not say that the Lord ransoms the souls of his servants?" asked the master.

"Nathaniel," said the master in a calmer and more controlled tone, "some are attracted by the desire of obtaining crowns and honours, others come to expose their different commodities to sale, while curiosity draws a third class with the simple desire of contemplating whatever deserves notice in that celebrated assembly. Thus on the more extensive theatre of the world, while many struggle for the glory of a name and many pant for the advantages of fortune, a few who are neither desirous of money nor ambitious of fame and are sufficiently gratified to be spectators of the wonder, the hurry and the magnificence of the scene."

"We are both of the latter category, methinks," answered Nathaniel.

"If you are still here next week," said the master, "I shall explain more of metanoia at the Temple of the Muses. I shall tell you what Zoroaster himself taught me."

"Much as I would like to, my friend, it is impossible for me to attend the temple."

"You will not need to attend the temple, Nathaniel," he answered assuredly, "for my message will resound far beyond these realms. It is a secret I have held for more than fifty years. And I am pledged to keep it so, but I am sorely torn. I cannot understand why I should have been entrusted with such a secret that I must now simply take to my grave. It doesn't make sense. The Pythian priestess herself said that my wisdom would never be exceeded. Does it not fall to me, therefore, to reveal the secret?"

"If it serves you to share this confidence with me, Sir, I shall undertake to mention nothing until it is in the public domain."

Nathaniel agreed to stay with the master for two more nights before conducting business to the east of Metapontum and then returning south to the sea ports. And the master did share the secrets, which he was soon to reveal, with the Jew.

~~~ الـ صمت من الـ عهد ~~~

The fierce wind lashed the citizens of Metapontum with rain and hail but nobody felt its sting as harshly as the creatures that lived on the hilltops above the city. The younger she-goats had not felt the biting hailstones before and were frightened by the roar of the sea below. But Germano stood proud and erect, staring glassy green-eyed away from the strong wind. His age and experience caused him to sense something in the mist;

perhaps a wolf, for that is where the wolf would approach from; hidden by the mist, downwind and made silent by the roaring sea. Just at the moment the old ram lost interest in the distant outline, Tiro noticed what had taken his attention.

High on a hilltop above the city of Metapontum, where the Bradamus River snakes endlessly in search of its mother the sea, another meeting of great consequence was to take place. A rider approached from a charcoal skyline at a gentle pace. Shrouded in a hooded cloak against the mist-like rain that fell from the blackened heavens, he came slowly nearer. The sun withdrew behind the blanket of cloud that lay ensnared on the hilltop where a farmhouse stood and the figure appeared and disappeared as the mist fell about his shadowy image.

Tiro guided a ram away from the cliff edge and, leaving his watch over the goat herd, limped painfully to the house as quickly as his crippled leg would permit, calling to his master as he ran.

"What ails thee boy?" replied a disconsolate voice from the doorway.

"A rider approaches, Master."

"I see no rider, you barmpot," said the man, looking into the mist. "Get back to your labour, boy."

Tiro chose not to argue with his master, knowing well the harshness of temper that accompanied his bad moods.

It was only when the irritable old man turned back to cross the threshold that he caught sight of the rider. He was taken by the unhurried advance. Although visitors were infrequent to his decaying homestead, he was sure he did not recognise the gait or bearing of this particular horse and rider.

Tiro received no apology, for the man was as ill-mannered as he was ill-tempered.

Moliones stepped onto the rain-sodden patch of land at the front of the house, picked up the pitchfork that lay against the wall and stood with the tines deep in a heap of straw that lay there. He did not want to provoke a fight but he wanted to be ready in case the stranger harboured malicious intent. This was a lonely place and Moliones was aware of how violent man could be.

One judges others in accordance with his own principles and values, thought Peritas, as his horse came to a halt outside the house.

"It's late," he called as he approached, "and I wish to break my journey if you would extend a welcome to a traveller such as I."

"Do you have business hereabouts?" asked Moliones.

"In the city of Metapontum," he answered.

"Is it good business, Sir?"

"I trade in copper from Dilmun in your homeland."

"You travel light," answered Moliones.

"I don't carry my wares with me. I come to arrange a sale, not to deliver it."

"And your name, Sir?"

"You ask a great many questions, Sir." The visitor paused, still sat upon his steed. He was used to procuring information rather than providing it.

"Tattannu. And you won't need the pitchfork. It is too late for the goats to feed and you need to cover the straw from the rain, not turn it."

Tiro watched the exchange with interest. The pitchfork, he thought, would be of little use against the stranger. He was quick witted, strong and fleet of foot. The overweight and aged Moliones would be no match for their visitor, even were he to be equipped with more apposite weaponry.

47

"Two drachma will get you a bed in the barn and a hearty meal, my Lord," said Moliones, throwing the pitchfork on top of the straw.

"And make me a poorer man, too."

"For two drachma, Tiro here will tend to your horse and my wife will tend to yourself if it suits you, Sir," he said with a wink of the eye.

"It does not," replied the stranger.

"Or I have my servant here if a boy suits you better, Lord," Moliones answered pointing at Tiro.

"Indeed it does not," Peritas answered firmly, as Tiro mumbled that he was no man's servant.

Moliones shrugged his shoulders. "He is less a servant and more someone who would starve to death if I was less generous."

"I will pay you three obulos," he answered, "for a bed, a meal and some care for my horse who is showing some lameness."

The farmer held out his hand and, seeing the purse, warned the visitor about the dangers of travelling alone.

"If you lack the law and justice to accompany it," he replied confidently, "then I will administer my own. So do not trouble yourself on my behalf."

Tiro led the horse to the stable and Peritas took in his surroundings. Moliones had been drinking from the still. Peritas could smell it in the air.

Moliones did not question why the visitor had stopped just a few miles short of his destination. It was an opportunity to earn some easy money, so he assumed the traveller did not know how close he was. The boy knew better than to question a stranger without the permission of his master. But Tattannu, or Peritas as he was really known, because he had lied about his name, knew how far he was from the city. And he knew he was more likely to find out what awaited him from these peasants than from a suspicious and guileless band of coastal dwellers, whose brains had been softened by the world and all it offered in this, their new home.

"I have a dove we can cook for our meal," called Moliones as he returned towards the house.

Peritas decided that it was time to extract some useful information from his hosts.

"I'll eat no flesh of the animal," he said, knowing that he risked associating himself with the one he searched for.

"You eat only the fruit of the Earth?" asked Tiro.

"No, but flesh disagrees with me at this time," he lied, for he was indeed a vegetarian. The subject was designed to establish whether Tiro knew of the one for whom he was searching, for he too ate no meat. He succeeded.

"My master eats no meat," said Tiro, preparing to make a fire for the night.

"Then why does your master prepare a dove?" replied Peritas, knowing well that Tiro referred to someone else, but pretending otherwise.

"No," replied Tiro, "not him, he is no more my master than you, Sir. I mean my master in the city. He is an astrologer, a philosopher and a poet."

"And what is his name?"

"The master lives in exile, having been sent from his homeland by Polycrates of Samos. He lives under the constant threat of death, so we are forbidden from mentioning his name. But you have heard of him for sure, Sir, because he was named by the Pythian priestess herself."

"He was named by the Pythian priestess but cannot now be named in public. Is it a riddle you use to identify him, for I am

49

sure I know the man of whom you speak?" answered Peritas, adding, "and what have you learned from the master yourself, Tiro?"

"Much, Sir. Too much, maybe, because I am slow of learning and must confess to not understanding all that he teaches. But he is much interested in the human mind and takes great interest in his students. He charts their habits, how they act and what they say. We must first attain knowledge and that knowledge may then lead us to wisdom."

Tiro paused as he tried to remember the many lessons he had learned from the master.

"The master teaches us to free ourselves from everything that binds us to the material world. He ministers to our moral and spiritual welfare and directs us to our true destiny; towards the light and away from darkness."

"And, when he stops philosophising, does he speak of anything I would understand?"

"He speaks of two trees that stand in a garden, Sir," Tiro replied timidly, not knowing their significance.

"Only two trees. 'Tis truly a garden then, not an orchard," replied the visitor.

It was getting dark and Peritas asked Tiro to fetch some water from the well. The visitor then retrieved some root vegetables from his saddle bag and began preparing them for a meal. He invited Tiro to join him and so the young man told Moliones that he would not be eating with him that evening. Moliones wished them good night and locked himself in the house for the night. The fire that Peritas had prepared was now sufficiently hot to cook the stew. For some time the two sat in silence waiting for the meal to simmer. Eventually, it was the boy who spoke.

"You chose well to stay here for the night, for the path down the hill to the town is treacherous following the heavy rain of late." He went on to tell the stranger that his friend Gallus had made the precarious journey earlier to tell him that they would be clearing the pathway the next day if the rain ceased. Gallus had told him of the master's intention to reveal a great secret in the temple. The expression on the face of Peritas remained unchanged as Tiro spoke of his friend's news of the master's lecture in the temple earlier that day.

Peritas was schooled in the Magi arts from the age of five. Most novices do not join the order until they are twelve years old but Peritas's mother died and his father was a friend of Theas, who was to mentor his son for the next twenty years. It was Theas who named Peritas the gentle assassin because of his ability to solve problems and remove people without the need to kill them himself. He was a conduit for murder rather than a murderer. Peritas was a committed servant to the cause and he submitted himself to the will of his masters.

When he received his commission as Musteria in the Magi order at the Temple of Neptune at Babylon he was just twenty-five years old, the youngest the order had known. His training prevented him from taking pride in such an achievement, for he recognised the weakness that pride nurtured.

Peritas was one of only four Magi in the Musteria order. They were the keepers of the secret. It was they alone who were assigned with the responsibility to ensure it remained only with those committed to continue its confidentiality until evil itself had been defeated. Only those four Magi were authorised to take whatever action was necessary to guard that secret. Each in due time was to be replaced so that the number remained at four, the number of justice and retribution.

The silence was broken by what sounded like a baby crying close by. It was a young goat. Tiro went to fetch the kid but Peritas stopped him.

"He cries from fear," Peritas told the boy.

"All the more reason to comfort him."

"Do you keep a bow?"

"Of course," the boy replied and Peritas told him to fetch it.

When Tiro returned, Peritas handed him a black scarf and told the boy to blindfold him. The visitor, still clad in a dark cloak against the elements, sat a short distance away from the fire, looking towards a copse some eighty metres away. The boy went to speak, to ask him what his purpose was, but Peritas told him to be quiet. And so he remained for ten minutes, sitting in silence with a dark blindfold about his eyes, holding the bow and arrow that the boy had handed him. Then, almost in one movement, he stood up, removed the blindfold quickly, took aim with the bow and fired an arrow into the darkness. A scream-like howl filled the stillness of the night. Tiro stood, amazed. The visitor had killed a wolf with a single arrow shot into pitch darkness. His mind was full of wonder and questions, but he could not speak, such was his awe at the skill shown.

A few minutes passed and the boy finally summoned enough courage to ask how he had managed to kill the wolf in such darkness.

The blindfold, explained the Magus, helped to accustom his eyes to the darkness for he had not sat with his eyes closed but open against the scarf. On removing the blindfold he simply looked into the distance for the reflected light of the wolf's eyes in the darkness. He knew the sound of the arrow would cause the wolf to turn and retreat into the woods but, as the animal did this, the arrow struck him in the neck. In the morning, Tiro would see from what had not been eaten of the wolf, that the visitor spoke the truth.

Tiro retrieved the young goat and held it towards him, stroking its velvet coat and long ears.

"How did you know the kid was affeared, Master?"

But the Magus was not willing to reveal this part of his secret art, for sensing fear in another being, whether it be animal or human, is a skill best retained by those of conviction. Tiro did not ask a second time, but changed the question.

"Are you a Magian, Sir?" he asked.

"A Magian is a sorcerer. Do you think I am a sorcerer?"

"Well, not a Magian. What is the word? Are you a Magoi then, Sir?"

"What will it serve you to know my answer?"

The boy shrugged.

"There are those who are enemies of the Magi, Tiro. So, if I were indeed a Magus, it might harm me to admit it."

"But I know nobody, see nobody," replied Tiro.

"Then my answer will not serve you at all. So I shall answer not."

"Then you are a Magoi."

"Because I refuse to say I am not, then I am. Is that your logic? For if it is, you must see it is flawed. If I ask you if you are a landowner or a King and you refuse to answer, does that mean you are?"

Tiro shook his head and concluded that his visitor was not a Magus, but was clearly someone very special.

Peritas picked up a stick and prodded the fire.

"I know a Magoi," Tiro said after a spell of silence. "It is the man I spoke of earlier. The man whose name we must not mention, my master in Metapontum. He was taught by the Chaldean priests and studied in Babylon for twelve years."

"Babylon," answered Peritas convincingly. "He has travelled far in his life."

"You must have heard of him, Sir," said Tiro. "For he is from our homeland and was born on the island of Samos."

"But you cannot speak of his name?" asked Peritas.

"We speak it not, Sir, for the master was exiled by the King himself. There are those in this world who would harm him."

"And you think I am one who would do him harm?"

"No, Sir, of course not. You do not know him."

"But you will not name him," said Peritas.

"Well, perhaps on this occasion," answered Tiro and was about to reveal the master's name.

"Please, speak it not for my benefit, for I have no interest in the man, other than to make conversation with you over our meal together."

"Very well, Sir," answered Tiro, "but you will have heard of him, for he possesses knowledge of the sacred sciences."

"The heirs of Zoroaster alone possess knowledge of the sacred sciences. Their temples are lit by the radiance of the gods," answered the visitor as he poured the stew into two wooden bowls. "Has this man studied you, Tiro?"

"He looks into my soul, Sir. He told me I stood in the mouth of Hades. He said that seven challenges await me and I am destined to fail six times. He says that above the entrance to the Temple of the Oracle at Delphi are two words: 'know thyself'. 'Think on these words,' he said to me, 'think on these words'. And I have done so, Sir, but I cannot fathom what he speaks of. What seven challenges await me? And how should I know myself?"

Peritas sat eating the stew and listened intently to the boy's ramblings.

"The master talks more frequently of late about his exile from Samos. He dwells on the memory of the place. Its pavilioned city abreast a great mountain on which stands the Temple of Neptune. He is filled with remembrances of its verdant coastline and wide bay where he once dined at the Palace of Polycrates, with its majestic colonnades."

The boy spoke of the very temple where Peritas had been tutored in the Magi arts. This is where he had been taught all he needed to know, including how to defend himself when necessary. Peritas stared out into the darkness and thought of the challenge that awaited him.

The Magi alone understood that the world had been created by God to entrap evil. God exists as eternal light and evil as the spirit of darkness. God knew that evil could not resist the challenge of turning his creation over to darkness. But, in doing so, evil would become entrapped in time and space. So life and death—not the simple mortality of the world, but true, eternal life and death—became the game pieces representing good and evil in this battle that had continued since the beginning of time. And the game board was the battle for the soul of mankind. There is only one outcome, of course, because Good is not constrained by time and space and can see the future. He knows that man will return to his divine origins.

At one time during his residence at Crotona, Tiro recalled, the master had remained in a pit for forty days and forty nights. Just a small shaft for air prevented him from being buried alive. Yet, when he was released, he recalled everything that had happened in Crotona during his imprisonment.

"The miracle marked him out as a devil," Tiro added, "he was expelled from Crotona for it and came here to Metapontum."

Peritas knew that it was a trick just like the one he had performed with the bow and arrow. There is always a logical explanation. The master had an accomplice who visited the chamber and passed food, water and news through the air shaft. The master read the notes by the light of a candle and then used the same candle to burn the message. When he returned to the surface after forty days he simply recalled all the information he had received from his accomplice.

When the boy had stopped speaking and Peritas had learned all he needed to know about the master, he began to make conversation with the boy, in order to win his confidence.

"What caused the injury to your leg, Tiro?" he asked.

"I was thrown from that cliff yonder," he explained, pointing towards the cliff edge. "It was when I was very small. I do not remember it myself, of course, but my parents were captured and enslaved and I was thrown, to my death, from the cliff. But, by the mercy of the gods, I was saved."

The farmhouse stood high up on the hillside overlooking the gulf. This face of the cliff was steep enough to prevent anyone walking down. Waves crashed against the cliff and it was easy to lose goats when the cloud became fixed on the hilltop. Tiro did not remember being thrown from the cliff. He learned of it from neighbours. Raiders from north of the mountains had taken away his mother and father and thrown him over the cliff. That is what everyone said, so that is what Tiro believed. When the story was elaborated on, the possibility of Spartans being responsible was mentioned. After all, Spartans threw their own children from cliffs if they failed to meet the high physical standards set by the warrior people.

Peritas listened to the boy's tale and concluded, without too much consideration, that the story did not represent the truth. Who would want to enslave a farmer and his wife? The boy's parents were thrown over the cliff with him. Except they did not become lodged among the rocks that formed its craggy surface. What did they have of value? They had no money, no belongings worth stealing and, by Tiro's accounts, even the goats were not stolen. The only person to gain from the incident was the present incumbent of the farm, Moliones. He could not have done the deed alone, nor would he have simply taken ownership of the farm without the permission of the local magistrates. Indeed, it was probably they who killed the boy's parents and sold the farm to Moliones.

"Did the law prevent you from making a claim for the land after you were recovered from the cliff face?" asked Peritas.

"I was only a child," insisted Tiro. "Moliones's first wife took me in out of the kindness of her heart and, after she died, Moliones himself kept me on to work on the farm."

"Workers get paid," Peritas rebuked him.

The boy waved his arms about him. "I'm fed and sheltered from the cold each winter, even when there is little work to do. Where would I go anyway?"

"Moliones killed your mother and father," said Peritas glibly without a hint of doubt, "or was party to the killing."

"No," replied Tiro, "It was the Spartans."

"Do you know how far you are from Sparta?"

"Farther than Metapontum I imagine."

"Tiro, you think you have knowledge. But only knowledge that is truth is worthy of the name," he added, thinking how far Tiro was from wisdom. "Have you ever sought to recover the property that is rightfully yours?" asked Peritas.

"The master teaches us that covetedness and avarice do not serve us well," he replied.

"They are your master's words, but they do not reflect your true feelings. Suppression of a natural desire for justice is not an antidote for avarice, young Tiro."

The words of Peritas were contrived to seduce Tiro and create dissonance and anger.

Tiro looked hungrily at the remains of the meal.

"May I have the last piece of bread, Sir?"

"The piece of bread is not mine, Tiro," answered Peritas, "but you ask for my permission to consume it. Yet this land on which we sit is indeed yours, but you do not ask for it."

The boy looked forlorn. "What good would asking for it do? My pleas would simply be rejected. Indeed, I would be fortunate even to receive an audience with the lowest clerk at the magistrate's office."

"Then you must barter," replied the Magus.

"But I have nothing to barter with, Sir."

Tiro ate the remains of the bread and Peritas allowed his words to take root in the shallow mind of the boy.

"Have you ever played dice, Tiro?"

"No, dice does not put food on my plate. It is hard work that does, not frivolous play."

"On the contrary, Tiro, dice can teach us much. As in life, dice is not so much about what we throw, but what we make of what we throw."

"You are a wise counsellor, Sir, and I would welcome your advice, but I understand little of what you say and do not see how it might help me to secure my rightful inheritance."

"Just like the game of dice, Tiro, you must use the circumstances that prevail at that time. Who is the chief magistrate for this region?" asked Peritas.

"Ceranus," answered Tiro, "have you heard of him?"

"I have not," admitted Peritas, "but all magistrates are of the same mould. How long has Ceranus held office?"

"Many years, Sir, before I was born."

"Then, if what I believe is true, it is he who conspired with Moliones to steal this farm from your parents."

Tiro was now beginning to hold fast to every word spoken by the stranger and, trusting in him, he began to understand that his conclusion was probably true. Before they retired to sleep, Peritas explained what Tiro needed to do. He was to seek a private audience with Ceranus or, better still, his assistant Kassandros and tell him that he knew what the master was to reveal in the temple next week. When Tiro met Kassandros, Peritas explained, it was important that he spoke as if he knew the events concerning the farm, rather than suspected them. He must be just as convincing that this was the very subject of which the master would speak in the temple the following week.

"Let no doubt be apparent. This is the key to success. Convince Kassandros of these two elements and this farm shall be returned to you," Peritas assured Tiro. But, in his heart, he knew that the godless lay in wait for the virtuous man.

By the time they retired to their bed in the barn, Peritas had succeeded in planting a plan in the young and easily corrupted mind of Tiro.

As he fell asleep, Peritas thought back to the last time he had seen the master.

Encouraged by his father Cyrus and the King's wise counsellor Zoroaster, the royal son Cambyses was taught in the ways of the Magi. So, when he became King of Persia, Cambyses summoned the wisest of men throughout the world to Babylon. But the venerable master refused and was taken there by force. His resistance was a deed he later regretted and he stayed voluntarily with Zoroaster for twelve years, gaining wisdom in astronomy and numbers. When he was fifty-six years old, the venerable master returned to his home city of Samos. It was during the final year of the master's stay in Babylon that Zoroaster himself died and he took up the mantle for the esoteric ideals of the mystical Magi. Peritas was only ten years old but remembered well the brilliant Pythagoras of whom Tiro now spoke.

Just as Peritas had fallen asleep thinking on the past, so Tiro entered the world of Morpheus thinking of the future, or a vision of the future that the visitor had planted in his mind. He must tell the magistrates the master's own words. The master confesses that he is a slave to the truth, he cannot deny it. He must warn them that the master intends to tell the truth about their deeds. "Won't that place the master in danger?" Tiro had asked Peritas. "They will repatriate him to Samos," Peritas had assured him, which is what he wants, is it not? Does Aspasia not say so herself; how he pines for his homeland. The magistrates will reward Tiro for his information. They will reinstate him as master of the farm his parents owned and Aspasia may then marry him as a man with income and position.

"What of Moliones?" Tiro had asked. "He will buy another farm with all the money he has saved up by not paying you a wage," Peritas had assured him. "Did the master not say 'know thyself'? What do you think he meant by that, Tiro? He meant know your position, know your rightful heritage. He intends to reveal that you are the rightful owner of the farm and you must warn the magistrates so that they might act before the council is defamed. They will welcome your help and reinstate you as the owner of the farm before they are publicly shamed by the master. Ask and you shall receive, Tiro. Know thyself."

Yes, thought Tiro as he drifted off to sleep. Know thyself.

~~~ الـ صمت من الـ عهد ~~~

Once the group of students had cleared the mountain path the following day, they returned to Metapontum for a meal. All, that was, except Gallus and Aspasia, who continued the journey up to the mountain top to see their friend Tiro. Kalisto scorned the idea of visiting a farm slave and returned with the others to the city.

Gallus and Aspasia approached the farmhouse tentatively. The mist that veiled the hilltop throughout most of the morning had now lifted under the influence of the midday sun. They could hear the familiar voice of Moliones berating young Tiro. As they drew closer to the house, they could see their friend conversing with a stranger as he sat in the open doorway of the barn.

"Get to your work, Tiro, or there will be no food for you tonight," called Moliones.

Tiro shuffled off past his friends to join the goat herd on the upper mountain.

"If I lose but one goat to this wolf," threatened Moliones, "you will not eat for a week."

Tiro thought about telling the old man about the killing of the wolf the previous night, but thought he would only earn a beating for his riposte.

"Tiro," called Gallus to his friend, "we have repaired the path. The passage to Metapontum is clear again if you wish to visit the temple."

But, affeared of Moliones, Tiro ignored his friend and continued on his journey up the mountain with the aid of a heavy stick.

I was born a shepherd boy and I have a shepherd boy's ways, he thought to himself as he obeyed.

Gallus walked to the well and drank from it as Moliones went about his business. He refilled the cup for Aspasia.

"Good morning," called Peritas as he approached the pair. "I am in your debt for repairing the road into town."

"Our master directed us to do the same, Sir," replied Gallus.

"The same man your friend Tiro spoke of over our meal last evening."

"The very same, I am sure, Sir."

"A master with no name," mumbled Peritas loud enough for them to hear.

"He is nameless, not through dishonour," replied Gallus, as Aspasia stood by silently, taking in each word that was spoken.

"The master is a virtuous man," continued Gallus, "initiated by the Magi as Zoroaster was before him. He was the first to be purified of his past lives by the Magi."

As they spoke, Aspasia was filled with foreboding. She had been taught to abandon those things we dislike in others, for it is not godlike to acknowledge evil in others but not to recognise it in oneself. She had studied under the master for long enough to realise that on this, her final journey, she could recognise evil in others as an essential part of her journey home. To acknowledge that evil exists and can be resisted strengthens the soul. So, sensing that the stranger might cause them harm, she hurried Gallus away under the pretext of needing to find her sister.

~~~ الـ صمت من الـ عهد ~~~

The heady scent of basil overpowered the still air on the terrace above the herb garden at the Temple of Ceres. Every

62

day, after breakfast, the master would walk around the gardens, enjoying the bouquet and glorious majesty and colour of the flowers that surrounded his house. But the thunderstorms of the past few days had left muddied tracks and deep puddles that the gathering heat had failed, so far, to extinguish.

So, on this day, he sat on the terrace contemplating his decision to finally speak of the secret after all these years. The undertaking given to Zoroaster himself had not been forgotten. But he simply could not understand why he had been entrusted with this great secret, only to take it to his grave. All things were to fulfil a purpose, he thought to himself, but this seemed to have none.

Pythagoras had been older than the others called to Babylon by the Magi. Those to be taught in the secret arts joined at the age of twelve but Pythagoras had ignored the call and had to be taken by force. But he did not resist captivity, choosing to succumb to the wishes of his captors. He relished in the enlightenment that surrounded this mystic place. He learned so much from his great mentor and many spoke of him as the natural successor to Zoroaster.

The terrace was now enveloped in sunshine and the heat and light disturbed him. So, moving to another balcony on the other side of the house, he stopped only for some water from a jug that had been placed next to his seat. It was quieter on this side and, therefore, more suited to his contemplation. His education had been delivered slowly, by degrees. So, when the revelation itself was delivered it did not, strangely, overwhelm him. Not all Magi were entrusted with the secret of the Tree of Knowledge. Those who were not understood why they had not been entrusted because of the teaching they had received. Complete obedience was the foundation stone of the Magi.

Each priest may be given one small part to play during their life. Their calling may, sometimes, be fulfilled by one solitary act.

Some Magi received very specific tasks, whereas others might live out their life without ever receiving the call. Pythagoras could not believe that this was the destiny chosen for him. He sat back in the chair and considered the enormity of the responsibility now placed on him. He closed his eyes so that the light did not distract him in his thoughts. Darkness held no fear for the Magi.

Three thousand years had passed since Good had enticed evil into the world of time and space that had been created for that purpose.

In the beginning when man, like God, was eternal, a river ran through Eden that divided itself into four rivers. On the banks of the river, before it separated, stood two trees, the Tree of Knowledge and the Tree of Life. By corrupting man, evil denied him the fruit of the trees. But good, in its wisdom, restored man's ability to return to his divine origins and placed the key to this knowledge in the hands of the Magi. The Magi were charged with keeping this secret through the ages, until man was ready to receive the secret of the Tree of Knowledge. Evil would ensure that man's journey would take him through eons of profound ignorance, where he would forego wisdom for knowledge. Only once evil was eternally ensnared in the material world would the Magi reveal the secret.

Pythagoras sat quietly for a few moments considering the decision that pressed upon him. Faith itself has been supplanted by ritual and practice. Surely this was a sign that it was time to speak.

Suddenly the silence was broken by a voice from the doorway.

"I must be leaving, my friend," called Nathaniel. "Your generosity will be recognised in heaven."

"May your journey be a prosperous one and your return home safe and speedy," answered Pythagoras.

"I need to make one last visit to the east and then I shall head south towards the coast and the sea journey home."

The pair embraced and Nathaniel joined his caravan for the onward journey, resolving to write a letter of thanks to his host without delay.

~~~ الـ صمت من الـ عهد ~~~

Tiro sat in the shade near the entrance to the office of Kassandros, waiting upon a chance to meet the assistant magistrate. Eventually, as the sun reached its highest point and Tiro began to worry about his absence from the farm, the assistant magistrate approached. Tiro got up and stood by the door. As Kassandros drew nearer, Tiro bowed. His gesture was ignored but his words were not.

"Sir," called Tiro as the magistrate passed, "I am bold indeed to speak with one of such high office, but I cannot stand by and allow the master to destroy all you have achieved for Metapontum."

"You are indeed bold to address me, boy," answered Kassandros, "but this is no more than I have come to expect of the pupils of Pythagoras." He paused and it occurred to him that this was the first such pupil to speak out against the master. So, on reflection, he ushered the boy into his office where they could be alone.

"Speak, boy," boomed Kassandros, "I am a busy person."

"The master has entrusted in me the secret that he is to reveal in the temple next week."

"I have heard that Pythagoras intends to disclose something of great importance," he replied.

"Yes," answered Tiro, "and did he not say that we dwelt with evil in exile from our true home?"

"So I am given to understand. And you know what he meant by this, do you?"

"Yes, Sir. That we live in exile from our homeland in Greece and there are those among us who deal in evil."

"And why should the master reveal this to you?"

"Because he believes I have suffered grievously at the hands of the evil ones and, in my own way, I too am exiled from my true and rightful home," answered Tiro.

"What home?" he asked, as he opened the shutters on the windows to let the light in.

"The hillside farm, now occupied by Moliones, of course."

The room went silent. Kassandros turned his back on his visitor and gazed out of the window, making sure nobody was lurking nearby.

"Your parents were taken by the Spartans, were they not? And you were then thrown over the cliff, as the Spartans are wont to do."

"Not so," stated Tiro boldly, remembering his visitor's advice. "Pythagoras knows the truth about the farm and intends to reveal that truth to all who will listen. He has said so, has he not? 'The truth is at the gates of the citadel' he said, my Lord."

"What evidence does he produce?" asked Kassandros nervously.

"Only his certainty that Moliones conspired with someone to kill my mother and father, and me too. But, by the grace of God, I survived the cliff fall. The master says he knows all and will reveal all"

"Moliones conspired with someone in a position of power at that time, to kill my parents, along with me. My master now intends to disclose the names of those responsible for this outrage."

"So, why approach me of such matters?"

"An honourable man like you, Sir, might avert the discourse this revelation might cause by returning the farm to me as the rightful owner and thereby resolve the matter before the master even speaks of it."

"Take care, young man. Do you dare make demands on me?"

"Of course not," Tiro answered in the same calm, assured manner he had conducted for the whole conversation.

Tiro looked at Kassandros as the older man considered his position. Tiro had thrown a good set of dice and had made well of them.

"You did the right thing in coming to tell me of these matters," said Kassandros eventually, before he finally remembered to ask his visitor his name. "Leave this with me, Master Tiro. We must ensure that justice is done without delay."

When Tiro returned to the farm, he found only Moliones and his wife. The stranger, with whom he had broken bread the previous evening, had left to conduct his business.

"Is he to return?" asked Tiro.

"Why would he tell me? He left without a word of thanks for my hospitality," said Moliones, who fortunately had not even noticed Tiro's absence. "Now get back to your duties, boy, the herd is to be fed."

Back in the city, the assistant magistrate waited, rather impatiently, to ensure that Tiro had left the area. He didn't want the boy to see the urgency he gave to the warning. He looked about the square to ensure nobody was around and walked quickly in the direction of the chief magistrate's office at the palace of King Syloson. He failed to notice the small figure of Aspasia standing in the shade of the temple. She had witnessed Tiro's visit to the assistant magistrate's office and was concerned at the possible reasons for it.

Kassandros went directly to the main office, almost forgetting to knock before entering. The building was cool and a gentle breeze swept through the open casement as Ceranus sat to listen to his colleague's message.

"The information that I have received," explained Kassandros, "is that Pythagoras intends to disclose a great revelation in the temple next week."

"Which is?" asked Ceranus.

Kassandros told him of his meeting with Tiro and reported all that the boy had told him.

Ceranus and Kassandros both knew and feared the wisdom of Pythagoras. The master had many followers who entrusted him with rumour and gossip. Little of what went on in the region escaped the knowledge of the great man.

"His followers are held in thrall by the persuasive eloquence of this Samian sage," said Ceranus.

The chief magistrate and his assistant had circumvented many laws in the advancement of their own positions and wealth. Any one of these misdeeds would be sufficient to bring about their downfall and they could not assume that the crime they committed all those years ago with Moliones was all that the master knew of their past deeds. Arrogance drove them to believe that whatever Pythagoras was to disclose would seek to injure their reputation because there was little mutual respect between the parties. That very day they resolved the fate of those who might reveal the darkness of their hearts. And the following day the seeds were sown as the chief magistrate's guards disguised themselves and joined the crowd in a public assembly outside the temple. Ceranus and Kassandros were the first to inflame the crowd that gathered outside the temple that day.

"Is he not subject to the same law that governs the princes and the people?" one called.

The guards reminded the crowd that he had been expelled from Crotona. "Why should the disgraced find harbour with us?" they called, shouting louder still, "Tarentum did not want him, so nor do we."

"The master's frequent references to a single omnipotent God is responsible for the thunderstorms and rock falls we have suffered of late. He alienates us with the gods and now he invites a Jew into his house to learn, presumably, more about the infidel's God, to whom he makes corrupt reference in the temple. He has angered the gods by doing so. He has gone too far this time and we must act on the part of the gods," cried Ceranus.

"The truth is at the gates of the citadel, he had said," called Kassandros, "but the truth is his own infidelity."

Incited by the words of the magistrates and by their guards, the crowd was filled with derision and anger.

"Death to the infidel," they cried.

Standing in the shade by the side of the temple was Aspasia, who was filled with fear at the sight of the crowd. Her first instinct was to find her sister and go straight to warn the master. But, that very morning, she had received a note from Tiro asking her to visit him at the farm. She was to be there within the next hour. She was concerned and, from what she saw of Tiro's visit to the magistrate's office, was now convinced that Tiro was implicated in the events outside the temple. What was it that the master had said to her only last week? "It is true, Aspasia," he told her, "that God works in mysterious ways but, for the most part, he relies on the practical intervention of people like you." Did he foresee in those words the events of today?

She sat for a few moments writing on a scrap of paper she kept with her to record her thoughts for the master. She rolled the paper up and sealed it with the wax of a candle in the temple. She then went to the home of the master, which she had visited many times and helped him in his work. Knowing her well, the servants allowed her in and gave her free access to the master's chambers. When she left with a small leather pouch containing documents, they assumed she was taking them to him.

Time was now of the essence and she searched the town for her sister. When she found Kalisto, she told her to take the letter and leather pouch to Tiro. Her sister reluctantly agreed and Aspasia went off to find the master. She had heard murmurings in the crowd that a large number of students were gathered with the master at the house of Milos, about one mile outside the city. Resigned to her fate, she hurried to ensure she arrived before the crowd.

Thirty-six students had gathered with Pythagoras at the house of Milos, a friend of the master who often made his large home available for lectures. Pythagoras was not sure if this would be his last day on Earth but he knew it could be. He was first among men with regard to mathematics and he had found the 'Rule of Seven', as he called it. But he had never revealed it to others for the fear that it may cause. So many secrets were to be taken to the grave with him. He had given signs to those he had met in his lifetime and some secrets lay awaiting discovery by future generations. But the Rule of Seven, he had never disclosed.

<div align="center">~~~ الـ صمت من الـ عهد ~~~</div>

Earlier that morning, around dawn, Tiro had heard what sounded like screams from the farm. He had spent the night with the goat herd on the hill and went to the cliff edge to see what the noise was but, in the darkness, he could see nothing. By the time the sun had risen and he had sight of the farm, the screams had stopped but he thought he could see three figures walking down the hill towards the city. As the sun rose he returned to the farm to find it empty. There was no sign of Moliones or his wife. Tiro suspected so much and knew so little. So he walked down the hillside to the city and, hearing the stirrings of the crowd, resolved to send a note to Aspasia. If what he feared was about to materialise, then she was in danger. So, he wrote a note to Aspasia asking her to meet him at the farm and, after passing this to her friend, he headed off to that same place.

He climbed to the top of the cliff so that he could see Aspasia coming and waited patiently for her to join him.

After two hours, he finally saw his beloved Aspasia in the distance, walking along the winding path up the hill to the farm. He followed her journey, losing sight of her as she passed through the wooded area close by. As she reappeared, he signalled to her to join him on the cliff top. It was only when she was a few feet away and spoke that he realised it was not Aspasia at all, but her twin sister Kalisto.

"I have a message for you from Aspasia," she said. "You might have walked down to meet me, instead of making me walk to the very top of this hill."

71

Tiro was speechless. He took the note from her and broke the candle wax that sealed it.

Tiro,

I believe you may have known what was to happen on this day. I am certain the master did and he knew that I had determined it also. This day has been chosen from all years to lament the loss of Pythagoras and I am pleased to have been chosen to depart this life with him. Think on this, Tiro; that, even if you did know and believed you had sent the master and Kalisto to their deaths with a great many others, I forgive you. The master has made it clear to me that this is my final journey on Earth and, by the time you read this note, I will be with him in the bosom of God. Whatever I may do for you and Kalisto from there, be sure that I will do it.

You are both at the start of a great journey. Six more times you will visit God's playground before joining me. Death holds only joy but you must seek to change your heart. Do this willingly and begin with Kalisto. It is easy to risk your life for someone you love. I challenge you now to do so for my sister as you would have done for me. You are both in grave danger, so take her back to Samos and begin again. Change your heart, Tiro, and through this Kalisto will change hers too.

There is one final duty I wish you to perform. Take the leather pouch I have given to my sister and, when you return home, search out the Magi, but never mention that word. Ask only for the Sons of Seth and, once found, hand them the pouch, telling them it is from the master. It is to be buried in the secret place in the fashion of the Magi.

We will not see each other for a long time but throughout those seven visits you carry with you my lasting love.
Forever,
Aspasia

As Tiro finished reading the note, Kalisto broke his contemplation.

"What is that smoke in the distance?" she asked. "it's about one mile outside town."

"It is the house of Milos," answered Tiro.

Kalisto walked forward to secure a better view.

"The house of Milos?" she asked as she turned back towards him and he had fallen silent.

"Why are you crying?" asked Kalisto hesitantly.

Tiro realised that he was responsible for the terrible events that were unfolding before him. Moliones and his wife had been murdered in the night by the magistrate's guards and now the master and his students were under attack from the crowd, incited by those same guards, led by Ceranus and Kassandros. An enormous sense of responsibility rested upon Tiro's shoulders. The immense and tragic consequences of his actions and his culpability flooded over him.

Tiro explained what he could to Kalisto and, fearing for their lives, the two fled the farm. When darkness fell on the city, they ventured in to find out what had happened.

Thirty-eight people had been in the house of Milos when the angry crowd set fire to it. The master, Gallus and Aspasia were among those who died the death of martyrs that unholy day in Metapontum.

After much heart searching, Tiro and Kalisto headed north at dawn and, after a heated discussion, they decided to keep going and try to find their way back to Samos or the Greek mainland. After a long sea journey to Sidon they found a caravan headed towards Assyria and joined it, hoping they may search out a Magus to fulfil the wishes of Aspasia. Eventually they reached a place called Edessa and, by fortune, safely searched out a man named Elohi, whose knowledge of the Magi customs was sufficient to convince them that he was indeed one of the Sons of Seth. Elohi lived about ten miles west of Edessa and, deciding to go no farther, Tiro and Kalisto settled in the very place where wisdom was buried and sprang into the Tree of Knowledge. And, even though they dwelt in a foreign land, they were both filled with a strange and overwhelming sense of having returned home. So, with the help of Elohi's family, they built a home close to a large cypress tree called Sarv-e- Šēṯ, which was Arabic for the tree of Seth. And they found consolation there.

When he was alone, Elohi climbed the hill and placed the pouch in one of seven arched chambers deep below the crumbled remains of a temple, where ancient parchments containing the doctrines of the Magi were kept. The seven chambers had been designed by Pythagoras himself many years before, when he had visited Edessa from Babylon. Before he left, he decreed that each cave be sealed in the way of the Magi so that, on opening again, the parchment records would disintegrate and the secrets of the Magi would remain with him and six other Magi whose names were known only to those seven.

~~~ الـ صمت من الـ عهد ~~~

After one day's journey, Nathaniel's servants set up camp near a river, close to the road that led to the port at the most southerly point of the country. From here he would return to his home in Capernaum, having secured several new business contacts and orders for ivory and rugs.

Once his servants had built a small fire, Nathaniel set about writing to his host to thank him for his hospitality. But he was not tired and he continued writing for nearly two hours, covering all the wonderful and mysterious subjects discussed with the master. Eager to despatch the letter to his new-found friend, Nathaniel instructed one of his servants to leave with the sealed message immediately in order that he could catch them up before the ship sailed.

The Jew carried little of value with him, so he was accompanied by only four servants on his travels. The one he despatched back to Metapontum was his personal assistant, a second cooked and cleaned for the caravan, a third acted as the guide and the fourth, a heavily built African named Ntomo, served to protect him. It was the guide who first heard the horseman approaching from the south towards Metapontum and he signalled to Ntomo, who rose to his feet and placed his hand on the hilt of the curved sword that hung from his waist.

The horse and rider approached slowly and halted several metres short of Ntomo.

"I wish you no harm, friend," he called. "I am a fellow traveller and would be grateful to share the warmth of your fire on this cold night. I travel to Metapontum."

By this time, Nathaniel had stood up and walked over to where the traveller was dismounting. "Shalom," he called and signalled to his servant to allow the man to join him by the fire.

"I am Sathas and travel from Samos with news for a man of great renown, who you may have heard of in your travels. He is called Pythagoras, so named by the Delphic pythoness herself in recognition of his wisdom and beauty."

Peritas had ridden all night and all day, travelling around and beyond the slow-moving caravan in order to initiate just such a conversation with the Jew.

75

"Then our meeting is fortunate indeed," answered Nathaniel, "for I have only recently left the same man of whom you speak and dined with him in his own home."

For a moment, the Jew regretted despatching his assistant with the letter to the master because Sathas could have taken it.

Nathaniel had left Metapontum at dawn on the very day of the events at the house of Milos. But news travels slowly and he was unaware of the death of Pythagoras. Once Peritas had satisfied himself of this fact, he set about discovering what had been discussed between the Jew and the master.

Just a few words stood between Nathaniel, his servants and whether they would wake to another morning. For Peritas it was all foretold and known only to God. Before they slept, Nathaniel spoke to Peritas of metanoia, of the Tree of Knowledge and the transmigration of the soul.

3

Any residual fear of a possible indiscretion in the hotel bar had been dismissed, but not forgotten, by the time Tyler returned home from the seminar. Nobody had mentioned his current, highly confidential work and he had made some useful contacts. Paul Gilligan was keen to write an article on the talented young Tyler Watson and Piruz Yilmaz, or Perry, had introduced Tyler to his influential boss, Oliver Carmichael. Oliver had suggested that they might have lunch together sometime and Tyler began to wonder whether he might be about to be headhunted by Codon Genetics Limited. But, although Tyler might be impressed by events at the seminar, Cally was oblivious to her boyfriend's meanderings when she arrived home shortly after him. She had other things on her mind, not least of which was a second interview with Chief Superintendent Alan Bent the following day. But she eventually found time to ask about Tyler's business trip. He was a little reticent to mention any possible indiscretion, so he focused on the other attendees.

Most of the people at the seminar specialised in one particular field of molecular biology. Many specialised in a single gene, just as doctors tend to specialise in one part of the body. But, just as one part of the body relies on another, so do genes, and Tyler was that rare individual whose job it was to understand the whole of the system; to place each piece of knowledge in context with the others. His work involved the genetic system in its entirety, the genome.

Tyler described the people he had met but spoke little of the subjects addressed at the conference.

"Did you learn anything?"

"We gain knowledge every day, Cally, but wisdom evades us at every turn."

"That sounds like a 'no'."

In spite of the concerns about her own job, Cally was her normal patient self around Tyler. It would be easy to seem patronising, but Cally was never that. What she felt for Tyler was not, perhaps, the urgent and passionate love of the body-changing teenage years, but it *was* love. A mature love that supplanted lustful urges with the satisfying bonds of friendship. A love rooted in ages past, as if they had always known each other.

That night they both slept restlessly. Cally trapped in a fruitless journey vainly trying to reach home in an allegorical dream of snakes and ladders, walking, cycling and running through the streets of her childhood that she had left at the age of twelve but were brought vividly to life in her dreams.

Tyler's apprehension only appeared towards the end of his dream. At that moment when he was forced to leave the wonderful land of his distant past. The awful sense of departure, with goodbye echoing into the shadowy night. He feared many things, such as heights, but nothing caused greater anxiety than to leave the world of his dreams.

When Tyler set off the next morning, his project was, once again, his preoccupation. He enjoyed his work, the company and the incredible insight and vision of his boss, William Trenchman. He knew that William did not share his more altruistic ambitions towards their work. Trenchman was a businessman who knew he had a star player in Tyler. He also knew that Tyler considered ultimate success in terms of curing the great illnesses of the world. Of course, he needed to share and contribute towards his boss's commercial ambitions, but eventually he would be released from these constraints to pursue a more philanthropic path. Perhaps, in his later years, he would become a professor and lecture on the subject himself. The genome, as he would eagerly explain to anyone who was interested, represented the complete set of instructions for every cell. As he sat on the fast-moving and crowded underground train, he suddenly remembered giving such an impromptu lecture in the bar on the night he arrived at the seminar. Each cell, he told his attentive audience, contained two genomes, one from each parent, but one was always more dominate than the other. The genome, in all but accidental deaths, will determine when someone dies. Genes make us susceptible to diseases such as cancer and cystic fibrosis. But while most research biologists were searching for a cure for specific mortality threats, Tyler announced boldly that he was looking at the broader picture. If the human race was to fully appreciate genetic factors on mortality, someone had to produce a complete inventory of all the genetic parts to the puzzle. No wonder his contemporaries attended on his every word, for the vast majority of scientists would have difficulty determining the fertilised egg of a chimpanzee from that of a human being, but the research Tyler undertook was significantly advanced of that stage. He was on his way to producing the assembly instructions for the perfect human being or, at least, for the human most resilient to disease. If you wanted to live forever, then Tyler and his boss William Trenchman were determined that Double Helix Limited would be the first to produce the patent. As the train pulled into his station, he clambered through the standing passengers and considered again that evening in the hotel bar. But he felt comfortable that he had not revealed the secret; that secret that he wasn't even sure of himself yet.

The offices of Double Helix were quiet, clean, bright and, more importantly, sterile. Tyler's office looked like an operating theatre, although it had a fairly ordinary desk in one corner. This housed his PC but had no drawers. Any paperwork needed to be locked away in what looked like safety deposit boxes along one wall. In the centre of the room stood a long flat table that was higher at one end than the other. A chair stood at the lower end and clearly the far end was for working while standing. It was here that Tyler prepared to begin his day.

Placing his set of instruments neatly on the top of the workstation, he went off to retrieve a specimen from the temperature-controlled storage room along the corridor. Trenchman had managed to secure a supply of human bones from a local disused cemetery when it was being redeveloped for housing. The transaction was possible only because the last burial to take place there was more than one hundred years ago and all known living relatives had been contacted and offered re-internment. Those human remains that were unclaimed were sold to Double Helix Limited for genetic research.

Tyler identified the remains of the person he was currently working on and retrieved a complete clavicle bone from the temperature-controlled drawer. He sat reading the notes he had produced the previous week. This was simple work and should have produced very predictable results. But when he had run the data through the DNA database, it had produced a perfect match. That was impossible. The bones he was working with belonged to a man who lived two hundred years ago and the DNA database was only created in recent years. The oldest data on the database was certainly less than one hundred years old. He had made a simple mistake; it was easy to do in such a complex operation. So he had left his work and gone to the seminar. Today he convinced himself that he would find completely different results. But he didn't. He felt frustrated; he skipped lunch, stopped drinking coffee and became totally immersed in his work. It was nearly five o'clock before he even looked at his watch. He stared at the screen of his laptop and sat wondering what the simple calculation was that he had got wrong in the process.

This work was nothing more complicated than the rules of inheritance; it was routine stuff, involving the replication process in DNA. It was something he had done many times before. When DNA is replicated in children, it is an extremely accurate depiction but it isn't perfect. It is never exactly the same. This genetic variation merely identifies the difference between the generations. But these two sets of DNA were not simply relatives; they were identical. Yet the person on the database was born in 1936 and the bone under his microscope belonged to someone born two hundred years earlier. How could that be?

Tyler got up and stretched himself. He hadn't realised how long he had been sitting at the workstation. He went to the cooler and filled a cup with water. Drinking all of it he threw the cup in the bin and walked around the room muttering to himself. Every child carries an equal genetic contribution from each of its parents. This identifies it as the child of those parents. But each characteristic of the parents is not visible in equal measure: one is more dominant. That's okay, thought Tyler. "Dominant is fine," he mumbled to himself, "but not identical." The DNA samples would normally be expected to provide further evidence of the ancestral chain so the prodigy will demonstrate a diluted version of its ancestors. But there is no dilution here, he thought, none whatsoever.

The only possible explanation was cloning, but that was impossible. Cloning began only recently, not in the nineteenth century. But what he was examining didn't involve cloning a piece of DNA, this was copying an entire genome; and this wasn't Dolly the sheep, but a human being; a human being who lived seven generations ago. How is that possible? This technology wasn't even considered before 1999. Just assembling the final sequence from all the pieces requires computational expertise that has only become possible in the past few years. How could it have existed in the early nineteenth century?

Tyler was becoming increasingly frustrated. He stopped to re-evaluate the situation. He loved difficult problems, which was probably why he was keeping the diary of his dreams. He knew he could never explain them but relished the challenge of trying.

Working on old DNA is complex, he assured himself. And he wasn't looking for viable DNA in the cells' nuclei as one might normally, but he was looking for it in something called mitochondria. Each mitochondrion contains one small section of DNA. It's the equivalent of microsurgery and it has big problems with contamination. He sat down, convincing himself it must be contamination. God, he thought, William will be furious with his staff. It's the one thing he prides himself on; 'non-contamination keeps us competitive' was his favourite expression.

Tyler locked everything away for the night and collected his briefcase. This never contained details of his work, as company rules prohibited any documents from being removed from the building. He locked his office, said goodnight to William and two other colleagues who were still working and walked down the corridor to the lifts. He decided to get some food on the way and cook a meal for Cally. He was still feeling a little guilty about leaving her alone for a few days and for not calling her on the first night. Cooking would help take his mind off work but, for now, he couldn't rid his mind of the confusion over the recurring DNA. He turned and walked back along the corridor to William's office and opened the door.

"Are you in tomorrow?" he asked.

"Yes," William answered, "but I'm meeting someone for lunch at one o'clock."

"Can you spare me some time? First thing?"

"Of course, Tyler," he replied.

Tyler had never looked at the world in wild surmise or relished in the fairy groves of romanticism. Any suspicion he harboured were of a practical nature and any mysteries that the world nurtured were just problems that he had not yet solved. So this scientific puzzle did not resemble, in any way, the enigmatic ambiguity of his dreams. In time, even that could be solved, so resolving the riddle of the bones and any possibility of recurring DNA was inevitable.

~~~ الـ صمت من الـ عهد ~~~

Cally's day had been equally frustrating and her boss was less sympathetic with his time than Tyler's. She had been subjected to a rigorous examination of her work in the David Hallet case. Chief Superintendent Bent had already been under

83

constant political and public pressure for several weeks to solve this crime and bring the killer to justice. It regularly featured in the national press throughout the investigation and public interest only grew when David Hallet was arrested. Ashley Bertoni had been berated in the press for actually causing the murder of Nelson Kosoto. They pointed to his ill-judged statement during his investigation of Charlene Hallet's murder, when Kosoto was released after prolonged interrogation by his team.

"The police are not seeking anyone else in connection with this murder," he had told the TV news reporter.

Nothing was said about that comment at the time. But, when Kosoto was found murdered in the same house where he was thought to have killed Charlene, the press vilified him. His statement had suggested that Kosoto killed Charlene, but he simply couldn't prove it. And when Charlene's father, David, was arrested for avenging his daughter's murder, nobody was surprised because of Bertoni's ill-judged comment.

All of this managed only to alienate Bent against the team, but none of it was relevant to his interview of Cally. It simply brought to question the capability of anyone working on the case.

She knocked on the door boldly and entered. The air conditioning unit on the wall fought vainly against the warmth of the sun that streamed through the window. Bent stood up and offered her the seat on the other side of his desk. She sat down but sensed that she might become trapped again. Trapped within the encircling light, like a fidgeting fly, wriggling in a futile dance of freedom. So she stood up and walked to the window. Bent considered his options but remained quiet. Cally found the cord and pulled it gently, turning the light to shade. Summer is made the darkest of seasons by the canopied oaks, just as winter is made light by the shedding of their verdant cloak. The harsh glare tapered away and they were left sitting as if in a shaded bower.

"David Hallet insists he has never visited 1 Wharf Street," said Bent. "So how did his DNA appear at the scene of the murders?"

"Well, he's hardly likely to admit it, is he?"

Bent looked unimpressed.

"Look, Miss Boyce, your colleagues have been suspended, H division is holding a viable suspect for the killing of Kosoto and all we've got is the DNA sample that you say you took from the body and wall."

"What do you mean, 'I say'?" she interrupted.

"Well you produce the forensic evidence, I assume."

"Yes, but you make it sound as if I made it up."

"Well, did you?"

"Of course not, Sir."

"Listen, young lady, I have to make a decision today on whether to release David Hallet. All we have is the DNA evidence and his denial that he ever visited the scene. The press are going to have a field day. Holding two suspects for the same murder." His voice was becoming louder and his tone less tolerant.

"Hallet had a motive, Sir. There is a motive, too."

"A motive? The man he killed was a drug dealer and a hardened criminal. If we arrested everyone with a motive, our cells would be full. Anyway, Mrs Hallet had a motive too and she didn't have an alibi either."

Cally sat in silence for a few moments. Anything she said simply seemed to make the matter worse.

"What evidence, other than DNA, did you find at the crime scene to substantiate his presence there?" he eventually asked her.

"None."

"So, no fingerprints, no witnesses placing him there."

"I'm not responsible for witnesses," she answered firmly but cautiously.

"No fingerprints," he repeated.

"No."

"And you found David Hallet's DNA in two locations. Under the torn wallpaper, which appeared to have been ripped by the murder weapon in the attack, and in the shoulder wound of the murder victim?"

"Yes," replied Cally.

"Could the DNA in his shoulder have got there by the body sliding down the wall?"

"Do you mean, could that have been the source of the DNA sample, the blood on the underside of the wallpaper?"

"Isn't it more likely than the other way round?"

"Perhaps, but how did the DNA get under the wallpaper?"

"Maybe it was on the blade of the machete," offered Bent, "and it was transferred from the blade onto the wallpaper and then on to the body."

"But, how did Hallet's DNA get onto the blade?"

"I don't know, but it would explain how his DNA was at a crime scene that he insists he never visited."

Cally shrugged her shoulders and sighed.

"Was there any other DNA or fingerprint evidence apparent at the crime scene apart from David Hallet's?" asked Bent.

"Yes, of course," she answered, "lots. It was a derelict house that was frequented by druggies looking for a fix."

"So how did you manage to find David Hallet's DNA among the thousands of pieces of DNA and fingerprint evidence?"

"Because I ran the sample of his DNA against some of the samples taken from the crime scene."

"And did you check for any other samples of DNA against the police database?"

"Yes,"

"And?" he asked

"Hundreds of matches," she confessed.

There was a quiet knock at the door and a young police woman came in carrying a tray of coffee. Bent stood up and closed the door behind her as she left. He poured two cups of coffee but didn't break his line of questioning. He wanted to know why none of these matches had been followed up. Cally explained that she had found DNA matching dozens, perhaps hundreds, of local drug dealers and drug takers who financed their habit through minor criminal activities. But, in any case, she had been told to stop once she had identified David Hallet's DNA at the scene as he was the obvious suspect, particularly as he was saying he had never visited Wharf Street.

"But how did his DNA get there if he is telling the truth?"

She shrugged her shoulders and explained that every minute of every day humans shed vast amounts of DNA through dead skin cells.

"They're cast on to the winds and end up, who knows where?"

"Is that the best you can come up with?" asked Bent. "Am I supposed to tell them that at the press conference?"

All evidence contains contaminants, she explained. DNA degrades in moist conditions and the murder took place in an old derelict and damp house. Cally watched her pleas in mitigation falling on barren soil. She sensed that the interview was coming to an end.

"DNA is a great tool in policing," said Bent as he rose from his seat, "but it's only as credible as the procedures used to collect it. You're suspended too, Miss Boyce."

"I'm on holiday, Sir," she said, looking at the still full cup of coffee.

"You're suspended. The press are going to have a field day with this one." He opened the door for her and hesitated before adding, "I shall call you when I want to talk to you again."

"Sir," said Cally, stepping back into the room, "may I just say something?"

"If it's relevant."

"I'm not convinced of Hallet's guilt, Sir. I never have been, in spite of the forensic evidence."

"I've heard all about this from Bertoni, Miss Boyce. The fact that Hallet doesn't swear and why would he do so in a text message. I suggest you stick to forensics and leave the detective work to your colleagues."

"But it's not just the swearing, Sir. It's the wounds too. The wounds were very different."

"Well they would be, wouldn't they. Kosoto was at least eight inches taller than Charlene. Of course the wounds would be different."

"No, it was more than that, Sir. The depth of the incision and the trajectory of the impact were completely different."

"Well, perhaps it was Mrs Hallet then?"

"Perhaps, Sir," she answered a little too timidly.

"I'm joking," stormed Bent, who was clearly unimpressed and sounded as if he was desperate to bring the meeting to a close. Cally again worried about the effect of any suspension on her career.

"Sir," she asked, "can you at least keep my suspension confidential? Perhaps until this thing blows over?"

He sighed. "I'll do my best," he said and closed the door behind her.

As she began her journey home, she switched on her mobile phone to find a text message waiting for her. It was from Tyler telling her that he had picked up some food on the way home and was cooking dinner. She replied to tell him what time she would be home and the fact that she had been suspended.

Cally was grateful for a sympathetic ear when she arrived home after a crowded journey on the London underground. Tyler listened to what she had to say. He had always believed in the honesty of numbers and science, but less in the honesty of people. Cally and Galen were the exceptions. Tyler was the one person who could appreciate that her work was not as precise as the public believed. He assured her that the work she did was just as difficult as his. He was working on DNA that was hundreds of years old but it had been stored in a coffin for most of that time. Cally's evidence had been stored in a damp, derelict house.

"Trying to extract DNA in those conditions is extremely difficult," he explained in a comforting tone. She felt reassured by his kind words but knew in her heart that his work was entirely different from hers and much more challenging.

"Could you be confusing David and Charlene's DNA?" he asked tentatively.

"No, it's definitely David Hallet's DNA. Why do you ask?"

"Oh, it's just something I am working on at the moment. Anyway, don't get too downhearted. Even samples stored correctly only remain stable for a few years, so extracting DNA from a body in a place like that is unreliable," he assured her, adding, "surely your bosses understand that?"

But Cally was not one to be patronised.

"You are being too kind, Tyler, and I don't need your sympathy. I know your work is more complex than mine, so you don't have to remind me by saying otherwise."

"I'm only a scientist, Cally. A scientist can only explain the world; it takes a poet to understand it."

But Cally would have none of it.

"I did touch on some of the stuff you do at university, Tyler. The genome is the sum of the parts of humanity. It is the most important work taking place in the world today. And you're at the very forefront of that research. I'm so proud of you," she said. "Let's forget about me, how has your day been?"

He held her in his arms, looked into her deep dark brown eyes and kissed her.

"Well, it's true I am past experimenting with peas and the fruit fly," he said, trying to sound modest and reflecting back to their days at university together.

"Oh," replied Cally, "that's a pity, because I know how much you enjoy sexing a fruit fly under a microscope." She pulled him closer to her and nuzzled his ear with her mouth.

"Do you know," she whispered, "that sixty per cent of sperm is DNA and the rest is protein?"

"Ooh, I love it when you talk dirty," he replied and carried her upstairs, hoping that the potatoes would not boil over.

~~~ الـ صمت من الـ عهد ~~~

Cally wasn't an extrovert but she was less introverted than Tyler. He was bookish but not nerdish. The two were very natural together. Almost like brother and sister. Neither was particularly tactile. They rarely kissed in public, nor did they hold hands. This was not born of an unchivalrous nature or because of liberal views. It was just that neither saw a need to publicise their love for each other. But they laughed a lot together and enjoyed each other's company. They were school friends who went to the same university on a similar degree course. Some felt they shared a house just to save money. But neither of them was that mercenary. They were easy in each other's company too. They didn't speak for the sake of making conversation. They could sit together in silence, reading and just looking up occasionally to smile. If one wasn't too engrossed in their reading, they would get up and sit alongside the other just to be closer to them. The dynamics of the relationship were subtle. Sex was never overly passionate but fun. It didn't detract from the romance for either to laugh during sex. Their work was similar but diverse enough not to present any conflict of interest. On the contrary, Cally would often bounce problems off her partner.

Their jointly mortgaged two-bedroom town house was on the fringes of the more expensive docklands area of London. No views of the river, no scenic vista of the Thames, or even one of the canals that threaded through the capital. But it was a nice area with good transport services and the mulberry trees lining the street outside gave it a suburban feel, even though it was close to the city. The second bedroom did not suggest that there were any plans to start a family. It was used as an office by whichever one needed it at the time. Cally brought work home more frequently than Tyler, but then Tyler's work was confidential and commercially sensitive. His employer imposed strict rules about taking material away from the office. This didn't stop Tyler sitting for long periods thinking about work and going through the various possibilities in his mind. Cally's work was ninety-nine per cent perspiration and one per cent inspiration, whereas Tyler's was almost the reverse of this.

The second floor had a view of a park, where football was played at weekends. There was a small balcony and on midweek summer evenings it provided a quiet shady spot to think. So if one person was using the study room, the other normally sat on the balcony until they ate dinner together.

They never referred to each other as 'darling' or one of the more modern equivalents. They didn't have pet names for each other. He rarely shortened Cally and he was always Tyler. But, although their relationship bordered on the sibling, they rarely argued. They were rational, reasoned adults, who rarely expressed their love for each other outside the home. But inside, it was an undemanding love, born of a deep, lasting relationship.

Cally and Tyler both dreamed a lot in their sleep. Perhaps everybody does, but not everyone remembers their dreams. Cally had anxious dreams where she couldn't find her way home or she had lost something. Her dreams always seemed real when she was experiencing them. The steering wheel falling off of her car was real, even though bizarre. Having to climb up sheer cliff faces to get home from work were real experiences in her dreams. Tyler couldn't stand heights, so climbing a cliff or mountain was frightening, but Cally had to confront such challenges every night in her dreams. Sometimes, in the dream, she even questioned the rationality of the situation but always concluded that it must be true; that it must be happening to her. There then followed the awakening into the real world.

Tyler's dreams were less anxious but were often about people he had never met before. But he knew them well in the dreams. It was like another life, with different friends in different places. Like living out another life in dreams. He felt a great sense of guilt towards Cally for sharing himself with someone else, very similar, in his dreams. He felt such strong affection for the fictitious woman that he was too embarrassed, as a scientist or a friend, to discuss this other woman with Cally. He spoke of the dreams, of course, but not of the strong feelings he had for the other woman in those dreams. Sometimes, when he didn't dream, or he failed to remember his dreams, he felt miserable and upset because dreaming for him was like returning to his true self. Galen once told him that ancient prophets believed strongly in dreams because they represented our previous lives.

After dinner, Tyler considered telling Cally about his findings but decided to share this with William first. Identical DNA could not appear in two different people hundreds of years apart; even Cally knew that, so what good would it do asking her opinion? So, he didn't discuss the cause of his anxiety but chose to talk about what was important to her.

"Look," Tyler said eventually, "it's your birthday on Saturday, so why don't we invite some people round for drinks to celebrate."

"I don't feel like celebrating," she answered.

"We're not celebrating this current nonsense that you are worrying about, Cally, we're celebrating your birthday."

"It's not nonsense, Tyler. I've been suspended and if that gets into the public domain, my career is finished. Suspended," she repeated, "how will that look on my CV?"

"Don't let it spoil your birthday."

"Well I don't particularly want to celebrate the fact that I'm thirty-seven either," she replied. "It's like a bloody road sign. Forty approaching, next stop: old age."

"Look, Cally, just phone round your friends tomorrow and invite them over on Saturday. It'll take your mind off things."

"Okay, but can we just keep it to the people who know about my suspension. I don't want to arrange a networking session to highlight my public humiliation."

"Call Galen, Steve and Ashley and I'll see if William and his wife are free."

<p align="center">~~~ الـ صمت من الـ عهد ~~~</p>

Tyler decided to take one more look at his calculations before seeing William about his incomprehensible conclusions. So, he arrived at work early the following morning. But it didn't matter how many times he scanned through the evidence, it still pointed to the two samples coming from the same person. He gathered up his papers and walked up to William's office.

"Come in, Tyler. How're things?"

"Fine," he said to begin with, then changed his mind. "Well not really. The sky appears to be falling in at the moment."

"Really, what's the problem?"

Tyler explained about Cally's suspension and asked William if he and Samantha would like to come to the birthday party on Saturday.

"I'll check with Sam and let you know tomorrow. I don't think we have anything on and we'd certainly like to cheer poor Cally up. Anyway, what's all this you've brought me?" he added, pointing to the documents that had been placed on his desk.

Tyler explained about his findings. The remains of a skeleton from the cemetery was a perfect match for someone on the DNA database. The skeleton was a man who died in 1802 and the man on the database died in 1999.

"So, what have we got?" asked William calmly and then answered his own question by reading the notes.

"Sidney Walter Clinchman, born 1740 in Stepney, east London and died there too in 1802. Not unusual," he added, "people didn't move far in those days. And James Henry Richards, born in Stevenage, Hertfordshire in 1935 and died in neighbouring Essex sixty-three years later in 1999."

William read through the paperwork, stopping occasionally to check some of the calculations. He was meticulous in his work and Tyler took the opportunity to exit the room to fetch them both a cup of coffee. When he returned, William was sitting back in his seat.

"If you're right," said Tyler's boss, "we cannot begin to conceive the commercial value of this discovery."

"Commercial value?"

"Anything as groundbreaking as this must have value, Tyler, anything that is truly new does."

"But the evidence must be flawed," declared Tyler. "It simply cannot be. Two people who died two hundred years apart cannot have exactly the same DNA profile."

"Someone once said that for an idea to be truly original it must, at first, appear to be ridiculous. And, anyway, when were you last wrong?" asked William before, again, answering his own question. "No," he stated firmly, "there's something in this and we're going to find out what it is. And when we do, I bet you it has a large dollar sign in front of it."

William then gave his considered opinion about the next steps.

"I want you to stay with this one personally, Tyler. This must remain confidential between the two of us alone. There's a bit of legwork to be done but I don't want to risk this information getting out by enlisting the help of someone more junior."

"But where do we go from here?" asked Tyler.

"You, my good man, must find out what the connection is between the late Mr Richards and the even later Mr Clinchman. Once we know that we can determine what to do next."

<div align="center">~~~ الـ صمت من الـ عهد ~~~</div>

Cally spent the day tidying up the house and making telephone calls. In spite of his suspension, Ashley seemed preoccupied with the Hallet case, or perhaps it was the Livingstone case now, but agreed to join the party on Saturday and to bring his partner, Teresa, if they were still talking.

"What else is there to do?" he said gloomily, then remembered something that was happening the following day.

"Did you know," he asked "that the Livingstone plea hearing is at the Bailey tomorrow?" Cally wasn't aware of that but wasn't surprised that Ashley was, as he had contacts in every nook and cranny in the criminal prosecution system.

"Do you fancy going?" he asked.

Cally agreed and Ashley suggested that he called Steve.

"Do you want me to ask him to the party?" he asked her.

"I'll ask him myself tomorrow."

Cally then phoned Galen. He had remembered it was her birthday and said he would join the party after the vigil mass.

"How's things?" she asked.

"Oh, quite busy today, I'm picking up a visitor from the airport this morning. He's a priest from Armenia who's staying in the parish for a couple of weeks."

"Are you sure you can get away on Saturday, then?" she asked.

"Of course, Cally, I've always got time for you. Oh," he said, remembering something important, "I was surfing the internet yesterday and found some information about the original murder at Wharf Street. The one back in the early eighteenth century. I'll tell you about it on Saturday."

~~~ الـ صمت من الـ عهد ~~~

Tyler left the house early again the next morning, saying he had some important work to attend to. Cally showered, dressed and left to meet Steve and Ashley at the Old Bailey.

The plea hearing seemed a formality. Nobody ever pleaded guilty to murder and suspected murderers don't get bail.

When the team arrived, Barnabas Cartwright, who was acting for Livingstone, was already defending a case in another courtroom, so Ashley suggested that they entered quietly and observed the defence counsel in action. In any case, they needed to get some idea of how long it would be before the Livingstone plea hearing would start.

The prosecution counsel had just finished questioning his star witness, a Mrs Prentice, who was the widow of a pedestrian killed in a car accident in a suburban high street several months previously. Cartwright was defending the driver of the car. He began his cross examination by offering his profound condolences for her loss.

"I would just like to go through the events of that fateful evening, Mrs Prentice," he told her. "I understand you and your late husband had gone out for the evening. Is that correct?"

"Yes."

"And did you drive or travel by public transport, or perhaps a cab?"

"We sometimes drive but, on this occasion, we decided to use the bus."

"So you sometimes drive?"

"Yes."

"But this time you chose to walk. And, was this a special occasion?"

"No."

"So, just an ordinary Friday night out?"

"Yes."

He asked her about where they had gone and she told him that they had a reservation at the Amalfi restaurant in the High Street.

"Is that the one the regulars call Carlo's?"

"Yes."

"Why is that, Mrs Prentice?"

"Because the owner's name is Carlo," she replied.

"Were you and your husband regulars then, Mrs Prentice?"

"Yes, a couple of times a month."

"Thank you," replied Cartwright, who, from Ashley's recollection, was being unusually polite to the witness.

"And what did you drink with the meal, Mrs Prentice?"

The prosecution counsel objected to the line of questioning but Judge Morrison overruled him and instructed the witness to answer the question.

"A bottle of red wine," she answered.

"And I believe it is the practice of Carlo to offer his guests a complimentary glass of prosecco before the meal. Is that correct?"

"Yes."

"And after the meal, Mrs Prentice, Carlo would offer his regular customers another complimentary drink. I imagine that if you frequented the restaurant *'a couple of times a month'* then you qualified for this. Is that correct?"

"Yes."

"And what did you and your husband have?"

"I had a limoncello and he had a strega."

"Do you not like strega, Mrs Prentice?"

"No," she answered, "it's too strong for my liking."

"Too strong for your liking," he repeated. "Yes, it is quite a strong Italian drink, isn't it?"

"Yes."

"Anyway," he replied, "you weren't driving on this occasion, so that's fine."

"Is that a question, Mr Cartwright?" asked the Judge rhetorically. "Please confine yourself to questions, Mr Cartwright and leave your observations to later."

Cartwright acknowledged the Judge's admonishment.

"Now, Mrs Prentice, this is where I have a little difficulty," he continued and she shuffled nervously in the witness box.

"You told my learned colleague that you planned to get a bus home but the restaurant and the bus stop are on the same side of the road. So, perhaps you could explain why you and your husband found it necessary to use the pedestrian crossing?"

The courtroom fell silent. Mrs Prentice looked at her own counsel and also towards the Judge. Neither offered any reason for her not to answer the question.

"We went to the pub across the road."

"You went to the pub across the road. Yes, of course, that would explain it. What is the pub called, Mrs Prentice?"

"The White Horse."

"And were you and your husband regulars there too?"

"My Lord," protested the prosecution counsel. But he ruled that it was a legitimate question.

"Fairly," she replied.

"What time did you leave the restaurant, Mrs Prentice?"

"I'm not sure."

"Is that because of the amount of alcohol you had consumed?"

"Pardon?"

"The reason you were unsure, Mrs Prentice, was that because of the amount of alcohol you had consumed?"

"No, I simply cannot remember. It was probably about nine o'clock."

"Fine. So you and your husband went to the pub at nine o'clock and came out around eleven o'clock, when the accident happened." He reinforced the word accident, replacing his learned colleague's expression of 'crash'.

She nodded and he continued his questioning by asking her how many drinks she and her husband had consumed. The prosecution counsel had another objection overruled.

"I can't remember," she answered.

"Well, perhaps I can help you there, Mrs Prentice. The White Horse is one of those pubs that offers you a bottle of wine if you buy two large glasses. Did you order two large glasses of wine?"

"Yes, I believe so."

"And did it take you two hours to consume that bottle, or did you order another bottle, Mrs Prentice?"

"We ordered another bottle," she answered timidly.

"So, can I just clarify, Mrs Prentice, you and your husband consumed three bottles of wine, two glasses of prosecco, a limoncello and a strega?"

"Yes."

"And presumably your late husband consumed around half of this, did he?"

"Yes."

Cartwright's tone began to change slightly.

"And then you both staggered towards the pedestrian crossing, did you?"

The prosecution counsel objected and this time, his plea was upheld. The Judge cautioned Cartwright against using provocative terminology such as 'staggered'. Cartwright apologised but had made his point to the jury.

"Was the crossing flashing green in your favour, Mrs Prentice?"

She admitted that it wasn't, but declared that the accused was driving too fast.

"Your husband stepped out into the road," suggested Cartwright. "Presumably he thought he had sufficient time to cross the road. But you stayed on the pavement, Mrs Prentice. So, your view was that it was dangerous to cross because my client's car was approaching. Is that right, Mrs Prentice?"

"Yes," she admitted.

"The lights were not in your favour. Your husband made a bad decision. He had been drinking heavily..."

The prosecution again objected and the objection was upheld. But Cartwright took the opportunity to point out that his client was only marginally over the drink drive limit but Mr Prentice was three times over that limit.

"My client was one glass of wine over the limit, m'Lord. The lights were in his favour. He had no reason to stop. Mrs Prentice made a good decision and her husband a poor one. Unfortunately it cost him his life."

The Judge dismissed his remarks and instructed him to continue his questioning of the witness.

"Your husband, Mrs Prentice, he had a drink driving conviction himself I believe."

She looked at the Judge but, in the absence of any assistance, answered, "yes."

"Yes," Cartwright continued, "six years ago, he himself was convicted of drunk driving, wasn't he. In fact he hadn't got his licence back until quite recently had he?"

"Last year," she answered reluctantly.

"Quite."

Ashley had seen enough. He looked at his colleagues and they all stood up, bowed to the bench and existed the courtroom.

"Jesus H," said Redpath a little too loudly, "the man's an animal. He just destroyed that poor woman in there."

There was no need for the others to agree with his assessment. Cartwright was an impressive barrister. They decided to have a cup of coffee while they waited the almost predictable outcome of this case before returning for Livingstone's plea hearing. Cartwright's client suffered only a fine and a one year ban from driving. He was found not guilty by the jury of causing death by dangerous driving.

A few minutes later, Livingstone arrived in the box and stated his name and address. The dark suit and tie he was wearing looked out of place with his unshaven face and dreadlock hairstyle. His accent was distinctly Caribbean.

Richard Barton-Smythe, acting for the Crown Prosecution referred to the seriousness of the charges and asked, almost too casually, that Livingstone be remanded in custody. Barnabas Cartwright, acting for Livingstone, rose to his feet and waited for his audience to focus their attention on him. He began by pointing out that the machete found at his client's home was a family heirloom given to him by his father. The police and forensic experts had found no evidence whatsoever to connect this item with the murders of either Charlene Hallet or Nelson Kosoto.

This was the first Bertoni and his team had heard of this revelation and Redpath mumbled a prediction that Livingstone was about to walk free from the court.

Cartwright then advised that Livingstone was not at Wharf Street at the time of the murders and had several witnesses to confirm this. Having dismissed the alleged murder weapon and produced an alibi, Cartwright continued to protest his client's innocence. He picked up and began waving a copy of today's newspaper towards his adversary and, speaking firmly, directed his next words to both the Judge and Mr Barton-Smythe.

"My client isn't the only suspect being held in custody for the murder of Mr Kosoto. Even the police don't seem to be entirely sure of Mr Livingstone's guilt in this matter, m'Lord."

The court was almost empty, but a couple in the public gallery, who appeared to be regular visitors, managed to interrupt proceedings by laughing excessively at the defence barrister's remarks.

Judge Michaelmas looked at Livingstone and took a few moments to read through his notes.

"I take your point, Mr Cartwright and I am prepared to release your client on bail." He paused again for a moment. "£50,000 and Mr Livingstone must report to the police twice each week."

There was a gasp from those watching, not least from Cally and her colleagues. Nobody had expected this. But obviously Bent had prejudiced H division's case by not releasing Hallet prior to this hearing.

103

Barton-Smythe objected but Judge Michaelmas would have none of it.

"Are we to incarcerate the entire population while the police decide which one of them is guilty? I think not, Mr Barton-Smythe, I think not. The defendant is granted bail in the sum of £50,000."

Livingstone's lawyer, Barnabas Cartwright, was ebullient as they left the courtroom. But Bertoni insisted Cally stayed as Redpath went outside to take a call on his mobile phone.

"What have you been talking about to Bent?" he said with a tone that suggested he knew exactly what she had been talking to his boss about. "Have you been going on to him about this swearing business again?"

"I haven't said anything…"

But Bertoni cut her short. "You most certainly have," he insisted.

"Let me finish, Ashley. I haven't said anything to Bent that I haven't already said to you."

Just as the conversation was getting heated, Redpath rejoined them.

"Is she going on about the swearing again?" he barked.

"It's not just the swearing is it," she answered. "There's other stuff as well. The wounds. The wounds are different in the two murders."

"And Bent told you why that was, Cally, didn't he? Kosoto is nearly six foot six and Charlene is about five foot seven."

But, before Cally could reply, Steve had decided to join in. "This isn't forensics. This is bloody speculation. You just fancy yourself as a proper copper."

Cally wanted to answer but decided it was fruitless. The direction of the wounds and the strength of the impact are forensic evidence. Steve wouldn't understand that. And, anyway, why would she want to be a proper copper if it meant being like him? Who would want to be a copper, she thought, if this is how you turn out?

Bertoni interrupted Steve's attack. "Listen, Cally, in future tell me first. Okay?"

"What are you talking about?" replied Cally, unable to contain herself anymore. "Of course I've told you. I haven't stopped telling you. But you didn't want to know. Hallet didn't swear. The wounds to Charlene Hallet and Nelson Kosoto were completely different even though they were caused by the same weapon. I've said that from the beginning. You just weren't listening."

She went to walk away but Steve couldn't contain himself any longer either and butted in before Ashley could reply.

"You should stick to forensics, Cally."

"I rest my case," said Cally, repeating her previous statement that the force and the direction of the wounds were forensic evidence. "But thick Steve here can't see that."

Steve wanted to hit her but realised it would cost him his job.

~~~ الـ صمت من الـ عهد ~~~

"We are bound by dint of blood," she says. These are the only words I can recall her speaking for my dreams are but silent visions of a distant world. A hill, a tree, a winding path. The same hill, the same tree, the same path. Once more she disappears and I am consumed by that recurring sadness. I cry for a lost friend. The end of a dream is always, presumably, what we remember on waking up.

This is not what I expected when I began recording these diary entries. This process should be less emotive and more rational. This is a scientific, an analytical, procedure and yet I am swept along in sentimentalism.   I must refocus and ensure this is a diagnostic enquiry.   Perhaps a list of single words would be preferable.   Record simply the people, places and events.   Fire, woman, falling from cliff, sunshine, earthquakes and marble halls, not these sketchy, unreliable anecdotes or reminiscences of a childhood that, upon awaking, I cannot recall.   This isn't my younger life, this is a book I must have read.

The dreams are divided into happy, sad and anxious experiences. But, even when they are of happy times, they end in sadness because she, the young woman, always disappears.   She can never accompany me into the real world.   Last night she was trapped in a fire.   This is an allegory, of course.   She is trapped in my dreams and I want her to escape and join me in the real world.

The concept of writing single words is worth considering.   But, even in itself, it reminds me of someone in my dreams.   An old man. No, not old, but infirmed.   What a strange antiquated word to come to mind, but it describes him perfectly.   An infirmed man, perhaps an old soldier, sitting in a pub, drinking from an old tankard.   It must be someone I saw in a pub and that memory stayed with me, subconsciously locked away waiting for him to visit me in my dreams. Someone spoke his name.   Do I know anyone called Samuel?

4

Memories fade and are consumed by the profound and vast ocean of life-filled days and star-charmed nights. But landscapes remain as constant as creation itself. And so, hundreds of years after the memory of the two runaways, Tiro and Kalisto, had been extinguished, the tree of Seth stood verdant on a hillside of scattered goats. Time thaws the frost of our memories but the rugged Earth lies ageless and unchanging against the mild stirrings of time.

Fourteen generations later, a young man had just completed a three-hour journey from the arable landscape of Potbelly Hill to the dusty and developing city of Edessa.

~~~ الـ صمت من الـ عهد ~~~

Dentrides tripped on the threshold as he left the untidy store, dropping two of the sacks of salt. He slung the other two sacks over the donkey's back and returned to retrieve those that had fallen to the ground.

"If you can't supply my cheese," called Kushi the storekeeper, "then I'll find someone who can."

The boy walked back into the store and held his arms out in supplication. "I *can* supply your cheese, Master Kushi. All these years my family has supplied cheese to your store. It is just this one time. My grandmother is old. She makes mistakes," he called in mitigation, adding, "she forgot to put the salt in, which is why I need only four bags this time."

"Yes," Kushi replied as he swept the dust from his doorway, "you buy less from me and you upset my customers who want to buy cheese. Now go, I have another customer to serve. I just hope he doesn't want cheese."

A stranger had walked into the shop as Dentrides was leaving.

"Do you?" asked Kushi.

"Do I what?" the stranger asked.

"Do you want cheese? Because this fool of a child has brought me none."

"No," he replied as he handed some fruit to Kushi, who weighed it. It was not unusual to see a stranger in town. Edessa was a cosmopolitan city on the main trading route to Antioch and the sea. This man looked no different to any other. He was about thirty years old, lean and dressed in a black hooded robe. He had tied his horse on the post left vacant by Dentrides's donkey as the boy walked away down the street.

"I need some information," the stranger said.

"Information is free. The fruit is two denari."

Silos paid Kushi and asked him for directions to Potbelly Hill.

"It's a few miles outside town. Follow the boy and his donkey for he lives there."

Silos caught up with the boy and asked if he could accompany him to Potbelly Hill. The boy looked up at him suspiciously and had to shield his eyes from the sunlight.

"I leave in one hour. Meet me at Ashok's well, outside the north gate of the city. I must get home before darkness falls."

Dentrides had gained a good knowledge of languages from his visits to Edessa and also from the frequent visitors to Potbelly Hill, or rather those who used it as an overnight resting place, for the closeness of a small community provided protection against the wild beasts and mountain bandits. The boy had a natural gift for languages and Silos recognised this in him.

Dentrides visited two other stores to purchase supplies for himself and feed for the goats, before leading his donkey through the north gate to the well. Ashok's well was a local meeting point where the residents, as well as the many visitors to Edessa, exchanged news. Dentrides filled his water bottles from the well for his journey home. It would take three hours in the hot afternoon sun.

"Have you heard the news?" called a lame beggar, who sat in the shade of the well. Dentrides looked for a small coin to place in his cup. He could get the news for free but he knew the old man would embellish the story and he could then relate it, in the same fashion, to his ageing grandmother on his return. It always pleased her to hear news from the city. The boy looked around, but could see no sign of the stranger who was to accompany him to Potbelly Hill, so he sat down in the shade next to the beggar to listen.

"A caravan arrived this very day from Alexandria with news of great tragedy and even greater sadness," the old man began. "Do you know of Alexandria?" the man asked Dentrides as an aside.

The boy thought for a moment. If he told the man he knew nothing of that city, then the beggar could, in the knowledge of his ignorance, tell him a story filled with falsehoods.

"Yes," he answered confidently, "I know a little of that place." The reply caused the man to hesitate and consider how he might proceed.

"Alexandria, as you may know, contains the world's greatest library, built in the reign of Ptolemy II, in ages past. It contains the greatest collection of books covering history, astronomy and all the other sciences."

"Yes, yes," said the boy, "and what of it? I must leave soon for home and all you have told me is that the world's largest library stands in a city many miles from here. What of it?"

Patience, thought the old man, had been lost of this boy. He should learn to be more appreciative of an hour lost in the company of his elders as he grew into manhood.

"It is destroyed," said the man bluntly, for he wished to tell the news at his own pace and was upset at being hurried. "Destroyed by a great fire," he added and went on to attribute the cause of the fire to the forces of Queen Zenobia of Palmyra, for she had plagued the emperor's army in that part of the empire for many years.

The boy stood up and saw the stranger approaching. "Just one question," asked Dentrides as he untied his donkey. "Was the caravan from Alexandria the only one to arrive at Edessa of late?"

"The only one since seven days hence," confirmed the beggar.

Once the boy saw that the stranger had seen him, he did not wait and began packing the supplies on the donkey and led the animal away from the city. Silos filled his water bottles, kept sight of the boy and followed on behind him, gradually making up ground until, after about one mile, he rode alongside Dentrides. The sun had long passed its highest point and was now on their backs as they walked. Silos thanked the boy politely for guiding him to Potbelly Hill.

"What is your business there?" asked Dentrides.

"I have no business there," he answered. "I simply intend to rest up before continuing my journey to Jerusalem."

The boy trembled at his words. He looked the stranger in the eyes and saw the essence of his own fear. He looked about him and thought for a few moments.

"Where have you travelled from?" the boy asked.

"From Babylon, in the east, beyond the land of Nod and, on my way to Jerusalem, I wish to visit the sacred grove where Adam dwelt, before the light was extinguished."

The boy did not understand much of the man's words. "From Babylon you say?"

"Yes," answered Silos and the boy remembered the final words of the beggar at Ashok's well. Knowing that Babylon and Alexandria lay in opposite directions from Edessa, the boy began to suspect his companion was lying.

Dentrides wondered how he could fail to notice the ensuing death of his father and the inevitability of his grandmother getting older and yet he recognised the subtle nuances in the behaviour of a stranger. Experience teaches us everything, he thought to himself.

After a few moments he asked, "have you been in Edessa very long?"

"Only one day. I was hoping to find a caravan travelling to Antioch or Jerusalem or, failing that, to secure the services of a guide to travel with me to that great city."

A ghost appeared in the mind of Dentrides. One that had visited him many times. One that had not walked among the living for three years. One that the boy knew he could never erase from his memory.

They spoke little as they travelled along the well-worn track towards the boy's farm on the lower slopes of Potbelly Hill. Fields of wild wheat grew in abundance and waved to them in the breeze as they approached the house. The small building stood in a fertile area of land at the foot of a hill, where a large herd of goats grazed. On the hill, a short distance from the house, stood an old tree that Silos recognised, even though he had never visited this place before. For it was just as it had been described to him during his seven years of training.

The goats saw their shepherd's approach and recognised the bags of feed. Once some had begun the journey down the hillside, the others followed. Now he would have to walk up the hill and scatter some of the winter feed he had bought for store, to set them grazing again. As they approached the house, the boy's grandmother rose from her seat in the shade of the house to greet them.

"What is your name?" Dentrides finally asked his travelling companion.

"Silos."

"And you're a Magi?" asked the boy knowingly.

"I am a Magus," he answered. "You are an astute young man. How did you know?"

"If you dress like a Magus and talk like a Magus, and you abide from Babylon, then you are probably a member of the Magi. We have many visitors from your kind."

"And what is your name?" asked Silos as he dismounted and offered his hand to the boy.

"Dentrides and my grandmother is Phila," he answered but did not take his hand. The stranger was unmoved by the rejection and continued to hold his hand outstretched until the boy took it reluctantly.

112

It was dusk and the boy gathered wood to build a fire outside the house, where a brick kiln stood. He walked to a rudely constructed well that stood a short distance away to the side of the house and poured the contents of one bucket into another. On his return he poured some of that water into a large pot that stood on the fire. His grandmother was introduced to the stranger and she began to fill the pot with vegetables and herbs.

Dentrides unloaded the rest of the supplies and tied the donkey up by the well. Silos prepared his bed for the night close to the blazing fire. Phila asked if he would prefer to sleep in the house, but he declined. The cloudless night sky was filled with bright stars and the warmth of the day began to diminish. The boy made sure there was an ample supply of wood for the fire and placed a large log on the embers. The flames threw a reddish glow on the boy's figure and, for the first time, Silos noticed the scars on the boy's wrists. The stiff ridges of flesh on the underside of his arm were obviously the result of an accident, for surely nobody would inflict such wounds on one so young.

Eventually they all sat around the fire and ate the broth, along with some small barley loaves that the old woman had made earlier that day. Silos offered to repay them for their hospitality but they would not take any money.

"It is a struggle to survive," Dentrides said, looking around at the harsh landscape beyond the verdant hillside farmland that surrounded the house. "But another mouth to feed makes no difference to our plight."

Phila told the visitor that the farm had belonged to her husband's father and his father before him. She had two sons and the older of the two brothers inherited the farm. The younger son, Demetrius, had left the family home more than thirty years ago to find his fortune. Her eldest son, Dentrides's father, had died ten years ago, when the boy was only four years old. Somehow the old woman had managed to survive in this remote place. Hard times befell them three years ago and she had considered selling the farm and moving into Edessa. The boy had thought about travelling to Jerusalem to find his uncle. But, in the end, they stayed and, as the boy matured, he was more able to manage the farm. He was now fourteen years old and it was he who did all the work. Phila showed the stranger her gnarled, arthritic hands and shook her head. Her face was weather-worn with deep creases in the reddened skin that could be likened to the marks on the boy's arms, but these were the natural scars of an outdoor life. Her eyes were translucent blue and though they appeared like ice, they had a rich warmth about them. Her hair was long but tied with a rag to prevent it falling about her rugged face. She showed the stranger her hands.

"I am no use to Dentrides anymore and it is difficult for him to manage on his own. He should sell the farm and make his fortune elsewhere. He is a clever boy."

"I am fine, Nana," he answered. "I want to hear no more of such talk." He paused. "Let us not burden our visitor with our troubles. Tell us of your plans," he asked of the stranger.

Silos finished his meal and told his hosts that he was travelling to Jerusalem in search of someone who had studied with him in the Magi temple at Babylon. He was a Jew who had lived at the temple for nearly twenty years, but had left three years ago to return to Jerusalem to seek out his cousin.

"Do you remember seeing such a man three years ago?" Silos asked.

"Many pass this way, but few visit the farm. Those who do are often your people. The Magi seem to have a particular interest in Potbelly Hill," answered Dentrides. "Perhaps you can explain why?" It was a question Dentrides had asked many times before without receiving an answer.

Silos seemed less secretive than the other Magi that had visited the farm in the past. He explained that the roots of the Magi were in this area for this was where Seth, the third son of Adam, lived and raised his family. The man spoke with certainty about things he could not be certain of.

"When Adam was expelled from the paradise that was Eden, his son Cain murdered his brother Abel and it befell the third son, Seth, to help man find the way back to the garden. The Magi are the Sons of Seth and it befalls us to fulfil that task."

"But you have found the garden for you say it is where Nana and I live."

"The garden is more than a place, young Dentrides. It is a state of mind, a way of life, a belief and resignation to the will of God."

"You are a strange man, Silos," said Dentrides. "I have met many Magi in my short life but none have taken the trouble to tell me of their roots."

"Some think that the best way to preserve a secret is to remain silent on all things. But, to protect a secret a man needs only to keep his counsel on that matter alone. There is little of secret among the Magi, Dentrides, but what is secret shall remain so."

Silos asked whether Dentrides had thought again about travelling to Jerusalem to find his uncle, as he had done these three years past. He shook his head and the grandmother explained that a Magus, just like Silos, had visited the farm three years ago and asked Dentrides to guide him to Jerusalem. The boy agreed and, in those hard times, Phila was to sell the farm and live in Edessa. But Dentrides returned a few days later, saying he missed home and they resolved to stay.

"You are three years older," Silos pointed out. "You are a man. Perhaps if Phila stayed here, you could travel with me to Jerusalem and find your uncle. My visit will be short and I will be returning this way. If you fail to find him, you may travel back with me."

The boy hesitated but his grandmother urged him to accept. She said he could tell Demetrius that his uncle's reason for leaving had past. His older brother had died and he could manage the farm with his nephew. She suggested that, in the meantime, her sister's daughter Haniata could help on the farm while Dentrides went to Jerusalem to find her son.

"I have lost one son. Perhaps the other is still alive."

She urged Dentrides to make the journey, but only he had seen the ghosts that terrified him so.

As the darkness grew Phila retired to the house to sleep and left the two men sitting by the fire drinking the stock of the broth to warm them against the cold night. Dentrides spoke of the uncle he had never known but who he felt he knew well through his grandmother's frequent remembrances. It was more than thirty years ago when a caravan stopped near the farm and suggested they needed a guide to lead them to Jerusalem. Demetrius saw this as a great opportunity to make his fortune, for they seemed like wealthy men. No word had been heard from that day to this, said the boy. Travellers returning from the great city in the west were always asked about him, but none knew of him. Jerusalem was a city of many inhabitants. It was larger still than Edessa and the fact that nobody had seen Demetrius did not quench their belief that he was still alive. The men he travelled with were astrologers and may have been Magi but his grandmother's recollection grew dim over the years.

In the morning, Dentrides led the herd of long-haired, hornless goats down from the hillside. As they went ahead of him he examined the bushes and trees to see how long the herd could feed on this hill before they would need to be moved farther afield. If he chose to accompany Silos to Jerusalem, he expected to return in less than two months.

He saw Phila rise from her chair on the porch outside the house. If he brought the goats down in small groups, perhaps he could convince her to let him milk them today, although milking was the only task left that she could undertake. She could no longer separate the curd and whey; the mix was too heavy for her to turn and the quality of the cheese was beginning to decline as a result of her laboured movement. Last month she forgot to put salt in the mix and the whole batch was lost. She was even finding it difficult to milk the goats, although she never complained. The joints on her fingers were contorted and she needed to sit in the warm sun for an hour each morning simply to release the stiffness in her body. She rubbed her hands together as her nephew approached the house. He called to her to remain sitting.

"There are but twenty goats to milk. It shall not take me long."

Silos offered to help with the work in payment for their hospitality and Phila reluctantly agreed.

It was only after the milking had been completed and the buckets emptied into the vat that Dentrides sat down to drink some cool water. It was then that Silos again put his proposition to the boy.

"Will you guide me to Jerusalem?" he asked. "If you help me find the Jew I am looking for, I will help you find your uncle."

It was only the insistence of his grandmother that convinced Dentrides to accept. The journey would be a long one; probably some five and twenty days if they followed a route along the Euphrates and Orantes rivers towards the coast. It would take longer than a more direct route across the desert but there was a constant supply of water and the verdant land alongside the rivers would provide them with ample food for the journey.

The following day Dentrides said goodbye to his grandmother and the two men then travelled together to Phila's family home a few miles away, to ask his cousin to stay with her during Dentrides's absence. As they approached the rudely built stone house, a girl the same age as Dentrides rushed towards the approaching riders and greeted her cousin by embracing him and kissing him on both cheeks, as she had done since they were small children together. Their mothers had been sisters and they had been born just two weeks apart. They were brought up more as brother and sister than cousins and they were clearly devoted to each other.

Having secured Haniata's agreement to stay with his grandmother, Dentrides set off on his donkey into the unknown. Alongside him rode Silos and they moved slowly towards the great Euphrates River that headed towards the coast. The Magus was older than the boy, perhaps five and forty years to his fourteen and they spoke little as they rode and sometimes walked along. Dentrides encouraged his companion to keep the river in sight. They avoided walking too close to it because, although there were not too many wild beasts in the area, those that did inhabit the region often visited the river to drink the water. But the greater hazard was the insects that lived in the hot, humid atmosphere around the river bank. Many were poisonous and those they weren't were still capable of inflicting illness. So they used the river as their guide and visited it only to fill their water bottles and catch fish for their evening meal.

There was a nervousness about the boy when they rested under palm trees for the night, close to the banks of the river. They always lit a fire, even though the nights were as hot as the days, for it warned any wild animals to stay away. Silos asked about Potbelly Hill and whether the boy had ever found any remains of a stone structure in the area. He had not, but he remarked on how strangely fertile the land was compared with that surrounding the area.

"How long has your family lived there?" asked Silos.

"Many generations," he answered.

"You seem very close to your cousin."

"Hani and I grew up together. We are bound by a great love for each other," confessed the boy from his heart.

"Do you love her?"

"Not in the way I think you mean," answered Dentrides. "We are bound by dint of blood and she is the closest friend I have, but it is someone else who calls my heart to be their own. Someone like Hani, but not her," he added, sounding strangely sure of his destiny.

"Who is this person of whom you speak?"

"I do not know, but I feel her presence," said the strange but beguiling boy.

"And your name, how did you get that?" asked Silos.

The boy shrugged and said his mother and father had given it to him, in the same way that everyone else had been given their name. "It was my grandfather's name and his grandfather before him, I believe."

"Do you know what it means?"

The boy shrugged again, half out of disinterest and half out of fear of the way their discussion was developing.

"It means the youth of the tree," explained the wise Magus. But Dentrides did not see the significance of this and feared that the conversation was getting too personal. So, in order to make conversation at all, he spoke of what his limited knowledge gave him most expertise in, the making of cheese. He explained to his travelling companion about the skin bags made from the animal's stomach and how the storage of the watery cheese in these bags made it curdle and ferment. He then explained about the pressing and salting of the curdled milk and, all the time, Silos was wondering why the boy was so nervous. Eventually, when the boy had stopped talking simply for the sake of talking, Silos asked him to explain what he was afraid of.

"Who can explain?" he replied. "Are we not all afraid of the unknown?"

Dentrides changed the subject quickly and went on to tell Silos about the rabbits he kept at the farm for food. When he was very small, it was the first work his grandmother gave him. He looked after the rabbits and recalled when one young doe had her first litter. He rose each morning to see if they had arrived. Then, one cold morning, he looked into the compound that protected the rabbits and found, scattered about, several small pig-like creatures.

"Pale pink they were. No fur. Tiny, fragile, vulnerable creatures, lying dead. I asked my grandmother and she explained that it was the doe's first litter and she was frightened of the unknown. It did not mean that she would be anything other than a perfect mother in the future. It did not mean that her fear would accompany her always. And her fears did leave her, for she had many offspring and was, indeed, a fine mother."

"How did you get the scars on your wrist?" asked Silos as soon as the boy stopped speaking, hoping to catch him off guard.

But, again, Dentrides felt unhappy about the way the conversation was going. "I don't need a friend," he shouted. And Silos struggled to put this seemingly unrelated statement into the context of his question.

"We are not friends, just travelling companions. It is a long journey and if the subject of our conversation does not change, I shall know everything about producing cheese and keeping rabbits and nothing of my travelling companion."

The boy did not answer, so Silos changed the subject.

"How much time would we save by travelling through the desert?"

"You need not ask of the time, Master," replied Dentrides in a trembling voice, "but of how much water we would need and how much food to survive such a treacherous journey."

They had finished eating and the boy decided he would take to his bed, which he did with much trepidation. Eventually he fell into a disturbed sleep and woke, still tired, in the morning.

The second day of the journey was spent in silence, apart from Dentrides cautioning his companion about losing sight of the river for, at this part of their passage, they travelled on a narrow path with the river on their right-hand side and the desert on their left. When they camped for the second night, the two sat in silence, sharing a meal of fish from the river before Silos made a proposal.

"We have many miles to travel together and I sense a lack of trust on your part. Let us each share a secret with the other. Then we will each have a hold over the other that, of course, we will never divulge as long as the other does likewise." He could sense the boy was sceptical so decided to divulge his secret first.

"Let me tell you," he began, "about the man I am following. Then I shall be indebted to you to keep it secret." Unhesitatingly, he then went on to explain that the man had left the Temple of the Magi in Babylon about three years ago to return to his homeland near Jerusalem. The Jew had been entrusted with a secret, the same as Silos had. News received recently from that part of the Roman Empire suggested that the Jew might disclose that secret and it was the job of Silos to find him and convince him to do otherwise.

"I cannot tell you the secret but, in telling you this, I have said more than I should. What I speak is the truth and must remain a secret between us." He then looked at the boy and his eyes suggested that a secret be given in return. But the boy simply shook his head.

"That means only that you have told me one true thing and one falsehood. Yet I have not yet told you a falsehood. Therefore I am not in your debt, Sir."

"What falsehood have I told you?" asked Silos.

"Babylon, like Edessa, stands on the banks of the Euphrates River does it not?" he replied, pointing to the near horizon.

"It does."

"So you must have travelled along this very river these past few days."

Silos began to suspect a trap and tried to change the subject. "The people of Bambyce hold the fish of the Euphrates as sacred and it has been so since the days of Abraham."

Dentrides ignored his companion's attempt to divert the point he was anxious to make. "Do you still contend that you travelled to Edessa from Babylon?"

The Magus was thrown off guard by the young boy's candour and began to explain, but Dentrides cut him short.

"It is not enough now to correct the falsehood. You must tell me also why you need to conceal your true purpose in visiting Alexandria."

Silos had never been outwitted by a youth before and realised he would now need to be totally honest with the boy.

"Very well," said the Magus, "this is the secret that you may hold over me until we meet in heaven." He then went on to explain to Dentrides that he had travelled to Alexandria to destroy a papyrus scroll that contained details of the secret that had been entrusted to him by his Magi teachers. The scroll had been purchased from the Delphic Oracle but never revealed to anyone other than the keepers of the secret. These, he explained, consisted of a small group of Magi, known as the Musteria.

"And you did so by burning down the greatest library ever constructed?" the boy replied as he laughed loudly. "Do you not consider that a little excessive?"

"You cannot possibly understand the magnitude of the secret. I am pledged, Dentrides, to do anything in my power to keep secret the knowledge that has been entrusted to me. Libraries will come and go, kingdoms and empires will pass, warrior and benign kings and emperors will rule and, for the greater part, be forgotten and destroyed by time. But the secret can never be revealed because it is not constrained by time."

He paused and suggested that the boy should now make his confession.

Dentrides tossed another piece of wood on the fire and resigned himself to revealing his greatest fear.

"Three years ago," he began, "a stranger such as yourself visited our farm. He claimed to be a Magus, just as you do. And, just like you, he was seeking a Jew."

The boy caught sight of recognition in the eyes of his travelling companion and added, "perhaps the same person you are now seeking." Dendrites went on to tell how he had accepted the job of guide to the man, even though he was but eleven years old at the time. Like Silos he asked about the journey through the desert and it became apparent to the boy that the Jew the man was seeking had taken this godforsaken route. On the first night, the man began to blame Dentrides for not catching up with the Jew and spoke of following him into the desert. Dentrides objected to travelling through the desert, but agreed to accompany the Magus for one more day before returning home the following morning. But when they made camp on the second night, the man drank heavily and raped the boy, before tying his feet and hands with cord.

"But I set myself free," he explained, "and returned home."

"How did you manage to free yourself?"

"I untied the cord around my ankles and then, using a burning stick from the fire, I burned the cords from my wrists."

"Is that how you received the scars on your arms?"

The boy nodded. But Silos could sense he had not heard the full story. The eyes of the storyteller revealed a further secret. One yet to be told to anyone.

"You were quick enough," said Silos, "to suggest that I had not told you the whole truth. If we each are to be bound by our innermost secret, then you must reveal the whole truth of what happened that night."

Several minutes passed as the boy considered his position. He walked around the trees they rested beneath and eventually found a date that was almost ripe enough to eat. He sat down again and tasted it. Silos waited patiently and, eventually, the boy spoke. He realised that Silos had confessed a great crime and even greater sin so, finally, he decided to do the same.

"I killed him," he said and there was another lengthy pause. "The screams from the burns would have woken him, so before I removed the binding from my wrists, I first picked up a large rock and smashed his head with it while he slept in a drunken state. It was very heavy. I don't know how I lifted it. I was given strength by the goddess of Nemesis. It was only then that I burned the cords from my wrists and returned home. I told my grandmother that I burned my hands preparing the fire and that was why I had returned home. I could no more tell her of what he did to me than I could tell of what I did to him."

"Firstly," said Silos after a few moments, "that man was not a Magus. He was an imposter. He, like others before him, hoped to capture the Jew and extract from him the secrets of the Magi. No Magus would do what that man did to you, Dentrides. This man was an enemy of the Magi and wanted only to gain the knowledge that had been entrusted to the Jew."

"Are your intentions not the same?" asked the boy, who was now trying to prevent himself from crying.

Silos explained that his mission was only to ensure the Jew did not disclose the one great secret that had been entrusted to him.

"The man you met wanted to obtain the secret even if the Jew was intent on keeping it. "

Silos stood up and, after telling his companion that they were now bound by the secrets they had divulged to each other, he lifted a piece of burning wood from the fire and held it to his wrist. Dentrides screamed at him to stop, but he did not do so, until the wrist was scarred like the boy. Silos seemed unmoved by the pain of the fire against his arm.

Before they slept, Silos told the boy more about the man they were following. He was a Jew, from Nazareth and he was returning to Galilee to find his cousin who he intended to work with. The Nazarene was a wise young man who was generous of nature and it was this generosity that Silos had seen as a threat to the secret. Like Silos, the Jew had studied holy scriptures at the Magi temple and was intent on doing good. He was a lauded student who would have made an excellent Magi master.

The following morning the two friends, because that is what they had now become, spoke of the route they would take to Jerusalem. They agreed to follow the river and cross the dry land that led to the Orantes River that flowed west towards the Libanus Mountains before stopping at Damascus and travelling across Mount Atabyoun to Jerusalem. Dentrides now felt comfortable with talking about the alternative route that they believed the Nazarene had taken. He explained to Silos that the Boreas wind from the north tormented the desert traveller, who would have nothing to eat or drink. The river trail had fruit and seed as well as plentiful water. But the desert traveller would have to live on locusts and wild honey alone to survive.

By the time the two reached the Orantes River several days later, they had become good friends. One night, Dentrides told his companion about the stories his mother had told him of his Uncle Demetrius. They spoke of the uncle's journey to Jerusalem as a guide to the group of Magi. When they had finished talking about this the boy asked Silos to tell him about the ancient man called Seth, who lived near Potbelly Hill.

"Before all the worlds were set in order," began Silos, "Adam was the first to be given the godlike gift of prophecy, through eating of the Tree of Knowledge, which grew somewhere near the land where your family now lives. He passed this knowledge to his third son, Seth, who passed it through the generations to Noah, who was famed for being delivered from the deluge. It was he who passed on that knowledge to the Magi. The Sons of Seth became the Magi and to them alone was bestowed the great secret. The man we now follow is himself a son of Seth. The Jew believes his coming was foretold by the Hebrew seer Isaiah in ages past. Perhaps the Magi your uncle accompanied all those years ago had read this too and understood what had been foretold, for many Magi are versed in astrology and have studied the history of the great religions. But the story does not end here," continued Silos, "for we cannot allow the great secret to be revealed even though the gift of prophecy shall pass. Sadly, wisdom is to be replaced by knowledge and intelligence, just as the gift of prophecy is to be lost to us."

Each night Dentrides learned more from Silos, but the great secret was never revealed to him. The boy listened intently as his companion spoke of Dentrides's homeland as a blessed place, where inscribed megaliths, the touchstones of truth, are protected by the sacred mulberry trees. Those megalithic stones were the ancient representation of man without life; man denied life. Not the life that we now know but the life enjoyed by Adam before he fell from grace. They lie deep below Potbelly Hill in the sacred temple of Eden.

The following day they reached Gennesaret, or the Sea of Galilee, now renamed Tiberius by the Romans, and travelled down the lake resting for the night in Et Tabigah, just north of the town that is also called Tiberius. The next day they arrived in Capernaum in the territory of Herod Antipas and stopped for the night in Ein Kerem, a village outside the great city of Jerusalem. It was late and, as they watered the horse and donkey at a well outside the town, a man sitting in the shade of a tree called them over.

"Alms for the poor, Sir. Alms for the poor," he called as he held out an empty cup.

The man was dressed only in a torn sackcloth blanket and his hair was unkempt. Neither Silos nor Dentrides had ever seen a leper and neither knew the law of Abraham that prescribed how a leper should dress and appear. The man lived outside the town and only visited the well at times when others did not. The two travellers noticed the scars that marked those parts of his body that they could see. A large part of his left foot was missing and they assumed it had been chewed off by an animal, for such were the dangers that lurked on the edges of small towns such as this.

Dentrides reached into his belt for a small coin and placed it in the cup.

"Have you any news from your travels?" the beggar asked, as he reached for two crutches and lifted himself up.

"It is I who have paid you for news, my good man," answered Dentrides.

"An exchange then," suggested the beggar and Dentrides told him about the great fire in Alexandria, just as he had been told at the well in Edessa.

"You are a fine storyteller, young man. You would make a good beggar."

"Better than you, I think," answered the boy, adding "now your news, for what it is worth." And he and Silos sat down in the shade to hear what the old man had to say.

He began by telling them about the terrible deeds of a band of Galilean bandits who lived in the hills outside the city, the leader of which had now been arrested. The beggar's delivery was as animated as his disability would permit. He balanced on the poorly made crutches and flayed his arms to give his story gravity. Then he told them that a hermit, who lived in the desert and preached the end of days, had also been arrested for denouncing the King as an adulterer.

"'Ahab with his Jezebel' he called the King and his mistress," the beggar told them, before going on to give his opinion of the King, the Roman occupation and the chief priests and Pharisees. But Silos was more interested in the hermit, for it sounded like the Jew he was pursuing who had, himself, ventured into the desert.

"'Prepare the way of Yahweh' cried the hermit," the beggar said, "and there were many who would listen to his words of resurrection," he added.

This final word gained the particular interest of Silos, whilst Dentrides was wanting to ask the old man about his uncle.

"What did the hermit say of resurrection?" asked Silos.

"He stood in the Jordan and cleansed people with water, telling them that they would live again. His younger cousin had lived before he said and he cured the sick, but I could not get close to him for the crowd stoned me if I got too near," he added casually. "He said he was not the one, but that another one would come after him."

The beggar then went on to tell them about the beheading of the hermit for his abuse of the King.

Silos questioned him further about the younger cousin, who he began to realise was the Jew who had left the Magi temple three years ago.

"He claimed," explained the beggar, "to be the re-incarnate of the prophets. 'Who do people say I am?' he asked his followers and they said to a man that he was Elijah or Jeremiah reborn and walking among us." He paused for a moment. "Some have said recently that he is his cousin, the hermit, reborn after his beheading. But many others saw them together. I doubt he was any of them, but he had many followers who believed otherwise."

"And what became of this man?" asked Silos.

"After the King lost what little patience he had with the hermit he had him taken to the fortress of Machaerus and beheaded. The younger cousin returned this way only a few days past. This one preached in a quieter tone than the hermit and was greatly affected by his cousin's arrest and execution. In fear of his life, he escaped into the desert from whence he came."

"And what of him now?" asked Silos.

"He is either still in the desert or is being hidden by his followers."

The beggar told them many things about the cousins but he knew nothing of Dentrides's uncle for, without a description, it was difficult to identify a man who had arrived some thirty years before. So the pair decided to go into the city and ask there.

"Is the older cousin the man you are seeking?" asked Dentrides.

"Do you not listen? The beggar told you the hermit's words, did he not? 'I am not the one' he said. No, the younger cousin is the one I am seeking, I am sure of that."

Silos suggested that they went their separate ways in the city for he had other business to attend to. They agreed to meet at the Pool of Siloam before dusk and walk back to Ein Kerem together.

As they approached the city walls of Jerusalem, they saw a countless number of camps. Beyond the gates, the city thronged with thousands of people and they wondered how so many people survived in such a small space.

"We are seeking a man who settled here from Edessa some thirty years past," Dentrides asked anyone who would listen. Occasionally he said Demetrius from Mesopotamia, or Demetrius of Assyria. And sometimes, he tried 'a man who came here as a boy from Potbelly Hill.' But few people had heard of Edessa, let alone Potbelly Hill. He learned that there were not many Assyrians or Mesopotamians who had settled in Jerusalem but, after thirty years, any identity he had with those places had probably been lost. But however he delivered the question nobody had seen or heard of his uncle. In fact, most people he spoke to simply said they were strangers themselves.

Under the midday sun, it was unbearably hot in the city and so Dentrides decided to take some shade at an inn near the Gennath Gate, close to the Maccabean Palace of Herod Antipas. The inn was so crowded that there was barely room to stand. He asked the publican if the city was always this crowded.

"It is Passover in three days," he answered. "Come back in four days and I will find a seat here for you," he added sarcastically, waving his arms to suggest the inn was full.

Dentrides's question about his uncle was met with a shrug of the shoulders by the publican, but was overheard by a man standing close by.

"I know the man you speak of," said a red-faced and rather stout man who had clearly been drinking heavily for some time. Unbeknown to the boy, Silos had returned and loitered just within the doorway to make sure that Dentrides was entirely safe. Silos was suspicious of the stout man's intentions and listened as closely as he could without being discovered, in order that his young friend was not deceived by the man.

"He is often here at this time," the man added. "Demetrius of Potbelly Hill we call him. In truth, there can only be one with that name. He works for Joseph Caiaphas, the son-in-law of the High Priest, Annas." The man paused and added, "I hope I was helpful to you young man," and placed his empty jug on the bar. The boy called for the publican to refill it.

"Thank you kindly, young Sir," he added with a hint of sincerity, before adding, "and he will, for certain, be here today, because I happen to know he has business with that man there." He pointed to a man holding a cloth purse, who looked furtively around him. He did not know his name but knew him as a follower of the cousins the beggar had spoken of.

The boy waited at the bar until a man entered and, after looking about the room, approached the man with the purse. The fear of disappointment prevented Dentrides from moving.

Staying out of sight of the boy, Silos walked across the room to take up a position nearer to the two men, so that he could overhear their conversation. It soon became clear that Dentrides's uncle, if indeed it was he, wanted information from the other man as to the whereabouts of the younger cousin. His employer, Caiaphas, feared an uprising during the Passover festival. Caiaphas held hopes of promotion to the office of High Priest and knew that it would please the authorities if he could dispose of this troublemaker. The man with the purse spoke of the great support that his master had. He described a crowd of 5,000 men gathering in the hills outside the city. But in spite of the offer of money and the threat of injury, the man with the purse refused to betray his friend. Silos failed to hear the end of the conversation over the noise that filled the inn. And, when

Caiaphas's servant left the inn, the boy followed, leaving the other man looking distraught and abandoned.

The boy caught up with his uncle just before he entered a building close to the inn.

"Uncle Demetrius," he called and the man turned round and looked closely at the boy. A few seconds passed before the older man recognised the likeness of the boy to his brother as a child.

"I was not born when you left, Uncle," Dentrides said. "Come home, Uncle. There is only your mother and me left now and we need your help with the farm."

The boy's pleading fell on a heart that had remained barren for many years but by dint of blood he searched into its dark recesses and took pity on Dentrides.

"What is your name?"

"Dentrides."

"'Twas my father's name and his grandfather before him," the man answered.

They embraced and the heavily built man held the boy's shoulders to take a closer look at him. There was no doubt that he was who he said he was and tears filled both their eyes.

They talked, at length, about the uncle's changed life since he travelled to Jerusalem. He had been given employment by Annas and then by the High Priest's son-in-law, in recognition of a service he did for them on his arrival in the city. The men he guided to Jerusalem all those years ago turned out to be enemies of King Herod and sought to overthrow him. Demetrius had told Annas all that the Magi travellers had told him during their long journey from Edessa. He was offered a place in the palace, employment and one hundred silver pieces if he agreed to murder the travellers on their way home. This he agreed to do, but could not do it. The Magi travellers had assured him that they had completed their business and never intended to return to Jerusalem, so he had simply reported back to Annas that the men had been killed and their bodies disposed of in the desert. Every day since, Demetrius had lived in fear of Annas finding out the truth, but he never did. But, despite the wealth and position he now enjoyed, he still feared that the truth would be revealed. He saw, every day, the torture inflicted by Annas and Caiaphas on their enemies but could find no way of escaping.

Demetrius told his nephew about the man he met at the inn and how Caiaphas wanted to capture the younger of the two cousins for fear he would cause a riot in the city. Dentrides suggested that Demetrius offered to deliver the cousin over to Caiaphas in exchange for his freedom in order that he could return to his homeland. The man with the purse had become disenchanted since the beheading of the hermit and might agree to betray his master for the reward that was being offered by the High Priest and Pharisees. Demetrius agreed and set off to meet Caiaphas to discuss his plan.

After Dentrides had followed his uncle from the inn, Silos approached the man with the purse, suggesting that he had seen him in the company of the young cousin when he was preaching in the hills. The man was reluctant to admit this at first, but was soon won over through the guile of the Magus. It was clear that he harboured worldly ambitions.

"He told me," he said as he fidgeted with the purse, "that he came not to send peace into the world, but to send a sword. Yet he has us living in abject poverty. When we sat on the banks of the Jordan at Bethsaida, we had more than 5,000 followers who he fed with a few barley loaves and fish. Five thousand men, all prepared to march with him to victory, but where is he tonight? Eating at the house of Simon the leper in Bethany."

He told Silos that Demetrius had told him that the chief priests and Pharisees had issued a decree that if any man knew where the Nazarene was they should report it to them so that he might be arrested.

"Is it true?" Silos asked, "that your master spoke of rising from the dead and being born again?"

"He did, Sir," replied the man and Silos feared the great secret may not be safe.

From that moment the Magus was resolved in his purpose.

"And did he speak of the significance of the number seven?"

"He said that he was predestined for greatness because great men occurred every seven generations. Starting with Adam, then Enoch seven generations later, Abraham at twenty-one, King David at thirty-five and the master himself was seventy-seven generations after Adam. There had been fourteen generations between Abraham and David and fourteen again between David and the deportation to Babylon, and fourteen again from that point to my master's own birth."

It was clear to Silos that the man was distraught and saw shadows in every corner of his life. His mind was easily manipulated.

"Fourteen is twice seven," he added nervously.

"And seven itself. Did he mention that?"

"He fed 5,000 people gathered on the hill with just seven loaves and seven fish." At this point the man began to meander, as he thought about what the significance of the number seven might be.

"There are seven spirits of God, seven seals," he continued, "seven angels with seven chalices. The sacred Menorah has seven branches. There are seven classes of furniture in the Tabernacle. It took Solomon seven years to build the temple in Jerusalem." He stopped his feverish chattering for a moment, before adding, "how many times must I forgive my brother, we asked him. Is it seven, Lord? He answered that it was seven times seven. Seven times we are to be forgiven."

The man began to see that the one he followed had walked this Earth six times before, as Abraham, David and the great prophets. That realisation was apparent to Silos and it became the man's death warrant. The Magus knew that both this man and his master must die if the secret was to be protected.

The ramblings of this clearly troubled man were enough to convince Silos that he must act. He could not allow the veil to be removed so easily, from a secret that had been kept safe for so long. The man began speaking more loudly now and was attracting the attention of the crowd in the inn.

"How are we to throw off the shackles of oppression when we go about penniless? We live in abject poverty. I held hopes of high office. A treasurer in the new kingdom that he promised us. And now I find myself an outcast, stoned and condemned by the authorities."

Silos calmed him down. "Then hand him over to those authorities," answered Silos quietly in his ear.

"They will behead him like his cousin. I could not be responsible for that."

"But you have a friend who has the favour of Annas and his son-in-law. Demetrius told me he can secure your master's freedom."

"How will he achieve that?"

"Is it not the practice of the Romans to release prisoners at the time of the Passover. Who better placed than Demetrius to secure your master's release? Tell Demetrius where he can find your master tomorrow night and, in return, ask for his promise of acquittal. There is even a reward. Thirty pieces of silver. That is a fund with which to throw off the shackles of oppression."

~~~ ~ ال صمت من ال عهد ~ ~~~

By the time the two companions had returned to Ein Kerem that evening, the mad man at the inn had accepted the reward of thirty silver pieces and told Demetrius where his master would be the following night. Caiaphas insisted that the arrest took place during the hours of darkness, when there would be few followers accompanying the Nazarene.

Dentrides and Silos stayed at Ein Kerem for five days until Demetrius arrived. On the fourth day they saw the beggar who they had met at the well on their arrival. But the man seemed greatly changed, so they stopped him to ask how it was that he was now able to walk, for his foot appeared to have grown anew and all the scars had disappeared.

"'Twas the hermit's cousin," he said. "The prophet. He came out of the desert and walked to the well." He paused, as if he still could not believe what had happened to him.

"He told me to fetch him a cup of water from the well. 'Fetch it yourself', I answered, 'as you are a more able man than I'. But, he just looked at me, with such love that I had never seen and I felt the strength return to my legs and I was able to walk. When I awoke the following morning, I was fully recovered. It is truly a miracle."

Remembering how the beggar had delivered his stories with such animation and ability four days before, they both laughed and mocked him by applauding. Clearly, he was some kind of wizard who had fooled them when they had previously met.

When Demetrius arrived the following day, they purchased supplies and set off on their long journey back to Potbelly Hill. The three companions travelled back along the river route towards Antioch and then on towards Edessa. On the way, Dentrides told his uncle about the beggar and the uncle told them of the events in the city during the Jewish feast of Passover. The Nazarene met a similar fate to his older cousin and was crucified by the Roman authorities for treason, along with some of the bandits from the hillside. And the man with the purse had indeed been mad, because he killed himself the day after his master's arrest. When Demetrius left Jerusalem, the High Priest was deciding what to do with the thirty silver pieces that had been returned to him after the mad man was found hanged. As blood money it could not now be accepted by the authorities, so they were discussing how it could be disposed of without corrupting the high office that the priests held.

On the twentieth day, when they had crossed the mountains and made camp, they each went to wash themselves in the clear waters of the Euphrates River. It was there that Silos noticed the scabs that began appearing on his body. But he was unfamiliar with the cause and it was Demetrius who knew what was wrong, for his many years in Jerusalem had made him familiar with the pariahs that the Jews called lepers. Silos insisted that Demetrius told him the truth of what was to happen to him. In the morning, the Magus decided to head north towards Babylon, where he could seek help at the temple.

Before leaving, now knowing the truth of his fate, he bequeathed a gift to Dentrides. A small purple-coloured amulet hung by a chain around his neck. Silos explained to the boy that it contained a small fragment taken from the Tree of Knowledge before Adam was expelled. It had been passed by him to his son, Seth, then on through the generations to Noah and his descendents. After coming into the possession of Zoroaster himself, it came to Silos through fourteen generations of his family. Having no family himself, he entrusted it to Dentrides, telling him that he still had many journeys to make but assured him that they would meet again.

"Keep this amulet always. If I had failed on my mission I would now be asking you to return this to my master but if I fail to return myself, and fail to return the amulet, my master will know I succeeded but could not return."

The Magus told Dentrides that the contents of the amulet were returning home. The boy did not understand and Silos left without explaining but he knew the amulet and its contents would now return to their true home on that poor farmland where life itself began.

"What will you do now?" the Magus had asked Dentrides before leaving.

"I was born a shepherd boy and I have a shepherd boy's ways. So I shall be a shepherd, like my father before me."

"Then be a good shepherd," he replied.

The boy opened the locket and removed the small piece of wood it contained. As he did so, he caught his finger on the clasp and drew blood, which stained the piece of the tree. He looked, rather apologetically, at Silos who simply placed the wood in the amulet and closed it. He planted it once more into the boy's palm and closed his hand about it.

The boy thought himself clumsy but Silos knew there was a purpose for everything that happened.

"You have a long journey to make, Dentrides."

"But I am only going home," he replied.

"Yes, you are," said Silos wisely.

"And what will you do?" asked Dentrides.

Silos examined the sores on his arms and hands. "All grief shall be repaid with joy in equal measure," he answered, but Dentrides did not understand and simply remembered the words and thought on them when he was next alone.

Demetrius was sceptical of the gift, but Dentrides treasured it for the rest of his life and shared its secret only with Haniata and eventually his grandson, who was named after him. Young Dentrides and the amulet dwelt within the shadow of Sarv-e- Šēt and he often recalled the strange stories that his grandfather had told him although he spoke only in his old age of his journey of adventure with the mysterious visitor all those years before.

5

The steps of the courtroom had been drenched by an unseasonal thunderstorm that freshened the air and, strangely, mirrored the reaction of the court to the Judge's decision to release Livingstone on bail. The sky still thundered loudly but the dark clouds drifted quickly eastwards and the sun began to reclaim the heavens.

A lack of physical evidence and the fact that the murder squad was already holding one suspect for the same murder clearly had a bearing on the judge's decision. The street-wise Barnabas Cartwright was not going to miss a photo opportunity like this. From inside the building, the fashion-conscious and egotistical lawyer despatched his assistant to ensure the waiting members of the press blocked their escape at the foot of the steps. He had learned from experience that a camera shot looking upwards always improves the profile, so he stopped, apparently shocked by the presence of the media, at the top of the steps.

The umbrellas were just being folded away and the sun's rays lit up the doorway behind Cartwright and his client. It was a superstar entrance, with the older man resting a comforting arm around Bunny's shoulder as they stepped out onto the rain-sodden steps. From the smiles and confident posture, one might easily have concluded that Livingstone had just been found not guilty, rather than simply made bail. Even a tiny mistake would have been capitalised on by the experienced defence lawyer, but this was a much more significant error.

"These are trumped up charges," declared Cartwright. "The police have Kosoto's murderer. They even said they were not seeking anyone else in connection with that murder when they arrested him. Now they choose to arrest my client, who is entirely innocent of the crime. Why? Why do you think that is?" he asked as the cameras flashed. "Well I think we all know the reason why my client is being hounded," he said before anyone chose to offer an answer. "They think they have a better chance of prosecuting my client because he's black."

He moved a little closer to the crowd of photographers. "Come on, step forward," he called, like a market stall trader to the reporters in a sarcastic tone, "who else wants to be arrested for these murders?" Then, just when he knew he had their full attention, he delivered the punch line, the very line he knew would fill the tabloid headlines the next day. "What is this, pick-and-mix policing?"

He ignored the empty steps to his left and right and carved his way through the throng of reporters, still with his arm draped around his protected client. The barrister had enjoyed many such scenes before in his illustrious career but, apart from the time that someone thought he was the drummer in Bob Marley's backing group, Leroy Livingstone had not and it suddenly occurred to him to grab his fifteen minutes of fame. He wrestled himself from his lawyer's comforting arm and snatched the microphone held closest to him.

"*You know what day finking man,*" shouted the tall and highly animated West Indian. "*Day juss see sum black guy. 'Yoo a brudda'; 'yoo from de i-lanns'; 'yoo weapon o choice a machete'; 'yoo black'; 'so id muss be yoo black boy', that's what day finkin.*" His heavily rhythmic pronunciation was consciously designed to capture his Jamaican ancestry, even though he had never lived there himself.

Cartwright led his client away through the crowd, continuing to proclaim his innocence, but the reporters and cameramen were already rushing away themselves, with the following day's headlines firmly imprinted in their minds, just as Cartwright had planned it. As they did so, they left the lawyer getting into his chauffeur-driven car and missed Livingstone climbing into an old, but very large Mercedes, driven by another gang member.

When Chief Superintendent Bent caught the Cartwright interview on the early evening news that night, he immediately began preparations for a press conference. A call from the commissioner of police insisted on it. The police needed to put their case across and it fell to Bent to lessen the damage caused. He knew from experience that the words 'pick-and-mix policing' would dominate the following day's headlines.

Once he and his team of media advisers produced their case and decided how it was to be delivered, he called Bertoni, Redpath and Boyce and ordered their attendance at the press conference, which was to be held the following morning.

~~~ الـ صمت من الـ عهد ~~~

That evening, when he returned home, Tyler found Cally tidying up. This was a little unusual because they both normally tidied as they went, so spring cleaning was rarely

143

necessary. But she was suspended from work, so he concluded she probably just had some time on her hands. He dismissed the matter and concentrated on his plan, before remembering that it was the birthday party at the weekend and Cally would want the house to be presentable.

"Did you get caught in the rain?" Tyler asked, knowing how she hated getting wet. Cally preferred the summer. She never walked in the shade where she could bathe in the sunshine. She loved to feel the warmth of the sun on her.

"No, I've been in the lab all day, going through the Hallet case files for the press conference tomorrow."

He went to remind her that she was suspended but chose not to. He wasn't tactful by nature, so needed to consciously remind himself not to be too negative in the current climate. Tyler had decided to enlist the help of Cally in his efforts to establish whether there was any connection between Clinchman and Richards, so he wanted to stay in her good books. It would mean him trusting her with details of his work but he simply didn't have time to trace the family history of Sidney Clinchman himself while completing the other elements of the DNA testing and there was nobody else he could trust to keep the matter confidential.

Tyler went into the kitchen, put down the bag of shopping and switched on the oven. As Cally tidied a chest of drawers, she fired a string of questions at him before he even had time to remove his suit jacket.

"Can I throw these scribbled pages away?"

"No, give them to me, I'll put them in my briefcase and check them before I throw them away."

"Can we replace some of these glasses? I don't think we have four the same."

"If you like."

144

"Oh," she suddenly said as she picked up the old egg-shaped brooch she found in the drawer earlier. "Is this yours?"

Tyler was busy reading the pages Cally had just given him, so she held the object up and called to him again.

"Can I throw this old brooch away? It's only taking up drawer space."

"No!" cried Tyler as he ran into the room to retrieve it.

"It's okay," she responded, keeping hold of the worn and lack-lustre piece of jewellery. "What is it anyway?"

"My grandfather gave it to me."

"Grandfather? Not your grandmother?" she asked, convinced it was a piece of women's jewellery.

"It's a family heirloom," he answered as Cally fiddled with the egg-shaped object.

"And it was your grandfather's?"

"I'm not sure," answered Tyler, taking it from her. "But we're not throwing it away, it might be worth some money. It could be a Fabergé egg."

"Fabergé? A minute ago," snapped Cally, "it was a family heirloom."

"Yes," Tyler answered, "and a minute ago you wanted to throw it away."

He made sure the brooch was placed safely back in the drawer.

"Did you know your grandfather?"

"When I was a child, yes," he replied. "He died when I was about twelve. I was, allegedly, named after him."

"Is that where Tyler came from?"

"No, not really, my grandfather was named Tyrone and apparently he was very keen for me to be named after him. I always thought he had been named after his grandfather, but my grandmother told me he was named after Tyrone Power."

"Tyrone who?"

"An old movie star, Tyrone Power."

"Sounds like a blue movie star to me, with a name like that."

"Very funny. Now may I return to my cooking?"

He emptied the shopping he had got on the way home and began chopping and slicing in preparation. He retrieved some saucepans from the cupboard and waited until Cally came into the kitchen for some cleaning cloths before putting his proposal to her.

"Cally," he asked tentatively. "If you have time to tidy up, is there any chance you could undertake some research work for me?"

"Don't you think I've got enough on my plate at the moment," she answered swiftly enough to convince him that she had given his request very little thought. She began to regret it until he tried a clumsy attempt at persuasion.

"But you're suspended. You have got time on your hands, Cally."

"You know what, Tyler, you can be incredibly insensitive at times," she said as she continued tidying the room.

"Well, I'll help tidy up if that helps."

"I'm not talking about tidying up. I'm talking about my career being flushed away over this Hallet case."

He realised he was in danger of upsetting Cally, so changed the subject and asked how she wanted her liver.

"What are the options?" she asked.

"Bacon, mushrooms or both."

"I better just have the mushrooms," she answered. "Working with Bertoni and Redpath is seriously damaging my figure. You wouldn't believe the rubbish those two eat in a day."

While Tyler busied himself in the kitchen, Cally continued to tidy up the lounge. Clearing out old, unused items was less cathartic for Cally than Tyler. It was a functional, unemotional process. She didn't dwell on the past as Tyler did, although his reference to his grandfather caused her to reflect on her own grandparents, or rather the one she could remember. The headstone Cally's parents ordered for her grandmother's grave contained the usual information, of course. But they had chosen to add three words to describe the woman who had lived with them for the last ten years of her life. At the time, it seemed a little disrespectful to abbreviate someone's life in such a way. But their objective was clear. They wanted to convey what type of person she was on what limited space was available on a headstone. It is probably the wrong time to consider doing such a thing. The risk of over-sentimentalising would overwhelm most people as it did on this occasion.

She began to wonder how she might choose to describe Tyler in just three words, or how others might define her. What a perfectly circumscribed world it would be if we were permitted only three words to record someone's influence on it. Your three greatest attributes to gain access at the gates of heaven. Would anyone be forthright enough to tell the truth?

'Loving', 'kind' and 'dependable' they resolved on after much reflection, recalled Cally, who dwelt on the subject as she continued to tidy up. This was the way her grandmother would be remembered by those who passed her grave each day. Should a life be reduced to such trivial wordplay? Loving of whom? To love someone we like warrants little merit and the love of someone we dislike is probably at best grudging and at worst insincere. If it is simply our own children we love, who could expect less? Surely it is a prerequisite of parenthood

147

to love our children. No, admiration is greater than love. No less can be said of kindness for the word flatters to deceive. Kindness to our fellow man is mostly limited to those we like or it becomes patronising or sycophantic. And dependable, an expression one might just as easily use to describe a car. Staunch, trustworthy, loyal in its human form and yet we regard trustworthy as no more than honesty and staunch no less than stubborn or uncompromising.

Cally removed a vase from the cupboard and placed it in the kitchen to be washed. She needed to remember to buy some flowers tomorrow. It didn't occur to her that Tyler might buy her some flowers for her birthday. What three words would she use to describe Tyler, she thought. If the vase didn't prompt him to buy a bouquet, then inconsiderate might be appropriate, or inattentive. Sadly, both were true, but neither was particularly important to Cally. Perhaps the choice of three words says more about us than about the one they are dedicated to. It is less about what we think of other people and more about what they think of us that counts, she thought, almost imagining some long-forgotten teacher telling her so. *'What needs my Shakespeare for his honoured bones?'* she wondered, remembering a poem from school. Perhaps greatness awaited Tyler. He was certainly capable of achieving something special in his field. Dynamic conveyed a rather different personality to Tyler, so she dismissed that word. Clever, astute and resourceful were similarly discarded. There were just too many options. Perhaps if all three words needed to begin with the same letter, that would restrict the selection process. Imaginative, inspired and inventive were shortlisted but all referred to his work and rather suggested that he had no worth outside his employment, however important that work might be. Perhaps, after his earlier remark, incredibly insensitive idiot would suffice. Or perhaps short, slim and studious, except he wasn't short. Although he was only slightly taller than her and she reached his height only when wearing high heels. He was obviously not as slim as her and, to be honest, he didn't have to be studious because knowledge came to him as easily as leaves to a tree.

Cally disposed of a half-empty bottle of Baileys, wondering whether it had a use-by date and not wanting to take any risks. Not that she could imagine Steve or Ashley drinking Baileys; insufficiently macho. She gave up on the search for three words to describe Tyler but couldn't resist contemplating her own memorial. What did Tyler think of her? How would he describe her in three words? She hoped that short, slim and studious would receive less consideration than she had given them. Would we not all choose something more poetic, more heroic for ourselves? Belligerent, bigoted and bloody-minded loomed ahead of brave, beautiful and beloved.

Tyler placed two plates on the dining room table and Cally thought about introducing her three-word challenge over dinner. But she was intercepted by a conversation of more practical value.

With less time to think about it, Cally would have considered Tyler temperate, clever and likeable both inside and outside work. But, as usual, she thought too much about everything. Tyler would choose diminutive and amiable, but too self-reliant to be described as congenial. She had a delicate beauty and her kindness and patience were seen as weakness by her work colleagues. But, to her long-term friends who knew her best, such qualities singled her out as someone they could trust and rely on. For the moment, though, he simply looked at her across the table and noticed that her youthful skin

149

was only a shade lighter than her fawny brown hair. He smiled at her and she smiled back.

Later on, after dinner, Cally retreated a little, as she always did in their relationship, to ensure Tyler's career remained on course, normally ahead of her own. The downcast turn of his lip and subtle change in his demeanour did not go unnoticed by someone who knew him so well.

"What is it you need doing?"

"Tracing some family history."

"What, the family heirloom; the brooch?"

"No, something from work. I've uncovered something really interesting; groundbreaking perhaps. And I need to trace the family history of a guy called Sidney Clinchman who was born in 1740 and died in 1802. I need to trace his family history right up to date if I can."

"Sounds like something for Galen, rather than me."

Tyler explained that it was strictly confidential at the moment and he wanted to restrict it to a limited number of people.

"It's just William and myself at the moment," he explained.

"But Galen's our oldest friend, Tyler. You know you can trust him. Anyway, I don't even know what work you are referring to. All I know and all Galen would know is that we are tracing the family history of someone named Clinchman. How can we possibly be breaching any confidentiality?"

Tyler conceded the argument and agreed to discuss it with Galen the next day. Perhaps Double Helix Limited could make a donation to the African drought fund to compensate him because he knew Galen wouldn't take any money in payment for his work.

~~~ الـ صمت من الـ عهد ~~~

150

The following morning, just before the press conference began, Chief Superintendent Bent told Bertoni, Redpath and Boyce that their suspension had been lifted, Hallet would be released and they would be given charge of the murder investigation again. Anything else would look like they were going right back to the start again. But, in reality, that is exactly what they were doing. More importantly, any denouncement of the team would reflect very badly on Bent. Bertoni assured him that they would sift through all the DNA and fingerprint evidence from Wharf Street and interview everyone known to have frequented the premises. Bent listened patiently to the plan before turning on the three of them on his way to the door.

"Get it right this time, or the only thing you will be in charge of is a school crossing."

He stormed out of the room and stepped up to the small stage erected for the press conference. He was joined by his three suitably chastened colleagues. The room fell silent and Bent announced that Hallet was to be released while the investigation proceeded. He further announced that Bertoni's team would take charge of the enquiry, including the work previously completed by H division after the arrest of Livingstone.

"Isn't the arrest of Livingstone simply further evidence of institutionalised racism in the Met?" asked one reporter.

Bent expected a lot of difficult questions and had decided to deal with all of them, rather than let them simmer on.

"We recognise in the Met that the number of young black men being arrested is disproportionate to the demographic makeup of the city," he began to explain. "But then we are all aware of the gang culture that exists among that sector of the community."

"Is there a link between Livingstone and Kosoto, then?" came a second question.

"We are only just beginning to understand the level of co-ordinated activity between these London gangs. The 2011 riots were clear evidence of this," he continued. "It is no coincidence that the riots broke out in Tottenham and Croydon almost simultaneously. It is clear that launching concurrent riots at opposite extremes of the Met Police area was designed to fully stretch our manpower and resources. It is clear that gangs are prepared to work together if it suits their purposes."

"So that's a yes then, is it?" asked the reporter again.

"Both Livingstone and Kosoto have a record of gang involvement. We cannot dismiss the idea that there is a connection just because they happen to be black. And we are determined to produce the evidence that either convicts or frees Mr Livingstone."

"Why wasn't the house in Wharf Street boarded up or guarded after the first murder there, Chief Superintendent?" asked another reporter.

"Once an investigation had been completed and an arrest made, the house continued to be a crime scene only until we had retrieved what evidence had been necessary."

"But that investigation has been re-opened, hasn't it, Chief Superintendent? And now the evidence is corrupted, isn't it?"

"I can assure you that all the evidence we need for a conviction is safely stored in our forensic department." Cally winced at his answer, hoping not to be questioned on it herself.

"The conviction of who?" a voice cried out from the crowd.

"Our investigation is ongoing. The murder team has only just taken over the work of H division. And I am confident that progress will be made in this case very soon," answered Bent.

152

"Detective Inspector Bertoni," another voice called out, "do you suspect anyone other than Livingstone or Hallet?"

"Yes, Inspector," called another voice before Bertoni had time to answer. "How many suspects do you have?"

"Is this a new 'pick-and-mix' style of policing, as Mr Livingstone's lawyer suggested?" called another and Bent could sense the meeting losing its focus. Suddenly, he could see the next day's headlines flashing in front of him.

"Thank you for your attendance today," Bent said loudly as he rose to his feet and signalled to the others to leave. "We shall keep you informed of developments in this case."

The cameras flashed as Cally, Ashley and Steve followed Bent from the platform, having contributed nothing to the meeting. One photographer made sure he had some close-up photographs of the four people on the platform, while his colleague scribbled down their identities from the place names lined up along their table.

~~~ ال صمت من ال عهد ~~~

Tyler's morning was as unproductive as Cally's. After postponing the start of his work until he had telephoned Galen to arrange lunch, he was interrupted by a call from Perry Yilmaz, who wondered if they could meet for a meal sometime.

"I'm pretty busy with something at the moment," he said, making a mental note not to discuss any details of his work. "Is there anything in particular you want to discuss, Perry?"

"Well," he answered, "I'll cut to the chase. Oliver has asked me to contact you personally about a research post we have available. He was very impressed with you at the seminar, Tyler. It's a great opportunity." He paused, waiting for a response.

Tyler told him that he was very flattered but he couldn't consider changing jobs at the present time. He explained that he was working on something that he wanted to see through to the end. Perry understood, or at least said he understood, but wouldn't let Tyler go until he had agreed to meet for lunch or dinner in a couple of weeks' time. A meeting was agreed in principle but Tyler made sure no actual date was set.

He had only just restarted his work when his mobile phone rang again. He thought about switching it off but looked first to see who the caller was. It was Paul Gilligan, the freelance journalist he had met at the seminar so, slightly intrigued, he pressed the green button and answered.

"Hi, Paul, how are you?" He tried to suppress a sigh and looked across at the work that was awaiting his full attention.

"Tyler, the editor of *Research Today* is really interested in producing a feature article on you," he explained. "It won't take up too much of your time. An interview over lunch and some photographs is all we need. And it would put you on the map for sure."

"Fine," said Tyler hesitatingly and hoping the call would not last long. "But I can't make it this week."

"That's cool. I'll call you next week to make the arrangements. Perhaps we can meet at your office and we'll have some lunch. It should only take an hour or so."

Tyler agreed but, after two interruptions, he decided he didn't have time to make any progress with the project before his lunch appointment with Galen. So he called Galen and agreed to meet at the restaurant. It was a little early for lunch, so the place was less than half full. They were offered a table by the window, but Tyler asked if they could have the one in the far corner. Galen looked at all the empty tables and followed his friend to the remote one farthest away from the other customers. He began to understand the reason when Tyler started to explain about the strict confidentiality of his work. But Galen, like Cally, simply said he had no knowledge of the work Tyler was doing. All he knew was that Tyler wanted him to trace the family history of Sidney Clinchman.

"That bit's not confidential, is it?" he asked.

"Well, I'd just rather we didn't involve anyone else, Galen. It's confined to my boss William, you, me and Cally. It would be great if we could just keep it there, a sort of inner circle."

"Okay," said Galen, "but I've never done any work on family trees before."

"But you're an IT geek, Galen, if you don't mind me saying. And, surely, that is all there is to tracing a family history now. It's all out there on the World Wide Web isn't it?"

"Probably. Everything else is."

The young priest clarified what was needed and Tyler explained that all he wanted him to do was trace all the ancestors of Sidney Walter Clinchman and produce a list of their names and, if possible, their whereabouts.

"The whereabouts part might involve Cally," added Tyler.

"Why?" Galen asked, but realised what his friend was suggesting. "Surely you're not going to compromise Cally's job, Tyler. She's in enough trouble as it is."

"No, I didn't mean that," answered Tyler, a little unconvincingly. "I can get someone to trace them once you have produced the list. It may not be necessary because I know the name of the person I am trying to link him to."

"Oh, what's the name then? Perhaps I can start from that end of the problem and work my way back to Clinchman."

"No, I'd rather not say at this stage. I'll know whether the project has been successful the moment you say that name."

"Fine," said Galen, "I'll start right away and I'll let you know at the party on Saturday how I'm progressing."

Tyler considered reminding him again about the need for confidentiality but decided he had emphasised this point sufficiently. So they returned to their meal and chatted about what Cally would like for her birthday.

~~~ الـ صمت من الـ عهد ~~~

It was a hot, humid evening on the last day of August and, as the party went on past midnight, the music got louder, more windows were opened and glasses were being refilled faster than politeness had allowed earlier on. Cally was a little upset that Galen had elected to bring a visiting priest, who nobody knew, to her birthday celebration. Sianos Kalash was from Armenia and spoke enough English to join a conversation, but he was a quietly spoken, introverted individual and a vegetarian. Fortunately, Cally had provided a vegetarian option in the buffet food but his lack of conversation was a greater challenge. He certainly wasn't as tolerant as his fellow priest when it came to bad language. Cally and Tyler often considered themselves a little too liberal in the company of Galen and so they tried to moderate their language in front of his guest.

Cally felt obliged, as it was her party, to make her uninvited guest welcome. He was a strange but surprisingly interesting young man in his mid-thirties. He was born in what he described as the beautiful land of Armenia close to the famous mountains of Ararat, upon which Noah's ark is said to have rested after the flood. He spoke in a softly rhythmic voice of a land he clearly loved. She offered him some wine but he refused and tried to explain that he did not drink alcohol.

156

"We Armenians introduced wine to the world 4,000 years ago. We are responsible for what it has done to the world," he said in good, but slowly delivered English.

Cally couldn't tell from his face whether this was a joke or a carefully considered piece of useless information that he carried with him to make conversation. So she asked about his family and listened patiently while he explained that his parents had died in the war, as had his brothers and sisters, so he was now alone in the world. Cally wanted to ask what war he was referring to, but thought she was supposed to know so she nodded expressively. He had suffered a difficult childhood, he told her, and was a young teenager when Armenia declared independence more than twenty years ago.

"A year after independence," he continued, "the Soviet Union was dissolved and Armenia's self rule was officially recognized. But, with control of the Russian state removed, a territorial war broke out. We lost our home and many members of my family were killed. The country was plagued by economic difficulties after the war with Azerbaijan. Then the Azerbaijani Popular Front forced a rail and air blockade against Armenia and the economy collapsed. When Turkey joined that blockade the situation worsened and people in the countryside began to starve."

Cally felt embarrassed that all this had appeared to have happened unnoticed in her world.

The war ended, he explained, after a Russian-brokered ceasefire. He was just seventeen years old and had witnessed the worst of humankind. He rejected the world and went into a closed order before deciding to join the priesthood.

Having condensed a painful life into a brief conversation, Sianos decided to ask about Cally's job and she thought about telling him of her problems at work. But she chose not to, even though he appeared to be a good listener and had a sympathetic tone. It all seemed a little trivial after his rendition of his childhood. So she kept her silence and introduced him to the other guests. But they were less comfortable around priests than their hosts, so Tyler ended up with the job of looking after their Armenian guest.

"You have a nice house."

"It's convenient. Neither Cally nor I are bound too tightly to the material world. We have what we need."

"That's good. Contentedness is a lost grace, Tyler."

And, from that innocent beginning, the conversation somehow moved from how Tyler met Cally to relationships in general and finally got round to soul mates and the role of destiny in determining our partner.

"You seem very comfortable together, Tyler," remarked Sianos, referring to his relationship with Cally. "Your rapport seems to exceed a simple loving relationship."

"We have known each other since our school days. Galen, Cally and I all began senior school on the same day and became lifelong friends."

"You have travelled a great distance together," he replied. "And what of Galen — he chose a different path?"

"We always remained in contact even when Galen went to Rome for six years to study for the priesthood. My relationship with Cally grew more serious, I suppose, when we were left alone."

"That sounds less like destiny and more like convenience."

"Yes, it is strange, but we seem to have an almost sibling relationship at times," confessed Tyler.

"Your Martin Amis once described long-term marital relationships as sibling, interspersed with sex," said Sianos, much to Tyler's embarrassment. He was used to such talk from Galen, but it was unexpected from his visitor.

Eventually Tyler broke the silence that followed the word 'sex' with a statement that he found surprising even to himself.

"I truly think we like each other more than we love each other, if that doesn't sound too unromantic." He paused. "I'm not sure I would have confessed that to Cally," he added.

"There is nothing wrong about a love created from friendship," said Sianos. "Sometimes I think there is truth in the concept of soul mates. Perhaps it is something deeper than life itself."

Tyler felt he should be becoming more embarrassed by the direction in which the conversation was moving but, in reality, he became increasingly comfortable with the stoic young Armenian.

"I'm sorry," said Tyler apologetically, "I don't normally talk to strangers like this, but you're right. I have always sensed there is someone on my shoulder, someone whose love for me is greater than Cally's. I cannot explain it."

Sianos looked directly at Tyler and then across to Cally. "This feeling," he said eventually, "it does not diminish what you feel for Cally. Do not punish yourself for such feelings, nor concern yourself about sharing them with me."

Tyler felt slightly discomfited by his guest's strange directness. He tried introducing Sianos to his other guests, but the young man seemed disinterested and chose to remain in the company of Galen and his two hosts.

The release felt by the team after their suspension had been lifted was tangible. Ashley's partner had decided not to come. He made an excuse for her absence but everyone knew that she just didn't feel comfortable in their company. Teresa had never been seen at parties and nobody expected to see her tonight. So

Cally and William's wife, Samantha, were the only two women at the party. The two of them still made as much noise as the men as glasses were refilled at a greater pace. William never seemed embarrassed by his wife's excessive drinking. He had given up trying to moderate her behaviour at parties years ago. The first signs were when she started referring to herself as Sam, rather than Samantha. Much later, it became her opinions on policing in the modern era that began to alienate her from the other guests. She stood just to the right of Genghis Khan in this respect.

Sat in one corner, drinking heavily, Ashley and Steve spent almost the whole evening in deep conversation about the case and, when they managed to enlist Cally into the conversation, they had to accept Samantha too. It was a dangerous mix.

"I still don't fancy Hallet for Kosoto's murder," Cally insisted. Her mind was a little addled by alcohol and she hadn't given any thought to the obvious reaction of her colleagues to her rash remark. Her statement was like a red rag to a bull. Steve was an aggressive person by nature and had a short fuse. It was a dangerous combination. He was a boxer in his youth. He reached the English Schoolboy Boxing Championships but never progressed to the more challenging levels of the Amateur Boxing Association Championships. He lacked the physical attribute of a long reach and the mental quality of patience. The combination of the two produced a record that contained more defeats than victories. He wasn't good enough to box for the police team when he joined as a teenager. But his early service with the force presented numerous opportunities to express the aggressive aspects of his character. Riot control and policing football matches rarely passed without the prospect of violent behaviour. This was met in equal measure by the young Redpath and it had the added attraction of overtime pay too.

"Oh, you're not going on about Hallet not swearing again are you?" screamed Redpath loudly enough for everyone to hear. Bertoni turned away, fearing the worse, and filled his glass. "Everyone swears sometimes. He was angry," Redpath continued.

"Look," answered Cally, "you interviewed him for hours and hours and he never swore once. Why would he send a text message with the 'f' word? It's so out of character. I don't think he sent that message."

Tyler sighed and looked heavenward. The last thing he wanted on Cally's birthday was a row about work.

"You're trouble, Cally," Redpath insisted, jabbing his finger towards her. "You think you're some sort of profiler. You're not, you're just forensics. I think Bent is right about you, you should stick to what you know and leave the detective work to me and the guv."

"What?" Samantha said, jumping into the conversation with both feet. "What detective work? What science is there in what you do?"

"Plenty," retorted Steve, as Ashley turned round to look for something to eat and to try to stay out of a worsening situation.

"Rubbish. It's the bloody emperor's new clothes," declared Samantha. "The police just sit back waiting for someone to grass the villains up or maybe stumble on a piece of evidence. There is no bloody detective work."

"I think you've been watching too much TV," answered Steve as politely as he could with several drinks inside him. He hadn't met Samantha before this evening so was unsure who she might be. She might just be a magistrate, he thought, so he moderated his tone. But Samantha took that as a sign of weakness.

"One of you probably sold Charlene's mobile number to the tabs. That happens all the time. How did they get all that information about the text message?"

"It wasn't me," said Ashley, rejoining the conversation.

"And it wasn't me," protested Steve a little too quickly and even more loudly. "Anyone could have fucking done that. It could have been the desk sergeant. If you don't mind me saying, you sound like a typical Daily Mail reader."

He continued to speak loudly enough to draw everyone's attention. Galen was unmoved by the foul language. He wasn't the common-or-garden Catholic priest, he held liberal views that were catholic with a small 'c', rather than a large one.

Steve's face was immediately in front of Samantha's. She wasn't fazed by it, she was somehow anaesthetised by the alcohol. But she did mind him saying that and she was just about to tell him so.

"Alright," said Tyler as he stepped over to try to calm the situation down. But, before he could restore order, he was unceremoniously pushed across the room by Steve and he crashed into a bookcase. Watching Tyler sprawl backwards meant almost everyone missed what happened next, mainly because it happened so quickly. As they looked round, Steve was himself lying prone on the floor where he had stood a second earlier. It was apparent what had happened, but the movement had been so quick that it was more an assumption than anything anyone had actually witnessed. Sianos Kalash, the quiet Armenian priest who had accompanied Galen to the party, had in one swift and effortless movement floored the police sergeant. It wasn't a punch, just a flick of the arm, so deft that nobody could quite understand how easily Steve had been unceremoniously laid out.

Steve was unharmed, apart from his pride. But the fall seemed to sober him up and the disturbance gave him a few moments to recover himself before he apologised to Tyler for his action. But, as the two shook hands, it was Sianos that everyone was looking at. Cally restored the music and refilled the glasses in an effort to return the party to some kind of normality. She deliberately separated Samantha from Steve and returned her to the company of William, who was now in deep conversation with Sianos, hoping to understand how the feat had been performed. But Sianos would not speak of it. Apologies were exchanged around the room and, rather than bring the party to a close, it simply livened it up. Cally left Steve and Ashley in a similarly intense discussion about the case and joined Tyler and Galen, who was keen to talk about the project Tyler wanted him to undertake.

"I've found your Mr Clinchman," he declared, a little too loudly in Tyler's view, who wondered whether William had heard him declare the name of the man at the centre of their investigation.

"Galen," interrupted Tyler, "this is highly confidential work. My boss might hear you."

"But William knows, doesn't he?" asked Galen.

"Yes he does, but he doesn't know you know. We need to keep all this between ourselves."

"Okay," he replied, a little too nonchalantly. "Anyway, Clinchman," whispered Galen, "married Ivy in 1764 and they had six kids. I'm tracing them now, but it should get easier because the first real census took place in 1820 and I'm hoping they will all be on it."

"That's great, Galen," said Tyler, "let's meet up in a few days to see how it's progressing. And don't forget it's confidential."

"Okay. Sianos doesn't understand English very well anyway."

Tyler thought for a second about what his friend had just said before realising what it meant.

"Have you told Sianos?"

"Only about the research. He follows me everywhere and wanted to know what I was doing on my laptop."

Tyler pleaded with him again about the need for strict confidentiality.

"I spoke with Sianos earlier, Galen, and his grasp of English is very good."

"Okay. Okay," said Galen, "I understand. I won't tell anyone."

Steve and Ashley came over to fill their glasses and Steve apologised again to Tyler. Ashley diffused the situation by talking more positively about the case.

"Tomorrow," he said, "we will go through all the forensic evidence from Wharf Street. The fingerprints and the DNA. Let's put Hallet to one side and build up a list of everyone who was in that house. Then we can compare that list with police records and cast our net a bit wider."

Cally and Steve agreed and they clinked their glasses as if they were beginning a new journey together.

"We also need to go through the files that H division has sent over," suggested Steve.

"Yes, that too," said Ashley. "Apparently they have a lot of good stuff on Livingstone for Charlene's murder, but less on the killing of Kosoto. If we get him for Charlene he might confess to Kosoto too."

"Why would he do that?" asked Tyler innocently.

"Because," answered Ashley, "if he is going away for one murder, he may as well go away for two. After all he will get no credibility inside for killing a woman, but for killing another gang leader? Now that really would give him some standing with the other inmates."

"Jesus, Ashley, you are so cynical," said Cally shaking her head.

Ashley was the first to leave the party and, as with most parties, once one person left, others began to follow. It was nearly one o'clock in the morning before Cally and Tyler had cleared up sufficiently to face what devastation was left in the morning. They sat down for one last drink and to talk over the events of the evening. Sianos was a strange character, they were both agreed on that much. Steve was hot-headed and Samantha was mad, bad and dangerous to know when drunk.

Tyler told Cally about the two calls he had received from Paul Gilligan and Perry Yilmaz. He didn't want to sound too boastful or make Cally even more depressed than she was. But her suspension had ended and, as he assured her, it probably would never appear on her record.

"I think Paul might want a photo of the two of us for the article," said Tyler hesitantly.

"Oh, do I have to?" pleaded Cally.

"Not if you don't want to, but he intends to mention you in the article, I think, just for a bit of background."

"So, I'm relegated to a 'bit of background' in your life, am I?"

He went to apologise, but she was only joking.

"If I'm around, I'll be in the photograph."

Then she asked about Perry and Tyler told her what he knew about him.

"Codon is a big company. I'm not sure I'm cut out for that sort of set-up."

Cally agreed and reminded Tyler how good William had been to him in the past.

"He clearly sees you as his right-hand man."

"Well, I'm not going anywhere at the moment," he assured Cally. "I'm too deeply into this current project to think about anything else."

~~~ الـ صمت من دال عه ~~~

It is difficult to remain objective about dreams for they are both corruptible and fragile. Perhaps the emotional recollections are an important part of the analytical process. Recalling emotions may be as necessary as places, people and events. They are all part of the same jigsaw puzzle. Last night was a landscape of joy, sadness and anxiety. A heat haze over a desert so wide I cannot not see the horizon; there is a sense of helplessness. Then, gradually, the heat haze changes with the temperature. The desert transforms to an English countryside; a hoarfrost on a fairy grove; silence, peace, a happy pastoral scene, with one exception; a dark, cloaked figure, a chimera arrives on horseback and a joyous scene capitulates to anxiety once more. It is that interlude between summer and winter. Patchy fog on an October field. We are searching for something and anxiety changes to sorrow in an instant. An overwhelming feeling of melancholy sweeps across the dream and the desert reappears. Thousands, perhaps millions, of people fill a vast valley. They are starving or dying from the plague. I am trying to escape the hell that surrounds me and I see the path. I recognise it from previous dreams. That same dusty, winding path that leads away from the torment towards her, the young woman who haunts my nights. I haven't seen her for a while. She had been absent from recent dreams. I can't see her but I sense she is present. Then

166

suddenly I see her, on that familiar hillside, sitting beneath a tree with sweeping branches. The sun is rising and the tree casts a long shadow up the hillside. Suddenly the goats that she is tending scatter and the bells around their necks clatter loudly.

The dream ended to the sound of bells and my alarm was ringing as if the dream is influenced by external forces.

6

Five centuries after Dentrides sat among his many children and grandchildren in the shade of the Sarv-e- Šēṭ, telling them of his adventures, the tree stood undiminished on the hillside. The girth of its trunk had broadened and its branches widened. It had seen generations come and go, new religions created and others slip into oblivion.

Sitting below the tree and forming a small posy from the wild flowers she had picked was a girl of just six years. Her mother was kneeling farther up the hillside milking a goat.

The tales told by Dentrides may have long since been forgotten but little Barika, by some strange act of nature, carries the features of her long-lost ancestor, those same features that would distinguish her as her father's child. But, just as nobody recognised her resemblance to Dentrides, few recognised her likeness to her true father. Her mother looked up from her work to see Barika sitting under the great tree and she recalled a starlit night on that same hillside just seven years past. The little girl smiled and her mother saw again that same smile on another's face and wondered where he was today.

~~~ الـ صمت من الـ عهد ~~~

169

"What was your sin, Yasir? What caused you to be sent here with me to die?"

But Talib's words hung, unheard, on the stagnant, still air that hovered in the heat of the tent. He did not have the strength to lift himself from the bed. He was a man in the midmost point of his life. But his blotched and inflamed skin resembled that of someone twice his age. He, like many others in the once small but now overcrowded village of Dijla, had succumbed to the ravaging effects of the plague. Dijla, so named simply because it was closer to the Tigris than the Euphrates, once sat in the most fertile area of the world. Birds would migrate thousands of miles to rest here. Its name directed you to life itself because life here was dependent on knowing the shortest route to any source of water. But now the Tigris, like the poisoned air above it, carried disease and sickness. Now its function was to direct its inhabitants not to life but to their death. By the time its inhabitants realised they needed to escape it was too late. The plague drained life from the people slowly, so one could barely see and feel it ebbing away.

Talib knew the answer to his question anyway. They shared the same sin, just as they now shared the same tent. Yasir had been banished here for the same reason and purpose as himself. As punishment and to silence any voice that might reveal the secret, anyone who may even hint at the truth. Feeling in the pocket of his cloak, he removed the purple amulet that his grandfather had given to him when he left home at such a young age. He rolled it in the palm of his hand recalling those happy days of his childhood. He winced as the edges of the locket rubbed against the festering and bleeding sores that were commonplace in this seemingly godforsaken place. The blood trickled and congealed on the amulet's intricate gilding as the stagnant heat of the tent drained the moisture from the air. He wanted desperately to scratch at his sores but had neither the energy nor the dexterity to do so. There were no bandages left and he had now come to learn that reusing the old ones only served to spread the disease faster. He wondered what Yasir would think when he found the amulet on him when he died. He would assume, of course, that he was one of them. A member of that mysterious group of men who frequented the monastery. He wondered whether he should tell his friend how he came by the relic and its contents. But, in truth, he did not know himself. Fragmented memories of his grandfather's incredible tales provided an unreliable remembrance of the truth. Quite how he had come by the object had been lost in the mists of time.

The scent of incense outside the tent evoked memories of his years at the monastery. All he had to fear in Antioch were the earthquakes and rock slides. But death came silently in Dijla, not suddenly with a roar or a tremor. In his early days there, he had overcome his fear of heights every day, climbing the rugged cliff edge back up to the monastery after collecting provisions and the ink for the scribes. Then, when he became a scribe himself, there were other fears to contend with. Fears less tangible. Fears that dwelt in the shadows of the mind.

It is spring. The seasons turn and new life is ushered in. But not here in Dijla, where each season brings its own misery. Here, life is ushered out, unceremoniously and with every agony imaginable. Those whom hunger is too slow to take are consumed by the plague. An invisible contagion walks among the condemned, or rushes towards those more fortunate.

That evening, when Yasir finally returned to the tent with some water and a little food, Talib made one final request of him. In truth, Yasir was surprised to find him still alive.

171

"Write a letter for me, Yasir, for I am not long for this world. But let my emotions be muted for the sake of delicacy. Let it not speak of love but of friendship, of an old childhood friend, not one who was loved most dearly on my part and with a consuming passion, but one for whom passion is a distant and diminished memory."

Yasir agreed, if it served only to relieve his friend's anguish, even though he doubted that the letter would ever be delivered. For who would deliver it? In any case, there was no paper, no quill and no ink. He looked at his companion and saw a young man withering in the mouth of death. A man with no family, other than those he had shared a monastic life with at the Monasterion Lucienus.

"Who will deliver it, my friend?"

Talib suggested that Yasir should take it himself. He assured him that the service he performed would be regarded highly in heaven. But, in reality, he simply wanted his friend to escape the hell that was Dijla and to escape the risk of the plague that took so many victims with each passing day.

"There is no paper, no writing materials," Yasir finally confessed.

"Then listen to the account of my life and tell it, in your own fashion, to the person to whom I shall direct you, the lady I shall name, who lives near Edessa."

"Begin," said Yasir, as he lay back hoping for sleep but knowing it would not come.

"Have patience, my friend. I was born a shepherd boy and I have a shepherd boy's ways. I will tell my story, from those humble beginnings, until this day when humility and all other graces are consumed by disease."

And so, after they had eaten what little food they had and Yasir closed the entrance to the tent, Yasir sat, unable to sleep

172

anyway in the insufferable heat and listened as Talib recalled his earliest memories of his childhood on a farm near Potbelly Hill. He realised that his friend's recollections were an idealised reminiscence of a harsh upbringing. The third son of a farmer, Talib's only contemporaries were his brothers and sisters, a few cousins and a girl, several years his junior, from an adjacent farm. He was obviously gifted and this aptitude for learning was noticed by visitors who would stop at the farm overnight, for it was located close to the main trade routes used by those from the east. He harboured cherished memories of the girl and he always believed, even from a young age, that they would marry.

Talib recalled harvesting the wild wheat that flourished in the fertile land and the joy of his friendship with Aisha. He had learned much from the family, particularly his grandfather, who favoured Talib and spent many hours teaching him all he knew.

But, one day, a visitor from the enchanted city of Babylon arrived at the farm and was generous of his time. He spent two days talking to Talib and then spoke at length with the boy's grandfather, who he seemed to know from many years past. He offered to provide the boy with an education at a Christian monastery near Antioch. He would serve a seven-year apprenticeship and might then be offered employment and perhaps work as a teacher in later years. No fees were required for his education and Talib would be permitted no personal belongings. But then he had none to speak of and the farm could not provide for everyone when all the children grew up. Before he left, his grandfather entrusted to him a precious jewel that he instructed the boy to keep safe for it had great personal value to him. He concealed the purple amulet on his person and never mentioned it to anyone at the monastery.

Talib was twelve when he left home with the man, who he learned was a Magus. They spoke about what life would be like at the monastery and, although Talib's heart was torn, he realised the great benefits that such an education would accrue. It would permit him to live in relative comfort in his adult years and, more importantly, to marry Aisha and raise their children beyond the hardship that they had both known.

The young boy travelled with the man and eventually, after many days' journey, the monastery appeared in the distance like an ancient fortress embedded in the side of a steep hill. It was unlike the hillside of his home. This was a harsh, rocky terrain far from the fertile land from where he had travelled. It was both imposing and alluring. It was a mysterious place, inhabited for the most part by mysterious residents.

Many of the young men who lived there had recognised the beauty and truth of silence. Those who had taken the vow wore a blue ribbon edging to their white alb. They led a monastic life, whilst the remainder were divided into those studying for the priesthood, who wore plain white vestments and those, like Talib, who wore a black hooded alb. This indicated a life of duty to God and the monastery, such as a scribe or a translator.

The hood was an indication of the secular aspect to their vocation and was a visible sign that they were not constrained to life within the walls. Those with hooded vestments could move freely outside the monastery, with the hood symbolising protection against both the weather and sin.

One of the blue-ribboned students, a convert from Judaism named Saul, knelt daily on a rough rectangular-shaped rock that stood in front of a small grotto in the cloister. He had carried the rock there himself from the foot of Mount Silphius on which the monastery stood and had sworn to kneel all day, every day, until he felt his prayer had fully engaged with God. He had been doing this since before Talib arrived and was now more than thirty years old. He looked much older and hobbled, rather than walked, to his supper each day before retiring and returning to the stone after breakfast the following day. More recently he had to be helped into his place of worship at the grotto and lifted from it again at sunset. The shorter days of winter offered him some consolation but the long summer days of kneeling before the crucifix would weary even he who was favoured with unconditional faith.

After a time, Saul was no longer considered strange but simply dedicated and uncompromising. Other visitors were, however, considered strange or, more accurately, enigmatic. The Magi had an aura of mystery about them and none more so than the appropriately named Musteria. Nobody really understood their purpose and nobody was prepared to ask. They wore dark, hooded vestments as Talib did but all carried an amulet around their necks. He recognised the dark-coloured brooch immediately, of course. It was identical to the one his grandfather had given to him. But something in his heart told him not to mention it to anyone. One day, he believed, he would find out what the purpose of the amulet was but, for now, it must remain his soul's secret.

When he first joined the order, Talib came to recognise these strange monks, whose hooded tunics were used as blankets on their travels. There were only four members of this particular order, that much was known. All were quite young and received intensive training in a remote and isolated part of the college. The training lasted for several years and Talib determined they were only appointed on the death of one of the four existing members of the Musteria. This ensured that there were only ever four such men fulfilling their purpose in the world. What that purpose was had never been revealed to the other occupants of the monastery. Their rule was made known only to those training to replace them. Even those considered suitable for training in the order were not told, it seemed, until their training had proved them worthy of the trust to be placed in them.

The Musteria was not a silent order vocation, but they never spoke of their duties or their experiences outside the walls of the college. Sometimes one would not return and, after a period of time, another would be appointed. Occasionally, when one failed to return, a stranger would arrive and return something to the master of the order, whose role was to oversee the training of the Musteria. One day, when Talib was sitting near the main gate drinking water from the well, he saw a man appear there and return one of the purple amulets that were worn around the necks of the Musteria. The return of the amulet seemed to signify something and these were the only occasions when a trainee was appointed without delay. Talib concluded that the owner of the amulet had died. But the reappointment of a trainee did not occur with such haste after the disappearance of a member when the amulet was not returned. Talib never understood why this was the case and often wondered how his grandfather had come by the one he had passed to him before he left home.

By the time, Talib returned home at the age of nineteen, having completed his seven-year apprenticeship, his grandfather had died and Aisha had passed the time of betrothal. He learned that she was to marry a wealthy merchant named Rasmi Akram, who was almost twice her age. Talib postponed his return to Antioch in order to attend the marriage. At least that was what he told everyone. His true intention was to persuade Aisha to reject Akram and to marry

176

him. But she was an obedient child and could not betray her father's promise. One night, explained Talib to Yasir, they found themselves alone together, sitting on the hillside overlooking the farm. There, among the goatherd, they watched the stars flicker in the night sky above them. Sitting beneath the large tree that dominated the hill, their bodies longed for each other. With her heart pounding, Aisha explained that she wanted children but they must be the offspring of her husband. But love overwhelmed them and the passion they had felt for each other for so long submerged them in desire.

"I could not suppress the feelings that had been buried those seven years past. There were tears but little regret for our actions," Talib explained, believing that this would change everything. But it changed nothing. The following day Aisha still married Rasmi in accordance with her father's wishes and after the loneliest day of his life Talib prepared to return to the monastery. Aisha gathered her courage about her like a cloak and went to wave goodbye to Talib. Taking a few of her cousins with her ensured that her emotions did not surface or overpower her. But, as his distant figure disappeared from the horizon, she stood gazing into the emptiness and felt that same emptiness in her heart. Even when the others left she did not hear their words but stood on the dusty, winding pathway. It was only the clattering of bells that awoke her from her daydream, as the goats ran down a nearby hill.

Suddenly she realised that she was now alone and began to cry. Her head told her that she would never see Talib again but somewhere deep in her inner being she knew she would. As sure as the sun rises and the sets each day, Talib told Yasir, she was certain that if she stood on that spot, one day, beyond their

177

imagination, he would return to her, for Talib knew that their souls could never be truly parted.

"I could no longer look upon her face, but could only imagine her beauty. Love may not be obedient but it is constant and eternal. She gained unfair advantage, Yasir, for in my mind she never aged. How unfair our God can be."

As the story unfolded, Yasir began to regret his promise. He soon realised that he was required to deliver this message to Aisha. Acting as a go-between in an illicit affair would not, he thought, be regarded highly in heaven as his friend had promised. Eventually, he stopped his friend's recollections and confessed his fears and reluctance to comply. The night fell silent for a few moments and Yasir thought he could hear his friend weeping in the darkness that now surrounded them.

"How can love be wrong, Yasir?"

The stillness of the tent seemed to resonate with his words and, eventually, Yasir relented and prompted him to continue.

"I travelled back to Antioch through the Orontes Gorge with a great sadness in my heart until, eventually, I arrived just outside the walls of the ageing yet once great Roman city of Antioch. I circled outside the walls and climbed the steep path up the side of the cliff and there sat the Monasterion Lucienus, awaiting my return. At that very moment, a tremor shook the foundations of the mountain and I feared for my life, for I had long believed that I would die in this way. I feared heights and often dreamed of being thrown from a cliff by my enemies. I almost wanted to be taken for I had nothing left to live for now that Aisha had been taken from me."

But, he explained, in due course, he found solace in the word of God. He committed himself to another fourteen years at the monastery, seven as a calligrapher working on the Codex Exegesis and seven teaching the art of calligraphy to novices.

178

He became particular friends with Ghalim Hashem, a scribe like himself who was working on the Hebrew Bible. Talib himself worked on the gospel of St Matthew, so the two had little in common through their work and they came from quite different backgrounds. Each resident occupied a small, windowless cell that was their home during their time at the monastery. They spent most of their time there working and praying. But there were common rooms and occasionally Talib met Ghalim there.

"It was several months later that we met you, Yasir, for you had just completed seven years of study in languages."

Yasir knew the Greek language well, but was one of the few workers who translated Hebrew into Latin, so he worked on various parts of the great project. When the three first met he was working on the book of Malachi and found that Ghalim was engaged on writing the same text that he had translated. It was this that caused them to talk about their work. It was not unusual to do this but not particularly encouraged by the masters.

Talib sat up, coughed repeatedly and paused to drink some water and to collect his thoughts about the next part of the story. Yasir explained that he knew what happened next, but Talib pleaded with him to listen. It was important that he cleansed his soul of the complete story. This was a cathartic process for the dying man and Yasir's silence acknowledged his friend's wish.

Talib recalled that in addition to their studies it was the duty of the novices to procure the ingredients for the ink used by the scribes. The acid produced by the local trees was mixed with vinegar and gum and then blended with coloured salt to produce the vivid reds and blues for the decorative work on the individually crafted pages. The production of the parchment

179

itself required greater skills than the average novice had developed. Apart from the actual flaying of the lambs' skin at the beginning of the process, novices did not involve themselves in the production of parchment, nor were they taught the skills required. Such skills were developed over a lifetime by the local tradesmen who served the monastery.

Ghalim was working from the Hebrew text of the old Bible and the Greek text of manuscripts discovered in an isolated convent near Mount Sinai, explained Talib to his patient friend, who knew well the events of which he spoke. Young priests, trained in the art of translation and calligraphy, laboured tirelessly in rewriting that text into Latin. Most of the monks had joined the monastery at the age of twelve like Talib to be educated and trained in the skills necessary for this one task. Many had, from a young age, committed to serve for twenty-one years: the first seven as a novice and scholar; the next seven as calligraphers or translators; and the final seven years were spent teaching and passing on those skills.

Among these was Talib, who sat in solitary confinement in his cell for many hours each day, meticulously transcribing the scribbled notes from the translator onto the parchment leaves that were to form an illumination of God's word. This version would be twice the size of the Codex Sinaiticus, with more pages than the 1,500-page original. Talib and his collaborators expected this magnificent manuscript to be the first ever Latin version of the complete Bible, comprising both the old Hebrew Bible and the new witness of Jesus Christ. It would be the gift of the monastery to the Pope. But Pope Felix was quite old now, so they laboured feverishly.

The head of theology at the monastery was Master Marwan Ghali, a severe and determined man. He was unwavering in his desire to be the first to produce a Bible in the new language of the faith. At first, Talib believed his haste was to achieve this before the great Pope died, but it was obvious that this could never be achieved. It would take at least two years to complete and he finally realised that Ghali's eagerness was that the gift should be produced in time, not for Pope Felix, but for the next as yet unnamed and unelected Pope. Ghali seemed to understand that the next Pope, the forty-ninth, was the one who should receive this gift, not the ageing Pope Felix.

Talib paused in his recollections to Yasir, to reflect on that number. Forty-nine, he thought, seven times seven. All the evidence he had found and, foolishly, taken to Ghali underlined the importance of the number seven and, particularly, seven times seven. He thought about elaborating on this to Yasir but decided it could only harm him.

When Pope Galasius arrived, a greater sense of urgency fell upon the inhabitants of the Monasterion Lucienus. Galasius wrote regularly to Ghali to enquire about progress on the Codex Exegesis, as it became known. Exegesis, the new interpretation. The Latin scholars Talib worked with must have understood what this meant. But they all stayed quiet. Their tacit agreement not to question the subtle changes being made to the text was essential. But Talib's limited knowledge caused him often to question those changes. Why was it necessary to ensure that the new text did not identify John the Baptist as the reincarnation of Elijah or Jesus to be the direct ancestor of Adam? And more importantly, by seven-times-fourteen generations, a son of Seth?

It had already been announced that the new Pope would make a declaration on suitable reading material. The 'de libris recipiendis et non recipiendis', the books to be received and not to be received. The Decretum Gelasianum. The canon of permitted scripture would be determined and dictated by Pope

Galasius and the new Latin Bible would be central to the new regime.

Yasir listened patiently to his friend and wondered whether he would ever have the courage to speak of those detailed recollections, but urged Talib to continue.

One day, Talib recalled, the three friends were in the refectory for their midday meal. He had found several references in the Bible to Elijah being St John the Baptist and wondered what this could mean for, at that time, it was but innocent meanderings.

The book of Malachi in the Hebrew Bible clearly stated that John is Elijah the prophet. Malachi said that Elijah will come again in another body.

And Jesus says 'who do people say I am?' He then spoke of the reincarnation of Jeremiah or Elias. Jesus said that Elias had come already and the people knew him not. But the Latin translation he was forced to write was less a statement and more an intimation of the soul's reincarnation. It simply said 'then the disciples understood that he spake unto them of John the Baptist'.

"The truth was not to be destroyed forever," said Talib, "but concealed forever. The truth recalled by the faithful followers of Christ, buried from view for all time."

Talib recalled the first time he visited Marwan Ghali. He had noticed that the beginning of the gospel of St Mark referred to the prophets as messengers, in the plural, but then this became 'he', in the singular, as if all seven prophets, or messengers, were the same person. He knew from Ghali's expression that he had uncovered something he should not have done. And, even if he had done so, should not have mentioned it to Marwan Ghali. What he did not know, at that time, was that this careless remark was to be his death warrant.

"Do you recall," asked Talib, "how we began to vary the places where we met to discuss our concerns? The chapel, the cloister, the library. Anywhere we could meet and talk in private."

"Speak on," replied Yasir. "You do not need me to confirm such matters." And his friend continued his tale from the point where Ghalim was translating the first book of the Old Testament. Chapter five, he reminded Yasir, set out the descendents of Adam. First Seth, then Enos, Cainan, Malcheel and Jared. And, after each one it stated how many years they had lived for and each sentence ended with an emphatic *'and then he died'*. But, when it came to the seventh descendent, Henoch, it did not say, as did all the others, *'and then he died'*. The Hebrew text was clear. Henoch's soul was subjected to metanoia. It was transfigured and reappeared seven generations later. But Ghalim was guided by Marwan to corrupt the text. So, instead, it said *'and Henoch walked with God and was seen no more because God took him'*. It was as if the truth was not to be extinguished but to be hidden in some way, so that it might be redeemed at some time in the future; revealed as the truth, when the time was right.

Yasir got up for a drink of water and gave some to his friend, to ease his ratcheting chest.

Talib continued his story with recollections of his own work on the gospel of St Matthew. This opened with the ancestry of Jesus Christ. Corrections were provided directly by Marwan Ghali, as was a reference to the prophets being a single messenger, a reincarnated soul, revisiting the Earth to deliver the same message. But this, like the other such references, was amended according to the instructions of Ghali. None was deleted, simply amended so that the truth might be concealed, secreted in some way in this new text. The reference to the

183

plural of prophets and messengers remained, but was subsequently referred to as 'he' instead of 'we'. Talib was young and never questioned the directives of his superior. He didn't feel comfortable in the presence of Ghali but there was nobody else he could turn to. But it wasn't this that tore at his soul. The memory of Aisha condemned him daily as a sinner. Guilt was added to guilt and remorse to remorse. Tormented by his grievous and carnal sins, eventually, the need to confess these overwhelmed him.

"I went to Marwan Ghali, our master, to confess my sins. To pour from my soul the most grievous of acts. I lived as a celibate for so many years, but I had already lost my virginity before I returned to Monasterion Lucienus after my seven-year apprenticeship. In any case, Master Ghali could not forgive my sins. He listened to them with what I believed was the intention of forgiveness, but he was unable to help. He said forgiveness was possible by God alone, so I should confess my sins again when I first saw his face on my deathbed. It was then that he questioned me about my work."

Ghali took advantage of the situation and, suspecting Talib of colluding with his fellow students over the new liturgy, questioned him regularly. Talib remained silent on the matter and it was Ghalim who spoke with the master on the subject, telling him of their concerns on the text. Nothing happened for a while. And then one day a stranger came. He was in the refectory when they were eating. He was eating there himself, so looked innocent enough, but he appeared again when they met in the cloister. He dressed in black and wore a purple amulet about his neck.

Ghalib Hashem disappeared the next day and, on the next, Talib and Yasir were summonsed to see Marwan Ghali.

And so Talib Al Balawi and Yasir were sent to the flood plains of the Tigris and Euphrates rivers in order to serve God and their fellow man. More than three million people lived on what was once the most fertile land in the world. But now, the floods and harsh landscape of the most densely populated area in the valley of the Nile served only in the transmission of human disease. Armed only with their knowledge of the word of God and enough food to last the journey, their task was to comfort the great number of humankind that had fallen victim to the plague.

As they passed over the top of the hill and looked down into the valley below, all they could see for miles was rudely constructed homes and what appeared to be a million people.

And there they stayed, administering to the sick and the hungry, and the poor in spirit and the weak of mind, until they themselves became sick and hungry, and poor in spirit and weak of mind. It was that same weakness that finally overpowered Talib and silenced his voice with sleep. Before he slept, Talib pleaded once more with his friend to visit his beloved Aisha and tell her of his fate. At that moment, he removed the purple amulet that his grandfather had given him from his pocket and held it out towards Yasir. He recognised it as the same one he had seen several visitors wearing when visiting the monastery but, like Talib, he had never asked its meaning. Talib explained that his grandfather had given it to him and he asked his friend to deliver it to Aisha for he had no son to pass it on to. He did not know its significance and was too frightened to ask the authorities at the monastery.

Yasir slept for just a few hours after Talib had finished his story, having resolved to deliver his friend's heartfelt message and the amulet to Aisha. Leaving what food and water they had, Yasir left with just a blanket and enough water to last him

185

until he arrived at the river. From there he began a three-day journey to Edessa, or rather a farm a short distance from that city.

~~~ الـ صمت من الـ عهد ~~~

Yasir met not a soul on his journey and, as he neared a farm, a young girl approached, leading a goat and a kid. Yasir recognised her immediately even though he had never met her, because the resemblance to his friend was undeniable.

"I am seeking your mother, Aisha," he said to her. The girl was surprised because she did not know the man. This was a remote place and the travellers who used to pass this way now journeyed by the river.

"You are the daughter of Aisha and Rasmi Akram, are you not?"

She nodded timidly and pulled the goat to her side.

"And what is your name?"

"Barika," she answered.

For a moment he went to say 'I know your father', but he stopped himself. And the girl led him to a house that stood at the foot of a hill, close to a tall cypress tree that cast a long shadow up the hillside. It was not the prettiest of God's creations but it certainly looked like the oldest. Goats rested in its shade and a ram stared at him from a large rock that formed a promontory on the slope.

Several members of the family came out of the house and other farm buildings to greet him, for they did not see many visitors. They looked concerned.

"Have you news of Rasmi?" they asked him but he shook his head.

"I do not know the man," he replied. "But I do have news from an old friend from your village called Talib Al Balawi, who left this place some fourteen years ago to work in the name of God at Monasterion Lucienus. Do you remember him?"

Some shook their heads but a beautiful young woman, who had taken the hand of the small girl, stepped forward. There was a quiet solicitude in her dark cinnamon eyes. Her drowsy look conveyed a foreshadow of goodness, a presage of virtue. She was beautiful and that beauty was replicated in her daughter, who clung to her side.

"We grew up together," Aisha said quietly as she and her family welcomed the stranger into their humble home. Once he had rested from his long journey, the whole community gathered together and sat beneath a copse of date palm trees to listen to Yasir's news. But first Aisha told him about the overdue homecoming of her husband. He was a merchant trading in silk and his return from a business trip to Jerusalem was long overdue. There had been no news, so they feared the worse. Bandits operated in the hills along the two rivers that led from Edessa to Jerusalem and Rasmi Akram had been attacked and robbed previously. As she spoke, Yasir kept looking at Aisha and her beautiful young daughter. He tried to pay as much attention to the others when they spoke but he was intrigued by them both. Aisha because he could understand completely now why his friend had fallen so deeply in love with her and Barika because she reminded him so much of Talib. Barika's face glowed with youthful exuberance and pleasure at meeting this visitor to her small and remote community. Aisha's eyes betrayed her fear that Yasir knew the dark secret of her past.

Once Yasir managed to convince Aisha that he was not the bearer of bad news about her husband, he had to tell her about

Talib. The young woman's instinct was to go with him to see her dying lover. She rose from her seat but, realising the surprise of the other women sitting there, she simply took Yasir's hand and offered her own condolences to him. She assured the others that Talib had been a childhood friend and one of the older women remembered him as a bright, intelligent boy of great promise.

Aisha had not felt such regret in her heart for many years. Barika had provided a constant reminder of her infidelity and she could now see the recognition of this on the face of their visitor. One only had to look upon the child to know who her father was. But Rasmi Akram had seen Talib only briefly at the wedding feast and it was several years later before Barika's expression, countenance and behaviour began to reflect her parentage, serving as a remembrance of Aisha's true lost love.

Yasir stayed for a few days, insisting that he worked for his daily food. He chopped wood, milked goats and tendered the same wild wheat fields that his friend had told him about. Each sunset he would kiss Barika goodnight and wondered whether both her true and her adopted fathers had died and met at the gates of heaven.

One evening, Yasir and Aisha sat up late drinking tea after the other family members had retired to bed. But neither of them spoke of her infidelity with Talib. Each knew that the other was aware of the subject that could never be spoken of. So, out of consideration for the other, they discussed other matters. Aisha asked about what life had been like for Talib at the monastery. She wanted to know if he was happy there and wondered whether he enjoyed his work. Yasir answered all her questions and asked what life would be like for Barika when she grew up. She told him that most of the families living around Potbelly Hill farmed and raised livestock. Some of the

188

larger farms sold produce in Edessa. When the children grew up they either moved away or married a distant cousin and stayed to live off the land. The opportunities to meet others were few. Once passers by had regularly stopped overnight on their travels but the trade routes from the east had changed some years ago and visitors were now rare.

"Which is why," she explained, "we were so pleased that you came to us with news of Talib. It was good of you to do this. It is always difficult to deliver bad news."

"Talib said I would receive a reward in heaven for undertaking such a task," he replied.

She smiled and could imagine Talib saying such a thing.

"Now," she said after a few moments of silence, "the only regular visitors we receive are members of the Magi. Occasionally they come simply to pray on the hillside and sometimes they will remove pieces of the great tree. But they never harm it. They remove only the dead wood, so they ensure no damage is caused. They seem to revere it and they often pay us and ask us to ensure the tree is never cut down."

Aisha insisted that they would never do this. The tree was sacred, she told him. She laughed when she recalled one such visitor who removed a complete branch that had withered. He had struggled to tie the long piece of wood to his mule but was very pleased to have it.

"He looked like a knight with a lance as he rode off," she smiled.

~~~ الـ صمت من الـ عهد ~~~

Eventually, Yasir decided to return to the valley of death at Dijla and hoped that he would yet be in time to console his friend with news of his beloved and the child he had never known. Aisha and Barika accompanied Yasir to the end of the valley at the edge of their homestead and Yasir handed her the amulet that Talib had given him. She placed it around Barika's neck and they waved goodbye to their visitor. As Barika ran back down the pathway towards her home, Aisha stood on that same pathway where she had stopped several years before to wave goodbye to her beloved Talib.

Aisha dwelt in that place, praying that one day Talib would return along that same path towards her. But it was not to be. Not in this lifetime. Not now, perhaps, but she hoped beyond hope that love, true love, never dies but, like the soul, enjoys immortality through God's good grace.

<div align="center">~~~ الـ صمت من الـ عهد ~~~</div>

It was nightfall when Yasir arrived back at the camp, still heavily laden with the memory of Aisha's languid dark brown eyes. He thought about spending the night in the hills and completing his long journey the following morning but he was anxious to learn whether Talib had passed from this Earth. So, hoping to impart his news of Aisha, he continued in the darkness back to Dijla.

Opening the flap to the tent, he was surprised to see Talib alive. He was pale and thin but seemed resolved to fight the spectre of death until his friend returned with news from his homeland. He tried to sit up when Yasir arrived and coughed violently. Pain ratcheted in his chest. He was anxious to garner any information of his beloved Aisha. Yasir patiently told him the whole story, ending with her farewell on the pathway. Talib began to cry but wanted to know more about little Barika.

Before they went to sleep, Talib became delirious. He constantly asked about a man who administered to him earlier that day.

"Who was he and what did he say?" asked Yasir.

"He dressed like us, Yasir, and spoke only once. He said 'pray for God's mercy'. He showed great kindness in my despair."

Yasir was tired after his journey and slept soundly that night. When he awoke, the first thing he saw was the empty bed. He ran outside into the morning sunlight, realising that Talib had tried to return to Aisha.

He raced along the well-trodden path and soon found the cold body of his friend. He lifted him up and spoke quietly to one whose soul had passed beyond this Earth.

"I now know we were sent here for a purpose. I have no doubt that I will see you again, my friend. The secret that we carry must be taken to the grave."

Once Yasir had buried his friend in one of the mass graves, he decided to travel back to the monastery. Stopping overnight, he made camp and was joined a short time later by a black-robed monk. Yasir recognised the dark-purple amulet he wore around his neck. The men ate some fish from the river and spoke little.

"Shall I pray for God's mercy?" asked Yasir, as he went to sleep that night.

7

There was a welcome moment of peace as the talking stopped and the engine of the car slowed down. Bertoni relished the moment. Experience sometimes felt like a yoke on his shoulders. In many ways, the past enabled you to foresee the future. Well, it certainly helped a veteran policeman to read the signs. Something ominous was on the way and it wasn't confined to the threatening dark sky that hovered on a not-too-distant horizon. Cally and Steve may have patched up their differences for now but that relationship was bound to spill over again at some point. A storm was coming in both a literal and figurative sense. Three successive days of the sun beating down on London's crowded streets contrived to produce a hot, humid atmosphere. The inevitable thunder and lightning would clear the air and cool down the day. But such a simple outcome seemed unlikely for the storm that was brewing over the Hallet case. Just as he was familiar with the intractable Mr Cruickshank, so DI Bertoni knew well the cunning of Barnabas Cartwright. The outcome of this case was as unpredictable as Mr Cartwright himself. The best Bertoni could hope for was that this particular storm arrived when he was not out in the open, exposed to the inevitable flak that would result.

"Number 1 Wharf Street," declared their driver as he brought the car to a halt.

"You're a policeman, Ratcliffe, not a taxi driver."

The car doors slammed as Cally and Steve got out of the back seats. Bertoni dwelt for a few seconds but that fleeting moment of inner peace was gone. He climbed out of the front seat a little less spritely than he had done in his youth. He looked up and down the untidy street and signalled to Redpath to open the door of the house.

The crescent-shaped Wharf Street reflected the unchanging face of Limehouse and it stood in stark contrast to the modern high-rise office blocks that had been built since the neighbouring docklands area of London had become a fashionable place to live and work. The odd-numbered houses stood on the south side of the street, facing north and, as such, never saw the sunshine except in the small yards at the rear of the properties. Number 1 Wharf Street was located on the corner, as if conscious but indifferent to its diminished status, but the shape of the crescent meant that one side of the building saw no sunlight. The first impression of the dilapidated house suggested that little sunshine had entered the lives of its occupants either.

As a Grade II listed building it was protected against structural change by those who would seek to diminish its historical, cultural and architectural merits. Adolf Hitler, his Luftwaffe and the east-end gangs that now frequented its ragged shell were exempt from such bureaucracy. The windows were boarded up and the front door served only as an obstacle to delay, rather than something that could prevent access. The adjoining house was habitable but empty. The 'for sale' sign had fallen over and it had obviously been vacant for some time. Its unattractive facade, although better than

194

number 1, deterred even the squatters who lived in several other houses at this end of the street.

The quality and appearance of the houses improved as the crescent curved out of sight from that end of the street.

Bertoni instructed the uniformed Constable Ratcliffe to stand outside the front door, not to prevent anyone entering while his team inspected the interior, but to make sure that nobody stole the patrol car that they had parked outside. This was a notorious neighbourhood, frequented by drug addicts, prostitutes and petty criminals. Having a squad car stolen would not look good on his CV and, more importantly, would subject him to ridicule among his colleagues. The contempt of his peers is something the DI would avoid at all costs. He took pride in his reputation. He wasn't going to stumble in the final stages of an otherwise distinguished career. Bertoni possessed a reflex intellect, functioning mainly on instinct but constantly monitoring the airwaves for gossip and rumour, particularly within the force itself.

The house had been built in the early nineteenth century by a sea captain. Many of the streets close to the docks, along the River Thames, contained grand houses that had been built by seafarers whose wealth had largely resulted from the success of the East India Company. But, as far as anyone could make out, the much-travelled captain had never occupied the house and it had been the subject of disputed ownership for nearly two hundred years. The property was caught up in litigation that would have been at home in a Dickens novel. In fact, the house itself made one think of Bleak House, if only because it so accurately reflected that name.

A nephew of the captain had, it was said, once occupied the house and had been murdered there. This made the dispute even more complicated because, like the captain, he died childless. Another relative, in the hope of acquiring the house, began renovating it in the mid-nineteenth century and one could see that little expense had been spared. The wallpaper, long since torn and soiled, looked like something designed by William Morris.

There was an intense smell of dampness and urine. A cat scuttled out of the rear of the house as they entered from the front. Ashley, Steve and Cally began making an ill-defined examination of the room where the murders were committed.

A building disfigured by bomb and blast retains a strange illusion of beauty. Like the dignity of a war veteran made legless and scarred by brave circumstances, it stands unmoved and defiant in spite of its experience. But however misleading any external damage might have been, once inside the building, the true nature of its fall from grace was apparent. The translucent darkness imposed by the boarded windows could not conceal the evident cause of its decline. Discarded needles and stained silver foil littered the floor. A clump of old newspapers created an improvised mattress in the corner. Floorboards had collapsed and, here and there, small worn pieces of carpet that once enjoyed a grander existence now provided a forlorn reminder of a previous life. Internal doors were missing, taken when they once had value, or at least enough to buy a fix, a ticket to another world for both the door and the seller. The banister was missing, along with some wood from the stairs. Access to the next floor was treacherous and only just possible, but Redpath's agile frame made the challenge look easy. The journey was unrewarded because upstairs was a replica of the one below, only with more dust and an eerie absence of light. He returned more cautiously with a shake of the head and a shrug of the shoulders. Bertoni was relieved. The discovery of another body would surely end his career.

Bertoni was overweight but vain enough to prefer a description of tubby to one of corpulent. Not that Redpath was likely to use the latter expression. Redpath was a man whose vocabulary rarely extended to words of two syllables. The young sergeant was a bristly, rough-hewn individual who was often uncouth and frequently churlish towards his colleagues. He did not respect rank but this was something that Bertoni had grown used to. The detective inspector was worldly, within the narrow confines of the police force. He was no more knowledgeable than one might expect from his thirty years in the force. The almost inevitable grey hair and failed first marriage that accompanies such long service in a demanding job were the only visible battle scars.

Very occasionally Redpath thought about the way he dressed. Clambering down from a dusty upstairs room was enough on this occasion and he took the trouble to dust himself down. He was the type of man who changed his shirt every day but was still the wrong side of smart and a long way from sartorial. He had only two ties, both Christmas presents from his mother. His reaction on both occasions was 'I don't do ties'. His mother knew otherwise. He did wear a tie but there was no more commitment to it than to some of his relationships. He had stopped wearing ties with a buttoned collar once he had passed his sergeant's exams. Now they simply hung, loosened, from his neck. There were many things Redpath 'didn't do', like commitment, or respect for his elders, which sometimes caused problems between him and Bertoni. Unlike his younger colleague, Bertoni's decision to change a shirt was based on a cursory visual inspection at the end of each day. The absence of stains or significant creases would permit a second wearing,

197

rather than the smell of the shirt. Deodorant, he mistakenly believed, could overpower even the hardest day's policing.

Redpath scrutinised the cuts to the once expensive wallpaper, now heavily stained in mildew. These were the cuts that had been made by the machete that killed Nelson Kosoto. He pulled the wallpaper away to get a closer look at what was underneath.

"Don't do that," said Cally sternly, "this is still a crime scene."

"What are you talking about?" he argued back. "There are all sorts of people in here every night. I'd be surprised if someone hadn't pissed on your crime scene."

Ashley thought for a moment that the storm he had feared was about to explode, but both Cally and Steve seemed to take a step back.

Cally looked at the plaster behind the wallpaper torn away by her colleague and noticed that blood stains continued down the wall.

"This blood was wallpapered over by someone," she told Bertoni.

"Possibly from the original murder, two hundred years ago."

"But some of it is on the wallpaper that is torn away from the wall."

"So?" he asked.

"Well maybe I lifted this old blood," she replied.

"But it matched Hallet's."

"Mmm," she mumbled, unsure of the significance of the old blood. "I'm going to take a sample anyway."

"We've already got two murders on the go, Cally," Bertoni replied, "we don't want another one that was probably committed by Jack the Ripper's granddad."

198

"But I don't remember anyone else's DNA from the wall and the wound. How did I avoid collecting some of this DNA when I lifted the samples from Charlene, Kosoto and Hallet?"

"Probably because 'Silly Bollocks' over there just tore the wallpaper to reveal it." Bertoni hesitated. "Look, Cally, don't make this any more difficult than it already is. We're not trying to solve some two-hundred-year-old murder, we're looking for DNA and fingerprints for Kosoto, Livingstone, Charlene, Hallet and any serious criminal on our database. Let's focus on that."

After collecting everything they needed, Bertoni instructed PC Ratcliffe to have the house boarded up while they went back to the station to begin examining the evidence.

Back at the station six cardboard boxes of documents were stacked in Bertoni's office. On top of them lay an evidence bag containing a machete. It took Cally about twenty minutes to establish that the machete was almost certainly not the weapon used to kill either Charlene Hallet or Nelson Kosoto. It had not been wiped clean and contained several sets of fingerprints and some DNA. But it wasn't the weapon. She ran the data through the various systems and found that the fingerprints were those of Leroy Livingstone and two other men with criminal records. They seemed to have no connection with the case. She reported the disappointing news to her colleagues in the next office and returned to the samples she had taken from their visit to Wharf Street. She began testing the samples taken from under the wallpaper, while Steve and Ashley sat in the office outside reading through the files of evidence sent over by H division. Reading was the least exciting part of Steve Redpath's employment and he grumbled quietly at his workload.

"There's a lot of evidence that Livingstone killed Charlene," said Ashley ten minutes later, "but very little to connect him with Kosoto's death."

"Motive and that's about it," replied Steve.

"Lots of people must have had a motive to kill Kosoto. He wasn't a nice person," answered Ashley sarcastically. He began to sound like Bent.

"Let's get Livingstone in and interview him."

"Too speculative, Steve," replied Ashley. "He has a great brief and we'll find out precisely nothing. No, I suggest we do a lot more groundwork and see how much evidence Cally can find of Livingstone being at Wharf Street. Then we'll interview Hallet again before we interview Mr Livingstone."

As the two men continued to read through the files sent over by H division, Cally worked in the adjacent room. Eventually she produced a list of all the visitors to 1 Wharf Street who were on the criminal records database. She then filtered them to identify anyone with any record of violence. She transferred the non-violent criminals to another list but did not dismiss them completely. She then eliminated anyone who was currently serving a prison sentence that began before the murder of Charlene Hallet. All the names on the list were local criminals, most of whom were known gang members. By the time she had finished producing the two lists, Steve and Ashley had said goodnight and agreed to meet in the morning to look at her findings.

When Cally discussed the case with Tyler that evening, she wasn't really paying attention to what he said. She was overwhelmed by the amount of evidence she had found at Wharf Street and how much of that evidence matched criminals on the DNA database. Tyler said that this was bound to happen when her team cast their net wider than the prime suspect. The only disappointment for Cally was that the samples taken from under the wallpaper at Wharf Street were spoilt by paste and damp so it was not possible to make a conclusive match.

"I'll take a look if you like, Cally. We've got some state-of-the-art technology at Double Helix and I might be able to succeed where you," he stopped himself from saying the word 'failed' and Cally was so engrossed in her work that she didn't notice.

When she told Tyler that the team were going to interview Hallet at his home the next day, he suggested to her that she asked him if he had any connections with Wharf Street previously.

"But he says he has never been there."

"I know, but it might be worthwhile finding out if he had any connection with it. Did his family come from that area?"

This slightly strange suggestion disturbed Cally's train of thought.

"Why?" she asked, raising her head from the paperwork momentarily.

"Oh, it's just something I am working on at the moment. Rules of inheritance stuff." But she was too engrossed in her work for his comments to register.

"Okay," she answered unconsciously and said she would send a sample of the DNA over to his office the next day.

"Did you hear any more from the reporter or your friend Perry?" she asked.

"No. I rather put them off for a week. I told them I was too busy at the moment."

~~~ الـ صمت من الـ عهد ~~~

Steve and Ashley had visited the Hallet household on several occasions but Cally had never accompanied her colleagues previously. Steve thought about questioning the need to have Cally with them but, having already annoyed her at the party, he decided to keep his head down. She had obviously asked Ashley if she could join them, he thought.

The first thing that Cally noticed, after Bertoni had introduced her to Sandra Hallet, was the complete absence of photographs in the room. She looked around the sparsely furnished living room to see if there were any other things that a less-observant person, such as Steve, might have missed. The house itself was like so many others she had visited in the course of her work. Normally she would be gathering samples of evidence, but today she was just observing. Most of those other houses had become shrines to a lost one. But this home lacked any evidence of that. No photographs, no candles, no floral tributes. Just an ordinary semidetached suburban house that appeared unloved and loveless. It wasn't just the absence of any photographs of Charlene that struck Cally, but the absence of any photographs at all. Where was the happy couple holding hands on holiday or sitting, sunburnt, sipping sangria? Where was the obligatory wedding photo? And didn't David serve in the army when he was young? Where was the picture of him in his uniform? He seemed the army type, thought Cally, even if he was a little undisciplined in his moods.

David Hallet had been aggressive and unhelpful from the outset. He had said all the normal things, if anything can be described as normal when your daughter is murdered. He had asked why the police weren't out there looking for the killer and questioned why they were wasting time interviewing him. But there was no shock reaction when he was charged. Little protestation, no cursing or swearing and, surprisingly, no threats of violence.

"It would be useful, Mr Hallet," said Ashley, "if you could give us a list of Charlene's friends or people she hung out with. Just off the top of your head if necessary, unless you have an address book."

"So you want my help now, do you?" asked Hallet. The 'my' instead of 'our' registered with Cally. This was a uniquely personal experience for David Hallet that he wasn't even prepared to share with his wife. "What's the point, you don't believe anything I say anyway. I didn't text Kosoto. It wasn't my mobile. I bought that mobile for Charlene, so she could stay in touch; so I'd know where she was."

Everyone had sat down at this point, but David Hallet was restless. He stood up and paced the room.

"She has an old address book upstairs," interrupted Sandra Hallet, "but she stopped making entries in it years ago."

"It might still be useful," answered Steve.

"Well," said Sandra as she considered the question again, because everyone had chosen to ignore her husband's outburst. "I think she saw a couple of her friends from school, Tina Baxter and Marilyn Pobranski. They'll be in the address book probably, but I don't think she has seen them for a year or two."

"More recently?" asked Ashley.

"I didn't know any of them," said Sandra, shaking her head and feeling guilty about not knowing who her daughter spent her time with. "I heard her speaking to someone called Demi on the phone once and I think she mentioned someone called Bunny, but they all have such funny names now. It's not John or Mary anymore and, if they were called John or Mary, they would invent other names, street names, that they were called." She was speaking nervously and more quickly now.

"I think we all know who Charlene was hanging round with, don't we," said David Hallet, who was still pacing the room like a caged lion. "Drug addicts, drug dealers, thieves, gangs of idle good-for-nothing youngsters with nothing better to do than mess my daughter's life up."

The word 'mess' registered with Cally and she thought again about how this compared with the word 'fuck' in the text message. She wanted to remind Steve and Ashley about her concern that David Hallet never swore. But she stopped herself and made a note to refer to it later if necessary.

"Can I ask you something, Mr Hallet?" she asked eventually. Steve puffed his cheeks out, but stopped himself from saying anything.

"You told us that you had never been to the house where Charlene was murdered, but do you have any connection with Wharf Street.? You live fairly close by, so has your family always lived in this area?"

Steve went to ask what that had to do with the case but, again, stopped himself. Ashley demonstrated even greater patience with his forensics officer.

"Yes, my family has always lived round here. In fact, my grandfather was born in Wharf Street."

"Now, Mr Hallet," said Ashley, wondering what the point of Cally's question was and deciding to move the discussion on. "Tell us about the mobile phone then."

Hallet sat down in a vacant armchair and told them that he had purchased the mobile phone and given it to Charlene so that she could stay in touch. She often stayed out late and he worried about the company she kept. He suspected she had probably traded it in for some drugs. Everything else he had ever bought her had been used to purchase drugs. She pawned items of jewellery he had bought her and once stole one of her mother's rings too.

"I never wore it anyway, Dave," Sandra said in mitigation of her daughter's offence, but her husband just tutted. "It doesn't matter now anyway, does it?" she added. "Our daughter's dead. What does one ring matter?"

Ashley got up to leave but Steve remained sitting.

"Just one last question, Mrs Hallet," he said, "Where were you on the night of 12 February?" David Hallet jumped up out of his seat. He was an emotional person, bordering on the violent at times but, even by his standards, his remonstrations were out of proportion to the question.

"So now my wife's the murderer, is she? You can't pin it on me, so you accuse my wife of that bastard's murder. Where do you guys get off harassing my family?"

His wife managed to calm him down, saying she had no problem answering the question, if it would help to find the killer of her daughter.

"I was at home all night."

"But your husband wasn't?" asked Redpath and David Hallet tutted loudly.

"No," she answered and paused before making a conscious and difficult decision to add to it. "Look, Officers, my husband was greatly affected by our daughter's murder."

She looked towards her husband but he simply left the room. Sandra relaxed a little and became more forthcoming when her husband had gone. "He couldn't talk about it, couldn't stop thinking about it, couldn't sleep or work. When your daughter is killed, life is suspended. The whole thing hung over us. Dave couldn't stand being in the same room as me. He couldn't bear to keep seeing the photos that littered the house." She waved her arms to indicate that all the photographs of their daughter had been removed. "All he could do was get in his car and drive around, aimlessly. Perhaps he thought he would find her."

"Find her?" asked Steve, "but she was dead, Mrs Hallet."

"I don't think he can accept that she is dead, Officer," she whispered in a lower tone. "I identified the body. Dave has never seen any evidence of Charlene's death. It is just all too much to bear. So he just drove around. He hasn't got an alibi. He hasn't got any witnesses. He knows that makes him your prime suspect, but he doesn't really care. In a way he would like to take responsibility for Kosoto's death because I know he wishes it had been him who killed him. I'm surprised he didn't confess to it, to be honest."

Mrs Hallet would have talked for several more hours had Ashley not intervened.

"I'm sorry to have taken up so much of your time, Mrs Hallet," he said, moving towards the front door. "We will keep you informed of any developments."

Just as they were leaving the house, Ashley received a call from H division to say that they had arrested a teenager called Mervyn Sissulu with a quarter of a kilo of heroin on him. He was believed to be working for Leroy Livingstone, so the team decided to have him transferred to their offices for an interview.

"Do you know anyone called Sissulu?" Bertoni asked Mrs Hallet as he stepped on to the pathway.

She thought for a moment. "No, why?"

"Oh, it's just someone we are interviewing in connection with the case."

Cally and Steve looked surprised because this was the first they had heard about anyone named Sissulu and the name did not appear on the main list Cally had produced from the DNA at Wharf Street.

206

On his way into the office, Tyler had slipped on the escalator when leaving the underground station. His ankle had twisted slightly and the pain distracted him from his work when he finally arrived at the office.

The DNA samples that Cally had removed from under the wallpaper at Wharf Street were in very poor condition. The high level of corruption was going to make it difficult to match it with anyone, let alone David Hallet. Errors were common in investigations of this kind. It would be easier, thought Tyler, to work on DNA from ancient Egypt because it is likely to have been stored in a sarcophagus. These samples hadn't been stored at all. The building was damp and there had obviously been a large number of visitors to the site.

The triple-repeat error was to be expected. This was like a stammer in speech. It produced multiple copies of the DNA just like a photocopier getting stuck. This often happened with samples taken from someone suffering from muscular dystrophy or Huntingdon's disease. When a cell divides it needs to copy all the DNA it contains and this is what causes the problem in samples taken from people with certain genetic diseases. He eliminated the random genetic drift and continued to narrow down the possibilities. But after four hours he was still no closer to clearly identifying the DNA from under the wallpaper and he concluded that he was never going to match it conclusively with any of the suspects in the case.

There had been plenty of cases where DNA evidence taken in cases before such evidence was permitted still identified the killer. In 2007, Tony Jasinskyj was found guilty of a murder committed twenty years before, simply because police had retained some samples taken from the scene. Tyler wondered what the police were thinking of at the time, but it certainly produced the right result, if a little late.

In the Wharf Street case, the best Tyler could conclude was that the DNA under the wallpaper was very old and unlikely to be related in any way to someone alive today. The reliability of DNA was almost entirely dependent on storage or the quality of that storage. DNA stored correctly was reliable but what he was looking at would certainly not stand up in a court of law.

Clinchman and Richards would present a similar problem. Clearly the names were different, so establishing a connection would require him to work outside the Y chromosome that linked the male line.

Tyler rubbed his sore ankle and wondered whether he should bandage it.

~~~ متال ص من ال عهد ~~~

Mervyn Sissulu had already arrived by the time the team returned to the station. He had been placed in the interview room by the desk sergeant and left there until Bertoni got back.

Ashley and Steve went into the small room adjacent to the interview suite and, from here, they could see Sissulu through the two-way mirror.

"Where's his parent or guardian?" asked Ashley.

"The duty solicitor has just arrived," answered the desk sergeant, who had brought them two cups of coffee.

They drank the coffee and joined Sissulu and his solicitor in the interview suite. Ashley switched on the tape machine and stated the names of those present and the time and date before adjusting his seat and beginning the interview. He had already checked with Cally and she had confirmed that Sissulu's fingerprints and DNA were found at the murder scene in Wharf Street. She hadn't recalled it because his name appeared on the second list of minor, juvenile offenders.

Sissulu was a cocky young man of West Indian descent trying desperately to grow some facial hair to make him look older. He felt protected by his gang connections and was accompanied by a young, smartly dressed woman with what appeared to be limited practical experience of the criminal justice system. Certainly, neither Ashley nor Steve had met her before.

"Our friends over at H division," Bertoni began, "tell us that they found five grand worth of 'H' on you, Mervyn."

"Taint worth no five," he answered boldly, "tree at most."

His solicitor looked at him sternly and suggested that he should consider seeking her advice before answering questions. But he laughed at her, saying he didn't need her help. He had the brothers.

"You're going to have me crying in a minute," said Steve before turning to his colleague. "The heroin market's collapsed, Boss. Poor Merv here might have to get a proper job."

"He won't be needing a job for the next few years. Dealing is a custodial sentence," answered Bertoni.

"It's for my private use," Sissulu mumbled eventually.

"A quarter of a kilo is not private use, Mervyn," said Steve.

"Don't call me that Mervyn shit man," he demanded, "dat ma slave name. I'yze Sweet Boy Sissulu."

"Okay, Sweet Boy," said Ashley, "as my colleague says, a quarter of a kilo is dealing, not private use. There isn't a judge in the land that wouldn't take that view. Trust me."

"Da one ting I aint doin' today man is trusting you." He laughed and leaned back in the chair until it nearly toppled over. Sweet Boy made it clear he was not going to trust anyone in that room, not even his solicitor. Ashley sat quietly for a few moments, looking through a file. Then he looked directly at the young man. But, before he could speak, youthful impetuosity took over as Steve interrupted his boss.

"Of course," said the young sergeant, "if you're not in a gang, then you're a juggler man. A self-employed street dealer. But if, on the other hand, you are in a gang, then we might take the view that you're just a soldier. Do you follow me, Sweet Boy?"

Sissulu thought about it but didn't speak. Ashley cast a reproving look in the direction of his impatient colleague.

"Your form isn't that bad, Sweet Boy," began Ashley. "I reckon you might get away with two or three years if you plead guilty. And a sweet boy like you will quickly make friends inside".

"Yeah," added Steve, "some great hairy-arsed lifer will love sharing a cell with you." The young solicitor flinched and Sissulu's face changed as he looked towards her for advice. She began to plead his case.

"Look," interrupted Ashley, "we're not interested in the drugs. H division will deal with that, but we can put a good word in for you. We're only interested in the murder of Nelson Kosoto."

"Who dat?"

"Oh, I think you know very well 'who dat', Sweet Boy. Your fingerprints and DNA were found at Wharf Street. From your accent, I would suggest that your weapon of choice is a machete." The young woman went to interrupt but Ashley ignored her and turned to Steve. "I think he can forget the two to three years, Steve," he said confidently. "This one's going down for killing Nelson 'who dat' Kosoto."

The change of emphasis paid dividends and Sissulu was soon telling Steve and Ashley about Kosoto and Livingstone. They were rival gang leaders. Kosoto controlled the streets of the Limehouse region in London and Livingstone had a gang in Mile End, a few miles away. Steve told Sissulu that they knew that already and, if he didn't come up with something new and useful very soon, they would be laying some serious charges on him.

"Bunny supplied Charlene with drugs," Sweet Boy said in the hope that they would now let him go.

"For the purposes of the tape, Sweet Boy, can you confirm that Bunny is Leroy Livingstone?"

"The same," he answered reluctantly.

"And, again, just for the record, do you know why he's called Bunny?"

"Bunny Livingston, man."

"Yes, but why?"

"You don't know much, man. Bunny Livingston was Bob Marley's drummer. And Leroy's name is Livingstone, so he's called Bunny too."

"And what about the mobile phone?" asked Ashley, whose question sent a visible shockwave through Sissulu's body. The boy was noticeably shaken by the question and neither Ashley nor Steve could understand why. Neither could the solicitor. Everyone noticed it, but nobody referred to it. His reaction hung about the room, like a thunder cloud waiting to burst, as the interview continued.

"Did Charlene have a mobile phone?"

"Yeah, she traded it in for a fix. It was brand new, too. Bunny saw her coming."

"Was Charlene part of Bunny's gang, Sweet Boy?"

"No way, man. She part o' Nelson's crew."

211

"She was in Kosoto's gang?" Sissulu nodded, wondering whether he was telling the detectives too much. He was surprised that they didn't seem to even know which gang Charlene was in.

"So why didn't she get her drugs from Kosoto then?"

Sweet Boy explained that Charlene and Kosoto were an item and Nelson wanted her to give up the drugs.

"Kozo wouldn't give Charlene any drugs, man. Dat's why he fell out wid Bunny. Cos Bunny pumped her full of 'em." He laughed but stopped when he realised nobody was joining him.

"Bunny and Kosoto fell out?" asked Ashley.

"Kozo told Bunny to stop selling drugs to Charlene, or else."

"Or else what, Sweet Boy?"

But Sissulu told Ashley he knew very well what he meant by 'or else'. In the gangs 'or else' meant only one thing.

"So," said Ashley, thinking he was now making some real progress. "Bunny then sends Kosoto a text message, saying 'you fucked with the wrong people'. Is that right?"

Sissulu clammed up at last.

"I aint saying nuttin' more," he said sternly, folding his arms to emphasise the point.

For the purpose of the tape, Ashley declared the interview suspended.

"Can I go now?" asked Sissulu.

"Definitely not, Sweet Boy," answered Ashley. "You stay right there. We are not finished with you by a long way."

With that, Ashley and Steve left the room to consult on their next move. They both agreed that the boy knew a lot more than he was saying, possibly enough to send Livingstone to jail for life. The next move was an important one and it was Redpath who came up with the idea of frightening the boy into telling them everything he knew.

Steve had seen this idea work before and was sure it would succeed again in this instance. They agreed to go back into the interview suite and immediately charge Sissulu with the murder of Kosoto. Neither Sissulu, nor the young solicitor who was representing him, had ever been in this sort of situation before and the detectives were confident that panic would cause the youngster to confess everything he knew. In the meantime they obtained a search warrant and sent Cally with another officer to Sissulu's flat to look for evidence.

They re-entered the interview suite and Ashley switched on the tape machine, stating that the interview had recommenced, with the same people present. He remained standing and looked down at Sissulu.

"Mervyn Sissulu, I am arresting you for the murder of Nelson Kosoto at Wharf Street, Limehouse, London on 12 February 2012. You do not have to say anything. However, it may harm your defence if you do not mention, when questioned, something that you later rely on in court. Anything you do say may be given in evidence."

Sissulu jumped out of his chair but Steve pushed him back down. The solicitor began asking questions about what this meant, how long her client could be held and what happens next.

"We can hold our suspect for thirty-six hours before we need to get a court order to extend this," answered Steve.

"For the purposes of the tape, Mervyn," said Ashley, "please state your age."

"I was seventeen last week."

"That's a spot of luck, Sweet Boy," said Redpath sarcastically, "we don't need to tell your parents. You're an adult." Sissulu instinctively felt for the adolescent hair beginning to grow on his face and seemed surprised by his promotion to adulthood.

"I didn't kill Kozo. You know dat."

"Well you'd better tell us who did then, Sweet Boy."

"I aint gonna say this in no courtroom," he answered, "but it was Bunny who killed Kozo. You guys know dat already. You said it, man, his 'weapon o' choice' is a machete."

Ashley went to ask Sweet Boy to confirm it was Leroy Livingstone who killed Nelson Kosoto but stopped himself because Sissulu was about to give them more evidence and he didn't want to put him off. So he just told him to continue.

Sissulu paused but then began telling them about events in February. But Ashley stopped him and told him to begin with the killing of Charlene back in December. Sweet Boy wasn't sure of the date, he said, but it was early in December because the Christmas decorations had just been put up in the main shopping street. Some threats had been made between the rival gangs. Charlene came to see Bunny for some drugs but she didn't have any money. Bunny wouldn't extend her any credit so she left. She had already traded in her mobile phone the week before and so she stole a ring from her mother and hocked it for fifty quid. Bunny gave her a packet and she left.

"A few hours later she came back, screaming at Bunny that he had sold her a load of blanks, you know shit stuff man and, unless he gave her some better gear, she was going to tell Kosoto that he was still selling drugs to her."

"And what happened next?" asked Ashley.

Sissulu assumed she had told Kosoto because some threats were made to Bunny. Bunny reacted and took a few boys, including Sissulu, over to Wharf Street because he knew Kosoto hung out there. But when they arrived there were just a few

214

drug addicts, including Charlene, sleeping it off. Bunny woke her up to find out where Kozo was and they were screaming at each other. All the other druggies left in fear of their lives and the place was empty apart from one of Nelson's boys, Donny Clarke, who was hiding in the next room.

"Bunny would have killed him too if he had known he was there," said Sissulu, adding, "then Charlene said something."

"What?"

"I don't know but it made Bunny real mad."

Bertoni pressed him on what she had called Livingstone, in case it had some relevance. He was convinced that Sissulu knew what had been said but was reluctant to propagate any slanderous comments about his idol.

"What could it have been? What did it sound like?"

"Pussy. Okay? She called him a pussy."

"And why did she call him that?"

"Bunny called her a bag bride and she said it back."

"A bag bride?" asked the DI.

"A crack-smoking prostitute, Boss," interrupted Redpath to update his less street-wise boss.

"Go on," demanded Bertoni and Sissulu continued his recollections.

"Bunny and a couple of the others had guns but one of his team was holding a machete. Bunny snatched it from him and took a swipe at Charlene. He was amping, man. He went absolutely mad and kept hitting her, even hacking at her as she lay motionless, dead on the floor." Sweet Boy explained that they all left Wharf Street and, in the car, Bunny used Charlene's mobile phone to text Kosoto.

"'You fucked with the wrong people'?" asked Steve.

Sweet Boy nodded and told them that things got much worse for a few months. Ashley asked him what happened in

215

February and Sissulu described a similar incident, where Livingstone visited Wharf Street, looking for Kosoto. One of Livingstone's dealers had been stabbed and robbed by Kosoto's team.

He described a bitterly cold February day when he and a few others, led by Bunny, went to Wharf Street to find Kosoto. Bunny still had the machete he had used to kill Charlene and intended to kill Kosoto with it too. He was going to taunt Kosoto by telling him how he killed Charlene. But, when they got there, Kosoto had a gun and, after shouting at each other, Livingstone had to run away. Kosoto shouted to him that he knew Bunny had killed Charlene because he had seen it for himself.

"What did he mean by that?" asked Ashley, but Sweet Boy was not prepared to say. So, Steve butted in.

"I think we still have more on Sweet Boy here than Livingstone," Steve said, before turning to Sissulu. "You're going down son; for life."

"It was Donny Clarke. It was all his fault. He filmed Bunny murdering Charlene on his mobile phone and started sending it around to other members of the gang, saying that Bunny couldn't kill nuffin more than a girl."

Ashley realised the importance of this information and the evidence on Donny Clarke's mobile phone, but felt the need to get back to Kosoto's murder.

"So," he asked, "if Livingstone ran off, how did Kosoto get killed?"

"Kozo's gang chased the Mile End boys away, but Kozo stayed in the house. He was trying to ring Donny Clarke to warn him that Bunny was looking for him. Bunny must have come back because you guys found Kozo dead; killed by the machete that Bunny took with him to Wharf Street."

216

"Did Livingstone say he killed Kosoto?"

"Yeah. Well, not at first he didn't. But then Bunny was going round saying he switched off Kozo's lights."

"What happened to the machete?" asked Ashley.

"Bunny had dropped it when the argument first broke out."

"When Kosoto chased them off?" asked Steve.

"Yeah. Bunny sneaked back and whacked Kozo with it while he was on the mobile to Donny."

"You know that?"

"That's how Bunny tells it."

Redpath could not wait any longer. He realised that Sissulu's reaction to the words 'mobile phone' was nothing to do with Charlene's phone but, Donny Clarke's. It was Clarke's phone that contained the damning evidence of Charlene's murder. So, he asked Sweet Boy where Donny Clarke lived.

"He's a ripper, man. Donny's hot. He sleeps with a different girl every night."

Ashley couldn't wait to start the search for Donny Clarke and his mobile phone but, just as he was thinking about wrapping the interview up, there was a knock on the door. It was Cally, so he suspended the interview and left the room. Cally explained to him that they had found several items of interest at Sissulu's flat, including the mobile phone that David Hallet bought for his daughter. It still had the text message on it that was sent to Kosoto.

Ashley returned to the room and told Sissulu they had found Charlene's phone in his flat, adding that any jury would assume he had sent the text message.

"Bunny sent the message!" he shouted. "He just told me to get rid of the phone."

"So, why didn't you?"

"It was brand new, man. I thought I would keep it for a while and sell it."

"Okay, Sweet Boy," said Ashley, "there's one thing that can get you out of here. Tell us where the machete is."

It took a few minutes of cajoling but Sissulu eventually told them. He had returned to Wharf Street trying to find other members of the Mile End gang and, when he got there, all he could find was Kosoto's body and the machete lying next to him. So he took the machete, wiped it with a rag and threw it over a fence onto some wasteland two streets away. He thought this would earn him some credit with Livingstone.

Steve managed to get a few addresses where Clarke was likely to be hiding out and they decided to release Sissulu back to H division to be charged with possession of drugs.

"You keep your mouth shut now, Sweet Boy," said Steve as he and Ashley left the room. "Co-operate with H division and you can walk with a minor charge of possession and the rest of Livingstone's gang won't even know you've been here. But you say anything to anyone before we've lifted Clarke and we'll be back for you."

Sissulu was nearly in tears at this point but understood what was expected of him.

Most of the addresses he gave Steve and Ashley were in the Limehouse area of London so, as they were in the neighbourhood, Ashley took a few minutes to call at Hallet's house to tell them they were going to charge Livingstone with the murders of Charlene and Kosoto. He told them that they had found the mobile phone David had bought for his daughter and could trace that to Livingstone.

Just before he left, Ashley received a call on his mobile from Cally telling him that she had located the murder weapon where Sissulu said he had thrown it. She had bagged it and was taking it back to the station to conduct DNA and fingerprint testing. At last, things were starting to move in their favour.

But that joy was short-lived because, in spite of thorough searches of all the addresses given by Sissulu, Clarke could not be found. Extra officers were brought in to search CCTV footage in the areas frequented by Clarke but, by the end of a long hot day, they were no closer finding him. To ensure word did not get to him, Ashley arranged for H division to hold Sissulu overnight. He then spent the next couple of hours ringing round all his contacts to try to locate the evasive Donny Clarke.

Cally was exhausted when she finally arrived home that night but was keen to recall all the events to Tyler. She grabbed a large glass of wine and told him about finding the machete and what Hallet had said about Wharf Street. She was pleased to be right about Hallet's innocence but wondered what the significance was of whether he had a connection to Wharf Street.

Tyler told her he had found no connection between Hallet and the DNA sample from under the wallpaper at Wharf Street. But Cally still couldn't understand what the purpose of the tests was.

"What difference does it make if Hallet's grandfather was born in Wharf Street, or whether his family originally came from that street?"

"I don't know, Cally," answered Tyler. "It's just something I am working on at the moment. I'm not sure if it's significant."

So, to Tyler's relief, she dismissed the matter.

"How was your day, anyway?" she asked as she offered him a glass of wine.

"Not as productive as yours. There's so much I don't seem to understand about the project I'm working on at the moment. Anyway, there is some consolation," he added, "Galen called today to say that he may have made some progress tracing the family tree of Mr Clinchman."

Apparently, Tyler explained, Galen had also been successful in uncovering the history of 1 Wharf Street. It had, indeed, been built by a sea captain and one who had served under Admiral Nelson. After a distinguished military career, he sailed the world on trading vessels and rarely stayed in London for more than a few days. He died of a rare disease in the Far East before the building of the house was completed. Following a long and acrimonious legal battle, a nephew took ownership of the house but, after the lengthy litigation, he had little money left for the upkeep and furnishing. It remained just a shell until, one day, an argument ensued between the nephew and a cousin who claimed ownership of the house. He, like his famous uncle, had been travelling the world. He had spent years on the Grand Tour, never wishing to come home. But he had enough money to dispute the ownership of a house that he believed was rightfully his and title to the property again became the subject of a legal dispute.

So, when the wealthier cousin finally returned to England, he challenged the newly appointed owner to a duel, which was fought out with swords, in 1 Wharf Street. The travelling cousin had gained just the skills he needed during his long sojourn in Italy and cut his opponent to ribbons. The newspaper records at the time made graphic reference to blood splattered walls following a gruesome encounter between the duelling cousins. The only winner, it seems, was the house, because the victor at least had the necessary fortune to decorate it in the manner to which it had originally been designed. No expense was spared. The best Regency furniture, wallpaper by William Morris, rugs from the Middle East and great works of art adorned the elegant rooms.

But the legal system failed to recognise justice by the sword and ownership was never entirely or satisfactorily established. So, when the cousin – who was, after all, only a distant relative of the original seafaring owner – died, the property again became the subject of litigation. Legal fees mounted as lawyers sought the rightful owner. In the end, the few possible heirs all refused to take ownership of the house because of the enormous legal bill that was now attached to it. So, it remained in mournful disrepair for many years. Undernourished, overgrown and unloved.

The last word resonated with Cally. It reminded her of the visit to the Hallet home, which had seemed unloved to her. Two houses touched by tragedy and one of them the location of three killings. Why had the seafaring captain built the property if he had no intention of living there? Cally mused on the subject but felt herself drifting into a morbid state of mind, so snapped out of it as Tyler continued his news from their friend.

"Galen also mentioned some strange stuff about his visitor. You know what Galen is like, he's been searching the internet for information on the religious order that Sianos belongs to. He didn't have any luck at first, then some really weird stuff turned up on a website, but when he went back to the site later it had disappeared completely."

Tyler explained that, from what Galen remembered, the website seemed to be run by a radical religious group because it sought to set out a plausible explanation for the meaning of life.

"Oh really," replied Cally, "not too heavy then."

"He remembered the opening lines verbatim."

"Typical of Galen. I'm surprised he didn't remember all of it."

"Well he remembered quite a lot. 'Before the world began', it started, 'before the universe was created, only good and evil existed. Good, in an attempt to entrap evil, created time and space'. The creation of mankind, it seems, formed part of that temptation."

"So the story of the Garden of Eden was right, then. Eve and the apple and all that."

"Something like that," replied Tyler. "But it seems God, or good in this case, took pity on man and granted him eternal life."

"Well, it's not the most radical theory I've ever heard."

"There was a lot more to it. Galen's going to try to recover the file. He's only sorry he didn't print it off."

"And it was all to do with the religious order that Sianos belonged to?"

"So Galen said."

"Well he seemed a nice guy to me," she replied. "Why doesn't he just ask him?"

"You know Galen, he likes to turn everything into a crisis."

Tyler got up to go to the kitchen for a glass of water and Cally noticed he was limping.

"What's wrong with your leg?" she asked and he explained that he had tripped on the way to work that morning.

"Do you want me to take a look at it?"

"No," he replied. "I've put a bandage on it for support. I'm sure it will be fine".

Cally's thoughts drifted for a moment and she was gazing into space when Tyler returned to the room. He looked at her and asked if she was okay.

"I just had a strange feeling of déjà vu," she answered. "It was seeing you limping."

"But I don't remember having a limp before," he laughed.

"Well," she replied, "that's déjà vu for you. I don't suppose you can explain it."

Tyler raised his foot onto a chair and they sat talking about their best friend until they both nearly fell asleep.

~~~ الـ صمت من الـ عهد ~~~

Fragments of a dream are all I have left to record from last night's restless sleep. A desolate scene from an African famine, the statue of a man frozen, kneeling before a living Virgin Mary, like dream and reality reflected in a mirror. Changing seasons, a shadowy spirit lurking in the darkness of a moonless night. Sadness, fires, snakes, disease and that painfully anxious search for something or someone. The only coherent element appears with that recurring pastoral scene. A group of people are collecting fruit from trees as they walk along a narrow country lane. They are dressed in roughly made cloth and appear poor. They are happy in spite of their poverty and I am sad despite my expensive clothes. A man who looks much older than his years keeps shouting out words like 'death' and 'cry'. We arrive at a country pub and I expect to see the young woman who frequents my dreams. But she is not there. I search everywhere. Suddenly everyone is running, searching for something. Something has been lost and everyone is looking for it but I am looking for the young woman. Both searches prove fruitless and we all cry together but for different reasons.

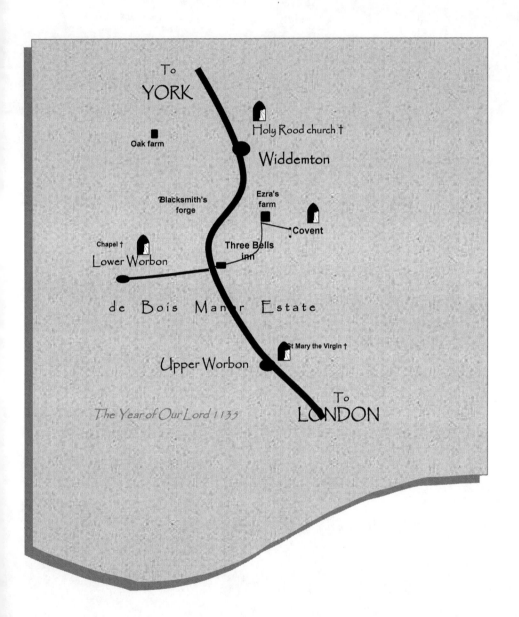

To
YORK

Holy Rood church †

Oak farm

Widdemton

Blacksmith's forge

Ezra's farm

Covent

Chapel †

Three Bells inn

Lower Worbon

de Bois Manor Estate

St Mary the Virgin †

Upper Worbon

The Year of Our Lord 1135

To
LONDON

8

Ezra and Samuel pushed their way through the crowd in the market square, as the stallholders loudly hollered the price of their wares. The snow of last week had melted but her pale sister the frost cast an icy footing through the town's narrow cobbled streets.

"Two farthings for a rabbit and three for a hare!" called a stout, rosy-cheeked man in a blood-stained hide apron, adding, "you'll find none better for less." The sleeves of his dirty shirt billowed in the frosty wind but he was unmoved by the cold.

Poaching would be cheaper, thought Ezra, who fretted on the fact that he could not keep for his own the wild beasts that wandered about his smallholding.

The rabbits and hares that the stout man shouted of were hanging from the crudely made frames slung against the walls from which mutton and, occasionally, beef were sold. Bags of millet, barley and buckwheat were traded by local farmers and the market reeked with the aroma of cardamom, cumin, nutmeg and cloves.

As the two men stumbled through the wool market, tradesmen produced roughly carved furniture and ornaments, whilst an old woman with large earrings sat telling a young woman's fortune. Ezra remembered the old woman's less-than-revelationary conjecture on his future, which had not been worth the farthing he'd paid her. Close by, a younger woman sat cross-legged in front of a ragged sheet on which she had spread her wares. Ezra stopped and wondered whether any were capable of healing his friend's malady. Chokeberries, elderberries, loganberries and rosehips had been garnered from the hedgerow during the autumn and transformed into remedies and treatments for all forms of malaise. Her bony fingers stretched forward and upward urging him to take one of the preparations from her. He had tried many such treatments in the past. None had been as effective as those he brought from his homeland, although they only provided temporary relief by way of hallucination and delusion. Some honey mead at the tavern would do as well, thought Ezra and they continued their way along the busy street.

Not far from where the woman worked her magic sat a blind man at a wooden box that he used as a table. He sat close enough to the doorway of the building to prevent access. Ezra did not want to enter but felt aggrieved at a stranger, particularly a beggar, causing such an obstruction. Ezra stared at the man but did not recognise him and, whilst strangers were not uncommon, it was unusual to see one trading in the market place alongside the local merchants.

"Away with thee, beggar," demanded Ezra.

"Foe," cried Samuel.

"I'm not a beggar," insisted the blind man.

"Then what is your purpose?" asked Ezra.

"Mine eyes are not corrupted by your appearance, Sir. Riches or poverty do not influence what I hear and I have the gift to foretell what lies beyond the threshold of this day. The truth doth await you, Sir. Only your eyes may betray the message of the oracle."

Ezra wondered what an oracle might be and went to walk on.

"I am a seer," the man said knowingly, almost reading Ezra's mind. "And you are right to fear the future, Sir. As we grow ever closer to perfection, one vicious act by a man is enough to prompt another to kill. Beware ire for it takes you from the mouth of heaven."

Ezra placed his hand on Samuel's shoulder and told him to stop.

"Halt!" Samuel cried loud enough to startle the strange fortune teller, who continued to hold out his open hand.

An oracle is just a beggar by another name, thought Ezra, who placed a farthing in the man's hand and sat on the empty chair by the improvised table. As he did so the man held on to his hand and felt the rough skin of his palm.

"You are not of noble birth, Sir."

"If that is the extent of your gift, I shall have my farthing back," declared Ezra.

"A man comes," the wizened old man announced and secured Ezra's attention. "He acts silently and disappears like the pale frost at sunrise. He is a man who walks frequently with death. But this time, it is not the sadness of death he leaves behind. Yet I foresee a loss."

"What is his purpose and how does it affect me?" asked Ezra tetchily.

"He simply takes what is rightfully his and his deed harms not your flesh but scars your soul forever."

"What is his name?" asked Ezra.

"He carries a false name, yet you will know the man of whom I speak. This is all I am able to say."

As Ezra left the doorway, the oracle called gently from the darkness. "Ne'er Ab'ram in his time e'er considered such a crime."

Ezra felt the words in the darkness of his heart as if they were God's own spies. Abraham considered killing his own son. What crime could be worse than that?

The wool market was used on different days of the week for the sale of sheep, sheep's wool and slaves, although sometimes furniture could be purchased there too. The slaves came from less distant lands than the spices that filled the air, but sufficiently faraway to warrant the label of thrall instead of slave. The Normans, who purchased most of them, understood that word better than slave. But in Ezra's eyes they were slaves just the same. It was important that the slaves understood their place. They were whipped harshly to demonstrate how submissive and compliant they were, but they understood nothing of the language. Thrall or slave, it made no difference to their meagre existence.

Ezra slung the two hares he had purchased over his shoulder and called to Samuel to keep up. The old solider mumbled to himself in sentences of one word and most words of one syllable. He appeared detached and oblivious to his surroundings as they headed off towards the inn for their lunch.

"Forward," he called, glassy eyed, into a void as Ezra handed him a sack of cheese to carry.

It was about a mile to the inn and then a further mile to home.

"Stay on the path," Ezra warned Samuel. "For a man could be lost forever in Worbon Forest."

Ezra stopped, looked into Samuel's glazed eyes and cautioned him again, more patiently this time, not to wander into the wood, although he knew his friend could read the forest well from his childhood near Nottingham. He wondered whether Samuel even thought about returning to his childhood home but knew, in his heart, that his childhood had been lost in a foreign land.

"We'll stop at the inn for lunch, my friend."

"Foe," cried Samuel loudly, thinking himself a guard at the gates of a distant but well-remembered city.

It was a cold day and the walk kept them warm. Ezra in front and Samuel marching three paces behind. The frosty wind reminded Ezra of a similar December day in Antioch when he would have been grateful to pay a full penny or more for a rabbit.

The once verdant bowers of the forest, which provided welcome shade on the hot summer days before harvest time, stretched leafless in the grip of winter and now shed light in equal measure. The ash, oak and horse chestnut began to thin out as they neared the crossroads and turned slowly into wooded thicket made similarly translucent by the season. The blackbird and fieldfare had emptied the hawthorn of berries and made ready for the bitterness of sloes that stave off famine. The foliage of warmer days now crushed and crumbled by the two heavy-footed friends as they continued on their way.

Ezra often thought of taking Samuel back to Nottingham. But he could not be certain that any family that remained there would treat him with the compassion that he and Rosalind did. Anyway, in truth he knew that Samuel would never leave Antioch for his mind was imprisoned by the siege, no less than those trapped so long within the walls of that once great city. Nobody asked what ailed him for it was obvious to all what unrelenting pain had been inflicted upon him. His actions and, more poignantly, his words bore adequate witness to his

229

entrapment between past and present.   Where was the promised honour? Where was the glory of triumphant victory?

The Three Bells inn stood by a fork in the road that provided the traveller with three options. The first road, which was the widest, headed northwards through the market town of Widdemton, from where the men had just come and then on to York, which was about two hundred miles to the north. It was along this path, to the south, that the two men travelled that late December day. The second road passed through Upper Worbon on its way to London. And the smallest of the three roads was no more than a drove road that headed west for just one mile before it expired in the tiny village of Lower Worbon.

The two men crossed a narrow ford and, as the road widened, they reached a large grey stone that had been rudely shaped to provide three sides with the distance to each of the villages carved upon it. They were all of equal distance from the inn, so-named because the bell of each of the three churches could be heard on a still day. Lower Worbon housed just a tiny chapel, rather than a church, but it still had a bell paid for by his Lordship that it might serve as a warning of invasion, rather than to toll the imminence of a church service. The parish church at Upper Worbon was dedicated to the Virgin Mary and a procession was held there for the three villages on the first Sunday of May each year. The largest town of Widdemton boasted a church, built some thirty years before by the invading Normans, with a prominent square tower that housed the loudest of the three bells. The bells tolled for the dead, they announced new life and rang out for marriages and mass on Sunday. But it seemed they tolled loudest for the feast days that provided so much joy for the people of the three villages. All three would chime tomorrow on the last Sunday of Advent,

230

when the fourth candle would be lit and the parishioners would sing of herald angels and shepherds who came to pay homage to a child King. But tomorrow, the bells would be twice blessed, for they would chime also for the coronation of a new King.

Ezra was more than fifty years old but could not remember exactly how old he was. And, although his friend looked older, Samuel was in fact two years younger. But the soldier had suffered cruel injuries in the war and was greatly affected by his experiences during the Crusades. The scars to his body and mind had both changed and aged him greatly. The former could be covered by clothes but the latter were apparent for all who had eyes to see.

"He is an old soldier to whom the war did grave damage," Ezra would explain to anyone who asked of his affliction. "You will see few physical wounds upon his body but his pain cannot be hidden."

"We are created of the same experiences, Samuel," said Ezra. "But, by comparison, I was born under a shining moon and you under a waning one."

As they rounded a bend, they could see the crossroads and the inn. His defining character, thought Ezra of Samuel, is like his vocabulary, best expressed in a single word — loyalty — for there was none braver than him in battle and none so steadfast.

Samuel had returned to England with Sir Guy de Bois after the great siege of Antioch and had brought Ezra and Rosalind with him. Ezra and Rosalind were not their original names for, although they were Christians, they formerly lived in Antioch. For some strange reason or misplaced guilt perhaps, Samuel believed himself responsible for the deaths of Ezra's family and friends. The war-ravaged soldier was bound by restitution. But all repentance is imperfect and his no less than others, for he could never bring himself to speak of his service under Tancred and the evil he was called upon to do in the name of God.

Ezra, Samuel and Rosalind returned from the Crusades at Antioch about thirty years ago. Ezra had acted as a translator to Sir Guy and, because he spoke some French and English, decided to return with Samuel to start a new life. For his loyalty, Ezra was granted a small piece of woodland by Sir Guy that he could cut down to use as farmland if he wished. He and Rosalind took pity on Samuel and together they built a farmhouse and shared their home with him. They grew some crops and worked on his Lordship's farms, ploughing, seeding and harvesting, because their smallholding was insufficient to provide them all with an income.

Ezra collected two jugs of mead from the bar and the friends settled down in two heavy wooden chairs close to a raging fire in the hearth. Each took one of the hares and began plucking the fur from its body and throwing it on the fire. As they did so, the fire flickered and sparked and Samuel continued to live his life in one hundred words, speaking of courage, mercy, wisdom and death, as Ezra looked upon him with heartfelt sorrow. It was lunchtime and in the absence of any other customers, they were soon joined at the table by Tom, who owned the inn. A few minutes later Father William Henry, the parish priest from the church of the Blessed Virgin at Upper Worbon, joined them too. Much to the displeasure of the priest, Ezra began to gossip about the inhabitants of the three villages thereabouts.

"Speak not ill of your neighbours," the priest corrected him.

"Did you poach those hares?" asked Tom, much to the displeasure of Ezra and the priest.

232

"I am not a poacher for poachers are hanged by his Lordship's authority and pleasure. Mercy, I'm not even allowed to keep the rabbits and hares that run about my land, for his Lordship claims they are his property and he gifted me only the land, not the beasts that inhabit it."

"I think he regrets gifting you that land, Ezra," remarked Tom.

"'Tis not I, but that old reprobate Edward who does poach his Lordship's stock, as you know very well, Tom, because 'tis you he sells his stolen wares to."

"Ted was in here yesterday," began Tom, "and he returned all my money in exchange for several jugs of honey mead, so who is the cleverer of us?"

"You really shouldn't speak of such things in my presence," said the priest.

"Privacy of the confessional," said Tom.

"This inn is not a confessional," replied William Henry.

Tom chose to ignore him and continued with his talk of the poacher.

"Ted said he saw the golden hare again on the hillside."

"There is no such thing as a golden hare. It was probably an ordinary hare and the sun just glistened off its fur."

"He swears by it and swears too that he will catch it one day. 'Tis his fortune, he says".

"Nonsense," declared William Henry. "There is no such creature as a golden hare. Nor is there any truth either in the tale he tells about the feast of St Mark."

"Oh, I've heard that tale too," said Ezra. "Ted will say anything for a free ale."

"But he does tell a good tale, Ezra. He told me of the new curate at Widdemton who took to growing flowers in his garden to please the priest and his Lordship."

"Can't eat flowers," said Ezra.

"Anyway, Ted said the curate asked to borrow his cousin's sheep to eat the grass so that he could see his pretty flowers all the better."

"And did he do so?"

"He did indeed and the blessed sheep ate all his flowers."

"Well, someone should have told the poor man that sheep don't eat grass by choice but out of necessity."

"Ted received his comeuppance," said Tom. "He was gored by a wild hog trying to steal its piglets. Very tender are they."

"Was he harmed?" asked William Henry.

"Not as much as the curate, I suspect," said Ezra.

"The curate learned an important lesson," said Tom.

"It was a dreadfully unkind act and a sin against God," said William Henry. "He's too clever for his own good. Once man ate from the Tree of Knowledge, he could no longer eat from the Tree of Life. Eternal life was denied him and he was banished from Eden. It says in Genesis: 'in the day that you eat from the Tree of Knowledge you shall surely die'."

"Talk not of dying on such a cold day, Priest. For a pennyworth of wit you could stir my good humour back to the fore," joked Ezra.

"Death befalls us all," replied the priest.

"Yes, but with God's grace, not today, Father."

Ezra supped his ale, continued to pluck the hare and began to tell the others about his visit to the fortune teller. William Henry tutted his disapproval.

"Just when he gets close to perfection," the seer told me, "one vicious act by man is enough to prompt him to kill. Beware ire it takes you from the mouth of heaven."

William Henry asked Ezra not to speak of such matters in the presence of a priest. The gift of prophecy was lost to man, as St Paul had foretold. So it was ungodly to speak of such matters.

"Nay," added the landlord, "tell us instead of your time at the Crusades. I shall put a log on the fire and we can eat some of this cheese you've purchased at the market, Ezra."

"I'll put up the cheese, if you put up the mead," he answered.

Tom spat in the palm of his hand and offered it to Ezra, who took it heartily.

"If no money changes hands then no Norman taxes need change hands neither," said Tom. The priest tutted his disapproval and felt in his cloak, but Ezra said he would not take the holy man's money.

"Have you any of the hazelnut cake remaining from Holy Rood day?" asked Ezra politely, "for Samuel here is smitten by it, Tom."

"'Twas gone by All Hallows, but I have some hedgerow pickle to accompany the cheese."

"Good, then sit on this cold Advent day and I shall tell thee of the evils and sad consequences of war." As he spoke, he continued to pull the fur from the hare and throw it on the fire, which spat back in anger.

Samuel gazed into the distance, whilst plucking absentmindedly at the animal in his large hands and simply said "pain." He, too, continued supping his mead as his old friend considered where to begin his story.

"Tell us," said William Henry, "of your service under Tancred."

Ezra finished eating a piece of cheese and washed it down with a large mouthful of mead. He cleared his throat and prepared to tell his friends, not for the first time, the story of his adventures in the Crusades.

"I served in a monastery on Mount Silpius outside the city walls of Antioch," he began, raising his hand skyward to indicate how far up the mountain the monastery was. "My Uncle Pergamon was a skinner and, being one of ten children, I was sent from our farm near Edessa to serve under my uncle and learn his skills. I served under him until the siege began in the October of that fateful year. Everyone from the monastery took shelter within the walls but I stayed with my uncle for we thought this would be a short-lived battle."

"Battle," repeated Samuel, adding the word 'fire' a few moments later.

William Henry, like the others, ignored Samuel's ranting and went to interrupt Ezra to ask how he could possibly know that the battle would be short-lived, but Tom intervened.

"Let the man speak."

Ezra took another mouthful of mead.

"After the siege had raged for a full month, Sir Tancred arrived with reinforcements. An elegant man he was, sat astride a white horse. By that time those outside the walls were almost starving."

Remembering those times of famine, he paused to eat another piece of cheese and to moisten his throat once again with the mead. He explained that he had learned some Greek, some Hebrew and even some French from the students at the monastery. So, desperate for food, he offered his services for what they were to an officer under Sir Tancred. But, in spite of the wealth of provisions brought by the invading force, little food was forthcoming in the days after his recruitment. Even then he fared only a little better than before, for there was insufficient food for everyone.

236

"We turned much into little and little into none. Nobody considered how quickly such an army could consume such great quantities of food."

After a few weeks, he explained, the soldiers took to eating their horses, but Tancred ordered an end to this inhuman practice when there were fewer than 1,000 steeds left. But strangely, Ezra pointed out, the food kept coming. Many wondered where the meat came from. Some said it was manna from heaven and others a miracle because it was around the time of the festival of the Immaculate Conception.

"Many claimed it to be an intercession by the Virgin Mary herself, but soon they realised that they had, in fact, been eating the flesh of the fallen foe. Turks were being eaten by the Christians simply to stay alive, although many of the knights refused to continue eating when they realised the truth and a great number starved to death before further supplies arrived, which was not before Twelfth Night."

Ezra paused, drank from his tankard and looked at Samuel. He wished he had not spoken of such deeds for he knew how much such remembrances hurt his friend.

"To add to our pain," he continued, thinking more of Samuel's pain than his own, "five days after the worst Christmastide known to man, an earthquake struck the city."

"Torment," said Samuel to himself, for nobody was listening to him.

"I was used to it, of course," continued Ezra, ignoring his friend's mumblings. "Earthquakes and tremors were frequent visitors to the mountain."

"Pray," said Samuel mournfully and his words were finally recognised by Ezra, who placed his hand on his friend's shoulder and spoke softly into his ear.

237

"He who would die well never considers death to be his neighbour."

Then, realising he had finished plucking the fur from the hare, he replaced the dead animal in his sack and examined the one Samuel had been working on. His strong rough hands had removed not only the fur, but also some flesh from the creature. Ezra placed it in the sack with the other one ready for gutting and continued with his story.

"By the aforementioned Twelfth Night three hundred souls had perished by the will of God and the actions of the Earth below our feet. 'Twas not valour, perhaps, but simply an instinct to prevail in spite of adversary and self pity that kept us alive. Each day, those who would raise the cross of St George knocked at the gates of the graveyard. They lived for the noblest of purpose and died in despair and sorrow. Their innocence lost. Life loosened from its human form. The red cheeks and bright eyes of youth now dimmed. If God is truly present in all places, I saw him not that Christmas. But, through good fortune and great bravery, the crusaders repelled a series of attacks during the famine and lived through the first week of the New Year until food arrived at the port."

He went on to relive many battles and adventures. As the weather improved and summer approached, the crusaders, with the aid of newly arrived siege engines, took the city.

"We kept the fortress for one year and one month. There were great signs. One starlit night a star fell from the sky into the walled city of Antioch."

It was never clear whether Ezra had ever actually met Tancred. The great Tancred. The Prince of Galilee, as he was known to his soldiers, rarely spoke to the lower ranks. But Ezra was an interpreter and, having improved his spoken French and English in the six months of the siege and the thirteen months that followed, Tancred agreed that he could accompany him when he finally returned home.

"But what of the Holy Lance?" asked William Henry, recalling Ezra's previous tales from the Crusades.

"Ah yes," said Ezra, realising he had forgotten an important episode of the tale.

"Hunger," said Samuel, but the word was overpowered by the crackling wood on the fire.

"When spring arrived," continued Ezra, "I was sent with a small force up the mountainside to secure the abandoned monastery that clung perilously to the hillside. Sent in spite of the earthquake three months before and," he continued, lowering his tone, "I was there that very day we discovered the Holy Lance. In one corner of the cloister it lay in a locked box. We were seeking food but found this branch, wrapped in the finest purple cloth. It gave off a radiance such that I had never seen. Pieces had been broken from it and it now formed a straight rod, almost like a small lance, which was how they covered up its true identity in the end. But we knew what it was from the small piece of parchment wrapped with it. The words were not in Greek or even Latin, but in Aramaic. An old local man was able to translate some of it. I alone now know the truth. Some said it was the Holy Lance. Others said it was the tree on which the Christ was crucified. But I know the truth."

Ezra still carried with him many of the Arab ways. He spoke of things his fellow companions had never heard of, of prophecy and the significance of certain numbers. Seven, he assured his friends, was the greatest of numbers.

"There are seven petitions in the Lord's Prayer and every wild beast known to man gestates in seven-day cycles," he told his eager audience. "The mouse and the hen carry their young for twenty-one days, the hare and the rat for twenty-eight; the duck for forty-two, the cat for fifty-six and the dog for sixty-three. Sheep for twenty-one times seven and man himself for forty-two times seven days."

But the others knew not of what he spoke.

"It's a piece of the one true cross," said William Henry, referring again to the piece of tree brought home from the war. "And now it is kept in the church of the Holy Rood."

"Named so because of it, too," replied Tom.

"Pain," said Samuel and Ezra again placed his hand upon his shoulder.

"We dwell too long in the affairs of the world," said Ezra, seeking to change the subject that had caused Samuel more melancholy. He placed his arm around his friend.

"I was born to be a soldier and I have a soldier's ways, my friend."

William Henry, who had sat a little impatiently throughout the tale, then looked at the troubled figure of Samuel and spoke.

"Anger rises in the breast, but to excuse the faults of others brings peace."

"Yes, let us forget the anguish of remembrances past," declared Tom, who had listened patiently throughout, "for tomorrow is the twenty-second day of December and our new King is to be crowned at Westminster Abbey that very day."

Tom refilled the jug and they spoke of Stephen of Blois who was to be crowned King after the death of Henry Beauclerc, who it was reported had died at St Denis-en-Lyon in France.

"King Henry was a good age," said William Henry. "Almost seventy years on God's good Earth."

"How did he die?" asked Ezra.

"It is reported that his death resulted from an excess of lampreys," replied the priest.

"What are lampreys?" asked Tom

"It's a slithery eel," replied William Henry. "These Normans eat anything."

"Is Stephen his son then?"

"No, but he's a grandson of the Conqueror. That's all we need to know."

"Why is not Stephen's older brother, Theobald, to be King?" asked William Henry.

"He is too weak," replied Ezra, "a first-cycle soul."

"What do you mean by such an expression, Ezra?" asked the priest.

"Ignore me, it is the ale talking," replied Ezra, hoping to conceal the words of his loose tongue.

"Theobald is blessed with the grace of contentment. He does not seek the crown," said Tom. "No, Stephen is a Blois, so Stephen shall be King. Anyway, he has the support of the Barons does he not, and that is what counts."

"My Rosalind thinks Matilda should be Queen, for she is Henry's daughter."

"Maud? I think not, Ezra," said the priest. "On the first part she is a woman and on the second part she is the wife of Geoffrey Plantagenet who would then be King in all but name."

"Let us pay homage to Stephen," declared Tom.

"King Stephen," they called and drank their fill.

A moment's silence fell on the men as they considered whether life would change after the coronation. Eventually, Ezra spoke up.

"I served Stephen's father in the Crusades."

"You served Tancred," declared Tom.

"We all served St George," said Ezra, "English, French, Romans and Spanish too. All in the service of God and St George."

"When will it be done?" asked Tom

"When will what be done?" came Ezra.

"The crowning of the King, of course."

"You'll hear the bells ring out. That'll tell us we have another Frenchman telling us what to do."

"Anyway," added Ezra, "his father went for the glory at Jerusalem. He didn't suffer the hardship we did at Antioch."

"Cold," said Samuel.

"Yes, it's getting cold. The sun is setting," said Ezra. But Samuel had noticed neither the setting of the sun nor the fall in the temperature. He was recalling some distant December day at Antioch. A day filled with regret and sadness.

"Let's be off home, Samuel," Ezra added as he said farewell to his friends and the two men began to walk away from the inn.

Just as they did so, Sir Guy de Bois, Lord of the three villages, rode passed and called out to them.

"Forget not the Christmas feast. Shall I see you there, my friends?"

"You shall indeed," called back Ezra and his warm breath, like pious incense, rose heavenward as it met the cold air of winter.

The knight looked suspiciously at the two plucked hares Ezra was carrying and his tenant thought about explaining that he had purchased them at the market. But Sir Guy simply rode off and Ezra called "God save the King!"

Ezra never believed the glowing ball that fell on Antioch that night to be a falling star. It may indeed only have been a fire ball from a siege engine; and all the other miracles and wonders could have been falsehoods to rouse the Christian forces too. But the tree was different. And it wasn't the Holy Lance, or the True Cross. It was none of these things. It was older still than these. The fruit of God's own work. 'Twas the Tree of Knowledge, thought Ezra, as he walked home that day. The Tree of Knowledge that stood in God's own garden alongside the Tree of Life. The True Cross of Christ was discovered by St Helena herself and was kept in the Church of the Holy Sepulchre in Jerusalem; so how could anyone believe that the piece of wood in our own Holy Rood church was the True Cross of Christ?

As they stumbled, full of honeycomb mead, along a straight path through the wood, a horseman approached and stopped in front of them.

"Where are you bound, Sir knight?" called Ezra, as Samuel felt instinctively for the absent sword at his side. The man was dark-skinned like Ezra and could easily have been from Assyria or somewhere near that distant land.

"I have business in York, but seek a bed on this cold night."

"An inn lies just along this road, Sir, the Three Bells. Ask for Tom. You may rest there for the night."

The traveller thanked them and proceeded in the direction of the inn.

~~~ الـ صمت من الـ عهد ~~~

The three hamlets surrounding the inn shared a plough and a mill and, on Christ's birthday, they shared a feast through the goodwill and courtesy of Sir Guy. All were welcome but each knew their place. The lords sat at the head of the table, then the landowners and the clerics and holy men of the three parishes. Next to them were the craftsmen and tradesmen and finally, the farthest from the fire, were the peasants. The lords drank French wine in flasks, the clerics drank local wine taken from a large oak barrel and the rest imbibed of honeycomb mead. Each guest took their own knife to hack away at the mutton and pheasant. There was sufficient for all but the best meat had gone by the time Ezra, Rosalind and Samuel gained their places at the serving table. The piece of land given to Ezra did not grant him the privileges of a landowner for it had been gifted to him by his Lordship.

The first of his Lordship's tithe barns to be emptied was used for the Christmas feast. The raging fire was fuelled by the hazelnut shells still left over from Holy Rood day. It was only when the fire subsided a little that Ezra could see the person sitting between William Henry and Tom the landlord.

"Is that the man we saw on the road three evenings past?" asked Ezra. Samuel looked and felt again at his side for an absent sword. He didn't need to speak. His actions confirmed it was the same man. Later that evening, after the revels and dancing had ceased, William Henry, Tom and the stranger joined Ezra and Samuel. Rosalind had left for home a few hours before, but Samuel, Ezra and the others were still there at cockcrow having spoken on many subjects, but mainly of the Holy Rood. Baldano, for this was the stranger's name, had learned from the locals of the old soldier who spoke in sentences of one word. A Saxon knight who spoke only of pain, death, wood, life, tree, wisdom, knowledge, betrayal, mercy, anguish and occasionally God. He had heard, too, of Ezra the great storyteller and the stranger pressed him to repeat some of the stories he told.

As the dying firewood crackled and the cock crowed outside, old Samuel stood up and raised his cup. "King." It was the most animated he had been for many a year.

~~~ الـ صمت من الـ عهد ~~~

When Ezra awoke in his own bed, the winter sun sat low in the sky and cast a crimson light through the shutter. He could not remember travelling home, nor could he recall what it was they had been speaking about the previous night. Had he been preaching again on the number seven? Had he been recalling again all he had been taught by his grandfather, so much of which he had forgotten and yet recalled under the influence of alcohol? He remembered speaking of his service at the monastery and could visualise Baldano listening patiently but Ezra struggled to recollect the detail of their conversation. He had spoken of the number seven, but was interrupted by William Henry. The priest recalled a reading from Job. *'He shall deliver thee in six troubles. Yea, in seven, there shall no evil touch thee.'* These were the priest's words but what else did they speak of?

In time, Ezra put the conversation, or what he could remember of it, behind him. And he did not think about the stranger again until spring. Then, one day, much of that Christmastide came to his mind again. Ezra was sure it was the work of the stranger. Had the man not spoken of travelling to York? And didn't Rosalind see him riding towards Upper Worbon a few days later? And that isn't the way to York. He was never seen again. Of course, there had been many travellers since. Most stayed overnight at the Three Bells on their journey. Some had used the blacksmith and some had asked about the history of the three villages. But none had appeared so furtive. None had made Ezra think so long on his grandfather's words. None caused him to think also of the blind man's warning.

245

Ezra and Rosalind had three children, or three that had survived at least, for there were as many more who had died. Two small girls passed from this world with a fever three winters ago. Their eldest child, Elizabeth, died in childbirth last year, along with the child in her womb. It was a frequent event where a baby was simply too big to pass into the world. The young mother-to-be died of exhaustion under the constant eye of Rosalind and the child inside her never saw the light of this world.

The three remaining children appeared healthy and were all looking forward to taking part in the procession from the parish church at Upper Worbon on the first Sunday of May. The youngest, Fanny, held hopes of being the May Queen one day but such an honour was rarely endowed outside the craftsmen of the three villages. The boys, John and Richard, were to be guards of honour and would follow the flag emblazoned with the red cross of St George. John was sorely affected by the death of his eldest sister and the little baby he was so looking forward to playing with. He took himself off to work on the land, day after day, digging and chopping down trees, returning to the house only to sleep and to sharpen the blade on his axe. He forgot it was Sunday and set off to the lower field as he had done each day since Elizabeth died and Ezra had to go after him.

"It's the Sabbath, John. You cannot work today, boy. In any case, there are no more trees to fell."

"There's a young sapling growing down by the convent wall," he replied.

"Let it be, John. It shall remind us of Betty and the little one. A constant reminder to you that life ends and life begins. It is the way of things, John."

It was only then that the boy cried. He had been unable to do so till that moment, unable to accept that his beloved sister had left this world. So they did leave the sapling and John tendered it as well as the vegetables he grew behind the house. It stood straight and tall, growing quicker than the boy could and, in later years, he would sit under it and remember his sister.

Everyone enjoyed the feast days when the villagers gathered together to celebrate their faith. The May Queen procession was the last such feast before the hard work of the summer that ended with the harvest. Every man, woman and child would take to the fields in August and September to fill the barns of Sir Guy, so that all could be fed through the winter.

Between the harvest and All Hallows on the first day of November fell Holy Rood day, when another great procession would be held, signalling that only the hazelnuts remained to be harvested.

And when that day came, Father William Henry, along with those elected to the three parish councils, went into the Holy Rood church at Widdemton to unlock and carry the Holy Lance in the procession.

It was on that day that Baldano's heinous crime was discovered. Not until the feast of the Holy Rood, when the Holy Lance—the very spear that pierced Christ's side—was removed from where it had been stowed for safekeeping, in a locked trunk in the presbytery, was this unholy deed revealed. Today this great and most sacred relic would not be paraded through the three villages after holy mass.

Sir Guy, who waited outside the church alongside two knights carrying the flag of St George and the flag of the de Bois family, roared his anger at the news. A third knight, appointed

247

to carry the Holy Lance through the three villages, swore an oath of retribution.

All the villagers were questioned about the loss of the relic but none knew of its whereabouts or how it could have been stolen from the church.

That afternoon, the folk from the three villages set off to gather hazelnuts; the same hazelnuts that Ezra had collected as a child to make the red dye used by the scribes at the monastery in his homeland. The same hazelnuts whose shells were used to provide warmth against the winter snow at the Christmas feast. The same hazelnuts that made the cake that fed the villagers on cold autumn evenings. But there was no joy in the gathering of nuts that Holy Rood day, just a sadness after searching the church and its graveyard. And a reproachful tone from William Henry and a reproving look from his Lordship. Who would steal their treasured possession? Ezra thought he knew and he feared that his own loose tongue, on the evening of that last Christmas feast, may have been the cause. So he kept his peace and decided not to speak of his suspicions.

His grandfather had told him of such men. The Magi, he called them. Those men who would protect the secret that Ezra had never revealed and, even now, could remember little detail of. A secret he promised to take to his grave. Their treasured possession had not been the one True Holy Cross. Nor had it been the Holy Lance, the spear that pierced the side of Christ. Older still than this was the ancient wooden branch he had brought back from Antioch, back from the monastery where he had learned of its origins from the Aramaic writing on the piece of parchment. This was no spear, nor a cross, but a bough from the Tree of Knowledge, that same tree from which Eve plucked the fruit that promised eternal life. And Ezra knew who had taken it. He had seen that purple amulet before, around the necks of infrequent visitors to the Monasterion Lucienus.

He stayed awake that night whilst all the three villages slept. Sitting in the small, overcrowded scullery, holding an identical purple amulet in his hand, he recalled the earliest memories of his childhood, even before he left the family farm at Potbelly Hill to work for his childless Uncle Pergamon at Antioch. He was only thirteen years old but, as the second eldest boy and with nine siblings, there were simply too many mouths to feed. His grandfather had told him that the amulet contained a piece of the Sarv-e- Šēṯ, the Tree of Knowledge and it would keep him safe. By rights it should have been passed to his elder brother along with everything else, but his grandfather took pity on a child being sent from his family home to a distant city.

Ezra, or Ezekiel as he was known then, had some experience of skinning goats and other animals so his uncle was pleased to secure his services, particularly as Antioch was now a thriving city that served the pilgrims who travelled from Europe to Jerusalem. For many such pilgrims a journey was essential at least once in their lifetime if they were to secure a plenary indulgence, or free passage through purgatory. Ezra was not certain that this was simply another of his grandfather's stories but, as he grew up in Antioch, he did meet many who were travelling to and from the holy city. His grandfather had also told him stories of the men who wore the purple amulet but, in some strange way, Ezra knew that these were not the fantasies that the old man normally related to him.

Ezra rolled the talisman in the palm of his large hand. He would give that amulet to his eldest son John if he should survive him and, perhaps, he would even reveal the secret of its origin in order that such a mystery did not die with him. But

249

he would never disclose what he knew of the loss of the Holy Lance. He recognised in his heart that he had all but witnessed this malicious enterprise and had remained silent for fear of what might befall him. For he knew that the eyes of the Magi were ever watchful.

9

Darkness enveloped the bedroom. Cally stretched out her arm and felt Tyler next to her with the tips of her fingers. She lay still, listening carefully and thought she could hear her mobile phone ringing downstairs. Normally she brought it to bed with her in case of emergencies but she must have forgotten. She had sat up late with Tyler, talking about Galen's strange tales of religious cults and his mysterious visitor, until she became overtired and was desperate for sleep at the end of a long day. Perhaps it was Tyler's phone, she thought for a moment, wondering whether to wake him. But then she remembered that his mobile had a different ring tone. She was only slowly awakening and her thoughts were still jumbled in her mind. The phone stopped ringing and her head slumped back on the pillow. She lay there for a few seconds but realised that there was no chance of returning to sleep while she was left wondering who might be calling her in the middle of the night. She got up, put on her slippers and went downstairs, turning the lights on as she went. Tyler remained in a disturbed sleep, mumbling about strange-sounding places and people.

There was one missed call. It was Ashley. She poured herself a glass of water, drank most of it and called him back.

"Have you seen the newspapers?" he asked before she had time to speak.

"Are you mad, Ashley? It's..." she paused to look at the time, "four a.m., Jesus," she said. "Ashley, it's four in the morning, what are you talking about?"

"Cally, the tabloids have got your face all over them, along with Livingstone and Hallet."

Cally couldn't grasp what Ashley was talking about. What newspapers?

"Ashley, look, I'm sorry, I'm still half asleep. What are you talking about?"

"Get dressed and get yourself a newspaper, Cally. And do it now."

"How did you get hold of a newspaper at this time of the night?"

"Some mates who work up on the press called me. Look I've got to go. Give me a call later."

Cally got dressed, grabbed her keys and managed to leave without waking Tyler. She returned a few minutes later, pale and shaken, and clinging on to several tabloid newspapers that had just been delivered to the local newsagents. She went into the kitchen, threw the newspapers on the table and switched the kettle on.

Tyler came downstairs, half asleep and in the opening stages of getting dressed.

"Where were you? I was just getting dressed to go and find you. You left your mobile here."

"I went out to get the newspapers."

Tyler looked at her strangely, as if she had lost her mind. For a moment he wondered whether he was still in one of his dreams. He didn't speak but the expression on his face required an immediate explanation.

252

"Look," she said, pushing the stack of newspapers towards him.

He took one and scanned the front page. He grabbed another, then another. There were slight variations but most contained photographs of Hallet, Livingstone or Cally or, in most cases, all three. One carried the headline: *'Spot the difference'*. It went on to describe how Metropolitan Police forensics expert, Cally Boyce, mistook a middle-aged, middle-class, white man for a young black man half his age. It went on to criticise the failure of police to apprehend the murderer of either Charlene Hallet or Nelson Kosoto, who had died in separate incidents in the same house two months apart. Some reporters asked why the murder scene of the attack in December was left open and allowed to be used by drug addicts and the homeless, destroying important forensic evidence. This serious failure, the article read, was repeated after the second murder. The house, it said, was now the location of three separate murders, but it failed to state that the first was nearly two hundred years ago.

The articles condemned the efforts of Bertoni and Redpath, censured Chief Inspector Bent, but saved their harshest words for Cally. She had been singled out for the severest of criticism for claiming to have found the DNA of David Hallet at the house, when he had plainly never visited the premises. The newspapers then stated that the officers involved then arrested Livingstone for the same murder, before releasing Hallet. Her incompetence, said one newspaper, was beyond belief.

"That's just not true," said Cally. "H division arrested Livingstone, not us. This is such a load of rubbish. I didn't pick them out in an identity parade. I would have noticed if one of them had been black. I was sorting DNA. And not any DNA, but DNA that had been corrupted in a damp and dirty wreck of a house."

Tyler threw the newspaper on the table with the others and put his arms around Cally. Nobody spoke, he just stood holding her for a few minutes. Neither felt like going back to bed, so they showered and sat drinking coffee and pulling apart the wildly inaccurate reporting of the tabloid press.

Ashley called her back an hour later to tell her that they had received a couple of leads on the whereabouts of Donny Clarke. He was going to pick up Steve and check them out.

Tyler tried a little vainly to console Cally and told her to try to forget about the press, before reluctantly admitting that he was having lunch with a reporter that day.

"It's that guy I met at the seminar, Paul Gilligan. I told you the other day that he wants to produce an article on me for *Research Today*."

"Be careful, Tyler. Look what just happened to me. You don't need the publicity. After all, other firms are already trying to headhunt you."

"What harm can it do?"

Cally picked up some of the newspapers on the table. "Quite a lot, Tyler, quite a lot. Anyway, think about it. You had that trouble with the animal rights activists a couple of years ago."

"That was all a misunderstanding. We don't even experiment on animals."

"I'm just trying to be helpful, Tyler. Be careful what you wish for," she added, pointing at the bundle of newspapers on the table.

~~~ الـ صمت من الـ عهد ~~~

Fortunately it was another hot and sunny day so Cally didn't look out of place in the sunglasses she wore as a partial disguise. Most of her fellow commuters were reading one of the tabloids she had seen earlier that day. But, fortunately, none made the connection on the crowded underground train.

Tyler spent most of the morning trying to make contact with Galen to find out whether he had any more news on the Clinchman project. Galen was conducting a funeral and, after an embarrassing incident a few years ago, he always ensured his mobile phone was switched off during such proceedings. So little work was completed before Paul Gilligan called to say he was waiting outside the office block. Tyler went straight down and they walked the short distance to Ristorante Gallura.

The restaurant was strangely busy for midweek and Tyler thought about suggesting they went elsewhere. But he had reserved, so he just asked for a quiet table. That wasn't possible and their discussion began under the distraction of noisy diners and, more significantly, of Tyler continually thinking back to Cally's problems with the press.

Conducting the initial interview over lunch had seemed a good idea, in spite of the babbling crowd, so Tyler tried to relax and portray an image of self-assured confidence. He reminded himself not to drink too much wine.

"What are lampreys?" asked Paul as he scanned the large menu.

"Eels," Tyler replied knowingly.

"You have an incredible mind, Tyler. How do you know all these things?"

"I don't know. I just seem to retain so much rubbish."

"Actually, the vegetarian option looks good," said Paul when the waitress arrived at the table to take the order.

"And I'll have the sea bass," added Tyler, before asking Paul if he wanted wine.

"I'm fine, actually."

"Just water then, please."

Paul covered all the usual information about education, achievements and any particularly innovative or groundbreaking work that Tyler had been involved in. But, just as things seemed to be going well and at the moment their main course was placed in front of them, Paul delivered a question that Tyler had not anticipated.

"When we were in the bar at the seminar," asked the reporter, "you mentioned some interesting work you were doing around the concept of DNA repeating itself. You said you thought that DNA might not be personally unique like everyone currently believes."

Tyler was thrown for a moment and his reply wasn't particularly plausible or persuasive.

"I can't recall that, Paul. Are you sure it wasn't Perry who said that?"

"Yes. Perry was there, but it was you who mentioned it, Tyler. Something about some lab work that showed an identical genome in people who were born a couple of hundred years apart."

"Oh, yes," he replied rather unconvincingly. "We got to the bottom of that. Contamination, I'm afraid, but please don't mention it in the article. My boss is obsessed with controlling contamination. He reckons it is the one thing that keeps us competitive."

"Fine. No problem."

"Erm," stuttered Tyler, "what did Perry think of the idea?"

"I think he was very impressed. I wouldn't be surprised if Codon tried to headhunt you, Tyler. Perry was singing your praises to his boss the next morning over breakfast."

"Yes, I have had a couple of calls."

They finished their meal and Paul explained that he needed to visit the Double Helix office soon. He wanted to get an action photograph for the article and repeated his earlier suggestion that Cally might like to be in it too.

"I think she's trying to avoid the press at the moment. You've seen today's newspapers, presumably."

"I didn't know whether to mention it. It'll blow over. These tabloid reporters lose interest in stories very easily. One day dog attacks are headlines and the next day they're not. Fickle bunch. Tell her not to worry."

Despite his hesitant response, Tyler thought he had handled the tricky questioning at the end of the interview rather well.

Paul arranged to visit the offices of Double Helix Limited the following week. The actual date needed to fit around the availability of Cally, which Tyler said was a little unpredictable at the moment. Paul explained that the editor would not sanction the cost of a professional photographer to travel over from the States for one shot, but their picture editor could work wonders with digital photographs, so he could make even Paul's work look good.

That evening, Galen called at the house to report back to Tyler and Cally about his research into Clinchman's descendents. He had received the numerous messages left by Tyler that morning and could sense a little desperation creeping in to the latter ones. But he also wanted to provide some counselling and succour to Cally. She had been pestered by press photographers at regular intervals during the day, but Bent spoke to her in the morning about dealing with it. He warned her not to avoid the camera as this makes you look furtive. So she smiled at the photographers but didn't answer any of the questions shouted in her direction. She was pleased to get the day over and equally pleased to have the company of her two favourite men for dinner.

"I'm not sure I can eat very much," confessed Tyler. "I had quite a big lunch with Paul Gilligan. I didn't get much work done today."

"Cook some pasta, Tyler," replied Cally, "Galen and I can eat most of it."

"Not too much cheese for me, please," called Galen.

"Tyler loves cheese. I sometimes think he is addicted to it. And he so enjoys making fresh pesto. It's the smell of the crushed basil. He says it reminds him of some distant place, so far beyond his earliest memories that perhaps it happened in his dreams, rather than his childhood."

Once they were all sitting down together, Galen explained how he had traced Clinchman's descendents. He began with Sidney Walter Clinchman himself, who was born in 1740 in the London Borough of Stepney and died in 1802. Stepney, said Galen, had its own borough status at that time but was later merged to create Tower Hamlets. Tyler grew a little impatient with the peripheral information Galen insisted on reporting but decided not to complain.

"Sidney married Ivy Leghorn in 1764 and they had six children. Which was not unusual at that time," Galen pointed out.

Then he took them through the history of the six offspring. Two had died in childhood from consumption, or tuberculosis as it is now known.

"It was quite contagious, so it's surprising it didn't spread throughout the family. Some people seem to have a natural resistance to it, I think, or perhaps a guardian angel was protecting them."

He had managed to trace all of them, largely through the census conducted in 1820 and was confident that he had found all the offspring of the four remaining children right through to the present day.

"And?" asked Tyler.

"Absolutely no sign of Mr James Henry Richards, born in Stevenage, Hertfordshire, in 1935 and who died in neighbouring Essex sixty-three years later in 1999."

"You're sure?" asked Tyler.

"Absolutely," he answered confidently and he opened up a large sheet of paper on which he had set out a complete family tree of the descendents of Mr Clinchman. "No sign of Jimmy Richards at all."

Cally could see the disappointment on Tyler's face. She wanted to change the subject to avoid further discussion on something that had obviously upset Tyler and also to sidestep any further talk about her own publicity, but Galen began to fill in the details of his investigation, explaining about his work with parish records and even calls to the crematorium.

"The four surviving children of Sidney and Ivy Clinchman all had children of their own. I managed to trace the names and birthdays of all their ancestors. There were four direct relatives born around the time of James Richards."

"Just four?" questioned Cally.

"Yes, it was seven generations on from Sidney Clinchman. There were no actual Clinchmans, but there certainly weren't any Richards either."

"But, just four?" asked Cally again in disbelief.

"Yes, Cally," Galen answered, "Just four. You must remember that this was between 1920 and 1940. Vast numbers of young adult males were killed in the Great War. Those who survived then became victims of the influenza contagion that swept across Europe after the First World War."

Galen could see the disappointment on Tyler's face. He looked as if he had reached another dead end in his current project. Galen could contain himself no longer.

"What is this all about, Tyler?"

But Tyler remained silent, obviously still contemplating whether to share his thoughts with his oldest and most trusted friends. The silence lasted a few seconds before Galen began taking him again through the various names on the family tree, but Tyler called Galen's informative talk to an end. He had heard enough to concede that both Galen and Cally needed to know about his recent findings regarding Clinchman and Richards. He poured himself a glass of wine, topped up Cally's glass too and began telling his friends about his discovery. He explained that he believed, rather reluctantly, that DNA replicated itself in certain descendents and, perhaps, it could be that this occurs every seven or fourteen generations. He took them through the various tests he had conducted on the old clavicle bone and told them about the exact match on the DNA database.

"Your two sets of identical DNA were taken from two men directly related and separated by seven generations," said Galen.

"Well, so I thought," answered Tyler. "But you have now told me that the two men were not related. So it's back to the drawing board."

"So, if Richards was the seven-times-removed grandson of Sidney Clinchman, you think that would prove that DNA recurs every seven generations? Is that what you are saying?" asked Galen. Tyler nodded.

"I'll have that drink now," said Galen, taking the bottle and pouring some into his glass.

"But you've just proved the theory wrong, Galen."

"Perhaps. But what if Clinchman, or indeed one of his offspring, had a child out of wedlock? That would explain it wouldn't it?"

Cally and Tyler had not considered that explanation. Cally picked up the large sheet of paper outlining the family tree. She wondered where such an indiscretion may have occurred. Were people any more promiscuous in the eighteenth century than the nineteenth or twentieth? But, of course, it could have happened at any time in that long period. Tyler's countenance brightened at the possibility of a solution to the puzzle even though the chance of finding the evidence was remote. But he was used to solving the most challenging problems with ease. He assured himself that there must be a logical explanation.

"How would we ever find that out?" he finally asked, unable to clear that particular question from his mind.

"I don't know," answered Galen, "but I'm certainly going to have a good try at doing so. This is great stuff," he added, jumping up out of his seat.

Then, suddenly, they both noticed that Cally had stood up, walked into the kitchen and was pacing up and down.

"Are you okay?" asked Tyler.

"No, I am not bloody okay," she said loudly and turned round to face him.

"You knew all along, didn't you?" But Tyler didn't have time to answer. "That's why you wanted me to ask David Hallet if his family had lived in the Wharf Street area, wasn't it?" Again, she didn't leave time for a response. These may not have been rhetorical questions in the true sense, but Cally certainly didn't require answers. She had worked those out for herself.

"You absolute bastard!" she screamed. "You let the tabloids bloody destroy me. You stood by and let them screw my career and you did nothing. You didn't even tell me what you suspected. You knew that the DNA I collected from Wharf Street wasn't Hallet's at all, didn't you? That DNA came from under the wallpaper. I see it now. When the killer struck the blow, the machete tore the wallpaper, revealing the old DNA and this was smeared on the body as it slid down the wall. Now tell me you hadn't worked all that out, Tyler. And don't forget, I know just how clever you are."

Galen stood in silence, watching his friends' relationship crumble in front of him and, despite his training in such matters, he felt helpless.

Galen was not the archetypal self-deprecating young priest. He was a modern IT-literate pastor, trained in restoring broken relationships. But this wasn't anything like the examples he came across during his training. This was his best friends breaking up their relationship right in front of him. Tyler accused Cally of becoming obsessed with David Hallet's innocence. She was, he said, pre-occupied with the conclusion that Hallet did not kill Kosoto. It was destroying her relationship with her colleagues and now it was going to destroy their relationship too. There was only a million-to-one chance that his theory of recurring DNA was true, Tyler told her as forcefully as his sanguine temperament would allow. And there was a ten-million-to-one chance that it occurred in the case of the Wharf Street murders. But, for Cally, it explained everything. It suited her to believe it, because it fitted into the tiny world she had created where David Hallet was innocent. Tyler's words cut like a knife but Cally did not permit him to take the high moral ground. She rounded on him for his lack of trust in Galen and herself. She repeated again the nightmare she had gone through without Tyler once considering that he should share the information he had.

As the argument raged on, the gaps between the insults grew longer and Galen thought about filling those gaps with attempts at reconciliation. But few peace treaties are signed in the heat of battle. In every battle there has to be a winner and a loser although, in reality, everyone loses.

It was getting late but Galen was reluctant to leave them in case one of them left the family home. His training had taught him that much. Keep the unit intact, retain the family group. It is much easier to repair a damaged partnership if the couple concerned are still co-habiting.

Eventually it became so late that he had to leave. He begged them not to make any rash decisions and they assured him that they wouldn't.

The argument between his friends had prevented him from telling them about the website he had found the previous day. Galen had managed to recover the file about the religious sect and it contained one piece of information that registered with him, particularly after what Tyler had said earlier. The strange website claimed that man would live for fourteen-times-fourteen generations. It referred to something called metanoia, a type of reincarnation of the soul. It also contained sections from the gospel of St Matthew. There were many references to the Magi, who it referred to as the Sons of Seth. But who were the Sons of Seth?

~~~ الـ صمت من الـ عهد ~~~

The following day Redpath finally located Donny Clarke and brought him in for questioning while two constables searched the flat he was currently sleeping in for evidence. They found his mobile phone, but if there had been any footage of Livingstone killing Charlene, it had been deleted.

While Bertoni and Redpath interviewed Clarke, Cally examined the mobile phone and continued her work on the machete. When they stopped for lunch it was apparent that Clarke was going to admit nothing. The phone provided no evidence to help the case and two young women came forward to provide alibis for Clarke and Livingstone for the day Kosoto was murdered. The case against Livingstone was disintegrating as quickly as the previous case against Hallet.

Bertoni called his colleagues at H division to tell them that Sissulu must be lying. He instructed them to interview him again and suggested they gave him a particularly hard time. Bertoni needed to make sure that Sissulu was lying before he released Clarke.

Cally examined the machete again but found no fingerprints. She found the DNA of both Charlene Hallet and Nelson Kosoto on the blade, along with some fragments of the wallpaper and some plaster. She found the DNA of two other people, but neither was on the database and the samples looked very old.

The handle had been wiped clean with fabric, perhaps the sleeve of a coat. Using tweezers she removed some fabric fibres and made a note to try to match these with Sissulu's clothing. Whoever had done it had wiped the blade too, but they had been careful to avoid the sharp cutting edge. It was from here that the DNA specimens were taken. Closer examination showed that a small section of the blade had been blunted and Cally assumed that this was where it had struck the wall, as it was surrounded by tiny particles of plaster and wallpaper. There was some earth and brick on one side of the weapon and some cat's hairs on the other. The brick did not match the samples taken from the walls of Wharf Street and Cally concluded that this had happened when Sissulu dumped the machete on the piece of wasteland.

Each fragment of evidence was placed in a sterile container and labelled. The blood samples were divided and separate containers used with different coloured labels. These extra samples would be made available to the defence counsel if required. Finally, Cally took small samples of Charlene Hallet's and Kosoto's blood and set about trying to establish the approximate dates these had appeared on the blade.

Suddenly the door opened and Bertoni's head appeared.

"We're off to pick up a friend of Sissulu," he told Cally. "Sweet Boy just told H division that Clarke sent the murder footage to his friend, Ahmed. We've got a couple of possible addresses for his whereabouts."

After he left, Cally re-examined Clarke's mobile phone but all the records had been deleted and there were no contacts in the address book. She sat looking at it wondering if there was any way of retrieving old data.

Cally's laboratory was adjacent to her colleague's office and this led into the main part of the station. With Bertoni and Redpath out she was able to work in silence, except for the murmur of distant voices in the main office. She returned to the machete and was studying it closely under the microscope when she was startled by a phone ringing next door. She considered ignoring it but thought it might be Bertoni calling her for some assistance. She left her work and went through to the next office. It was Bertoni's line and she picked it up, almost expecting to hear his voice.

A nervous voice told her his name was Ahmed and he was scared. He was asking for police protection.

"I want to go into the police protection scheme," he said in a trembling voice as if the words had been learned by heart.

She wanted to tell him he had been watching too much TV but discretion encouraged her to choose not to.

"Where are you, Ahmed? I'll get Inspector Bertoni to pick you up."

Wrong choice of words, she thought, before changing the context.

"I'll get my colleague to meet you."

"No, I don't want Bertoni or his idiot sidekick. Sweet Boy told me all about them. You meet me," he demanded.

She hesitated, wondering whether to call Ashley on her mobile while she kept Ahmed on the line.

"You come or I go into hiding. You'll never find me. I want guaranteed protection from that murderer Livingstone."

"Have you got the mobile phone with the evidence on it, Ahmed?" she asked softly.

"That's my million dollar chip. I want a new identity, the works. For the mobile, I want a new life."

"We're going to get Livingstone for both murders with or without your help, Ahmed, but I want to help you. Will you let me help you by sending Inspector Bertoni?"

"Both murders?" he asked and she tried again with the same proposal, trying to ignore his last remark. But Ahmed was resolved. Either Cally met him and took him somewhere safe or he would wipe the footage from the mobile phone.

Cally agreed and he gave her the name of a pub just outside the gates of Victoria Park in Hackney. She was to be there in fifteen minutes. She thought about calling Bertoni but decided

266

she didn't want to do anything that might cost them the footage on the mobile phone.

When Cally pulled up outside the pub, there was nobody to be seen. Well, nobody she thought fitted Ahmed's description. She realised he was probably hiding, waiting to see if anyone else was around. He was the type to suspect a trap. Then, suddenly the passenger door opened and a young Indian-looking boy jumped in the seat next to her, shouting at her to drive. Paranoia filled the car and she drove off looking around to see if anyone saw him get into the car.

Ten minutes later Cally parked the car in a quiet side street and explained that, if Ahmed wanted a deal, she would need to call Bertoni.

"I'm just the forensic officer, Ahmed, I don't have the authority to do deals. I certainly don't have the authority to set you up in a safe house," she added, thinking he would be impressed by this comment. He was.

"Okay, do the deal. But no wise stuff. I just have to press this delete button and the evidence of Bunny killing Charlene is history, lady."

"Yes, Ahmed, and you'll be history too." Cally turned the car engine off, worried that he was about to destroy evidence that could secure a prosecution. She was losing her patience with him. "Think!" she screamed at him, "without that phone clip you have absolutely nothing to give up and you'll be thrown back to the wolves."

The boy, for that was all he was, trembled at the thought and was unsure about what he should do. Eventually, he pleaded with her to end this nightmare, so she called Ashley and they agreed to meet back at the station. Fifteen minutes later Cally drove the car into the safety of the police car park.

"I want protection 24-7!" shouted Ahmed at Bertoni from the passenger seat. "A safe house and a new identity."

"What is he going on about?" Cally heard Steve ask his boss in the background.

All Cally could think about on the drive back was Ahmed's reaction when she told him that they would get Livingstone for both murders. She wanted to press him further on the matter but didn't want to prejudice the case. The most important thing was to get hold of the evidence on the mobile phone that Ahmed was clinging to. But she was preoccupied with Ahmed's reaction to her statement that Livingstone was to be charged with both murders.

Perhaps Tyler was right. Maybe she was obsessed with David Hallet's innocence. But if Livingstone didn't kill Nelson Kosoto, that left only Hallet.

The interview with Ahmed took only a few minutes but, in the absence of his parents, they had to wait for a youth worker to arrive because he was only fourteen. Fourteen, Cally thought, yet exposed to such a violent life of crime. Even if they were able to provide all the protection he wanted, nothing could prevent the sort of person Ahmed was going to become without a life-changing intervention.

That afternoon, with the video evidence of Charlene being violently murdered safely in their possession, Bertoni and Redpath went to arrest Livingstone. The evidence also proved that the footage was sent from Donny Clarke's phone, so he was arrested at the same time. They were interviewed briefly and kept overnight before being charged in the morning. The two young women who had provided them with alibis were also interviewed and, eventually, retracted their statements. Chief Superintendent Bent made his presence felt on the successful arrest of Livingstone. He hovered in the background as Livingstone, Clarke and the women were questioned.

Faced with the overwhelming evidence from the mobile phone and the DNA evidence from the machete, even the resourceful Barnabas Cartwright could do little to prevent his client being charged with the murder of Charlene Hallet.

~~~ الـ صمت من الـ عهد ~~~

With Bent around, Cally arrived at the station early the next morning. It was going to be a big day and she wanted to be part of it. She walked into her colleague's office with the intention of telling them that she now believed that David Hallet murdered Kosoto. That would make Redpath feel good, seeing her change her position so radically. But she never got the chance. As she stepped into the room, Ashley couldn't wait to tell her his news.

"Livingstone has confessed to both murders. Double bubble, Cally." He was so ebullient that he failed to notice her reaction.

Cally retreated to her laboratory but she couldn't concentrate. All she could think about was that Hallet had killed Kosoto. Her whole body screamed out to her. But common sense told her to ignore this overwhelming conviction and walk away from an almost impossible situation. Any suggestion that Hallet was guilty was only ever going to end in disaster. She needed time to think, so she stayed away from Redpath and Bertoni. For the moment, she went back to collating the evidence that proved Livingstone guilty.

In the end, it wasn't a particularly busy day for Cally. There was a hurriedly arranged press conference, of course, but she was not expecting any apologies. She didn't receive any and went home feeling somewhat less pleased with herself than she expected or deserved. Hallet's guilt still bothered her, but she never got the chance to find out why Ahmed was so surprised at Livingstone being charged with both murders. And obviously now that Livingstone had confessed to them nobody would want to complicate what was a very straightforward case. She had to consider her position. Taking an opposite stance to her colleagues had only managed to alienate her before. However strongly she felt, perhaps staying in step was the safest way forward.

But Cally was never someone to simply toe the line. She could never keep her own counsel. So, while she was waiting for Tyler to return home from work, she called Galen and asked him for a favour. She wanted him to try to find out what he could about David Hallet's army service. She was still perturbed by the absence of any photographs at the Hallet home. Surely there would be a photo of him in uniform.

"Just between you and me," she suggested to Galen, before she realised she was actually expecting him to take sides in her argument with Tyler.

"Sorry," she said, "I shouldn't have asked that."

"I don't mind, Cally, but you really need to sort this thing out with Tyler. This isn't something that should bring your relationship to an end."

By the time Tyler arrived home, Cally had resolved to bring their argument to a close. She told him about her conversation with Galen and realised that she was behaving no differently to him.

"Although," she added, "you had a reason for keeping that information to yourself. Of course you have a need for confidentiality in your work," she hesitated, wanting to continue with her offer of peace. Tyler seized on that pause and intercepted her apology.

"Let's just put all that behind us, shall we?" asked Tyler and they kissed. It was more a kiss of friendship than passion for they were friends first and lovers second. This wasn't a case of making up by making love. Simple day-to-day arguments ended up in bed. This incident left scars but they were only there to remind them both of how much they loved each other.

Later that evening Galen called to find out if Cally had made the peace with Tyler. He was pleased to learn she had.

"Oh, by the way," he added, "finding out about Hallet's army service was quite simple. Dishonourable discharge after serving three years in military prison for manslaughter."

The words made Cally gasp. She tried to stifle her reaction. At the risk of re-opening the wounds that created those scars, Cally decided to share Galen's news with Tyler. He turned out to be just the right person to consult. He put aside the argument and listened to Cally's thoughts on why Hallet killed Kosoto.

Obviously there was no record of Hallet killing someone while in the army. These were army records and not a police matter. According to police records, Hallet did not have a criminal record, even though he had actually killed somebody. She then told Tyler about Ahmed's reaction to her telling him that Livingstone was going to be charged with both murders.

"He obviously thought that Livingstone had not killed Kosoto," she said, then changed her mind. "Not thought," she added, "he seemed to know Livingstone had not killed Kosoto."

Tyler just sat and listened while Cally expanded on her various theories. They all seemed to fly but a crash landing was inevitable because even she couldn't explain why Livingstone would actually confess to a murder he didn't commit.

"That's an easy one," said Tyler. "If he goes down for Charlene's murder, he's simply a woman killer. Not much credibility in prison, I suspect. But killing a rival gang leader — that probably gets you heaps of respect inside. And, if he is definitely going down for one murder, why not two? The sentences will run concurrently anyway."

Cally recalled a similar comment by her colleagues and had to agree that this made sense. But what about the machete? How did Hallet get his hands on Livingstone's machete? Again, Tyler had the answer. The scenario he presented was equally as plausible. Hallet went out driving and, in all likelihood, often went to Wharf Street where his beloved daughter had been murdered. He had sat outside in the car on many occasions. Then, one day when Kosoto and his gang were inside, Livingstone arrived with the Mile End gang. There was a big fight. In his escape, Livingstone dropped the machete. Hallet realised that Kosoto was probably alone in the house, so he went inside, found the machete and murdered Kosoto. He dropped the weapon, which Sissulu later found and wiped clean because he thought it was used by Livingstone. Then Sissulu dumped the weapon.

"Everyone assumed that Livingstone returned to the house and killed Kosoto. And Livingstone isn't going to deny it, is he?" asked Tyler.

With two perfectly logical explanations Tyler was, once again, Cally's hero. Now it really was the sort of argument that ended up in bed.

Later that night it was Tyler's turn for a confession about his indiscretion at the seminar. It was now apparent to him that he had told Piruz and Paul about his discovery and he was really worried about the consequences. He tried to dismiss his concerns by returning to Cally's dilemma. She was convinced of Hallet's guilt and Tyler now supported her view.

"Why don't you just speak to Ashley about it?" he suggested. "He is your boss."

"What, take Steve out of the loop? Anyway, technically Bent is my boss."

"Do it outside of work then. Pop round to see Ashley. Tell him how you feel. Tell him that, if he doesn't agree, you will walk away and not mention it again."

She looked at him and went to protest. How could she walk away from her conviction that Hallet was guilty?

"Come on, Cally, just tell him calmly the logic behind your beliefs."

~~~ ال صمت من ال عهد ~~~

As Tyler left home the following morning, fragments of a dream from the night before began to connect, forming a strange landscape of ancient ruins. Perhaps he had been dreaming about a holiday he and Cally had taken in some foreign land. As the tube train clattered through the stations, he quietened his mind and tried to reconstruct the dream.

The offices of Double Helix were fully air conditioned. The walk from the underground station was only a little more bearable than the train journey. It was a hot, early September morning and it was a relief to step into the cool reception area. Tyler placed his ID card against the reader and the glass doors swished open. The offices were spacious and cool, and he nodded to his colleagues as he walked to his office.

Once he had logged on to his computer, Tyler began writing up his report. For added confidentiality he decided to do this himself. William always insisted on a written report. Everything needed to be documented. Tyler had done this at various intervals during his investigation. He referred to his earlier notes as he began the section on Clinchman's ancestry, but his mind kept returning to the dream.

Tyler stopped writing mid-sentence. He could hear a buzzing sound, then realised it was his mobile phone. He had switched it to mute to ensure he was not disturbed. But he couldn't resist looking to see who was calling for he was already finding it difficult to concentrate. It was Galen. Tyler thought it might be connected to his investigation, so took the call.

"Hi, Tyler, I thought you weren't going to answer for a moment. I was just about to give up."

"What's the problem, Galen? Have you found something out about Clinchman?"

"No," answered Galen, who then began to explain something unconnected with Tyler's work. As usual it started from the very beginning and Tyler wasn't really listening. His mind began to reconstruct his dream from the previous night. The places seemed so real. He had visited them many times. He felt guilty for missing his night-time friends during his waking hours. There was a madness about the whole concept. *This* was the real world. The world of his dreams was distant and vague. Sometimes, like last night, the locations reminded him of some past holiday. Ancient ruins, temples, mysterious places in a strange and distant world. The locations in his dreams changed but the people remained the same. Cally was always there, or rather someone like Cally. In his dreams he knew it was her but she didn't always look like Cally.

"Are you listening, Tyler?" Galen asked before explaining that he was in the coffee bar around the corner from his friend's office. He didn't want to talk on the phone, so wouldn't tell Tyler why he needed to meet him so urgently.

Tyler was upset at having to leave his work but, as Galen had been instrumental in the success of the project, he closed his laptop, put it in his briefcase and took it with him, rather than locking it away.

The cafe was empty apart from a young foreign woman who spoke only enough English to take an order for a coffee. Galen was just purchasing a croissant when Tyler arrived. He looked pale. At first Tyler thought he had been spending too much time on his laptop. But it wasn't anything as obvious as that.

"Not the most popular place in town," Tyler remarked as he looked around the dimly lit and empty cafe. But he soon realised that Galen had deliberately chosen this unpopular venue for their meeting. He wanted to talk to Tyler in complete privacy.

"What's all this about, Galen? Cally and I are fine now. We don't need any more counselling. Although we are grateful of your help," he added, thinking he sounded a little ungrateful.

Galen shook his head and Tyler realised it was not about Cally. "Have you found something out about Clinchman and Richards?" Tyler asked with a renewed sense of urgency.

"No, it's nothing to do with your project."

"Well, what is it then?" he answered a little too disappointedly.

"It's Sianos Kalash. Do you remember, the Armenian priest on the exchange visit? Although there has been no mention of my going to Armenia," he added cynically.

"How could I forget him?" answered Tyler, "after what he did to Steve Redpath at Cally's party."

As always, Galen started from the beginning. Tyler was anxious to return to his project back at the office but tolerance, patience and the great respect he had for his oldest friend prevented him from cutting Galen's explanation short.

"Sianos was born in 1977," he began and Tyler wondered whether he was to learn the entire history of his friend's visitor before Galen reached a point of interest. He sipped his coffee and tasted a piece of the almond biscuit that rested in the saucer. It was as hard as a rock and he decided against damaging his teeth on it.

"He told me he joined the closed order when he was seventeen, after the war in Armenia. But that wasn't true. Why would he say that? He joined the order when he was twelve in 1989, having been identified as a special student. It was then that he was sent to a closed-order monastery to be educated, when he was twelve not seventeen." He looked at Tyler, expecting a comment. He did not receive one.

"Well," he continued, "what does that remind you of?"

Tyler shrugged his shoulders, wondering what the relevance was.

"Oh, of course, you didn't study theology did you?" Galen commented almost absentmindedly and went on to provide his friend with some examples from history, including the brilliant mathematician and theologian Pythagoras and, of course, Jesus Christ.

"Christ was sent to a Turkish monastery to be educated?" asked Tyler in disbelief, expecting his friend to say 'of course not'.

"Yes, well, in a way," replied Galen, much to Tyler's surprise and went on to explain that the story of the three wise men was a romanticised version of the truth. The Magi hadn't attended the birth of Christ as was widely believed. They arrived a few years later, after hearing of this special child.

Tyler shook his head and asked what the relevance of all this was.

"If you look at theological history," Galen explained, "the massacre of the innocents took place when Jesus was a child, not a newborn baby. The Christmas story of the three wise men, the Magi, is fiction. Historically it has been proved to be false. No, the visitors from the east came to take the child away, to educate him in the ways of the Magi, probably in Babylon and certainly years after his birth. How else do you explain the complete absence of any records of Jesus between the ages of twelve and thirty?"

"I assume the Catholic church denies this?" asked Tyler.

"We don't talk about it."

Tyler began to see the strange logic of his friend's suggestion but still didn't understand the relevance to Sianos Kalash.

"There are so many stories surrounding the Magi, Tyler. They are less a religious order and more a secret society. They existed for hundreds, if not thousands, of years before Christ. They could easily exist today."

"So what has that got to do with the visit of your Armenian priest, Galen?"

"He has shown a great interest in your project, Tyler."

This comment secured Tyler's full attention. He looked rather disappointedly at his friend.

"What have you told him?"

Galen convinced Tyler that he had told Sianos very little. But his visitor had shown considerable interest when he had mentioned that Richards was the seventh generation after Clinchman.

"It clearly had a significance. I could see his face change. It was as if you had discovered something incredibly important."

"Well I have. If DNA recurs every seven generations, it *is* significant. But how could he have known about my work? He arrived before I told another soul about it."

Galen said he thought Sianos had come for another reason but had certainly developed an interest in Tyler and his work. He had even asked Galen to bring him to the party.

"What did he come to the UK for then?" asked Tyler.

"I'm not sure. The only other interest he has shown is Buckingham Palace. He's been there a couple of times. I notice he had a newspaper article about a gift presented to the Queen by the Pope for her diamond jubilee. It is an ancient Bible."

"Is there any reference to seven-generations theory in the Bible?"

"There are plenty of references to seven in the Bible, Tyler. It is mentioned fifty-five times in the book of Revelation alone. And there are seven loaves and seven fishes and seven baskets. Jesus cured Mary Magdalene of seven devils. There are references in almost every religion to the number seven. In the Jewish religion, Naaman bathed seven times in the Jordan, the ark rested on the seventh month and the dove was sent out on the seventh day. The Menorah has seven branches and there are seven great holy days. In Egyptian mythology, Ra has seven hawks, there are seven houses of the underworld and seven is the sacred number of Osiris. Apollo's lyre has seven strings, Pan seven pipes. In Hinduism, there are seven jewels of the Brahmans and seven gods before the floods and seven wise men were saved from the flood. In Islam, the perfect number is seven. And there are seven doors to the cave of Mithras, seven altars and a ladder with seven rungs. Don't you see, Tyler, this goes beyond the Catholic church, it transcends religion itself."

Tyler was trying to take it all in, but Galen had not finished.

"Seven is mentioned so many times in the Bible. I did a search on the internet. There are seven ages of man, seven wonders of the world, seven days of the week, seven pillars of wisdom. The list goes on and on. And, if you go back to the guy I mentioned earlier, seven becomes very significant."

"Who, Jesus?"

"No, Pythagoras. He was perhaps the greatest ever mathematician and he had very strong beliefs about numbers in general and the number seven in particular."

"Where is all this leading, Galen?"

But Galen didn't seem to know. He shook his head.

"I don't have the answers. Just a lot of questions. But what I do sense is that you are in danger. The knowledge you have is significant. There are powers who would, I believe, seek to suppress that information. You need to take care, Tyler."

"And you too, my friend," replied Tyler as he stood up and shook his hand before leaving. "If you find out anything please let me know."

"Oh," replied Galen in a positive tone, "one thing is certain, Tyler, I intend to find out what all this is about."

When Tyler got back to the office, he had a visitor waiting in reception. It was Paul Gilligan. He had been passing and called in to see if they could agree a date for the photo shoot.

"I need to check with Cally if you want to include her," said Tyler a little impatiently.

"Okay, give me a call. I'd prefer a photo of both of you." Gilligan paused and seemed distracted by what Tyler was carrying. "I've got that laptop and the same briefcase as well," he commented, pointing at what Tyler was holding. "Where did you buy yours?"

"At a shop by the train station."

"Anyway, give me a call when you have spoken with Cally," said Gilligan as he left the building. "See you soon."

Tyler made a mental note to check Cally's diary that evening.

~~~ الـ صمت من الـ عهد ~~~

She finally returned to my dreams last night but remained as distant as ever, beyond my reach. There is a fire but not like before. This time I am the one trapped by the encircling flames. People are screaming derision at me. But she looks on, unmoved, staring at me from an arched window just as she did in the previous dreams. The fire is gone and I am left without her, walking in a large green area, like Hyde Park in London, bound by woodland and at the foot of the hill is a crumbling stone wall with a large oak framed against it. Bells are ringing out and I walk into a large barn. It is Christmas and everyone is celebrating. Across the floor a dark figure waits in the shadows. The solution to this puzzle is identifying him and the woman. She is the dream-like version of Cally but who is he?

10

The signs of new life ran unchecked through the hedgerows of England's vast countryside. The land had remained unchanging for centuries, subjecting itself only to the sovereignty of the seasons. Men still ploughed the fields with the aid of domesticated beasts and children's hearts still raced with joy at the first indication that winter's reign had ended. And spring still spurred desire in a young woman's breast.

The wheels of the carriage crackled against the small stones that provided an unmuddied journey up to the main house and past several of the new students at Thorneycroft College. Groups of two and three young men walked together, introducing themselves to their new friends. But Alice's attention was drawn to the lonely figure of a nervous but attentive young man whose attire set him apart as perhaps one of modest means. Alice wondered what would have become of her had her husband's first wife not died and had she not been approached to take her place. She was, of course, a distant cousin of Lord Thorneycroft, but her side of that large family was landless and her father worked to feed them. So it would have been unthinkable for Alice to reject such a proposal. Her parents were permitted to visit the estate only once each year on her birthday and, even then, Lord Thorneycroft always ensured he was away on business at the time.

The carriage drew to a halt outside the house and the sound of her husband calling in the distance woke her from her daydream. As she stepped down from the carriage, the young man was passing and doft his cap to her ladyship out of politeness. She seemed to recognise something in his countenance and stared for a moment until her husband's voice again stirred her from her imaginings.

"Mr Wyatt, Mr Wyatt," called Sir Josiah loudly as he walked animatedly down the slope towards a group of men who were surveying the surrounding area.

Mr Wyatt did not wait for his Lordship to come to him but seemed to skip, rather than walk, as quickly as he could back up the steep incline, towards the smartly dressed man.

"Show me again," Sir Josiah said, flapping his arms, "that drawing."

Mr Wyatt called to his assistant to bring the drawings, which he handed directly to his Lordship who, on checking them, threw two to the ground and rolled open the other one to show the architect. The assistant quickly retrieved the other two documents before they were blown away by the wind.

"You have the dimensions completely wrong, Mr Wyatt. My view from the house should be one of a landscaped garden, Sir. I don't want to be looking out of the house at a forest. Continue cutting the trees back for another furlong. Make the changes, make the changes," he demanded as he thrust the paper back into Wyatt's hands. And, with the fresh instructions delivered, his Lordship walked back to the main house, berating a gardener on the way.

Having completed the building of Thorneycroft College, Wyatt had been retained to improve the landscape of the garden and the view from the front of Upper Worbon House. He had little experience of such projects but was unable to deny the wishes of his Lordship, however demanding and misplaced they were.

On the death of his father ten years earlier, Sir Josiah Boise had inherited the title of Lord Thorneycroft along with the estate and a significant fortune. He could trace his family back to the Norman conquest of England. To those in high office and position, he portrayed the image of a great benefactor, but he was capable of even greater malevolence. His forefathers had not attained their status through philanthropy but by every instrument at their disposal to keep the local peasantry in their place.

The Thorneycroft estate consisted of more than 1,000 hectares. Sir Josiah's ancestors had taken increasingly more of the land with each generation. All that now remained outside his ownership was the market town of Widdemton, a blacksmith's forge, the Three Bells inn, Oak farm, Ezra's farm, the convent and the church of the Holy Rood. Apart from the owners of Oak farm and Ezra's farm, all the local farmers were tenants of his Lordship and earned just enough from their labour to feed any offspring who survived the harsh cruelty of childhood.

At the eastern end of the estate stood the Convent of the Virgin Mary, which had been built by his Lordship's great-great-grandfather when a church of the same name, along with the village of Upper Worbon, had been destroyed in a fire. At the centre of the estate, where the tiny hamlet of Lower Worbon had stood, was Upper Worbon House, where Sir Josiah lived in an as-yet childless marriage to his wife, Alice, who was twenty years his junior.

His Lordship had two children from his first marriage. Rufus was the elder, who failed in his efforts to bully his sister, Estelle, who was both wiser and more articulate than her brother. In spite of this, Rufus received all the credit for the building of the new college. Nobody wanted a clever wife, so it would serve no purpose for Sir Josiah to espouse the merits of his daughter. Indeed, in his Lordship's less than modest view, obedience and blind loyalty were the only prerequisites for the perfect wife. So Rufus, who had contributed little to the design or the construction, would open the new building, which now stood at the northern end of the estate.

But, even before the first students had arrived, Sir Josiah was subjecting its newly appointed head to undue influences. His Lordship had paid for the new building and had provided the land, so why should he not be granted some benefits from the enterprise.

His first request was for a young student to archive the treasure trove of items collected by his ancestors over the past six hundred years. Once a first year student had been identified as suitable by Estelle and was spending most of his time under her direction, his Lordship found other work for his new tenants. Two more students were assigned to Rufus to redesign the interior of the banqueting hall of Upper Worbon House. And a fourth student, Gabriel Watt, was specifically appointed to Rufus to help in the translation of one particular document which, because nobody knew what it said, was considered unsuitable for translation by Estelle. Gabriel Watt, whose grandfather owned Ezra's farm just outside Widdemton, was sent to Rufus after Estelle's students had initially failed to make any progress whatsoever with this particular document and expressed concerns that it may contain immoral or licentious text and therefore be entirely inappropriate reading for her Ladyship. The long, fading piece of parchment was written in a language unknown to anyone at the college so Gabriel, who spoke French and Spanish and had a natural gift for languages, was commissioned — in an unpaid capacity of course — to work on its interpretation. After all, Gabriel had received a scholarship from his Lordship and assumed this did not come without some obligation on his part.

With the other members of her family suitably engaged, Lady Boise asked her husband whether she might occupy herself with some employment of her own. This was not received very well by his Lordship but, once she had convinced her husband that such duties would cease as soon as she was with child, her wish was granted. Sir Josiah decided that Alice should learn to speak French and, having recognised the aptitude of Gabriel for the language, it was he who was appointed to instruct Lady Thorneycroft on two days each week. This would leave one day for his duties in translating the document and the remainder of the week for his other studies.

At seventeen, Gabriel was the same age as Estelle and ten years younger than her Ladyship. He was shy and studious but had developed a structured procedure for translating almost any language. By identifying regularly used words and applying a phonetic interpretation, he was often able through laborious endeavours to construct a reasonable translation of even the most difficult transcripts of ancient languages.

This particular document, however, was to prove the most difficult he had been challenged with. At first it seemed to be a form of Hebrew dialect and Gabriel had spent many fruitless weeks as a result of this inaccurate assumption. So he curtailed his work and decided to approach it using a different perspective, one of logic and probability.

He was sure that the first four sections of the letter, for that is what it appeared to be, began with the same word. He decided to assume that this was the word 'I' or the first person singular.

One morning Lady Alice was late for her lesson and, when she arrived in the drawing room, she found Gabriel deep in thought at the desk by the window. Closing the door quietly, she stood in benign silence for a few minutes, watching him work. Suddenly he stood up and turned towards her, intending to retrieve a reference book from his case. He was startled to see her standing there, simply observing him at his duties.

"I'm sorry, your Ladyship, I didn't hear you come in," he said as he stood and bowed respectfully.

"Please don't concern yourself, Gabriel, do finish your work," she replied patiently.

But he gathered up his papers and hurriedly placed them into the case he had collected from the floor.

"We should begin, your Ladyship," he said as he pulled a chair out from under the table for her to sit on.

"May I see what you are working on?"

"It's the document I am translating for Master Rufus, your Ladyship."

"Gabriel," she said as she sat down, "would you be so kind as to call me Alice."

"I'm not sure I should, your Ladyship," he stuttered.

"Just when we are alone, then, when we are in this room at our studies, perhaps."

He chose not to answer and wondered if he might manage to avoid saying 'your Ladyship' or, indeed, 'Alice' at all in order to maintain propriety.

"You seem to enjoy your translation duties far more than my futile attempts to learn French, Gabriel."

"Not at all," he said, stopping to see if he could avoid adding anything without sounding rude. "And I hope they are not futile."

"Won't you please show me what you are working on?"

"I believe it to be a letter from a Jew to a Greek, for it seems to be written in Hebrew interspersed with what Greek the person knew at that time." He had assumed this context explained the use of both languages in a single document.

"How old is it?"

"Probably 2,000 years old. It's a very ancient form of Hebrew, if it is indeed Hebrew at all."

"How do you begin translating a language that nobody speaks anymore?"

Gabriel's nervousness subsided under the influence of discussing his favourite subject.

"It is difficult but, take this letter, each of the first four paragraphs begins with the same short word. One might assume that it was the word 'I'. Hebrew for 'I' is, I believe, 'adham'."

"Like the first man?"

"Yes, I suppose so. 'Hayah' means 'existed' or 'was' in Hebrew. So this first word," he added, leaning across Alice to show her the word he was referring to, "is 'ehyeh'. I have seen this translated from bibles as 'I am'." He was enthusiastic about his work and seemed, in her view, to be excessively pleased with himself for translating just a few words.

Alice was looking up into the young, handsome face of Gabriel as he stood next to her, pointing at the letter. He suddenly realised that she was not reading the letter but was, instead, looking directly at him. The closeness of her face and her pale beauty startled him and he stepped back, dropping the letter on the floor. Alice reached for it, as did Gabriel and their cheeks touched.

"I'm sorry, your Ladyship."

"Alice," she replied.

Gabriel placed the letter back in the case and retrieved a text book. He flicked through the pages trying to locate the place where they had ended their previous lesson. She reached across and placed her hand on his. The strange roughness of his palm seemed out of place on such a well-mannered youth. He pulled his hand away and gave her the book.

"Forgive me, my Lady, if I lack the necessary graces for my duties. I was born a shepherd boy and I have a shepherd boy's ways."

"And a shepherd boy's hands, too," she replied. He pulled his hands away at her words and tried to hide them in his pockets. But he realised immediately that this made him look slovenly and disrespectful, so he placed them behind his back and continued with his instruction.

~~~ الـ صمت من الـ عهد ~~~

With each week that passed, Gabriel felt increasingly comfortable in Alice's company. He did, indeed, begin to call her by her Christian name and the intimidation he felt to begin with became a self-consciousness that itself evaporated as their friendship developed.

Alice learned sufficient French to convince her husband that the young man was a suitable tutor. But, in reality, they spent less time each week studying French and more frequently discussed each other's past or interests. He told her about his grandfather, who wanted Gabriel to receive an education in order to avoid the hard life of a farmer. They laughed as he recalled to her some of the fantastic tales of adventure his grandfather had related to him as a child. And he introduced her to poetry, just as his grandfather had opened that wonderful new world to him. She had read Chaucer, of course, but was less familiar with John Donne. As a shared love of Donne grew, so did the fondness between them. Their age difference was disregarded because reference to it would only have suggested that their relationship was more than platonic. A friendship grew in spite of the difference in class that Gabriel always saw as a screen that prevented any embarrassing situation developing.

Spring had now taken a firm hold and the hedgerows turned from brown to green. The oaks were the last to begin their transition and the stockmen and shepherds prepared for new life on the estate's farms.

Shortly before the official opening of the new Thorneycroft College, Lord Thorneycroft received a letter from King James himself. He wished to donate a new Bible to the college and Sir Josiah was to collect it from Hampton Court Palace the following week. The invitation extended only to Sir Josiah, Bishop Beaumont and Jeffrey Goodenouth, the first head of the college. Lady Alice Boise was not required to attend but, in order to impress the King, Sir Josiah intended to take as many servants as would seem appropriate, without appearing ostentatious.

Alice wanted to be a good and obedient wife. She had never set out to fall in love with her young tutor. But she had not raged against it, thinking it something beyond possibility. It would remain, she believed, a fantasy she could dream of in the certain knowledge that it could never become reality.

Often, when making love to her husband, Alice would think about Gabriel. The thought of now being left almost alone with him for two days stirred a volatile passion within her. And, for the first time, she flirted with the idea of realising those dreams. But she still felt in control. It was simply a walk to the edge of a cliff in order to look over into a new and dangerous world. She would never go there, of course, but the thrill of going so close overpowered her. She found an excuse to change the days for her French lesson the following week and sent a message to Gabriel through a servant. *'Owing to circumstances beyond my control'*, the message read, *'I shall need to change the arrangement for my French lessons next week. Kindly call on me on Wednesday and Thursday'*.

The message left no margin for refusal or comment and it was not as if Gabriel had anything else to occupy him. The letter from her Ladyship was sufficient for him to absent himself from his own lessons.

~~~ الـ صمت من الـ عهد ~~~

Once Alice had pictured events in her mind, her passion overpowered any hesitation or misgivings. She did not intend to force events but simply to facilitate them. She dared to make her dream possible, but in that possibility slept a developing resolve to ensure the dream became reality. For it not to happen now would be unconscionable. So, when Wednesday came, she sent her maid on an errand that would take most of the day. And, when Gabriel arrived, she was sitting alone in the drawing room reading Donne.

"Could you explain this to me?" she asked as he entered the room and she read aloud from the book.

"*'Unlace yourself, for that harmonious chime*

Tells me from you that now it is bed time.
Off with that happy busk, which I envy.'
What is a 'busk'?"

Gabriel believed she knew what the word meant and was teasing him.

"Where did you get that book, your Ladyship? For I know it to be banned by the authorities."

"Alice," she reminded him, noticing he had referred to her as 'your Ladyship'. "It came from a rather obnoxious friend of my husband, who presumably appreciated Donne for all the wrong reasons. Now do please tell me what a 'busk' is."

"It is an explicit phallic reference, Alice. But then I think you know that."

"Don't be harsh with me, Gabriel," she pleaded gently. "Read for me."

She pressed the book into his hands.

"There, continue reading from 'that happy busk, which I envy'"

She stood in front of him and looked into his eyes. He appeared nervous but read as he had been instructed.

> "*'Off with that happy busk, which I envy,*
> *That still can be, and still can stand so nigh*
> *Your gown, going off, such beauteous state reveals,*
> *As when from flowry meads th' hill's shadow steals.*
> *Off with that wiry coronet and show*
> *The hairy diadem which on you doth grow:*
> *Now off with those shoes, and then safely tread*
> *In this love's hallowed temple, this soft bed.'*"

She stood nearer still to him.

"And what is a 'hairy diadem which on you doth grow'?" she asked, touching his lips with her finger. He quivered and she removed her finger, but only to press it against her own lips.

"Continue," she asked.

> "'In such white robes, heaven's angels used to be
> Received by men; thou, Angel, bring'st with thee
> A heaven like Mahomet's Paradise; and though
> Ill spirits walk in white, we easily know
> By this these angels from an evil sprite:
> Those set our hairs on end, but these our flesh upright.'"

"Is your flesh upright?" she asked and pressed herself against his body.

Without letting go of his hand she lowered herself to the floor and with her eyes pleaded with him to join her. His throat was dry and a hollowness filled his chest.

"Chaucer never aroused me as Donne does," she whispered as they lay next to each other on the floor.

They were soon joined in the nakedness described in Donne's poem. She had longed for him since that first day they met and, up until this moment, he had been too frightened to realise his own desires. They plummeted into a sea of irresistible passion and lust.

The following day the maid was again despatched on an errand and the pair spent even longer consummating their love.

In the days that followed, Alice was inspired to do well at her French studies, in order that her husband would retain the services of Gabriel and perhaps even allow her to study Spanish under his guidance too.

One evening, when the family was joined at dinner by Bishop Nicolas Beaumont and Jeffrey Goodenouth, Sir Josiah suggested that perhaps other students could benefit from

Master Gabriel's tuition instead of his talent being confined to a classroom of one. It was a telling moment because the shrewd Estelle read well the expression of disappointment on her stepmother's face. That look told her something that she had hardly dared to suspect. But she was a perceptive individual who knew that anything she might accomplish would undoubtedly be the product of her sharp astuteness. Estelle knew she was to rely on her endeavours and could expect no favour from her father or her brother. She resolved to determine the true feelings of Alice.

"Have you succeeded in translating the ancient parchment, my Brother?" she asked Rufus as she sipped her wine.

But, before he could answer, Alice spoke up.

"I believe Gabriel is making some progress," she answered in his place.

Sir Josiah was too busy cutting his venison to have noticed but Estelle did.

"Master Gabriel," she commented, emphasising the word 'Master', "must be the brightest of our students, Father."

"Indeed," answered his Lordship a little absentmindedly. "And what does it say?" he added, changing the subject back to the translation of the ancient document.

"Oh," said Rufus, "he has only managed to interpret a few words, but he is convinced it is a letter from a Jew who lived in Capernaum, which was sent to the great mathematician Pythagoras."

"And how has he determined this?" asked his father.

"Apparently, Sir, proper nouns are quite easy to translate because, at that time, they were almost always written in Greek. So words such as 'Metapontum', which was a place in Italy where Pythagoras dwelt and the words 'geometry' and 'astronomy' seemed to confirm it, for the great man was prominent in those sciences."

His Lordship was disappointed that more progress had not been made and asked Jeffrey Goodenouth if it might not be appropriate to allow Master Gabriel some assistance.

"Of course, of course," he said. But fortunately, before Alice could protest, Bishop Nicholas intervened.

"No need," he said confidently. "I have the very person."

"And who might that be?" asked his Lordship.

"I have an esteemed visitor next week, your Lordship. Monsignor Pietro Bellano is an envoy from the Vatican itself and he intends to spend a few weeks with us as part of his education. He is spoken of very highly indeed and is currently visiting Yorkshire before travelling south to stay with me. I have laboured for some time in an effort to find him something of interest to do during his stay with us. This could benefit us all."

The bishop and Lord Thorneycroft knew well that any inhospitality shown to a papal delegate would not go unnoticed by the King, for diplomacy between the monarchy and the Vatican was still in a delicate state.

Alice thought about intervening but decided against it. But Estelle noticed the change in her countenance and her suspicions intensified. The following week those same suspicions rose in the mind of Monsignor Bellano, who noticed too the sparkle in the eyes of Alice at the mention of Master Gabriel. His discerning eye saw also how the two behaved in each other's company, for the Italian priest shared the same dark heart as Estelle.

Gabriel was authorised by Mr Goodenouth to devote more time to the document during the priest's visit to Thorneycroft.

Shortly after Monsignor Pietro Bellano arrived at Thorneycroft College, he was invited to dinner with his Lordship, where he was presented with his first sight of the manuscript accredited with being sent to Pythagoras. Somewhat surprisingly he made a judgment after just a cursory look.

"It appears to me to be a combination of biblical Hebrew and a latter dialect, which dates the document around the time of Pythagoras. The Old Testament book of Nehemiah was written in such a language, but without the Hellenistic and Roman influences that emerge from this document. The written form of biblical Hebrew continued but ceased being used as a spoken language after this period. So this is a rare document, not only because of the person it was written to but also because of the language it uses. This dates it quite precisely and so affirms its authenticity."

"But is it a letter to the great Pythagoras?" asked his Lordship.

"Yes," answered Bellano confidently, "and it certainly has value for this reason alone. But it contains little of interest beyond that."

In spite of his reservations about the merit of its content, his Lordship was still pleased to hear the priest's words and the bishop took pride in having introduced his Lordship to such a knowledgeable individual.

And so Bellano and Gabriel worked together on the parchment. The Italian priest agreed with the young man's assessment that this was a letter from Nathaniel of Capernaum to the great mathematician Pythagoras. However, he disagreed about much of the content and was sceptical of the student Gabriel's techniques.

Gabriel told him that he thought the letter made references to mankind once being immortal and how the soul migrates across generations before rising to heaven. But Bellano dismissed such fantasies and discredited Gabriel at every opportunity.

"It is one thing, Master Gabriel, to speak a language and quite another to translate it. To translate one needs to express the true sense of a word, to elucidate its true meaning."

Gabriel kept his own counsel but resolved to continue his translation in his own style. And Bellano, for his part, also began to produce his own translation of the whole document, which differed in many respects from Gabriel's. The young student protested to Mr Goodenouth but was told to show more respect for his elder. Gabriel was determined that the true translation should not be lost for he began to feel it contained an important message. When he learned that Monsignor Bellano had been asked to prolong his stay to complete the translation, Gabriel could barely contain his disappointment. So he decided to work in secret on the document and act in a more compliant tone when he was working with the priest.

~~~ الـ صمت من الـ عهد ~~~

One warm, early summer evening, Sir Josiah proudly announced over dinner that Lady Alice was with child. Estelle looked deep into Alice's eyes as the words were spoken, determined to extract every last nuance of information from her expression. The downward glance and contrived smile confirmed all she had suspected. She began to spy on Alice's movements in order to determine what substance lay beneath those suspicions.

Through guile she soon learned from Alice's maid of how the dates of her lessons had been changed to coincide with the master's absence. Any suspicions were confirmed when she learned how the maid was sent on errands to ensure Alice was left alone with Gabriel.

Estelle concealed her evil intent from all but Monsignor Bellano, who recognised an opportunity that served his purpose. He found many reasons to prolong his stay at Thorneycroft and became a confidant of Estelle.

When the hot summer days began to shorten and the estate workers' thoughts looked forward to a successful harvest, the prospect of a new son put a spring in his Lordship's step. A cold winter seemed less harsh and the barns would be full. So, for now he would enjoy the autumn and all its fruitfulness. His position was elevated by the new college and his only concern was, perhaps, his misguided perception of his children and their prospects.

Then, one day, Sir Josiah received the most tragic news. His son and heir, Rufus, had been killed in a riding accident. He had taken the role of Master of the Hunt from his father only six months before and enjoyed the chase. Jeffrey Goodenouth and Bellano witnessed the appalling accident, which resulted from the saddle slipping as he jumped the dry wall fence that separated the lower pastures.

It was Bellano, of course, who had weakened the saddle strap, for he knew what evil would occupy Estelle's mind once her brother had died. The thought of losing her inheritance to the bastard son of her stepmother filled her with horror and she became vulnerable to Bellano's plans.

After the funeral, the cortege returned to Upper Worbon House and Bellano waited until Estelle was alone in the garden. He was forthright and uncompromising in his approach.

"Is the bastard child to inherit what is rightly yours?" he asked her.

"It may be a girl," she answered.

"Shall you wait then, Madam, and risk losing everything to a whore's child?"

She was shocked by his candour and frank words but allowed them to coil about her like a serpent. She suspected the priest was capable of great wickedness and wondered what price she would need to pay to secure his allegiance.

"What is it you want from me?" she asked.

"I seek nothing for myself. I want only to prevent a great miscarriage."

At first, she did not believe him and feared there would be a great price to pay for his services. But he convinced her otherwise and together they conspired to overthrow her stepmother. They gathered information, obtained a statement from Alice's maid and recorded times and places when Alice and Gabriel met to consummate their affair.

On his way to Thorneycroft, Bellano had travelled through the villages and towns of the sparsely populated Yorkshire moors. He had heard local rumours of great evil and knew well the inevitable conclusion to the practice of witchcraft, which he found in a small town near York called Stapleton. He needed just a few names, which he would recall to bring about the downfall of poor Gabriel. And one evening at dinner he spoke directly to Sir Josiah.

"With your grace, my Lord, I need to leave for a short time to visit a friend in Yorkshire. And yet I am at such a critical stage of the translation. I wish there was some other way."

"Can't you simply write to your friend and tell him what pressing duties you are encumbered with?"

"But, who would deliver the message, for I could not trust it to a stranger."

It took only the most subtle of suggestions before Sir Josiah instructed Goodenouth to assign Gabriel to the duty. And so Bellano stayed whilst Gabriel journeyed north to deliver the sealed envelope he had been given by the priest.

Bellano had spent just enough time in the remote Yorkshire villages before he travelled on to Thorneycroft to recognise the fear that had taken seed in the small towns thereabout. He had seen it many times in his travels across Europe. Rumour and gossip were the sowers of those seeds and persecution and murder were the harvest. The fear of witchcraft and Satanism had spread from Spain and Italy. And whilst the Inquisition had not yet landed in England, witches were still subject to hanging. Bellano knew too that petty treason was punishable by burning. So, by wording the letter correctly, he could implicate Gabriel in the latter.

The letter was written by a man recently hanged for witchcraft and was addressed to another who currently stood charged of the same offence. The contents suggested that the carrier of the letter, Gabriel, was a suitable recruit for their coven.

When Gabriel arrived at Stapleton with the sealed letter addressed to Benjamin Snooks, he was unaware that Snooks had been arrested for witchcraft. So, for fear of being associated with the witch, they sent the young man to Ralph Livesey, the Mayor of Stapleton, who was in charge of the assizes looking into accusations of witchcraft in the area. He decided to open and read the letter, in order to establish who Gabriel was.

The content and subject matter of the letter was sufficient to condemn both Gabriel and Benjamin Snooks as witches. It left Livesey in no doubt about their guilt and Gabriel was arrested.

The letter provided the final critical piece of evidence the townsfolk were seeking to rid themselves of such evil in their midst. Within a week, Gabriel, a stranger to the townsfolk of Stapleton, was accused, denounced and condemned. The mysterious death of a young boy in a neighbouring village was enough to warrant the sentence of burning at the stake.

So, as Gabriel's son was being born at Upper Worbon House, Gabriel was being burned at the stake in Stapleleton, just as Bellano had planned. Amongst Gabriel's possessions at the college the priest found the true translation of Nathaniel's letter.

Master Pythagoras

I am in your debt. To welcome me into your home showed great kindness and generosity of the heart. Your hospitality was unbounded and I hope, one day, to have the privilege and honour to welcome you to my own humble home. The inclement weather that accompanied my sojourn at Metapontum presented greater opportunities simply to sit and converse with you on the great issues of the world.

I shall recall forever our discussions on geometry, astronomy and your enlightening number theorem. If I remember correctly, the number one represents unity, two diversity, three harmony, four justice and retribution, five marriage and six creation. Beyond that I have no recollection. What rational and coherent sense this now makes to me and made thus by the generosity of your heart.

I was entranced by your explanation of metanoia and the transmigration of the soul. I shall not look at my fellow man in quite the same way in the knowledge that I now possess. The concept that each soul transverses this world seven times is beguiling and intriguing.

I hope, like you, that true faith shall not be supplanted by ritual and practice. Wisdom tells us that there is but one God serving us all. That same God of whom we spoke during my visit. The same one who created our earthly father Adam and settled him at Eden. It was that same Adam who caused both the Tree of Life and the Tree of Knowledge to be lost to mankind.

I have dwelt on your words as I travelled towards my home. Metanoia and the transmigration of the soul make sense to me now that I have your expert explanation. The message that eternal life is the inheritance and the reward of every soul that transverses this world seven times must be kept secret no longer. Our prize for enduring the challenges of a world of time and space, created by the eternal and all-knowing God, to enthral and entrap the eternal enemy evil is, as you say, eternal life with God.

I have thought upon your description of Eden. All great religions recognise that in the beginning, when man, like God, was eternal, the river that ran through Eden divided itself into four rivers. On the banks of the river, before it separated, stood two trees. In my mind I can visualise that great gift, that perfect land. There stood the Tree of Knowledge and the Tree of Life. It is now clear to me that by corrupting man, evil denied him the fruit of the trees. But God, in his wisdom, restored man's ability to return to his divine origins and placed the key to this knowledge in the hands of the Magi. The Magi were charged with keeping this secret through the ages, until man was ready to receive the secret of the Tree of Knowledge.

It is to our eternal regret that evil would ensure man's journey would take him through eons of profound ignorance, where he would forego wisdom for knowledge and, yes, the gift of prophecy too. But once evil is eternally snared in the material world the secret will be revealed by the one true God we all pray to.

I shall write again when I arrive in my homeland. If I should be honoured with a letter from my illustrious friend, I shall be twice honoured.

Your friend, always,

Nathaniel

The priest destroyed the young man's translation of Nathaniel's letter and his own rendition of the interpretation became the accepted version, for there was nobody to challenge it. Bellano's task had been completed and he left knowing that Estelle had no interest in learning the truth of the document.

The great joy felt by Sir Josiah at the birth of his son was short-lived. For Estelle presented to him the overwhelming evidence of infidelity by Alice.

"I gave her my name," he screamed, "and all she gave me in return was a bastard son!"

He consigned her and the child, who she named Oliver, to the convent, where they were to remain until he decided what would become of them. Even though they stayed out of sight and were never spoken of in the house, rumours spread about the villages. The unseen child became known as Watt's son.

As the years passed, Sir Josiah continued to postpone any decision to rid himself of Alice or the child. They remained in the convent and Estelle would visit her sometimes, just to witness her wretchedness. She scorned and mocked her about the death of her lover, the witch. And she ensured Alice knew what awaited her once Estelle's father died.

Sister Frances, the mother superior of the small convent, knew well how evil Estelle was and, realising that the baby's life was in danger, she went to see Gabriel's grandfather, who still lived at Ezra's farm near Widdemton. Together they arranged for Oliver to be spirited away and given to a distant aunt in Cornwall.

On the occasions when Estelle visited the convent she never suspected the child had gone. She only went to ridicule and threaten Alice. So, when Sister Frances convinced her that the child had died, it simply gave Estelle another reason to mock Alice. She wanted the child to be dead and so she willingly believed that he was.

Eventually, a few years later when Sir Josiah died, Estelle inherited everything. She didn't see the purpose of killing Alice but ensured that she lived in isolated squalor until she did eventually die, without leaving the convent ever again. Alice was buried in a single grave in the garden, close to the wall of the convent.

Oliver's grandfather outlived his own children but had a few distant relatives. When he died, Ezra's farm and all its contents were to be auctioned as part of his estate and it was purchased by a young couple from Cornwall. Estelle had died a few years before and her two children had squandered much of the family wealth, so the family were no longer financially able to acquire any further land. In fact, the young couple from Cornwall were able to extend their property by buying the land up to the wall of the convent, where a majestic old oak tree stood, which local people referred to as Betty's oak. The field contained a south-facing hillside that they thought suitable for keeping sheep or goats. The man had always dreamed of owning a herd of goats and perhaps selling cheese.

During the cleaning of the old run-down farm, an amulet was found that the man recognised. It reminded him of the incredible stories his grandfather had told him about when he was a child. Nobody ever recognised Oliver and he never revealed anything of his past life that he had been told of by his aunt. He thought about changing the name of the farm but remembered his grandfather telling him that Ezra's farm had, indeed, been owned by an ancestor of theirs named Ezra, who had been rewarded with the land for his service in the Crusades. But Oliver assumed that this must have been just another one of his grandfather's incredible tales.

11

Galen sounded even more anxious when Tyler called to invite him round that evening. His ramblings of the previous day about Pythagoras, Jesus Christ and the significance of the number seven suggested that Galen was having some sort of nervous breakdown. Cally was going to visit Ashley that evening, so Tyler decided to seize the opportunity for a quiet discussion about Galen's concerns. Calming his friend's anxieties seemed the best way forward. He resolved to dismiss these irrational and unsubstantiated fears that the young priest was harbouring. So when he arrived in the office he phoned to make arrangements to meet him.

"I'm glad you called, Tyler," he said when he answered the phone. "I've had a breakthrough on Clinchman."

After his strange behaviour yesterday, Tyler did not build his hopes up, but just agreed to meet that evening to discuss it. Perhaps Galen is suffering from something that caused mood swings, thought Tyler, when he reflected on the brief conversation.

A few moments elapsed and Tyler's mobile phone rang. He answered it without looking to see who the caller was, assuming Galen had forgotten something.

"Hi, Tyler, it's Paul. I was wondering if we could get a date in the diary for me to take the photograph."

"Sure, Paul. Sorry to keep putting you off. Can we make it at my offices on Friday afternoon? I'll square it with my boss and arrange for Cally to be there too."

"That's fine, I look forward to it. Oh, by the way, have you heard from Perry Yilmaz?"

"Not recently, Paul, why?"

"It's okay, I've been trying to contact him but he's not returning my calls. Don't worry, I'll see you Friday."

Tyler agreed to Friday only because he couldn't realistically put off the appointment any longer. It also gave him a few days to try to convince Cally to attend.

~~~ الـ صمت من الـ عهد ~~~

Cally had been occupied all morning, trawling through the DNA and fingerprint data to try to establish where in the house various visitors had been. It was a long and tedious task. She managed to avoid Ashley and Steve as they worked on the two lists Cally had produced and began to identify the possible witnesses they wished to interview. When Steve was out of the room and the best opportunity presented itself, Cally asked if she could call round to see Ashley that evening on a personal matter. Ashley seemed particularly reluctant to meet at his flat and suggested several other places. But Cally insisted it was confidential and would only take a few minutes so, grudgingly, Ashley agreed.

When she arrived shortly after seven o'clock, the absence of a female touch was immediately apparent in the flat. Ashley was busy trying to tidy up when she got there and Cally began to help.

"It's okay, Cally, sit down, let's have a drink."

"I don't mind, Ash, Tyler is very tidy and I don't get too many opportunities to demonstrate my domestic skills."

Ashley knew she was just being kind. The place was a mess and it was obvious that Ashley had been living a single life for some time.

He waited for her to ask and she waited for him to tell her. A few moments elapsed before Ashley eventually spoke.

"She left me," he said almost too quietly to hear.

Cally thought that much was apparent from the disarray.

"When?"

"A couple of months ago." He waited for her to point out that Teresa was supposed to have been joining him at her birthday party. She wondered why he had felt unable to mention it then.

"You didn't have kids did you, Ash?"

"No."

"That's a blessing then."

"It might have been the cause."

She went to say that kids shouldn't be the glue that keeps a relationship together but remembered what her mother used to speak about 'every marriage being its own mystery'.

"Are you okay?"

"Getting there," he answered and picked up a pink and yellow mug that had obviously been used by Teresa. If she had been gone two months, Cally began to wonder how long it was since any housework had been done. Ashley stared at it and sighed. Cally walked over, took it out of his hand and, opening the pedal bin, threw it in.

"Start again, Ash," she said.

"I'm fat and fifty odd."

"From what I see on the underground every day, the world's full of fat and fifty-year-old women, Ash. Take your pick."

"You're young, Cally. You don't understand. You can't just forget the past. If you do, it becomes an irrelevance, it makes everything you've done seem worthless. It makes you worthless."

"Okay. Don't forget it then. Just do it again, with someone else."

Ashley rummaged round in a cupboard and found a bottle of whisky. He showed it to her.

"Any vodka?"

He returned the whisky bottle to the cupboard and retrieved a bottle of vodka. He poured two glasses and Cally deduced that he clearly wasn't fussy about what he drank. She got up and looked in the fridge for some Coke. Finding none, she simply diluted the drink with tap water. Ashley made a mental note to do some shopping.

"What was it you wanted, Cally? Presumably it is something about the Hallet case, or Livingstone case as it is now, otherwise you would have told me in front of Steve."

She was momentarily thrown off balance by his astuteness. Her silence told him he was right.

"I've been doing this job a long time, Cally. If you want to remind Steve how right you were, go ahead. Be my guest, shove it down his throat. You knew Hallet was innocent all the time, so make the most of it. But just remember, one day the situation will be reversed, so be prepared to take it too."

"Ash," she said, to stop him talking before his assumptions embarrassed both of them.

"It's not that, is it?" he suggested rather than asked.

"What's the opposite of me being right?"

"You being wrong, obviously."

He sipped his neat vodka and sat back in the armchair waiting for an explanation. Cally sat opposite him and recovered her thoughts.

"Hallet *is* guilty," she said defiantly.

"Livingstone has confessed," he fired back at her. He paused and swigged the vodka. "You were so sure he was innocent. What's changed, Cally?"

"Sometimes a change of heart isn't such a bad thing."

After a brief exchange of stating the obvious, Cally began to outline her thoughts. She told Ashley about Ahmed's reaction when she mentioned that Livingstone would be charged with both murders. He clearly knew that Livingstone did not kill Kosoto. She told him of her theory of why Livingstone would confess to killing Kosoto and how this would increase his credibility in prison. And she told him that Hallet had served three years in military prison for killing someone.

Ashley listened to her suggestions then sat for a moment in silence. He placed his head in his hands.

"Why is life so bloody complicated? I suppose I'm going to have to tell Bent now."

"I'll do it if you like."

"No, Cally, that's my job. You can tell Steve," he added and laughed for the first time in many weeks.

~~~ الـ صمت من الـ عهد ~~~

Galen's behaviour when he arrived at the house did nothing to appease Tyler's concerns about his friend's mental health. He seemed hurried and nervous. He looked over his shoulder furtively as he stepped through the door, almost as if he believed he was being followed.

Tyler retrieved two bottles of beer from the fridge and began by asking Galen about the Clinchman case.

"Great news, Tyler. You were right all along."

"Clinchman had a bastard son then?"

"No. He had a legitimate daughter. His first, his eldest," replied Galen, rushing headlong into his story, instead of taking the long patient route he normally adopted.

"When Sidney William Clinchman married Ivy Leghorn," he began, "he was a widower, having been married previously to Charlotte. Charlotte had died in childbirth in 1762. A daughter, also named Charlotte, had survived. James Henry Richards was a direct descendent of that same Charlotte's eldest son, Walter Burgess."

Tyler tried to slow the proceedings down and sipped his beer. His friend's uncharacteristic rendering of his news suggested that he still had concerns about Sianos Kalash, his visiting Armenian priest.

"That's great work, Galen," he said, thinking that perhaps there was something significant about the firstborn child.

"And," blurted Galen, interrupting his friend, "Richards was seven generations after Clinchman. Six after Charlotte Clinchman—that's the daughter, not the wife, who married Walter Burgess. Seven generations," he repeated before taking a deep breath. "Well?" he added.

"I'll report back to William in the morning. Let's see what he thinks about this development."

There was a pause in the conversation and Tyler presumed that Galen wanted to discuss his Armenian visitor, so he was surprised by the next question.

"How are you and Cally?" asked Galen a little less anxiously.

"We're great thanks, Galen."

"Really?"

"Yes, really. All settled."

"No residual animosity?"

"None whatsoever. Cally and I are fine. We're always fine. There is nothing she can do to ever make me stop loving her. And I think the same goes for her, too."

"That's great," he replied in a tone inviting Tyler to ask him what he had been doing. He clearly had something he wanted to tell Tyler, but wanted to be asked.

"What else have you been up to, Galen?" he asked.

"Just surfing the Web as usual. Well, around my priestly duties, of course."

"Tell me something new," said Tyler.

Tyler sensed Galen's surfing, at least on this occasion, was probably connected to his ramblings of the previous day. Galen looked different, confused about what he had found on the Web, and it wasn't the work he had done for Tyler.

"What have you been doing, Galen?" he asked anxiously. "You haven't been hacking into US security or anything, have you?"

"Of course not. It's just that I can't seem to get something straight in my mind," the young priest began. "Following that other stuff I found, I was reading up on religions that existed before the time of Christ and found some quite interesting stuff about the Magi."

Perhaps it is natural, Tyler thought, for a priest to be pre-occupied with religion. Telling his best friend that he had become obsessed with the matter would only antagonise Galen and Tyler feared he would retreat into his shell. So he humoured him and continued the conversation.

"You believe Sianos is a Magi?"

"Magus actually, Magi is the plural." He paused and tried to put things into some sort of chronological order in his mind. "Sianos Kalash studied theology in the Middle East and said he belonged to the Order of the Holy Sepulchre. But I found out that he actually belongs to something called the Order of the Seventh Sepulchre."

"And what did you find out about that?" asked Tyler, as he went into the kitchen to get another couple of beers.

"Well, it repeated a lot of the stuff I found on that website before."

"What—Pythagoras, Christ and the significance of the number seven?"

"That and other things even more weird. The significance of time and space; the time and space we live in. There seems to be some complicated mathematical formula that determines how that time and space operates with regard to regeneration; to rebirth. At least that's what the Magi thought."

"Reincarnation, you mean?" asked Tyler, rushing back into the room.

"No, more complicated than that. The rebirth of the soul. Metanoia is the word they used. The transmigration of the soul."

"Look, Galen," said Tyler as he sat opposite his friend, "start from the beginning."

"Okay," said Galen, "people like the ancient Egyptians and the Magi," he began, but Tyler interrupted.

"Blimey, Galen, when I said the beginning I didn't think you were going to go back to the beginning of time," he said laughing. But the laughter soon ended as he realised that Galen was serious.

"The Magi and the Egyptians held identical theories on the subject of time and space. They both had the same beliefs about the measurement of time on Earth. They both built stone circles, like Stonehenge, in order to calculate time; these were remarkably accurate too and, in their own way, much more sophisticated than the way we measure time today. The Magi followed a calendar made up of three hundred and sixty days each year, then realised that they were five days short and created another. But it didn't supersede the first one. They ran them concurrently and believed there was great significance when they intersected. This occurred about every 1,500 years, or 1,461 to be precise. On its own that meant little until I remembered something I read in the press about the Queen receiving a gift from the Pope. The Codex Exegesis."

Tyler got up and walked about the room. He was used to absorbing and analysing complex data but even he was having difficulty taking all this in.

"And what's the Codex Exegesis?" he finally asked.

"The Codex Exegesis is a Bible written by monks at a monastery in Antioch in the sixth century. The translation is 'secret Bible'. It's housed in Buckingham Palace now. It is believed to be the first translation of the Bible from Greek into Latin. It became infamous, rather than famous, for some of the text in the gospel according to Mark. This is the gospel that talks about the ancestry of Christ. It suggests that something significant happens every seventh generation."

It was getting late and Tyler began to wonder if Cally would be home soon. He went to the fridge and returned with a bowl of olives.

Galen went on to explain that some people believed that this translation into the Latin was used to suppress certain information about the transmigration of the soul. But one monk was determined to plant certain clues in the Bible that would reveal the secret. Those clues are contained in any modern copy of the Bible today.

"Do you have one?" asked Galen, taking a sip of beer and placing the empty bottle on the table.

"Do I have one what?"

"A Bible?"

"The one my godparents gave me is around here somewhere," he answered.

"Then find it, because I know where to look."

Tyler lifted his hand to stop his friend talking.

"Hold on," said Tyler and he went to the kitchen to find a bottle of wine and two glasses. "I think we need something stronger."

"And I think we need a clear head for this," remarked Galen.

"You might, but I need a drink."

"Okay. I'll get the wine. You get the Bible."

Tyler returned with an old but rarely used Bible and gave it to Galen. Galen flicked through the opening pages to find the first part he was looking for and Tyler poured two glasses of wine.

"The two clues, or at least the two clues we know about, are located in the first book of the Old Testament, Genesis, and the first book of the New Testament, the gospel according to St Matthew."

He turned to Genesis and found the part in chapter five that he was looking for. Tyler took a large mouthful of red wine.

"Here," he said, "it records the descendents of Adam. Everyone ignores it because it is simply full of begets and begats Everyone skips this chapter. But, if you take the time to read it, there is a significant clue to the transmigration of the soul and the whole meaning of life. Look," he added as he began to read:

"*And Adam lived a hundred and thirty years, and begat a son to his own image and likeness and called his name Seth. And the days of Adam, after he begat Seth, were eight hundred years and he begat sons and daughters. And all the time that Adam lived came to nine hundred and thirty years, and he died. Seth also lived a hundred and five years and begat Enos. And Seth lived after he begat Enos, eight hundred and seven years and begat sons and daughters. And all the days of Seth were nine hundred and twelve years and he died.*"

"And so it goes on," said Galen, "through the six generations of Adam, Seth, Enoch, Cainan, Malcheel and Jared. And after each one, just like Adam and Seth, it says quite simply and specifically, '*and he died*'. But, when you get to the seventh descendent named Henoch, it says '*And Henoch lived sixty-five years and begat Methuselah. And Henoch walked with God and lived after he begat Methuselah, three hundred years and begat sons and daughters. And all the days of Henoch were three hundred and sixty-five years. And he walked with God and was seen no more because God took him*'. You see, Tyler, it doesn't say, like the previous six, '*and he died*', it says '*and he walked with God and was seen no more because God took him*'. Do you see, Tyler?" But, of course, Tyler did see.

Galen then pointed out enthusiastically to his friend that, if you continued reading the book of Genesis, there were fifty-six generations between Adam and Abraham.

"Now, look at this," declared Galen, turning the pages to the first book of the New Testament, the gospel according to St Matthew.

"This gospel begins much the same way as Genesis, setting out the descendents of Abraham. And it says: '*So, then the generations in all are, from Abraham unto David fourteen generations, and from David to the deportation to Babylonia'*, that's Josiah, and note that we are now in Babylon, home of the Magi, and it continues, *'fourteen generations from the deportation to Babylonia unto Christ fourteen generations.'* So, from Adam to Christ is seven-times-fourteen generations, Tyler.   Do you understand the significance of these clues?"

"And," replied Tyler knowingly, "seven-times-seven generations is about 1,461 years."

"Correct," said Galen.

Tyler sat with the Bible on his lap, reading through the text again. He drank his glass of wine and filled it up again. Galen had hardly drunk any of his wine.

"Are there any other clues?"

"Who knows? Who knows what was suppressed either?"

"The remarkable thing is," continued Galen, "that, strangely, the Mayan civilisation on the other side of the world held the same beliefs about time.   Ancient civilisations on opposite sides of the world, who had never met, believed in the recurring significance of 1,872,000 days, which is fourteen-times-fourteen generations. Some believe the world will end once man has lived for fourteen-times-fourteen generations."

Tyler went to interrupt but Galen stopped him.

"Just let me finish, Tyler," he said. "The Codex Exegesis suggests that Christ was the direct descendent of Adam, fourteen-times-seven generations later.   Now, when I was studying at the English College in Rome there was talk that a document existed in the vaults of the Vatican. It was a letter from a well-travelled Jew called Nathaniel who lived about 500 BC. It alleges that he met the famous mathematician Pythagoras and it also suggests that every seven generations a soul is reborn. It seems Pythagoras believed that a soul returned to Earth seven times before returning to its heavenly home."

"What has Sianos to say about all this?" asked Tyler.

"I intend to ask him tomorrow."

~~~ الـ صمت من الـ عهد ~~~

When Cally arrived home, Galen had already left and she told Tyler about her conversation with Ashley and how relieved she was when he agreed to tell Bent about her theory.

"I think I may have some bad news for you, then," replied Tyler. "Galen has proved the link between Clinchman and Richards. Richards was the seventh descendent of Clinchman and his first wife Charlotte, who Galen had missed on his first checks on Clinchman."

"That doesn't prove Hallet is innocent."

"No but the DNA from behind the wallpaper could have been Hallet's ancestor's."

"But you said it was a ten-million-to-one chance."

"Yes and I still think it is. I just thought you should know. Anyway, Hallet would need to be the seventh-generation descendent of the losing duellist at 1 Wharf Street for the DNA to prove his innocence. That happened around 1850. That's just over one hundred and fifty years ago, so that would barely be possible."

"I won't say anything to Ashley about this, Tyler. You need to do some more work on this theory of yours before it would be allowed in court anyway."

"You're right, Cally," he said and then told her about his concerns for Galen, even though much of what he was talking about seemed to make sense. It just seemed so bizarre, so unbelievable.

"So what is Sianos doing over here then?" asked Cally.

317

"Galen doesn't know. But he lied about the name of the order he belonged to and Galen says he has an unhealthy interest in Buckingham Palace."

"Is he a terrorist then? He is certainly familiar with martial arts. Look what he did to Steve at the party."

They both had to agree that there was something very strange about Sianos Kalash that they couldn't explain and Galen harboured strong concerns too. They tried to convince each other that all visitors to London are interested in Buckingham Palace, but however much they played it down, neither of them felt entirely comfortable about the strange Armenian.

~~~ سدكون حالة مـ يـ ثاق~~~

The following day, those concerns manifested themselves in the worst possible way. It seemed an ordinary day, but it was far from that. It was to become one of those days that remain forever in the soul. A never-to-be-forgotten day. A date that haunts you each time you see it on a calendar or diary.

Cally was working in her laboratory when Ashley walked in. She assumed he had some news from his meeting with Bent, but it was something much worse and she could see it on his face.

"What's wrong, Ashley?"

"It's your friends from the party. Galen and Sianos."

"What? What about them?" Cally asked anxiously.

"There's been a traffic accident." The world stopped as those words rushed into Cally's mind. "A copper from central London called me because he found your name and number on one of their mobile phones. So he called me. I recognised the name. It's unusual isn't—Galen?"

318

Cally looked into Ashley's eyes and waited for the bad news. To ask would be superfluous, unnecessary. He knew what she was desperate to ask him.

"Sianos is unconscious but Galen is dead, Cally. I'm so sorry."

He thought about holding her in his arms but a combination of self-consciousness and his former life as a teacher prevented him from doing so.

She placed her hand over her mouth and closed her eyes with her thumb and forefinger in a vain attempt to stop herself from crying. She failed, of course.

"Galen, Galen," she cried and handed her mobile phone to Ashley. "Call Tyler for me," she asked. "I can't."

~~~ الـ صمت من الـ عهد ~~~

Sianos lay in the hospital bed drifting in and out of consciousness. Galen's final words echoed in his mind. 'Help my friends'. He knew that Galen was now dead. It was the last thing he had witnessed before passing out and waking up in the ambulance, Galen lying motionless in the wreck and hearing his voice. 'Help my friends'. Sianos felt cold, very cold and continued to drift in and out of consciousness. The lights above him were bright. He thought about his mission, his failed mission.

The Codex Exegesis had lain in the Vatican museum, unread, for 1,500 years until the Pope presented it to Queen Elizabeth for her diamond jubilee, a symbol of when the world was united under one faith. If Michael Fagan could break into Buckingham Palace and sit on the Queen's bed, surely Sianos could gain entry and destroy the Codex?

319

When Tyler arrived the doctors told him of their intention to put Sianos into an induced coma to ease the pain. He might never wake up, but the pain was too much for him to bear at the moment. It was a risk they had to take. Cally arrived a few minutes later and showed the doctor her warrant card. The doctor should have suspected their personal involvement but he was preoccupied with his work. He removed a business card from the pocket of his white coat and gave it to Cally, telling her to call him if she wanted any further information.

"You have five minutes before we induce the coma. Please don't touch him," the doctor said and Cally and Tyler rushed into the small room where Sianos lay. They asked how he was feeling and told him that he was about to be put into a coma to ease the pain. He lay there for a few moments considering his next course of action. Eventually he spoke and told them that he had been taught to ignore pain from a young age and pleaded with them to delay the doctors' action until he had told Tyler all he needed to.

"Ironic, isn't it," said Sianos, "the training I was given will enable me to betray the very people that trained me. To reveal the very secret they charged me to protect."

"The doctors are coming," said Cally.

"Lock the door, for I need to tell you everything from the beginning."

In spite of his irrational fears, Tyler was always capable of action. He had always been bold of heart but rarely needed to call on it. Suddenly an alarm rang out down the hall and the two doctors turned and raced away. Clearly someone was in more urgent need of the doctors' attention and fate seemed to intervene. Having been literally rescued by the bell, Tyler closed the door.

Sianos told them that his mission had been to destroy the Codex that was given to the Queen for her jubilee. But he had been distracted from this when he had overheard Galen's call to Tyler and began to understand about the research Tyler was engaged in.

"The information you have, Tyler, places you in danger. Anyone who risks revealing the secret of the Sons of Seth becomes the target of the Musteria. Just as I was charged with destroying the Codex, so one of my brothers will be charged with destroying you, Tyler, and your work. Because you are very close to revealing the secret."

Tyler began to wonder who the other Musteria could be.

"There is a man called Piruz, Sianos, is it him? Is he a Musteria too?"

Sianos said he didn't know.

"There are always four Musteria in the world," he explained, "but they are not known to each other."

"Was Galen killed by this man, Sianos?" asked Cally.

"I don't think so. It was an accident, I think, but I cannot be sure. You may never find out, I think." He paused before asking Tyler to do something for him.

"Remove from my neck the amulet that hangs there. Take it and open it."

Tyler removed the chain from the neck of Sianos and opened the small purple amulet to reveal a small fragment of wood.

"Is it the True Cross?"

"No, much older than that. It is the Tree of Knowledge."

Cally and Tyler looked at each other.

"I have an amulet identical to this, Sianos. What does it mean?"

"Either your ancestor was himself a Musteria or knew a Musteria who completed his mission but, for some reason, could not return home. Otherwise the amulet would have been returned. It is a signal for the Sons of Seth."

In the few moments remaining before the doctors returned, Sianos told Cally and Tyler about the Sons of Seth. He had been born in the shadow of the mountain where Noah's ark came to rest. But years of Russian control taught him to keep his own counsel. He told them of a young Armenian, many years ago, whose family was originally from Antioch, who joined a closed order of monks. The monk, it was said, devoted his entire life to producing a small part of a handwritten manuscript, the Codex Exegesis. He and his brothers undertook to translate the first Bible from Greek into Latin and the order would then present the book to the Pope. The manuscript is said to reveal certain secrets of the Magi. The monk in question worked on St Matthew's gospel and it was this particular chapter that earned the manuscript its name, because it was here in this gospel that the secret texts are said to be contained. But there were other clues to the secret that had never been found.

"The Bible was eventually presented to Pope Galasius in the late fifth century," Sianos told them. "Galasius was the forty-ninth Pope and many people from the area where I lived believed it was no coincidence that he was the seven-times-seventh Pope.

When he had finished telling Tyler about the secret, he said, "take my amulet and leave it at the Temple of Ta'yinat on the Plain of Antioch in southeast Turkey. Do not speak to anyone. Just leave it in the temple. It will be found. It is a signal that I did not complete my mission."

Cally wrote 'the Temple of Ta'yinat, Plain of Antioch' on the business card that the doctor had just given her.

"Open your own amulet," added Sianos, "yours too will contain a piece of the Tree of Knowledge. I am going to where you will be soon, Tyler. Do not place too much value on your mortal body. Your soul is protected by metanoia. There is nothing wrong with the taking of a mortal body. The ending of a life when you know another life is to follow is permitted. But you will understand the great harm such knowledge can bring."

"I have no children," Tyler said, "how can metanoia cause my soul to reappear seven generations hence?"

"You know the answer. What is meant to be is meant to be, Tyler. As I say, you are to follow me soon. This is your final journey and Cally's too. You spoke at the party about someone else. I, too, feel the presence of someone who cares deeply about you both. Search deep in your souls and find the person that awaits you and you will soon meet again."

"Rest, Sianos, the doctors will be here soon to sedate you."

The door suddenly opened and two doctors entered. Cally and Tyler were politely told to leave, which they did with much trepidation. They went outside the hospital building and switched on their mobile phones. Both had several missed calls.

Tyler had forgotten, in his rush, to tell William where he was going. He returned the call and explained what had happened and told his boss about the Clinchman and Richards connection. William cleared his appointments for the afternoon and Tyler returned to the office.

Cally's messages were from Ashley, who had met with Bent to discuss the suspicions around Hallet.

When she arrived at the station, she received a message that Redpath and Bertoni had gone to pick up David Hallet for questioning. They wanted to know about his prison record in the army and why he had failed to mention this at his earlier interviews. Later that day they arrived back at the station alone.

"He's done a runner," shouted Redpath as he came into the office where Cally was sitting. "And his wife thinks he's armed."

"Armed?" asked Cally. "How is that possible?"

"His wife revealed everything," said Ashley, who went on to explain that Sandra told them her husband is determined to kill Livingstone. Apparently he lost it when he realised he had killed the wrong person. Now he's determined to kill Livingstone with a gun he took from Kosoto when he killed him.

"Sandra confirmed everything," said Ashley. "Charlene was Nelson Kosoto's girlfriend. Everything Sissulu told us was true. All David Hallet succeeded in doing was to kill the only other person who cared about his daughter."

The detective inspector paused for a moment. "Sorry, Cally, how's your friend Galen? Was the information correct?"

She nodded her head but couldn't say the words.

"I'm sorry. And the other guy?"

"In a coma."

She decided not to share all that Sianos had said to her and Tyler earlier that day. She didn't feel ready to do so. There was too much going on with the Hallet case.

Ashley told Cally to go home. There was nothing for her to do at the moment, at least until Hallet had been arrested. He picked up her handbag and pressed it to her chest.

"I'll call at the hospital on the way home to see how Sianos is," she said.

Tyler received similar advice from his boss and he also decided to call in at the hospital to see how Sianos was getting on. The pair was pleased to see each other and felt a strong need to be together and to spend some time thinking about Galen. The hospital seemed the only place to be at that moment. Tyler had forgotten to tell Cally about the call from Paul Gilligan. It seemed unimportant now. William had agreed that Tyler needed to start work afresh in the morning if he felt up to it. They agreed to conduct carbon-dating tests on both the amulets to see if they provided any proof of the information given by Sianos.

After receiving confirmation that Sianos remained in an induced coma, Tyler and Cally made some enquiries about arrangements for Galen. But the doctors said there would need to be a coroner's enquiry.

~~~ الـ صمت من الـ عهد ~~~

That evening Cally and Tyler tried to come to terms with the loss of their best friend. The death of someone so young is a shock at any time but, with their lives torn apart by the Hallet case and the incredible story related to them by Sianos, it was difficult to know where to start.

"Can we just sit and talk about Galen for a while?" asked Cally. "Let's just ignore everything else and think about the wonderful times we had together." She found a candle and lit it.

"He was such a great guy," said Tyler. "I'm not sure I will ever come to terms with it. But he was so worried about this stuff with Sianos. His whole personality had changed in the

325

last few days. He was obsessed with it and, having spoken with Sianos today, I can understand why."

"But Sianos was convinced it was an accident, Tyler. If he was a member of this secret society, or whatever it is, surely he would know."

"I don't know," confessed Tyler. "I've never heard of the Seventh Sepulchre or the Sons of Seth. Who are they? What do they want?"

"Well, if Sianos is right, one of the things they want is to stop you telling anyone about metanoia, the transmigration of the soul every seven generations. You need to be careful, Tyler. You need to tell someone."

"What would I tell them? Who'd believe me?"

"Well, at least discuss it with William tomorrow."

"Yes, perhaps he can find something out about this Piruz Yilmaz guy. He seems a little too interested in my work. If a colleague of Sianos is out to stop my work, it must be him."

"That could just be commercial espionage, Tyler. Stop looking for shadows."

"You're right. I'll talk to William about it tomorrow."

Just as they were thinking about going to bed Cally's mobile phone rang. It was Ashley.

"Cally, there's been a development in the Hallet case."

"Have you caught him?"

"No, Cally, he's still on the loose and we have concerns for your safety. Stay where you are and don't open the door. I'll be round shortly with a couple of police officers. We're going to station them at your house, unless of course, you want to be moved to a safe house."

"A safe house? Whatever for, Ashley?"

Tyler stood closer to Cally, wondering what the conversation was about and why a safe house was being discussed.

Ashley explained that they had spoken with Sandra Hallet that afternoon and she had heard from her husband. She had pleaded with him to give himself up but he was raving. He couldn't get at Livingstone, who was now being held in custody pending trial, so he wanted to take out his anger on anyone else he thought was responsible for his daughter's death.

"Apparently he blames you, Cally, for messing up the DNA enquiry. It seems that the articles on the front pages of the tabloids convinced him that you are in some way to blame."

"But that's ridiculous, Ashley."

"Listen, just stay there, we'll be there in a few minutes."

When Ashley arrived it was decided to leave Cally and Tyler in the house and simply station police outside. There was no suggestion that Hallet knew where she lived and moving them was only liable to complicate their protection further.

"We'll organise an escort to take you to work tomorrow, Tyler," said Ashley. "But I think it's better if Cally stays here until we have arrested Hallet.

~~~ الـ صمت من الـ عهد ~~~

In my dream I am writing a diary or journal just as I am now. Hallucination and real life fused together, one imitating the other, but which is reality? A sea voyage, a figment of my imagination because I have never made one. Completely unreliable data in any scientific terms, but authentic and realistic enough to produce tears. Dreams seem so real, she seems so tangible. I am looking for her, lost in a desert landscape in some foreign country, overwhelmed by the sense that I may never see her again.

A long pathway stretches towards the horizon, winding through a valley in a land I have visited many times in my dreams. As I reach the end of the valley the sun breaks through the shadows created by the hills on either side and I see her disappearing into the distance. She glances over her shoulder anxiously but, however quickly I walk or run, her figure grows more and more distant.

I slept erratically last night, breaking in and out of dreams, intervening in someone else's life. The sun is hot and the buildings ancient but intact and strangely new. I am on holiday in Greece or Cyprus yet I have never been to either. More unreliable data. And there is the burning house again and the screaming of the people trapped inside.

I got up early this morning and read through the diary notes I wrote last night. I have reread them several times recently and taken to carrying this diary with me in my briefcase. I could not wait until the end of the year as I planned. I needed to analyse the details, to find their true meaning. I now realise that there are several themes and think I know their relevance.

A burning house, a betrayal by me and another of me, a desert pathway to a familiar hillside and the shade of a tree. The young woman always disappearing in the distance. Forever on the path ahead of me. Unreachable.

12

Where once were endless acres of ancient forest, new communities now flourish. With each generation more trees are cleared and in the parishes once conquered and occupied by the Norman family of de Bois, only Widdemton prevails of the three hamlets that housed the local inhabitants. The Three Bells inn still stands at the crossroads but the significance of its name has been lost with the passing of time. It serves as a staging post now for the horsedrawn coaches that travel between London and York.

The Thorneycroft estate that flourished under the tyranny of the descendents of a crusading French knight is now completely turned over to the college authorities and the institution serves nearly two hundred students within its ancient grounds. The coronation of the new Regency King heralds a dawn of discovery, adventure and opportunity for young men of spirit and the land about the college now lies hushed in blissful occupation by students of theology, archaeology and the ancient order of things.

The old convent, now largely rebuilt, even now houses a secluded order of nuns and adjoining this building still lies a

329

pastoral scene of grazing sheep. Thorneycroft College has blossomed as the descendents of its original owners have all but disappeared into obscurity. Only the local farmers and tradesmen remain living alongside the scholars at the now celebrated seat of learning.

Seven generations have worked the land and managed an increasing flock of sheep since Oliver passed from this world and walked with God. He is buried in a small family plot alongside his mother Alice, although any memorial to their lives has long since perished with the passing of time. They who are remembered never die, but time is the all-conquering enemy of remembrance.

~~~ الـ صمت من الـ عهد ~~~

When Adam returned to the dormitory after the anthropology lecture, Thomas was lying naked on his bed, deep in thought and wistfully scribbling on a sheet of notepaper. His bright, blond curly hair hung about a pale face that was almost too pretty for a boy.

Thomas was not statuesque in the artistic sense. He was too slim and his physique could not capture the true extended contours of the classic body.

He turned towards Adam, lying on his side. He was not an exhibitionist. He had, he said, been lying there in the hope that Quirk would come in. He would then pretend to be terribly embarrassed and spend several minutes looking for something to cover his nakedness with. No, he was not an exhibitionist, but he was a tease and he loved pushing the boundaries of risk. So, he was far more suited for the trip than Adam, who felt no jealousy towards his friend.

He looked up from his writing and his eyes fell silently on his friend's face. Adam's dark hair and olive complexion contrasted completely with the features of his colleague. Thomas resigned himself to the fact that their sexual preferences contrasted completely too and dismissed any libidinous desires from his mind.

Adam decided to ignore his colleague's nakedness and thought, briefly, about tidying his locker. Instead, he began complaining again about the unsolicited attention of Professor Quirk and concluded that it was his indifference to the older man's indecent overtures that found him out of favour for the trip to the Middle East.

"You are so wrong," Thomas told him. "His prejudices lie in a completely different direction."

He was right, of course. Professor Quirk did not consider a scholarship boarder a suitable companion for his expedition to Assyria. It had nothing to do with his sexual preference but much more to do with his social prejudice. But he had a reasonable excuse to exclude Adam. A student of anthropology, even one with the natural gift for languages that Adam demonstrated, was superfluous to such a trip.

'We shall not be recovering human skeletal remains,' the professor had told Adam, adding that the indigenous population of Arabia was of no consequence to the purpose of the trip. The ancient caves said to exist below the long-lost Temple of Edessa contained antiquities of far greater importance to Thorneycroft College, the professor insisted.

Thomas pointed out that it was a long journey and Quirk would object to sharing the social graces with a grammar school boy, particularly in the confined spaces provided on a small sea-going vessel.

"Even as pretty as you, Adam," he added teasingly.

"No, he'd much prefer to share his bunk with you."

"I'm homosexual, Adam, not mad. The fact that I prefer men doesn't make me any more nymphaeaceous than you."

"That's as maybe but you need to be careful."

"Nonsense," insisted Thomas, "old Sir Percival just likes touching boys' bottoms Adam. It's innocent molestation," he added, wondering if there was such a thing. "He's not actually going to do anything. He'll find some nubile young Arab boy for that and pay him generously to keep his mouth shut, just as he did in Egypt last year. After all we wouldn't want to see the prof consigned to Reading jail, would we?"

The two friends were reaching the end of their three years at Thorneycroft and Adam was annoyed that he had nothing to do during the summer, other than to seek employment.

"What is that you're writing anyway?" he asked.

"A letter home, to my parents, telling them of my intentions after the expedition."

"And what career have you decided upon?"

"A life of minimal consideration of God and maximum consideration of self."

"And how will you achieve that, may I ask?"

"The priesthood, I think."

"Are you mad? You haven't the slightest inclination towards a religious life."

Thomas explained that it would enable him to stay on for a fourth year. Only theology students were granted a fourth year at Thorneycroft.

"I can't bear to leave this place, Adam. A college crammed full of pubescent young men is heaven to one of my sexual persuasion."

Adam protested at his friend's outrageous plans.

"Look," said Thomas, "you have to find employment and I have to find an excuse not to go home to my overprotective parents. Anyway, it's not as if I'm going to get married, is it?"

As a solution, thought Adam, it would at least prevent the need for his friend to excuse himself from the suitable marriage that his family certainly had planned for him.

"You're too cynical to be a priest," Adam said eventually.

"A priest?" laughed Thomas. "If I don't make bishop in five years mother will have Lovelace's balls for earrings."

Geoffrey Lovelace was bishop of Cripplegate, a member of the House of Lords and College chaplain at Thorneycroft. He was also Thomas's uncle and godfather.

"A position of influence," he continued, "and a generous stipend. Anyway, what are you going to do?"

"There's not much call for anthropologists," confessed Adam.

"I never thought of you as irresponsible. If you have to work for a living, you really should have chosen a more practical subject."

"What, like the priesthood?"

"Or the law. My cousin has a very substantial income from the law. The world is full of gullible people and the purpose of the law is to make them pay for their gullibility."

Adam finished tidying his locker and determined that he could get all his belongings into one suitcase.

"So what does the letter say?"

"I've told them that I want to be a missionary when I return from Assyria."

"God," replied Adam, "and do you?"

"Of course not, stupid. But if I start with that proposition, I can negotiate myself a much better position at home. They'll be so desperate to keep me close that they'll nag Lovelace until he grants me a position. Who knows, perhaps I could take up his role as chaplain. Think of that Adam; you could be confessing your sins to me."

"Your parents will never allow you to become a priest."

"Perhaps not, but who knows, they may even send me on the Grand Tour, just to keep me from becoming a priest. A year of predatory sex in Italy is infinitely better than a fourth year here."

"I like it here," replied Adam ruefully, as he removed the empty suitcase from under his bed.

~~~ ا ال صمت من ال عهد ~~~

The overnight rain had stopped by the time the six-mile cross-country race was about to start. The talk was all about whether Thomas Wenlock could become the first student to win the race in three successive years. This had been achieved only by a theology student in his fourth year, nearly fifty years ago.

Adam buried himself in the crowd of runners. He didn't want to be lured into a fast pace by Thomas and the other more athletic students.

Sir Arthur Mackenzie Wright had been invited to start the race. He dropped the flag and several runners sped off across the rocky terrain, followed by a large pack who seemed content, from the outset, to make up the numbers.

Thomas cruised along in third place, intent on taking the lead up the steep, testing hill around the midway point. Adam loitered around the centre of the pack, content to complete the course without embarrassing himself. After two miles he could see Thomas gliding along effortlessly with the leaders. Suddenly, through the crowd of runners, he could see several boys stumble on a downhill stretch of the path, where the

334

runners passed an old, dying oak tree that the students called Betty's oak. The rain had made the course slippery, especially on the more stony parts and roots from the old tree rose up close to the path causing some boys to trip. The murmurings were relayed back through the runners, who were now beginning to stretch out. But by the time the news reached Adam he could already see what had happened.

Thomas was sitting under the gnarled old tree with his right foot resting on a large root that may even have been responsible for his fall. The ankle was already swollen and beginning to turn purple. Adam stopped to see if he could be of any assistance to his friend, who was looking even paler than normal and was clearly in great pain.

This part of the course could not be seen from the start, so it became obvious to Adam that medical help might not arrive until after the first runners had completed the course. He picked Thomas up in his arms and began walking back down to the starting point outside the college. The slow return journey took twenty minutes until several members of the crowd saw them and helped carry Thomas back to the medical room in the main building.

Nurse Brent declared the ankle to be broken and began to bandage it with some stiff wooden splints to keep it straight.

The last thing on anyone's mind at that time was the expedition. Anyone, that was, except Professor Quirk, whose curse of 'damn' attracted the reprimand of those gathered around the injured young man and particularly Nurse Brent.

"Will he be able to travel?" the professor asked.

"Of course not," replied the nurse, who was still shocked at the professor's language. Quirk was comforted by his old naval friend Captain Tremaine, who had been engaged to transport the expeditionary force from Gravesend to Assyria. Tremaine had served under Admiral Nelson but now captained a merchant vessel, the *Saint Sebastian*, which moved goods and a few occasional passengers to distant horizons.

It was agreed that, after the opening of the new wing that afternoon, an emergency meeting would be held to decide on a replacement for young Wenlock, although Professor Quirk insisted on a second opinion before finally ruling out his favoured pupil.

Several students were approached by Quirk in the intervening period but most first and second year students had left for the term break and third years had, for the most part, secured positions following their graduation. Nobody, it seemed, had several months to spare for a dangerous journey to a distant land.

Eventually, it was the hardened and bewhiskered Captain Tremaine who was despatched to approach Adam, for Quirk could not bring himself to do so. Providence dictated that it was to be the grammar school boy or the trip would have to be cancelled.

Fearful of sharing a cabin and then a tent with the professor, Adam's hesitation almost caused Tremaine to take his lack of response as a rejection. But Adam, rather ill-advisedly, grabbed the captain's arm as he turned away. A snarl growled from beneath the beard and he removed it quickly.

"I'll go," he declared. "Of course I shall go."

"Good lad," said Tremaine heartily and he slapped the boy on the back.

~~~ الـ صمت من الـ عهد ~~~

When Adam visited Thomas later that day his friend was surprisingly cheerful. He was relieved that he would not be burdened with the reputation that may have accompanied an historic third win. For, whilst he blossomed in the light of others' attention, he did not seek fame. He understood how his sexual predilection would require him to avoid the spotlight as he matured into adulthood. Even Gods do not grow old gracefully, he told Adam.

Adam began to tell his bedridden friend the news of his inclusion in the expedition party but Thomas had already heard. Professor Quirk had sought his young protégé's blessing when he visited him earlier.

"And what did you say, may I ask?"

"What do you think, young Sir? I authorised it only if he limited his attention to heavy petting."

"God, Thomas, you are cruel. You cannot be serious about your priestly ambitions with a mind like yours."

"A broken ankle prevents me from returning home and, when I do, convalescence is bound to lead to the Grand Tour. One must take the warm Mediterranean sun if one is to make a full recovery." He paused and placed his hand on his friend's arm. "You shall visit me in Pisa in the autumn, after the professor has had his wicked way with you. Coleridge can bring the drugs and you can provide me with the nubile temptation, dear boy."

At the opening of the new wing, later that day, there were speeches from Professor Quirk, Bishop Lovelace and Sir Arthur Mackenzie Wright. In his absence, Thomas received generous applause at the suggestion of the professor, much to the disapproval of Bellington Minor, who had actually won the cross-country race. There was an incredibly brief reference to Thomas's replacement on the expedition and Bishop Lovelace spoke of the high endeavours of our age, before complimenting Mackenzie Wright on the design of his magnificent new wing.

The new wing contained a lecture hall and a museum on religious text. The long, straight north wall of the building featured windows made from a new type of glass, designed by Mackenzie Wright, which allowed natural light into the room without causing any damage to the exhibits. The college had many renowned benefactors, most of whom were former pupils and several of these had donated exhibits. Those exhibits spanned two millennia and included a letter written to the famous mathematician and theologian Pythagoras around 500 BC and a fifteenth-century German Bible that was believed to be owned by Martin Luther.

The letter had been donated to the museum by a French nobleman whose maternal ancestors had once owned Thorneycroft. His family allegedly took the letter and other artefacts from the Castel dell Angelo in Rome, when Pope Gregory was forced to leave hurriedly to save his life. The Normans had pillaged Rome and eventually set fire to the city. Buildings were ravaged as the Pope escaped to the Basilica of St John Lateran to the south of the city.

The stature of the family left no doubt about the provenance of the letter, although there was no corroborating evidence or attribution to support its origin. The German Bible was clearly genuine, with much anecdotal evidence to support the ownership of Martin Luther, but was given far less prominence because the donors were businessmen, rather than landed gentry.

In one corner, attributed as a relic from the Crusades, was a piece of parchment. The strange Aramaic dialect it was written in had prevented it from ever being fully translated.

Centre stage was afforded to a seventeenth-century King James Bible presented to the college by the King himself more than two hundred years earlier.

~~~ ~ الـ صمت من الـ عهد ~~~

Adam's letter to his parents expressed regret that his late selection for the expedition prevented him from returning home. His anxiety about a long and tedious journey in the company of two older men was compensated only by the knowledge that he might have the opportunity to meet many more new friends during his trip. He felt strangely drawn to Assyria, yet he had previously read enviously of that distant land only in order to converse with his roommate who was now prevented from travelling there.

After the thanksgiving mass for the travellers, Adam made one last visit to his friend. Professor Quirk was already at his bedside, stroking his hand along the young man's tight-skinned calf, checking to see that the bruising had extended no further.

"Make sure this doesn't happen to you," Thomas called to his embarrassed friend as he joined them. The double entendre was missed by the professor, who assumed he was referring to the breaking of an ankle, but was completely understood by Adam.

"I'll try," he answered.

The rest of that day was taken with the packing and checking of baggage for the trip. Professor Quirk had been corresponding with a Turkish archaeologist for the past year and it was he who was to provide the guide and the labourers that would be needed for the final part of the journey overland to Urfa and also for the dig itself.

The expedition force consisted of Captain Tremaine, the professor and Adam, until they arrived at Gravesend, where they met with the captain's motley crew. This consisted of seasoned seafarers and a young cabin boy who was likely to catch the eye of the professor.

At the dockside, Adam wondered how Thomas would have coped with loading the baggage onto the boat. But he knew, in his heart, that Thomas would not have been assigned such labours by the professor. Someone would have been hired for any manual employment. But this was Quirk's way of punishing Adam for taking the place of his beloved student. So, intent on proving his value, Adam lifted, carried and pulled the heavy bags and trunks onto the vessel.

The *Saint Sebastian* had been taken from the Spanish following one of the many sea battles with England. Its name was changed from the *San Sebastiano* and it was refitted for a renewed life as a merchant vessel.

~~~ الـ صمت من الـ عهد ~~~

The captain sailed south towards familiar waters off Spain and headed into the Mediterranean Sea. After six weeks and several storms it rounded the Straits of Gibraltar and, on entering calmer waters, made its first stop at Casablanca, where a slightly inebriated Tremaine needed to avoid the larger cargo ships heavily laden with wool as they left the busy port. A week later they stopped again, at Tunis, but departed without taking on provisions because of some unrest there. This forced them to make an unscheduled stop again at Alexandria because, by now, the crew's diet had been reduced to biscuits and water.

340

It felt good to eat a proper meal again and they were all looking forward to arriving at Jerusalem and then sailing on to Beirut, where they planned to stay for one day because the captain had business there.

At Beirut, Professor Quirk and Adam took advantage of the extended stop and went ashore. Quirk was keen to take some samples from the local pine forests and Adam made sure that he retained some leaves too, which he would keep in a special place later.

It was Adam's job to record the events of each day in a journal, in order that this could be read to the college students and left for posterity in the new museum. When they returned to the ship at the end of the day, Adam retrieved his journal and pressed the leaves in the page he was about to write on. He had been given licence to write as he pleased of events and the two older men enjoyed listening to his renderings at the end of each day. They made no objections to his references to the foul air in the cabin or the violent perspirations of its inhabitants during the warmest parts of the journey. Adam had a good writing style and a creative mind. The two older men were heartened by his frequent comments on the purpose of the expedition. That night he wrote: *'we hope, by every means possible, to locate the ruins of Gobleki Tebe and retrieve some suitable artefacts for the new museum'*.

~~~ الـ صمت من الـ عهد ~~~

Professor Quirk and Captain Tremaine were strange bedfellows, because it seemed to Adam that this is what they were. Quirk was a vegetarian and pacifist and his friend clearly was neither. The professor insisted that he could never injure a living creature, whereas Tremaine was obviously a man of war

341

and seemed to relish the memories of it. His past adventures easily made Tremaine the more romantic character of the two and many of his stories had been embellished to make them sound even more glamorous. Certainly, of the two, the captain showed the greater kindness to Adam. From his earliest memories, as a child, the captain reminded Adam of his late grandfather who would tell him stories and relate his own adventures.

At first, the professor was reluctant to tell Adam precisely what it was they were hoping to find at the ancient Assyrian settlement of Gobleki Tebe. But, as the journey proceeded, he was more forthcoming.

One evening, after Adam had read his daily entry in the journal, there was little of interest to discuss, so the professor entertained the captain and Adam with details of their mission. He made particular reference to his collection of tree samples at Beirut because this had relevance to their task ahead. The world believes, he explained, that a tree called the cypress of Abar Kuh, which had stood in Abarkuh, near Yazd, is the oldest tree in the world.

"It stands seventy-five feet high and fifty feet wide," he explained, "and is thought to be more than 4,000 years old. All that is true, of course," he continued, "except it is not the oldest tree in the world. For I have received a report of one even older, near Edessa. And I believe it to be one of the two trees that stood in the Garden of Eden. Whether it is the Tree of Life or the Tree of Knowledge is for us to determine, my friends."

"An adventure," growled the captain with a smile that leapt from his beard.

Quirk went on to explain to the captain and Adam that Sarv-e- Šēṯ is Arabic for the cypress of Seth. It is a Cupressus sempervirens tree in Gobleki Tebe, which roughly translated means Potbelly Hill. It lies in Assyria, close to where the professor believed the Garden of Eden stood.

"Seth," he continued "was the third son of Adam and Eve and the brother of Cain and Abel. He is believed to have been appointed by God himself as Abel's replacement when Cain slew his brother. Eve said of Seth that God had planted another seed to replace Abel and Adam is said to have given Seth secret teachings that would become the Kabbalah."

The professor added that Potbelly Hill was, in his view, the site of an altar and below that there were seven chambers that contained great treasures. Some of this he had learned from his previous visits to Egypt and Assyria and some from the letter written by Nathaniel the Jew, stolen from Pope Gregory and now on display at the new Thorneycroft College museum.

The two men listened in thrall at the professor's words. The captain's eyes brightened at the mention of buried treasures.

When the vessel arrived at its final destination at the sea port of Sidon, the captain left two crew members to tie it up for a few months and the professor went off to meet his friend and guide, Professor Riyad. But he was actually met by a man called Elohi bar Elohi, who spoke some English. Elohi sent another man, named Jahmal, to gather together the labourers that had been hired by Professor Riyad for the work.

After a good night's rest in an inn close to the port area, the party set off towards Gobleki Tebe, which was situated a four-day journey away, near to a hill several miles from the city of Edessa.

Elohi explained to Quirk that his master, Professor Riyad, had travelled on to Edessa to purchase some medicines and would meet up with them at Gobleki Tebe.

After three days' travel, they rested for the night and Elohi reported that the guide Jahmal had told him that they would reach their destination the following afternoon.

They rose early and set off before the heat of the day became too intense. Once the sun had travelled for one hour beyond its highest point, Adam felt overcome by a sense of urgency. Some unseen power seemed to urge him forward even though, in reality, he could not know which direction to go in. He shook the bridle and slapped his horse into a gallop.

As he reached the head of the caravan, a long winding pathway led directly towards a huge sun, made colourless by its glow. It sat on a near horizon before him and he went on ahead of the caravan, past Jahmal, still strangely compelled to rush onward, impatient to find something — or someone — who he somehow knew would be waiting on this very path.

Every step he had ever taken seemed destined to lead to this place. This consecrated moment, created by a million days past, lingered on the dusty path and, drawn forward into the sun, he rode on oblivious to the calls of those behind him.

The pathway led between two hills and, as it curved to the left, his way ahead was sheltered from the heat of the sun. He dismounted and, leading his horse, walked into a short valley. The hill to the right folded away and, as he strode once again into the sunshine, its radiance shimmered about a figure on the path ahead. With each step its form grew more distinct until he stood just a few feet away from a beautiful young woman. He did not know her but, in his heart, he had always known her and he somehow knew that she had always been waiting there, on that pathway, for him to arrive. Her name was Gharam and, like this pathway and the hills that surrounded them, she came from a life beyond his childhood.

Jahmal caught up with Adam and, together with Gharam, they led the party to a farm that stood at the foot of a hill. Jahmal explained to the family what the expedition party wished to do and, out of respect, the visitors met with the elders of the small community to consult with them. They sat beneath a small copse of date palm trees and agreed a price that would be paid to them for allowing the exploratory dig to take place. In return the community would assist in any way they could. Once the two groups of men had shaken hands in agreement, a group of women brought cups of a pale and perfumed tea. They sat for an hour with Jahmal translating as the elders told them of the history of the small farmland. Most of the inhabitants were cousins because few people left the safety of their homeland. As they sat and drank tea, Adam's attention was constantly drawn to the beautiful Gharam, who worked rather distractedly among the goat herd. She frequently looked towards him and he was just as transfixed by her gaze. Her sleepy dark brown eyes conveyed an essence of peacefulness, evoking a promise of kindness and quiet forbearance.

After he had unpacked, the professor eagerly walked to the south-facing side of the hill and saw, as he expected, an ancient tree with roots that rose and fell in the hillside about it. The tree was much older than the date palms they had sat under earlier in the day. It was just as Professor Riyad had described in his correspondence.

The supple branches and scale-like dark green leaves swayed and shimmered in the gentle breeze. The foot of the tree up until the first foliage was formed of knotted and gnarled roots. Like all members of the sempervirens species it was evergreen but everything else about the tree seemed unique. And the most surprising thing to him was the scent. How

345

could the hard, fibrous tissues of such an old tree continue to produce such a heady fragrance?

There was no sign of Professor Riyad but Elohi explained that he had probably been detained at Edessa. He was convinced he would join them soon. He then told Quirk, Tremaine and Adam that there was no wildlife to fear in the local area apart from snakes, which were extremely venomous. It was probably the antidote serum, he believed, that his master had gone to Edessa to purchase.

As with the beautiful Gharam, in his heart Adam believed he had met Elohi before, but this was impossible. His behaviour, demeanour and the locket or large jewel he wore about his neck held a resonance that Adam could not dismiss. He seemed to remember his grandfather holding just such a locket or talisman in his hands as he told stories to Adam as a child.

Adam was the type of person that missed the obvious signs but always noticed the nuances. Knowing this he wondered which obvious signs he had missed on this occasion. And, throughout the day, he considered the nuances that caused the suspicions he felt for Elohi.

At sunset, when they sat around eating, the professor affirmed his belief that this was the very place he had been searching for.

He explained to the captain and Adam that thousands of years ago Gobleki Tebe housed a hilltop sanctuary that had been built at the highest point surrounded by this plateau. It was some ten miles from Edessa but existed long before Edessa was ever conceived. It had originally been occupied by hunter gatherers at the beginning of time. Wild wheat grew here, just as it did to a lesser extent today, and this permitted sedentary farming communities to form.

346

"This arid hillside and these rolling planes will become a treasure trove for our new museum," he stated confidently. "Before the goats you see feeding here existed there were deer and gazelle that were hunted in the earliest days of man. Animal sacrifices were made here and wooden gods carved from the trees that grew around here. Altars were built, libations poured and invocations chanted."

The professor's assessment was right. The following day flint arrowheads were found nearby and the bones of deer too. But it became clear that the hunter gatherers were the victims of their own success because they were forced to a harsher life of farming when the population grew and the wildlife diminished. Animal husbandry took over but the wild wheat had never been exhausted. The local people still called it the bread of heaven. Adam wondered whether this was the root of the stories of manna from heaven in the Old Testament.

As the dig commenced they found coarsely built stone walls beneath the ruins of more recent domestic buildings that housed shepherds. The floors were heavily encrusted with lime. Then, suddenly, the following morning a great discovery was made close to a date palm tree and a few feet away from the stone flooring they had found the previous day. Brushing the dust from the ground a stone was revealed. The digging tools were discarded and a stone pillar shaped almost like a tree was slowly uncovered by hand. At first the professor thought it to be an altar, then he convinced himself it was part of a larger group of stones used to determine the date and time. Finally they realised that the stone aligned itself along the axis of the rising spring sun. Alongside it a shaft seemed to point towards Orion in the southern sky.

"Orion is associated with death and rebirth," declared the professor excitedly.

Then one of the labourers, who was clawing at the dust around the large stone, gasped and jumped up from his kneeling position. He pointed towards the stone and Tremaine clambered down on all fours to rub the dust away.

"Here's one for you, Quirk."

Tremaine called for a piece of paper and copied down the strange Arabic letters carved on the stone. He handed it up to Adam, who looked at the paper and handed it to the professor, who declared that he recognised the language.

"This is an ancient form of Hebrew. I'm not sure what it means though."

Quirk checked with Tremaine what he had written down and established that it was 'Etz haChayim'. The professor tried to contain his excitement.

"That means 'The Tree of Life'," he explained, with a questioning tone, as he wondered whether he had truly found Eden.

Adam helped the captain to his feet and he stood waiting for an explanation from Quirk.

"It is my belief, gentlemen, that man's fall from grace happened right here, on this spot where we are standing. We have, I believe, found the Garden of Eden and that tree over there," he added, pointing to the ancient tree, "could very well be the Tree of Life or the Tree of Knowledge."

"Then," said Adam as he looked about him, "this place is pre-everything."

"We cannot possibly compass what we have discovered here today," said the captain.

The others agreed and they called for some black tea so they could clear the dust from their mouths and discuss what this could mean.

"The book of Genesis," said the professor "says that Eden is in the west of Assyria and Gobleki Tebe is in the west of Assyria. Genesis also says that Eden lies where four rivers meet and Gobleki once stood where four rivers met."

Gobleki lies in the Plain of Harran," said Adam, "and Eden means plain."

"That's true, my boy," replied the professor and the captain slapped Adam on the back.

The three were joined by Elohi, who brought them some black tea and sat with them. He spoke good English and was able to help them with the more recent history of Gobleki Tebe.

"It is my belief," said the professor, "that we have found the location I have been seeking. Somewhere very close to here there are seven caverns, comprising of one outer chamber that leads to six others. The entrance to the outer chamber can be found only at the spring equinox. All I know is that there shall be a sign on that day to tell us where to dig."

The professor had always planned to arrive at Gobleki Tebe in time for the spring equinox because of the information sent to him by Professor Riyad. And now he did not have to wait much longer to bring his plan to fruition.

~~~ ~ الـ صمت من الـ عهد ~ ~~~

Two nights before the spring equinox, Elohi insisted to the professor that supplies were needed. He had calculated the time it would take for a party to travel to Edessa for provisions and return and he now insisted that a group should leave for the town the next morning. There was some debate about whether the party would be back before dawn on the date of the equinox but Elohi insisted that they certainly would be. So,

349

Quirk agreed and arranged for Tremaine, Adam and three local men to travel to Edessa.

The following morning, leaving Quirk with Elohi and some local workers engaged as diggers, the provisions party set off. Adam hoped that he might, by chance, encounter Gharam as they passed the farm at the foot of the hill. Whether it was by good fortune or design on the part of the young man they did, indeed, meet as the young woman was collecting goats from the hill for milking.

Allowing the party to continue ahead, Adam, with the aid of Jahmal, spoke with Gharam.

"Providence and fate were met on the long, winding path of my life when I saw you the other day," he began. "And the face I saw at my journey's end was not known to me, yet I recognised you. I am not sure how this can be."

At that moment, for someone to whom language fell as easily as leaves from a tree, he failed to understand what she was saying.

"Speak slowly," he asked in order that he might understand her directly, rather than through Jahmal.

"I too," she answered, "recognised you. Or rather, my soul did, for I have met you many times in my dreams. At first it seemed like a distant starlit night that began in my childhood but this was transformed from such a sweet memory to a distant one and finally a lost one."

And so there was a gradual realisation in both their hearts that every step they had ever taken was always going to lead them to this place at this time. For him all the obstacles, all the rejections of Professor Quirk, had been overpowered in that one moment by the Moirai that seemed to accompany him through every stage of his life. There was an inevitability of these events and she shared that certainty of the influence of fate for she

350

had, from an early age, resigned herself to be the handmaid of providence.

Their thoughts that had been subjected to much tribulation and anguish of spirit through their dreams were now at rest but the love they felt for each other was as busy and as active as fire.

Adam gathered his thoughts about him and rushed off with Jahmal to catch up with Tremaine and the other three men.

"May an angel go before you in your travels," called Gharam.

~~~ ال صمت من ال عهد ~~~

After they had left, Professor Quirk explained to Elohi that he hoped to recover from the chambers below the temple certain scrolls and other items left there by the Magi. The plan was to locate the opening of the outer chamber and build another cavern at that opening. Into this cavern they would insert a telescopic cylinder with special glass designed by Sir Arthur Mackenzie Wright at each end. This, the professor hoped, would enable him to read the documents without removing them from the chamber, which he believed may cause them to disintegrate.

"How are we to locate the opening of the outer chamber, Master?"

"At dawn on the day of the spring equinox, which is the day after tomorrow, a sign will be given."

He went on to explain to Elohi that the Sarv-e- Šēṯ tree, the cypress of Seth, would provide that sign.

By midday on the day before the spring equinox, the professor was getting anxious about the return of Adam and the captain. Most of the labourers had been sent to the camp to rest out of the noon sun, in preparation for the dig the next morning. So the professor sent one of the remaining workers to look for the provisions party and ensure their return to the site before dawn.

Quirk and Elohi stood by the tree that evening and the Arab explained to him that when the sun rises in the east the next morning, it will cast a shadow.

"Surely that will be the sign," added Elohi.

"You are a clever man, Elohi," replied the professor and the two of them set off up the hill to see if they could predict where the shadow would end, for that is where they believed the opening might be.

It was Elohi who cleared some dust to reveal a large stone. On it was an inscription, just as there had been on the one found previously by Captain Tremaine.

"What does it say?" asked Quirk.

"It is difficult to translate. It is a very old form of Hebrew, I think. I believe it says 'Out of nothing'," he declared.

At those words, the professor could not contain himself and leaped into the hole made by Elohi.

"Out of nothing," the professor repeated. "That can mean only one thing. This is where life itself began, out of nothing. Man created from the dust on which I now stand."

The professor began to dig furiously with his hands.

"I will go down the hill and fetch some spades," called Elohi as he ran away.

When he returned a few moments later he held a spade in one hand and dragged a sack behind him with the other.

As he reached the professor, he placed the spade on the ground by his feet and lifted some dust. He then threw this in the face of the professor as the old man turned towards him to speak. Then, into the small recess where the professor stood,

Elohi emptied the sack. Having been dragged along inside the dark sack, the large snake struck out at the first thing it saw and its venom was injected into the professor's calf. Quirk fell to the ground screaming and Elohi killed the snake by striking it with the spade.

It took about twenty minutes for the professor to die. A combination of the spasms that erupted around his body and his old age meant he was unable to resist death for much longer. Elohi did not want to have to kill him with the spade. That would be much too difficult to explain to the others.

So, when the last evidence of life disappeared, Elohi placed the spade in the hands of the professor's body to make it look as if he had been digging with it when the snake struck.

The party returned the next day just before dawn and Adam began to remonstrate with Elohi about his estimate of how much time the journey for provisions would take.

"If it had not been for Jahmal, we may have arrived too late for the sign at dawn!" he shouted.

"You are, indeed, too late," answered Elohi calmly. "I would have come to fetch you myself, for something terrible has happened to the professor. He has been killed by a snake."

Adam and the captain rushed up the hill and found the professor's body exactly where Elohi had left it. It was easy to conclude that the professor had been digging, when he was attacked by a snake.

"It is clear," explained Elohi, "that when the snake bit him, he killed it with the spade."

As they spoke, the sun rose behind them. It was dawn on the day of the spring equinox. The three of them waited to see where the long shadow of the tree would be cast. They sat alongside the body of the professor on the shaded side of the tree and waited until the shadow of the highest bower rested.

Before it had completed its journey up the side of the hill, Adam scanned the knoll where it seemed to be heading. Then, just before the shadow began to recede, they walked farther up the hillside scattering the goat herd that had grazed there since the beginning of time. Just where the shadow ended stood a rock jutting out from a hillock. An old glaze-eyed ram stood on the stone platform like a guard, a silent witness to the past, the keeper of the world's oldest secret.

Adam realised that the professor had failed to locate the seven arched chambers deep below the temple, where ancient parchments containing the doctrines of the Magi were kept.

Elohi had managed to protect the seven chambers designed by Pythagoras himself more than 2,000 years before, when he had visited Edessa from Babylon. The master had decreed that each cave should be sealed in the way of the Magi so that, on opening again, the parchment records would disintegrate and the secrets of the Magi would remain with him and six other Magi whose names were known only to those seven. Elohi's determination to prevent the discovery had managed, also, to prevent their disintegration. For now, at least, the Magi's secret would remain intact.

'It is better that some things are taken to the grave. Secrets that remain secret for so long have a natural resistance to the light', Elohi thought to himself.

The news that Jahmal brought from Edessa of Professor Riyad's murder by hill bandits had been almost forgotten but he was remembered, along with Quirk, when the captain said grace before the meal that evening.

After they had eaten, the captain and Adam considered their next course of action. They agreed that it was impossible to return the professor's body back to England, so they decided to build a pyre and cremate him here in Gobleki Tebe.

"Where life began," said the captain, "so his life shall end."

"And what of the expedition?" asked Adam.

"We cannot go on without him. It ends here, my boy. You shall write up your journal and we shall relate its contents to the college on our return. Some shall call this a failure, Adam, but we found the Garden of Eden. This was, indeed, the professor's greatest achievement, so how can it be called a failure?"

"You are right, Captain Tremaine," said Adam. "But just as the professor's journey shall end here, so mine must begin."

"How so, young Master?"

"The long, winding path that I have travelled so far seems, somehow, strangely straightened in the company of Gharam. And for her it seems she has waited a lifetime for me too. I am enchanted, beguiled and bewitched by her. But that does not mean the feelings I have are misplaced. This place has nurtured the beguiling ways of woman since the beginning of time. Woman's corrupting influence was born of a desire to please. A necessity to charm became an imperative for their gender. She has been left waiting in this place before and, now, it seems that waiting is to end."

"Well spoken. Life ends and life begins," replied Tremaine.

"I feel I am but a shepherd boy at heart and I am drawn to this place and its people. I still have a shepherd boy's ways about me, captain."

The following day, Adam asked Gharam to marry him and return with them to England for their new life together. She agreed and, following an ancient local ceremony, Gharam said goodbye to her family and the party left for the port of Sidon and the journey home.

It was only when he was updating his journal on the final leg of their journey home that Adam wondered about the snake. The captain had contemplatively reflected on the professor's death, stating how strange it was that he should be killed by a snake in the place where the Garden of Eden stood. Adam pondered this strange coincidence. Moreover, he couldn't accept that even after being attacked by the snake, the professor would kill it. He recalled what Quirk had said on the subject and how he could not bring himself to injure another of God's creatures. Perhaps, faced with death, he changed. But if he didn't kill the snake, that same snake that Elohi had made a point of warning them of, then perhaps the death of the professor was not all it appeared to be.

Adam's final entry in the journal before the vessel docked at Gravesend read:

'What do you think man would do if he learned the true meaning of the Tree of Life? If he truly understood God's purpose? Adam ate from the Tree of Knowledge and was denied the gift of the Tree of Life. But knowledge also has been lost to man. Knowledge is replaced by intelligence but wisdom is, itself, lost'.

~~~ الـ صمت من الـ عهد ~~~

Several years later, on the death of his father, Adam discovered a purple amulet amongst his belongings. He recalled Elohi wearing such a charm and wondered what its significance might be. By then Adam and Gharam Wattson had six children and fourteen grandchildren, who were frequently entertained by their tales of an expedition to a strange and wondrous land where goats grazed on the hillside and where time itself began.

13

Hallet is guilty, that much is certain.

Bertoni pulled up behind the parked police car, turned off the engine and savoured a moment of silence and solitude. When the lack of accomplishment in his life stared back from the mirror, he always blinked first. But today was going to be different. A rare sense of achievement was one small step away. He would rescue a damsel in distress and capture a murderer. Today he didn't blink. It was a clean shirt day. He got out of the car and, watching where he stepped, made his way to Cally's front door.

The berries that had ripened on the mulberry trees a few weeks before were now but a bloodstained patch upon the pavement on the street outside. A trail of purple smudges along the roadside where the empty police car stood provided a prophetic, but unnoticed, testimony of unwelcome footsteps outside the house. Autumn hurried the sun to rest earlier each day and the yellowing leaves were shed to protect the Earth from the bitterness of winter. Once again the white root slept in the Earth's dark core, life suspended in hibernation, as it waited unwearyingly for the distant promise of spring. Others of a less predictable nature showed similar patience and diligence to their undertaking as was evidenced by the crimson marks along the footpath.

A shard of light snaked through a gap in the curtains and the last vestiges of summer welcomed the day. Cally stirred, half held in her slumber and reached out with her fingertips into an empty space. She could hear voices in the kitchen downstairs and shrugged off the sleepiness that clouded her mind. Gradually the pieces of yesterday's jigsaw assembled in her head until she arrived in a new day.

The police guard that had been assigned to keep her safe through the dark night had completed his work and she could hear the sound of a familiar voice. But it wasn't Tyler. Bertoni was relieving his junior officers. It was Friday morning and the voices were asking Ashley about overtime over the weekend. He assured them that he would be arresting the suspect today, so there would be no need to authorise overtime for sitting in someone's house watching TV. The two uniformed officers duly communicated the absence of anything to report, but then neither had ventured into the shadows outside the house. Even if they had, they would not have noticed the footprints of someone on a desperate mission commissioned by Nemesis herself.

"Make yourself decent," Tyler called as he finished getting dressed.

"You're up bright and early."

"I've got a lot on today and I want to get it all done as quickly as possible, so I can be with you until Hallet has been apprehended."

~~~ الـ صمت من الـ عهد ~~~

358

Tyler was the first to arrive at the office and had already planned his day in his head. Paul Gilligan was visiting him that afternoon to take some photographs. The journalist specifically wanted Cally to attend, but that was unlikely while Hallet was on the loose. Tyler thought about calling Paul to tell him but didn't want to postpone the photo shoot any longer.

Once at his desk, he opened each of the two amulets, keeping them and their contents separate and identified with tags. He laid the desktop out like an operating table, with small polythene bags for the items he was to examine. He switched on his PC and immediately started the process of DNA checks and carbon dating. His own equipment was not as accurate as the main laboratory but it would be close enough and he wanted to keep this matter completely confidential.

A few minutes later the carbon-dating results appeared on the screen. The amulet belonging to Sianos Kalash was around five hundred years old, but the one owned by Tyler was much older. Too old to be true, thought Tyler. The result suggested it was more than 2,000 years old and he wondered whether man had the capability or technology to make such objects that long ago.

The contents of the amulets, the two pieces of wood, were older still. They were the same age, with the results suggesting they were at least 4,000 years old. He examined them with tweezers under the microscope. They were simply two small, uncorrupted pieces of a tree that appeared to have been broken, rather than cut, from a branch. Perhaps they had been taken from the same tree if they were the same age. That would be very easy to prove with the right equipment. Tyler leaned back in his chair and tried to clear his mind. Something was troubling him; some distant memory niggled away inside his head. What was the significance of two pieces of tree? He remembered the tree in his recurring dream. A solitary tree, casting a shadow down a hillside. He concentrated harder, trying to picture the hillside. There were sheep, or goats and then, like the lens of a camera focusing, he saw her, the young woman who regularly haunted his dreams. In his dream she was Cally but she didn't look like Cally. For a moment he closed his eyes and could visualise two people lying under a tree, making love on that very hillside, below a starlit sky. But, in a second, the vision disappeared. He poured himself some water from the cooler and dismissed the relevance of a dream before returning to his work.

Tyler printed the DNA test results off and retrieved them from the printer. He then ran the results through the national DNA database. There were no matches on the amulets themselves or on the wood from Kalash's amulet. The wood in Tyler's amulet contained his DNA. He wasn't too surprised by this at first. After all, he had touched the wood when he removed it from the amulet, so it was possible the DNA was from that contact. He looked at the flesh-tight, sterile gloves he was wearing, took them off and put another pair on. He just assumed the outside of the gloves had picked up his DNA when he put them on and then this had transferred to the wood. After all, he was looking at tiny fragments of evidence.

On further examination he found microscopic evidence of blood both on the contents and the outside of his own amulet. He checked the other amulet and its contents again but found no such evidence there. They were just miniscule flakes of blood that could be seen only through a microscope. With meticulous precision, he first removed a tiny fleck of blood from the piece of wood for DNA testing and then, with the same care, did the same with the amulet. He decided to have a coffee before continuing so, carefully placing the items into small plastic pockets, he left the room. Other members of staff were arriving but he couldn't see any signs of life in William's office. He returned to his office, sat back in the chair and tried to think about something else. He wondered about trying to trace his own family back for seven or fourteen generations and considered, for a moment, what he might find. Presumably a recent ancestor was the son of someone called Watt, until the time came when an increasingly transmigratory people required second names, so that people with the same first name could distinguish themselves from each other. At that point, first Watt's son and eventually Watson was created. But, who was the original Watt, he wondered.

Tyler unpacked the items he was examining again and returned his attention to the tiny sample of blood he had taken from the piece of wood contained in his grandfather's amulet. He examined it again under the microscope and removed sections for DNA testing for carbon dating.

The DNA results appeared on the screen immediately. Just like the earlier sample, the DNA was his own. The possibilities appeared in his head. Was this an error of contamination or was it a case of recurring DNA? A further test proved that it was either his DNA or an exact genome match to his own. The carbon-dating test would provide the answer but instead of hastening towards that result, he stopped, realising that he was standing at the threshold of an important discovery. This wasn't about him, this was about mankind, the transmigration of the soul—metanoia. The results would be extraordinary and revolutionary and he wanted to savour the moment. He began the process meticulously, leaving no room for error. He sat back in his chair and pressed the enter button as if it would take him into another world, another galaxy or, perhaps, another time.

The blood DNA sample was approximately 2,000 years old. Tyler gasped when the result appeared on the screen of the PC. He went through the same procedure with the amulet, removing the blood sample and testing it for DNA before carbon dating it. It was his own DNA but, strangely, this time the carbon dating suggested the blood sample was around 1,500 years old. He sat in silence for a few moments contemplating the possibilities. These were two blood samples about five hundred years apart that had identical DNA to his own. He calculated quickly that five hundred years could easily represent fourteen generations and thought back to his conversations with Galen and Sianos.

He looked at the clock and realised that William would not have arrived yet. He could barely contain his joy and desire to tell someone. But, instead, he began putting the items back into their sterile containers and packing away his equipment. He placed the DNA and carbon-dating printouts on his desk and waited for William to pass by his office. After twenty minutes he went to William's P.A. and found out that his boss was meeting a supplier on the way into work and would not arrive until around lunchtime. Tyler decided to wait and began writing his notes in preparation for his meeting with William.

~~~ الـ صمت من الـ عهد ~~~

Ashley explained to Cally that she was being moved to a safe house while they located and arrested Hallet. But first he needed her to formally identify Galen's body. He seemed to forget that they had been lifelong friends and expected, rather than asked, Cally to agree. They drove to the hospital with a second police car as escort, leaving the house empty. Cally grew tense as they approached the mortuary building that was adjacent to the hospital. She took consolation in the fact that she was saving Galen's parents from such a traumatic experience. She had seen crash victims before and was aware of the sight that awaited her. Hot, sunny days on campus; a cold snowy day spent Christmas shopping in London; drinking mulled wine and laughing; laughing a lot; laughing until she cried. A lifetime of happy memories, except that it wasn't a lifetime; it was a life cut short.

A man in a white coat checked the label attached to Galen's toe before pulling back the sheet that covered him. Cally looked at Ashley and nodded.

"Is this Galen?" he asked, indicating that he needed her to say it.

"Yes," she replied and sighed heavily, as if an enormous piece of her life had been cut adrift and was sailing away from her. In spite of all she had seen in her work, death had never appeared to be about her, or her contemporaries. Yes, she had seen young bodies lying on mortuary slabs before, but their age had almost been an irrelevance. Galen was different. He was like a brother to her. Death seemed closer to her than it had ever appeared before. 'We value our mortal life too much,' Galen had said to her once. He feared we treasured life too greatly. He felt we diminished its true worth because we couldn't accept that something so sacred as life itself could simply be a stepping stone to an entity of much greater value.

As they left the basement area of the building, Cally asked if they could visit Sianos in the hospital to see whether he was still in an induced coma.

"I think we should look through his belongings, Ashley. There may be some clues as to whether Galen's death was accidental or not."

"We don't have a warrant," explained Ashley.

363

"Just a look. There's probably nothing there. We don't have to take it. Just look at it and get a warrant later if there is anything that might be considered as evidence."

Ashley reluctantly agreed and they went upstairs to the wards. As they climbed the stairs Cally told her colleague about Sianos and the suspicions that Galen held about him. Ashley was a realist and found the whole idea of a conspiracy dating back thousands of years a little preposterous, but Cally assured him he would think otherwise when he saw some of the evidence.

"Sianos is an agent of some ancient religious sect that is pledged to protect a secret."

"What secret?" asked Ashley.

"I don't know. Sianos needs to destroy some evidence contained in a Bible that is now owned by the Queen. But this same secret had some relevance to the work that Tyler is conducting. Sianos feared that one of his colleagues was out there and Tyler's life was in danger. Galen was afraid, Ashley. I've never seen him so worried about anything before."

"Okay," said Ashley, "I'll conduct some checks on this Sianos guy. What's the name of his colleague?"

"I don't know, but I think it might be someone who Tyler came into contact with recently, a guy called Piruz Yilmaz."

They arrived outside the corridor that led to the ward where Sianos lay. Ashley's mobile phone rang just as they reached a sign reminding him that mobile telephones were not allowed in the wards.

"You go in to see Sianos and I'll take this call," he told Cally.

As the door closed behind her, Cally walked down the quiet corridor. There was little activity and, as she entered the private room where Sianos was, the only sound came from the heart monitor that bleeped consistently to indicate life continued. He was asleep, or still in a coma, so she went directly to the small locker beside his bed. She knelt down and opened the door. Some items had been put in a plastic bag, which she removed and looked inside. She noticed there was a watch and some other items and documents. She was about to get up and empty the contents when she suddenly felt something cold press against the back of her neck.

"Stay there," Hallet demanded and Cally realised that it was the cold barrel of a handgun she could feel.

Hallet leaned back and pulled the blinds on the windows that looked out onto the corridor.

"Phone your friend Bertoni," he demanded.

Cally went to protest but Hallet pushed the gun back on her neck.

"Ring him now. Tell him I want Livingstone. I don't care if I have to kill you, Bertoni, or this poor bastard here," he said pointing at Sianos. "But you can all live if he just brings Livingstone here to me."

"He's never going to agree," she pleaded.

"Just call him."

Ashley had just ended his call when the phone rang again. A passing nurse tutted her disapproval. He seemed calm when he heard it was Cally's voice, but her tone told him that something was wrong. She hoped he had been in this situation before.

"Tell him to give me five minutes. I need to speak to Bent."

Cally rested her mobile phone on the table but left the line open.

"What did he say?" asked Hallet, not caring if Bertoni heard what he said.

"He needs five minutes. He doesn't have the authority to arrange the meeting." She chose her words carefully. She understood it was not going to be a meeting, this was an execution that Hallet was trying to arrange.

Cally tried to begin a conversation with Hallet but he was having none of it.

"Shut up and simply arrange the exchange," he demanded.

"It's going to be difficult," she answered. But Hallet didn't answer. There was to be no compromise. He seemed resolved on killing Livingstone.

A long ten minutes elapsed during which Cally could hear Ashley's voice intermittently on the mobile phone lying on the table next to her. She was still kneeling in the same position with the gun pressed against the back of her neck.

"Cally," Ashley whispered once he realised she had picked her mobile phone up. "How far are you from the landline phone in the room?"

"Three," she answered, not wanting Hallet to know what the conversation was about.

"Metres?"

"Yes."

"I'm going to put someone else on the phone now. He's a trained negotiator. He wants to speak directly to Hallet. Pass the mobile phone over."

Cally remained kneeling and lifted the mobile phone above her head.

"They want to talk to you." She tried to sound calm.

"What?" asked Hallet in a menacing and impatient voice. But he took the phone with his free hand and pressed it to his ear.

"Mr Hallet, my name is Richard, my job is to resolve this situation to everyone's satisfaction. May I call you David?"

"Look," replied Hallet, "don't think you can charm your way around me. If you bring Livingstone here to me within one hour, I'll let your forensic officer go. Otherwise I'll kill her and everyone else who gets in my way." He waited, expecting an immediate rejection.

"I think a meeting between Livingstone and yourself is entirely possible, David."

"Okay, bring him here then."

"It would need to take place at the station, David, it would need to be supervised. But it's not unusual in these cases."

"You don't understand, Inspector Richards..."

"Richard, please, David," the inspector corrected him patiently.

"Look, you don't understand," repeated Hallet. "I just want Livingstone brought here. It's a straight swap for your girl here. You give me him and I'll give you her."

"That's not possible," replied the trained negotiator, who was trying not to appear obtuse. He knew exactly what Hallet wanted and was trying to circumnavigate an impossible situation.

"You heard me, Richard, or Richards, whoever you are. Eleven o'clock or she dies."

Hallet pressed the red button on the phone and placed it on the table next to Cally.

All the time Hallet was being kept talking, Bertoni had been organising a team of armed police marksmen who, along with their own commander, had positioned themselves in the office building immediately opposite the hospital ward where Hallet and Cally were. A special screen had been wheeled into the room that formed a bullet-proof, one-way glass. This enabled the marksmen to take up clear positions in the building opposite without Hallet being able to see them. Each of the

367

marksmen had headphones on with a microphone. They were instructed to keep Hallet in their line of fire and be prepared to shoot to kill. The commander sat alongside them with headphones, a microphone and binoculars. Each of the three armed police would call occasionally.

"Alpha, clear."

"Bravo, clear."

"Charlie, no."

A call of 'clear' meant they had an unobstructed sight of Hallet. Several other officers were hastily trying to establish whether they were able to get listening devices into the ward where Hallet was. They thought about lowering a microphone down from the floor above outside the window but rejected this idea in case it caused Hallet to look at the office building opposite. The last thing they needed at that moment was for Hallet to pull the blinds on the window.

The calls of 'clear' and 'no' continued and the commander kept watching Hallet, whose revolver was still placed on the back of Cally's neck. He would act only when all three marksmen had a clear shot and Hallet had removed the gun from the hostage.

At that moment, Cally's mobile phone rang and she answered it.

"Cally," whispered Ashley.

"Yes," she answered quietly but enough for Hallet to hear.

"Cally, tell Hallet that the police want to do a deal but we can't speak on the mobile in case it has been hacked. Tell him we will call him on the landline in the ward room where you are. Convince him, Cally, convince him he has won."

What happened next seemed to last a lifetime but actually took about one minute. Cally told Hallet that the police wanted to do a deal but they needed confidentiality and needed to speak to him on the landline. At that moment the landline rang and Hallet took three steps across the room. The moment he took the gun away from Cally's head and switched it to his other hand to pick up the phone, three voices in the adjacent building called simultaneously into their microphones.

"Alpha, clear."

"Beta, clear."

"Charlie, clear."

"Fire," called the commander and the screen in front of them was pierced by three bullets that smashed though the window opposite and hit Hallet in the forehead. Cally screamed, Sianos seemed to twitch in his bed and Hallet's head jerked backwards before he slumped to the floor.

A few seconds later, the small ward room was filled with police officers and Cally was being rushed off to be checked by doctors. The quietness that had occupied the building for the past hour suddenly exploded into noise and activity.

As Cally sat with Ashley in another ward room being checked over, she noticed Sianos being moved while police took photographs of the scene and wrote down statements from everyone involved.

"Have you told Tyler?" asked Cally.

"I thought it best not to. There was nothing he could do. He would have just got in the way and I knew it probably would be over very quickly. There was no way Hallet was going to temper his demands and, of course, there was no way we could agree. It was always going to end this way, Cally." He asked if she wanted him to call Tyler.

"No," she answered, "I'll go over to see him at his office, if that's okay?"

"I'm sure that's fine, Cally. We can get a statement from you later. They just need to check you over before releasing you."

"Tyler is being interviewed by a reporter from *Research Today* and he wanted a photo of us both together anyway." There was a hint of hysteria in her voice but she was trying desperately to make everyday conversation and bring her life back to normal.

"I'm surprised you haven't advised him against the media, Cally."

"I did," she said smiling, "but I'm not sure Paul Gilligan or *Research Today* intends to write an expose of my Tyler. It's a science journal, Ashley, not a tabloid newspaper."

Ashley then remembered what he had been doing when this situation had erupted.

"Oh, by the way, that call I received on my mobile earlier was about your man Yilmaz. He's exactly who he says he is. No police record, works for Codon as he says. Vouched for by the highest authority. So I think all that stuff that Galen was telling you is just rubbish off the internet."

~~~ الـ صمت من الـ عهد ~~~

Cally called Tyler to let him know she was on her way to his offices and told him about what had happened at the hospital. She arrived at the offices of Double Helix Limited just as Paul Gilligan was getting out of a taxi. She noticed him straight away because he appeared to be carrying Tyler's briefcase. They had never met but realised who they were when they both asked for Tyler at reception. They sat in the waiting area and chatted. Paul said he was pleased she was able to join them. He preferred to write quite personal biopics.

370

There were a lot of technical articles in *Research Today* and his task was to bring the human side to the magazine.

"Is that Tyler's briefcase?" she asked.

"No. It's funny but we both have the same laptop and case. We must have the same taste."

Tyler came down the lift and collected them. He desperately wanted to hold Cally following her harrowing experience. He also wanted to tell her about his findings but knew he had to wait to tell William first and his boss had still not arrived at the office. In any case, Cally began relating to Tyler, rather hysterically, what had happened to her at the hospital. Tyler was holding her when the lift doors opened and Paul seemed a little embarrassed to be with them at such an emotional time.

Cally stopped talking when the lift arrived on the next floor but still clung onto Tyler for support. It felt strange for him to hold her in such a show of public love. It was out of character for both of them but they both felt a strong need for support.

"All grief shall be repaid with joy in equal measure," he reassured her as she stepped away from him and used a tissue to dry her eyes.

"Where did you hear that?" asked Paul.

"Probably some school teacher in my youth."

Paul seemed shocked to hear about the killing of Hallet. Cally understood, of course, why that should be but there was something strange in his expression that she could not make out. As if the killing of Hallet had some particular significance to him. But she couldn't understand how that could be. It was a sign of recognition on his face when she mentioned Hallet. She dismissed it, thinking that Tyler had maybe mentioned it to him previously.

371

Paul wanted a photograph of them together but in a working environment. William Trenchman finally arrived and joined them in Tyler's office, before suggesting that they took one shot in Tyler's office and another in his.

Tyler's briefcase, containing his laptop and mobile phone, was underneath his desk. Paul placed his briefcase on top of the chair that stood next to the desk and took out his camera.

"Don't get those mixed up," called Tyler as he saw Paul had exactly the same briefcase as he had.

"I'll leave it on the chair if that's okay."

Tyler and Cally stood by the higher section of Tyler's workstation and posed for the camera. Paul took several photographs from different angles. They then moved to William's office for some more photographs until Paul was satisfied that he had what he needed.

Once Paul had checked the pictures on the camera screen, he asked if Tyler and Cally were available for some lunch at the restaurant where he had met Tyler previously.

"I can finish off the interview there and I'll send you a transcript for your approval in a few days, if that's okay."

"Sounds fine to us, Paul," answered Tyler and Cally nodded.

"Okay, I'll meet you there in half an hour then. You probably want some time on your own anyway."

William's secretary came in to escort Paul out of the building and he collected his briefcase from under the table in Tyler's office on the way out.

After he had left, William and Tyler heard the full details of Cally's frightening experience earlier in the day. William was his usual benevolent self, suggesting that the two of them should take a holiday where they could escape the memory of recent events. But Cally assured him that she would never forget Galen.

"Of course not," answered William. "Look, Samantha and I stayed at a great country house hotel recently. The Thorneycroft Country House Hotel, just off the motorway heading towards Yorkshire. It would be a great place for Cally to relax after her ordeal. Why don't the two of you take yourselves off for the weekend and get away from all this nonsense?"

Tyler assured William that they would think about it.

"Anyway," said Tyler, "that wasn't what we wanted to talk to you about actually, William."

"I hope you're going to tell me that Cally here is pregnant, Tyler."

"No, William, no, it's nothing like that."

"Because Samantha can't understand why you two have not started a family yet."

"Just not ready, I suppose, William," replied Tyler politely, trying to change the subject.

Tyler began by telling William everything that Galen had found out about Clinchman and Richards. He also told him about the strange stories related to them by Galen before he died and the additional evidence of Sianos Kalash from his hospital bed.

"But that's not everything," he added in a penitential tone, having decided to tell William about the approach from Codon, before giving him the incredible news about the tests he had conducted that day.

"I met a guy at the seminar, William. His name was Piruz Yilmaz. He worked for Codon." He paused for a moment. "Actually they tried to headhunt me, but that's unimportant."

"Well it may not be to you, Tyler," answered William.

Tyler raised his hand. "I'm not going anywhere, William. I like it here. We have some important work to do." Then, just as Tyler produced the printout results of the DNA and carbon-dating tests and began to tell William about his incredible discovery, he was interrupted by Cally's mobile phone ringing. He paused, wanting Cally to hear about his marvellous news too.

~~~ الـ صمت من الـ عهد ~~~

At the same time that Tyler and Cally were having their photographs taken, Bertoni was on the phone to *Research Today*. If Perry Yilmaz wasn't a hit man, then he thought he should perhaps check out the other person Cally mentioned, Paul Gilligan. But he wasn't having any luck. He had found absolutely no reference to him on the internet, which seemed strange for an international freelance reporter. So he phoned *Research Today* but the human resources department of the magazine were being particularly obstructive. They didn't give personal information out over the phone and suggested that the detective inspector should write to them.

"I haven't got time to write and I don't need a pen pal. Look," said Bertoni firmly, "I understand all about the Data Protection Act, but I need this information now. Paul Gilligan is a self-employed freelance reporter. I just want to know if he is working for you or has ever worked for you. As an employee or a contractor."

Ashley could be belligerent at times and he wasn't going to give up until the woman on the other end of the line realised she could not get rid of him and told him what he wanted to know.

A few minutes passed before he was handed over to someone in authority. Paul Gilligan had, indeed, been an employee of *Research Today*, or at least their publishing company. But Paul had died a few years ago after a short illness. Ashley went silent for a moment and the other person continued talking.

"What is your interest in Paul? I don't understand why the British police are interested in him. Can you please explain what your interest is, Inspector?"

But Ashley simply put the receiver down. He was still thinking about what this information could mean. If Paul Gilligan was dead, who was it that Cally and Tyler were meeting?

Ashley decided to call Cally to see if there had been a mistake. Just as she and Tyler were finishing up with William and Tyler was relating his fears about the mysterious colleague of Sianos's, Cally's mobile phone rang.

"Cally, are you sure about the guy you are meeting today? Did you say he was Paul Gilligan? Is he still there?" His questions were fired like a repeater rifle and Cally had to wait to get her reply in.

"Paul? Yes, he was here a few minutes ago. Anyway what's this about, Ashley?"

He told her he had made some enquiries and had been given some strange information about Paul Gilligan. He hadn't had time to check it out yet but wanted Cally and Tyler to wait for him and Steve to arrive.

"Ashley, there could be a quite reasonable explanation for this. Anyway we're meeting up with him in a few minutes, I'll ask him."

"Cally," said Ashley firmly, "wait there, Steve and I will pick you up. I just want to be absolutely certain about this guy."

Cally told Tyler and they decided to wait for her colleagues to arrive. Cally removed a document from her handbag. It was something Galen had given her when she last saw him. She gave it to William, telling him that this was the type of stuff Galen was digging up in his research.

William read it out loud. "'In our first life, the first part of the soul's journey, we experience a realisation, a desire to abandon those things we dislike in others. But it is not godlike to acknowledge evil in others but not to recognise it in ourselves'."

"Religious fanaticism," he said, but admitted that he could understand how Galen became so intrigued by such stuff, especially with him being a priest. "And that Sianos guy was a strange character, wasn't he? Look what he did to your friend Steve."

"Look, William," said Tyler as he and Cally decided to meet her colleagues in reception, rather than wait upstairs. "I'm not going anywhere, so don't worry about Codon trying to headhunt me. I feel we are very close to discovering something of great importance here. We're close to finding out the truth."

Ashley and Steve didn't notice the taxi pulling away from the offices of Double Helix Limited as they drew up in their car outside.

Paul had delayed his departure for a few moments as the phone in the briefcase he was carrying received a text message from Perry Yilmaz. It wished Tyler every success with his project and hoped they would meet up again soon. He deleted the message and asked the taxi driver to take him to Heathrow Airport. Paul looked in the briefcase and found a dark-red-covered desk diary. He already knew, when he learned of the death of Hallet, that he would need to go through with his plan. The contents of the diary only confirmed that he had made the right decision.

As the taxi turned left at the traffic lights into the next road, Paul took a mobile phone from his pocket and dialled the number of his own mobile phone, which was still in the briefcase he had left in Tyler's office. At that moment, there was a massive explosion and behind him the office block he just left was ripped apart. Glass and concrete showered down to the street below. Smoke and dust billowed and people screamed and ran for cover. Some hid in doorways and immediately began speculating about the possibility of a terrorist attack. Later, when they found out who the occupants of the building were, that speculation would change to animal rights activists.

"What was that?" asked the taxi driver.

"It sounded like a gas mains explosion," answered Paul.

"We could have been buried under the rubble," answered the taxi driver as he hastily drove off towards the airport, leaving the smoke-filled street behind him.

There was certainly something buried under the rubble, thought Gilligan, something that had been buried since the beginning of time.

What the critics said about

Lost in a hurricane

'A real page turner'

'No character and no observation is wasted in this novel. – everything ties together in the end'

'The plotting is complex (although it is by no means labyrinthine), but this is no airport lounge fodder thriller. OK, let's be clear, it's not Heller's Catch-22 or Salinger's The Catcher in the Rye, but it is better than any of the ghost-written celebrity 'novels' that clog up the Best Sellers charts'

'For a first effort, Lost in a hurricane is bloody good'

What the critics said about

Deathbed Confessions

'Deathbed Confessions, is a cracker and begging to be adapted for TV'.

'Deathbed is a sequel to the author's full blown debut Lost In A Hurricane and focuses on the hero of the first book, Jack Daly'.

'Deathbed Confessions is at times a taunt thriller, at times mystery, and at times touching renderings of life and human relationships'.

'This is a book with a tough heart, but a heart that at least twice brought tears to my eyes. Highly recommended'.

What the critics said about

The Unfolding Path

'The Unfolding Path' is a really terrific book. The author takes us on a journey of what is to me unrivalled detail'.

'This is a page-turning read, featuring present day (and timely), international issues based around a web of intrigue. Even telling you the main subject matter of this book I think would spoil it for the reader by giving too much away, but I will say that the ending is extremely powerful and vivid. 'The Unfolding Path' is brill, and would make a fantastic movie'.

Coming soon
Covenant of Retribution

Made in the USA
Charleston, SC
04 January 2013